JUL 2007

D1214975

30th Anniversary Anthology

Asimov's
SCIENCE FICTION®

30th Anniversary Anthology

Edited by

Sheila Williams

TACHYON PUBLICATIONS
San Francisco

The Asimov's SF 30th Anniversary Anthology
Copyright © 2007 by Dell Magazines, A division of Crosstown Publications
Introduction copyright © 2007 by Dell Magazines.

Cover illustration © 1990, 2007 by Michael Whelan
Cover design © 2007 by Ann Monn
Interior design & typography: Irene Lee
The typeface is Adobe Garamond

Tachyon Publications
1459 18th Street #139, San Francisco, CA 94107
(415) 285-5615
www.tachyonpublications.com

Edited by Sheila Williams
Series Editor: Jacob Weisman

ISBN 10: 1-892391-47-3
ISBN 13: 978-1-892391-47-6

Printed in the United States of America by Worzalla

First Edition: 2007
0   9   8   7   6   5   4   3   2   1

All stories originally appeared in *Asimov's Science Fiction*, published by Dell Magazines, a division of Crosstown Publications. Grateful acknowledgement is hereby made to the authors and authors' representatives listed below for giving permission to reprint the material in this volume.

"Air Raid" by John Varley writing as Herb Boehm, copyright ©1977. Reprinted by permission of the author.

"The Time of the Burning" by Robert Silverberg, copyright ©1982. Reprinted by permission of the author.

"Speech Sounds" by Octavia E. Butler, copyright ©1983, Reprinted by permission of the estate of Octavia E. Butler.

"Dinner in Audoghast" by Bruce Sterling, copyright ©1985. Reprinted by permission of the author.

"Robot Dreams" by Isaac Asimov, copyright ©1986. Reprinted by permission of Ralph M. Vicinanza. Ltd.

"Glacier" by Kim Stanley Robinson, copyright ©1988. Reprinted by permission of the author.

"Cibola" by Connie Willis, copyright ©1990. Reprinted by permission of the author.

"The Happy Man" by Jonathan Lethem, copyright ©1991. Reprinted by permission of the author.

"Over There" by Mike Resnick, copyright ©1991. Reprinted by permission of the author.

"Ether. OR" by Ursula K. LeGuin, copyright ©1995. Reprinted by permission of Virginia Kidd Agency. Inc.

"Flying Lessons" by Kelly Link, copyright ©1996. Reprinted by permission of the author.

"Itsy Bitsy Spider" by James Patrick Kelly, copyright ©1997. Reprinted by permission of the author.

"Ancient Engines" by Michael Swanwick, copyright ©1999. Reprinted by permission of the author.

"Lobsters" by Charles Stross, copyright ©2001. Reprinted by permission of the author.

"Only Partly Here" by Lucius Shepard, copyright ©2003. Reprinted by permission of the author.

"The Children of Time" by Stephen Baxter, copyright ©2005. Reprinted by permission of the author.

"Eight Episodes" by Robert Reed, copyright ©2006. Reprinted by permission of the author.

DEDICATION

For the writers and editors responsible for *Asimov's Science Fiction* magazine's first thirty years.

ACKNOWLEDGEMENTS

Thanks and praise are due to Brian Bieniowski, who offered wise counsel on the stories appearing here, and who put a great deal of work into preparing the book for publication. Thanks are also due to Irene Lee who helped design and lay out the book, and who came to my rescue on more than one occasion. Gratitude is due to Abigail Browning, Dell Magazines' subsidiary rights director, who set the deal for this book in motion and who cleared all permissions. Behind the scenes help from Lauren Adams, Meredith Bennett, Jessie Lawton-Crane, and Jill Roberts must be recognized with appreciation. Finally, a special debt of gratitude is due my own editor and publisher, Jacob Weisman. This book owes its existence to his support and conviction.

CONTENTS

INTRODUCTION

Thirty years! It's hard to believe that the adventure that began in the seventies—the advent of a new digest-sized science fiction magazine—has reached its third decade. Pulling this anthology together has been a joyful excursion for me. Opening the pages of past issues of *Asimov's* has felt a bit like stepping into my own time machine to memories of the past and the promise of the future. Images of time and place come flooding back. I first learned that the world included science fiction magazines in my teens through Isaac Asimov's loving introductions to the various volumes of *The Hugo Winners*. I knew then that I wanted to be a part of this world. Isaac had discovered SF in the magazines for sale at his father's candy store, and it was to the magazines that he and Ray Bradbury and Robert Heinlein sold their first work. Encountering an early issue of *Isaac Asimov's Science Fiction Magazine* in my college bookstore was a wonderful discovery, but given his ardor for those early periodicals, I was not surprised to learn that Isaac Asimov had founded a magazine of his own.

While science fiction magazines had been pervasive on newsstands when Isaac Asimov was growing up, their numbers had dwindled by 1977. The loss of the magazines, though, meant fewer marketplaces for professionals, and fewer openings for young writers. Joel Davis, the owner of Davis Publications, Inc., convinced Isaac that a new SF magazine with his name on it would have a healthy shot at survival and would provide writers with a new place to sell their fiction and give young readers a new chance to discover it.

Published initially as a quarterly, the magazine hit the newsstand with the Spring 1977 issue. The famous first cover sports a photograph of Isaac. The magazine's name blazes across the page like a streaking rocket ship. The founding editor was George Scithers, an author and well-regarded SF fanzine editor. As with any start-up venture, there were the usual predictions of imminent doom, but the magazine quickly became a financial success. By 1978 it had become a bimonthly and it achieved monthly status a year later.

While George Scithers's first intention was to publish an upbeat, all-science fiction magazine, he soon discovered that to fill a monthly magazine he would have to consider fantasy stories as well. Under later editors, the magazine would gain a reputation for publishing an even more eclectic range of stories.

For me, the first issue hit the ground running with John Varley's "Air Raid." With today's biotechnical advances, the story couldn't take place in 2007 in exactly the way it does in 1977, but the future it hints at is still pretty believable. It remains an almost unbearably tense story that must be read in one sitting. George discovered a number of new authors including Barry B. Longyear, Somtow Sucharitkul (also known as S. P. Somtow) and Sharon N. Farber, and worked closely with prominent authors like Robert Silverberg, Gene Wolfe, and Roger Zelazny. Within a couple of years, George had won science fiction's prestigious Hugo Award for Best Editor and the stories had begun to receive recognition as well. Indeed, his last issue as editor of *Asimov's,* February 1982, features a novella by Connie Willis that was to bring her the first of many Hugo and Nebula awards.

George employed staff members who would affect the future of the magazine as well. For the first six months, he was assisted by Gardner Dozois. A distinguished young author, Gardner would return to the magazine in another guise some years later. In late 1978, George hired Shawna McCarthy. Shawna was an able assistant who would have a long-term effect on the nature of the magazine.

George was succeeded in 1982 by Kathleen Moloney. In her brief tenure, Kathleen published important work by Connie Willis and David Brin, and continued to publish well-known authors like Robert Silverberg, whose still relevant tale from his famous Majipoor universe, "The Time of the Burning" (1982), is included here. She was the first *Asimov's* editor to publish works by new writers like Jack McDevitt and Esther M. Friesner. In the summer of 1982, she gave me my entrée into the world of SF magazine publishing when she took me on as an editorial assistant. By the January 1983 issue, Kathleen had turned the magazine over to Shawna.

Shawna McCarthy gave the magazine a literary reputation. She published the early works of Karen Joy Fowler and Lisa Goldstein. She introduced the works of James Patrick Kelly, John Kessel, Kim Stanley Robinson, Michael Swanwick, and Lucius Shepard to the magazine. During her tenure, Bruce Sterling published his first story for *Asimov's,* the opulent "Dinner in Audoghast" (1985); and Octavia Butler published her first award-winning story, "Speech Sounds" (1983). Shawna was also the first *Asimov's* editor to publish a story by Gardner Dozois, and Gardner picked up his first Nebula Award for his second sale to *Asimov's.* In addition to publishing science fiction and fantasy, Shawna began to publish the unclassifiable sort of tale that Ursula K. Le Guin mentions in her story note at the end of the book. Shawna won a Best Editor Hugo for herself before she left the magazine to pursue a rich and varied publishing career.

Shawna's successor was the aforementioned Gardner Dozois. Gardner would continue the magazine's literary reputation, and solidify his own reputation as well. In his nineteen years at *Asimov's*, he would win the Best Editor Hugo a record-breaking fifteen times. Gardner continued to publish classic science fiction stories like Isaac Asimov's haunting "Robot Dreams" (1986), Kim Stanley Robinson's "Glacier" (1990), and alternate history stories such as Mike Resnick's "Over There" (1991). He published hard to classify tales like Connie Willis's "Cibola" (1990), and Ursula K. Le Guin's "Ether, OR" (1995), and he, too, made room for first sales by then unknown writers like Kelly Link—"Flying Lessons" (1996)—and early sales like "The Happy Man" (1991) by Jonathan Lethem.

These stories had influences on science fiction and on literature in general. They encouraged authors to experiment and push their limits, while providing entertainment for the readers. Connie Willis says of the magazine, "What I've loved about writing for *Asimov's* is that they've always been open to all kinds of stories, from time travel to psychics and channelers to post-apocalyptic nightmares to comedies. I've never once thought, 'Oh, I can't send that to *Asimov's*. That's not the sort of thing they publish.' In the proud tradition of science fiction pioneers like Judith Merril, *Asimov's* editors have constantly worked to expand the boundaries of science fiction and encourage excellence in every kind of story."

This variety of stories has continued during the past decade. Michael

Swanwick's "Ancient Engines" (1999) shows the frustrating limitations of technology, while in "Lobsters" (2001), Charles Stross pushes hard in the opposite direction as he attempts to go beyond the conundrum of the Singularity. James Patrick Kelly tinkers with technology and its repercussions in "Itsy Bitsy Spider" (June 1997), and Lucius Shepard offers us an eerie brush with reality in his 2003 fantasy, "Only Partly Here."

I had been a part of *Asimov's* for twenty-two years when Gardner left in 2004. Although I'd always had a lot of input, it was exciting to finally have the chance to put my own imprint on the magazine. This book's closing stories are from my own era—Robert Reed's unusual television series "Eight Episodes" (2006) and Stephen Baxter's extremely distant look into the future—"The Children of Time" (2005). Although both stories are set on Earth, they are eventually separated by the passage of nearly a billion years.

In the thirty years since the magazine's inception, we have continued the tradition of publishing quality stories from well-known writers while searching out the same sort of stories from brand-new authors. Perhaps the biggest change the magazine has undergone was the loss of its editorial director at what is now the midpoint of its existence. Isaac Asimov never picked out the stories, but he wrote all the editorials and provided amusing commentary right up until his death in 1992. He lent a backbone of support to the magazine that gave it the strength to continue after his death. Thirteen years ago, Robert Silverberg assumed part of Isaac's mantle when he began to write a monthly "Reflections" column for *Asimov's*. He, along with the other regular columnists, is now a mainstay of the magazine. Another much more insignificant alteration has been to the magazine's full name, which is now simply *Asimov's Science Fiction*.

Stories from *Asimov's* have been honored with forty-four Hugo and twenty-five Nebula awards. They have also received World Fantasy, Theodore Sturgeon, and a host of other significant awards. This book, however, is not an attempt to recreate a Hugo Awards anthology or the Science Fiction Writers of America's annual volume of Nebula Award winners. Many of those stories are already available in numerous anthologies and collections.

If I were to attempt to reprint all the award-winning stories and all the ground-breaking tales that first appeared in *Asimov's*, this book would run to several volumes. Due to space limitations, there are no novellas here, and long novelettes are sharply curtailed. Room doesn't even exist for a short story from every year of publication. To comment on the amazing authors who are left out, like Nancy Kress and Kristine Kathryn Rusch, or Ian McDonald and Frederik Pohl, is to risk over-looking too many others. This book cannot provide a comprehensive history of the magazine, but it can provide a sampling of the terrific writers who have been a part of *Asimov's*.

This anthology has given me a chance to riffle through thousands of pages of *Asimov's*, reacquainting myself with untold numbers of vision-ary stories. Often, I remember exactly where I was when I first read a story, the thrill of a new idea taking root in my mind. These stories bring back the past while reopening windows on the future. Now, whether you're a long-time reader of the magazine holding a slice of your own history in your hands, or a new reader about to embark on discoveries of your own, I hope you will join with me in celebrating the thirtieth anniversary of *Asimov's Science Fiction* magazine.

AIR RAID

John Varley, writing as Herb Boehm

I was jerked awake by the silent alarm vibrating my skull. It won't shut down until you sit up, so I did. All around me in the darkened bunkroom the Snatch Team members were sleeping singly and in pairs. I yawned, scratched my ribs, and patted Gene's hairy flank. He turned over. So much for a romantic send-off.

Rubbing sleep from my eyes, I reached to the floor for my leg, strapped it on and plugged it in. Then I was running down the row of bunks toward Ops.

The situation board glowed in the gloom. Sun-Belt Airlines Flight 128, Miami to New York, September 15, 1979. We'd been looking for that one for three years. I should have been happy, but who can afford it when you wake up?

Liza Boston muttered past me on the way to Prep. I muttered back, and followed. The lights came on around the mirrors, and I groped my way to one of them. Behind us, three more people staggered in. I sat down, plugged in, and at last I could lean back and close my eyes.

They didn't stay closed for long. Rush! I sat up straight as the sludge I use for blood was replaced with supercharged go-juice. I looked around me and got a series of idiot grins. There was Liza, and Pinky and Dave. Against the far wall Cristabel was already turning slowly in front of the airbrush, getting a Caucasian paint job. It looked like a good team.

I opened the drawer and started preliminary work on my face. It's a bigger job every time. Transfusion or no, I looked like death. The right ear was completely gone now. I could no longer close my lips; the gums were permanently bared. A week earlier, a finger had fallen off in my sleep. And what's it to you, bugger?

While I worked, one of the screens around the mirror glowed. A smiling young woman, blonde, high brow, round face. Close enough. The crawl line read *Mary Katrina Sondergard, born Trenton, New Jersey, age in 1979: 25*. Baby, this is your lucky day.

The computer melted the skin away from her face to show me the bone structure, rotated it, gave me cross-sections. I studied the similarities with my own skull, noted the differences. Not bad, and better than some I'd been given.

I assembled a set of dentures that included the slight gap in the upper incisors. Putty filled out my cheeks. Nose plugs widened my nostrils. No need for ears; they'd be covered by the wig. I pulled a blank plastiflesh mask over my face and had to pause while it melted in. It took only a minute to mold it to perfection. I smiled at myself. How nice to have lips.

The delivery slot clunked and dropped a blonde wig and a pink outfit into my lap. The wig was hot from the styler. I put it on, then the pantyhose.

"Mandy? Did you get the profile on Sondergard?" I didn't look up; I recognized the voice.

"Roger."

"We've located her near the airport. We can slip you in before take-off, so you'll be the joker."

I groaned, and looked up at the face on the screen. Elfreda Baltimore-Louisville, Director of Operational Teams: lifeless face and tiny slits for eyes. What can you do when all the muscles are dead?

"Okay." You take what you get.

She switched off, and I spent the next two minutes trying to get dressed while keeping my eyes on the screens. I memorized names and faces of crew members plus the few facts known about them. Then I hurried out and caught up with the others. Elapsed time from first alarm: twelve minutes and seven seconds. We'd better get moving.

"Goddam Sun-Belt," Cristabel groused, hitching at her bra.

"At least they got rid of the high heels," Dave pointed out. A year earlier we would have been teetering down the aisles on three-inch platforms. We all wore short pink shifts with blue and white stripes diagonally across the front, and carried matching shoulder bags. I fussed trying to get the ridiculous pillbox cap pinned on.

We jogged into the dark Operations Control Room and lined up at the gate. Things were out of our hands now. Until the gate was ready, we could only wait.

I was first, a few feet away from the portal. I turned away from it; it gives me vertigo. I focused instead on the gnomes sitting at their consoles, bathed in glowing lights from their screens. None of them looked back at me. Withered, emaciated, all of them. Our fat legs and butts and breasts are a reproach to them, a reminder that Snatchers eat five times their ration to stay presentable for the masquerade. One day I'll be *built in* to a console, with all my guts on the outside and nothing left of my body but stink. The hell with them.

I buried my gun under a clutter of tissues and lipsticks in my purse. Elfreda was looking at me.

"Where is she?" I asked.

"Motel room. She was alone from 10 PM to noon on flight day."

Departure time was 1:15. She cut it close and would be in a hurry. Good.

"Can you catch her in the bathroom? Best of all, in the tub?"

"We're working on it." She sketched a smile with a fingertip drawn over lifeless lips. She knew how I liked to operate, but she was telling me I'd take what I got. It never hurts to ask. People are at their most defenseless stretched out and up to their necks in water.

"Go!" Elfreda shouted. I stepped through, and things started to go wrong.

I was faced the wrong way, stepping *out* of the bathroom door and facing the bedroom. I turned and spotted Mary Katrina Sondergard through the haze of the gate. There was no way I could reach her without stepping back through. I couldn't even shoot without hitting someone on the other side.

Sondergard was at the mirror, the worst possible place. Few people recognize themselves quickly, but she'd been looking right at herself. She saw me and her eyes widened. I stepped to the side, out of her sight.

"What the hell is . . . hey? Who the hell . . ." I noted the voice, which can be the trickiest thing to get right.

I figured she'd be more curious than afraid. My guess was right. She came out of the bathroom, passing through the gate as if it wasn't there, which it wasn't, since it only has one side. She had a towel wrapped around her.

"Jesus Christ! What are you doing in my—" Words fail you at a time like that. She knew she ought to say something, but what? *Excuse me, haven't I seen you in the mirror?*

I put on my best stew smile and held out my hand.

"Pardon the intrusion. I can explain everything. You see, I'm—" I hit her on the side of the head and she staggered and went down hard. Her towel fell to the floor. "—working my way through college." She started to get up, so I caught her under the chin with my artificial knee. She stayed down.

"Standard fuggin' *oil!*" I hissed, rubbing my injured knuckles. But there was no time. I knelt beside her, checked her pulse. She'd be okay, but I think I loosened some front teeth. I paused a moment. Lord, to look like that with no make-up, not prosthetics! She nearly broke my heart.

I grabbed her under the knees and wrestled her to the gate. She was a sack of limp noodles. Somebody reached through, grabbed her feet, and pulled. *So long, love! How would you like to go on a long voyage?*

I sat on her rented bed to get my breath. There were car keys and cigarettes in her purse, genuine tobacco, worth its weight in blood. I lit six of them, figuring I had five minutes of my very own. The room filled with sweet smoke. They don't make 'em like that anymore.

The Hertz sedan was in the motel parking lot. I got in and headed for the airport. I breathed deeply of the air, rich in hydrocarbons. I could see for hundreds of yards in the distance. The perspective nearly made me dizzy, but I live for these moments. There's no way to explain what it's like in the pre-meck world. The sun was a fierce yellow ball through the haze.

The other stews were boarding. Some of them knew Sondergard so I didn't say much, pleading a hangover. That went over well, with a lot of knowing laughs and sly remarks. Evidently it wasn't out of character. We boarded the 707 and got ready for the goats to arrive.

It looked good. The four commandos on the other side were identical twins for the women I was working with. There was nothing to do but be a stewardess until departure time. I hoped there would be no more glitches. Inverting a gate for a joker run into a motel room was one thing, but in a 707 at twenty thousand feet . . .

The plane was nearly full when the woman that Pinky would impersonate sealed the forward door. We taxied to the end of the runway, then we were airborne. I started taking orders for drinks in first.

The goats were the usual lot, for 1979. Fat and sassy, all of them, and as unaware of living in a paradise as a fish is of the sea. *What would you think, ladies and gents, of a trip to the future? No? I can't say I'm surprised. What if I told you this plane is going to—*

My alarm beeped as we reached cruising altitude. I consulted the indicator under my Lady Bulova and glanced at one of the restroom doors. I felt a vibration pass through the plane. *Damn it, not so soon.*

The gate was in there. I came out quickly, and motioned for Diana Gleason—Dave's pigeon—to come to the front.

"Take a look at this," I said, with a disgusted look. She started to enter the restroom, stopped when she saw the green glow. I planted a boot on her fanny and shoved. Perfect. Dave would have a chance to hear her voice before popping in. Though she'd be doing little but screaming when she got a look around . . .

Dave came through the gate, adjusting his silly little hat. Diana must have struggled.

"Be disgusted," I whispered.

"What a mess," he said as he came out of the restroom. It was a fair imitation of Diana's tone, though he'd missed the accent. It wouldn't matter much longer.

"What is it?" It was one of the stews from tourist. We stepped aside so she could get a look, and Dave shoved her through. Pinky popped out very quickly.

"We're minus on minutes," Pinky said. "We lost five on the other side."

"Five?" Dave-Diana squeaked. I felt the same way. We had a hundred and three passengers to process.

"Yeah. They lost contact after you pushed my pigeon through. It took that long to re-align."

You get used to that. Times runs at different rates on each side of the gate, though it's always sequential, past to future. Once we'd started the snatch with me entering Sondergard's room, there was no way to go back any earlier on either side. Here, in 1979, we had a rigid ninety-four minutes to get everything done. On the other side, the gate could never be maintained longer than three hours.

"When you left, how long was it since the alarm went in?"

"Twenty-eight minutes."

It didn't sound good. It would take at least two hours just customizing the wimps. Assuming there was no more slippage on 79-time, we might just make it. But there's *always* slippage. I shuddered, thinking about riding it in.

"No time for any more games, then," I said. "Pink, you go back to tourist and call both of the other girls up here. Tell 'em to come one at a time, and tell 'em we've got a problem. You know the bit."

"Biting back the tears. Got you." She hurried aft. In no time the first one showed up. Her friendly Sun-Belt Airlines smile was stamped on her face, but her stomach would be churning. *Oh God, this is it!*

I took her by the elbow and pulled her behind the curtains in front. She was breathing hard.

"Welcome to the twilight zone," I said, and put the gun to her head. She slumped, and I caught her. Pinky and Dave helped me shove her through the gate.

"Fug! The rotting thing's flickering."

Pinky was right. A very ominous sign. But the green glow stabilized as we watched, with who-knows-how-much slippage on the other side. Cristabel ducked through.

"We're plus thirty-three," she said. There was no sense talking about what we were all thinking: things were going badly.

"Back to tourist," I said. "Be brave, smile at everyone, but make it just a little bit too good, got it?"

"Check," Cristabel said.

We processed the other quickly, with no incident. Then there was no time to talk about anything. In eighty-nine minutes Flight 128 was going to be spread all over a mountain whether we were finished or not.

Dave went into the cockpit to keep the flight crew out of our hair. Me and Pinky were supposed to take care of first class, then back up Cristabel and Liza in tourist. We used the standard "coffee, tea, or milk" gambit, relying on our speed and their inertia.

I leaned over the first two seats on the left.

"Are you enjoying your flight?" Pop, pop. Two squeezes on the trigger, close to the heads and out of sight of the rest of the goats.

"Hi, folks. I'm Mandy. Fly me." Pop, pop.

Half-way to the galley, a few people were watching us curiously. But people don't make a fuss until they have a lot more to go on. One goat in the back row stood up, and I let him have it. By now there were only eight left awake. I abandoned the smile and squeezed off four quick shots. Pinky took care of the rest. We hurried through the curtains, just in time.

There was an uproar building in the back of tourist, with about sixty percent of the goats already processed. Cristabel glanced at me, and I nodded.

"Okay, folks," she bawled. "I want you to be quiet. Calm down and listen up. *You*, fathead, *pipe down* before I cram my foot up your ass sideways."

The shock of hearing her talk like that was enough to buy us a little time, anyway. We had formed a skirmish line across the width of the plane, guns out, steadied on seat backs, aimed at the milling, befuddled group of thirty goats.

The guns are enough to awe all but the most foolhardy. In essence, a standard-issue stunner is just a plastic rod with two grids about six inches apart. There's not enough metal in it to set off a hijack alarm. And to people from the Stone Age to about 2190 it doesn't look any more like a weapon than a ball-point pen. So Equipment Section jazzes them up in a plastic shell to real Buck Rogers blasters, with a dozen knobs and lights that flash and a barrel like the snout of a hog. Hardly anyone ever walks into one.

"We are in great danger, and time is short. You must all do exactly as I tell you, and you will be safe."

You can't give them time to think, you have to rely on your status as the Voice of Authority. The situation is *not* going to make sense to them, no matter how you explain it.

"Just a minute, I think you owe us—"

An airborne lawyer. I made a snap decision, thumbed the fireworks switch on my gun, and shot him.

The gun made a sound like a flying saucer with hemorrhoids, spit sparks and little jets of flame, and extended a green laser finger to his forehead. He dropped.

All pure kark, of course. But it sure is impressive.

And it's damned risky, too. I had to choose between a panic if the fathead got them to thinking, and a possible panic from the flash of the gun. But when a 20th gets to talking about his "rights" and what he is "owed," things can get out of hand. It's infectious.

It worked. There was a lot of shouting, people ducking behind seats, but no rush. We could have handled it, but we needed some of them conscious if we were ever going to finish the Snatch.

"Get up. Get *up*, you *slugs!*" Cristabel yelled. "He's stunned, nothing worse. But I'll *kill* the next one who gets out of line. Now *get to your feet* and do what I tell you. *Children first! Hurry*, as fast as you can, to the front of the plane. Do what the stewardess tells you. Come on, kids, *move!*"

I ran back into first class just ahead of the kids, turned at the open restroom door, and got on my knees.

They were petrified. There were five of them—crying, some of them, which always chokes me up—looking left and right at dead people in the first class seats, stumbling, near panic.

"Come on, kids," I called to them, giving my special smile. "Your parents will be along in just a minute. Everything's going to be all right, I promise you. Come on."

I got three of them through. The fourth balked. She was determined not to go through that door. She spread her legs and arms and I couldn't push her through. I will *not* hit a child, never. She raked her nails over my face. My wig came off, and she gaped at my bare head. I shoved her through.

Number five was sitting in the aisle, bawling. He was maybe seven. I ran back and picked him up, hugged him and kissed him, and tossed him through. God, I needed a rest, but I was needed in tourist.

"You, you, you, and you. Okay, you too. Help him, will you?" Pinky had a practiced eye for the ones that wouldn't be any use to anyone, even themselves. We herded them toward the front of the plane, then deployed ourselves along the left side where we could cover the workers. It didn't take long to prod them into action. We had them dragging the limp bodies forward as fast as they could go. Me and Cristabel were in tourist, with the others up front.

Adrenaline was being catabolized in my body now; the rush of action left me and I started to feel very tired. There's an unavoidable feeling of sympathy for the poor dumb goats that starts to get me about this stage of the game. Sure, they were better off, sure they were going to die if we didn't get them off the plane. But when they saw the other side they were going to have a hard time believing it.

The first ones were returning for a second load, stunned at what they'd just seen: dozens of people being put into a cubicle that was crowded when it was empty. One college student looked like he'd been hit in the stomach. He stopped by me and his eyes pleaded.

"Look, I want to *help* you people, just . . . what's going *on?* Is this some new kind of rescue? I mean, are we going to crash—"

I switched my gun to prod and brushed it across his cheek. He gasped, and fell back.

"Shut your fuggin' mouth and get moving, or I'll kill you." It would be hours before his jaw was in shape to ask any more questions.

We cleared tourist and moved up. A couple of the work gang were pretty damn pooped by then. Muscles like horses, all of them, but they can hardly run up a flight of stairs. We let some of them go through, including a couple that were at least fifty year old. *Je*-zuz. Fifty! We got down to a core of four men and two women who seemed strong, and worked them until they nearly dropped. But we processed everyone in twenty-five minutes.

The portapak came through as we were stripping off our clothes. Cristabel knocked on the door to the cockpit and Dave came out, already naked. A bad sign.

"I had to cork 'em," he said. "Bleeding Captain just *had* to make his Grand March through the plane. I tried *every*thing."

Sometimes you have to do it. The plane was on autopilot, as it normally would be at this time. But if any of us did anything detrimental to the craft, changed the fixed course of events in any way, that would be it. All that work for nothing, and Flight 128 inaccessible to us for all Time. I don't know sludge about time theory, but I know the practical angles. We can do things in the past only at times and places where it won't make any difference. We have to cover our tracks. There's flexibility; once a Snatcher left her gun behind and it went in with the plane. Nobody found it, or if they did, they didn't have the smoggiest idea of what it was, so we were okay.

Flight 128 was mechanical failure. That's the best kind; it means we don't have to keep the pilot unaware of the situation in the cabin right down to ground level. We can cork him and fly the plane, since there's nothing he could have done to save the flight anyway. A pilot-error smash is almost impossible to Snatch. If there's even one survivor, we can't touch it. It would not fit the fabric of space-time, which is immutable (though it can stretch a little), and we'd all just fade away and appear back in the ready-room.

My head was hurting. I wanted that portapak very badly.

"Who has the most hours on a 707?" Pinky did, so I sent her to the cabin, along with Dave, who could do the pilot's voice for air traffic control. You have to have a believable record in the flight recorder, too. They trailed two long tubes from the portapak, and the rest of us hooked in up close. We stood there, each of us smoking a fistful of cigarettes, wanting to finish them but hoping there wouldn't be time. The gate had vanished as soon as we tossed our clothes and the flight crew through.

But we didn't worry long. There's other nice things about Snatching, but nothing to compare with the rush of plugging into a portapak. The wake-up transfusion is nothing but fresh blood, rich in oxygen and sugars. What we were getting now was an insane brew of concentrated adrenaline, super-saturated hemoglobin, methedrine, white lightning, TNT, and Kickapoo joyjuice. It was like a firecracker in your heart; a boot in the box that rattled your sox.

"I'm growing hair on my chest," Cristabel said, solemnly. Everyone giggled.

"Would someone hand me my eyeballs?"

"The blue ones, or the red ones?"

"I think my ass just fell off."

We'd heard them all before, but we howled anyway. We were strong, *strong*, and for one golden moment we had no worries. Everything was hilarious. I could have torn sheet metal with my eyelashes.

But you get hyper on that mix. When the gate didn't show, and didn't show, and *didn't sweetjeez show* we all started milling. This bird wasn't going to fly all that much longer.

Then it did show, and we turned on. The first of the wimps came through, dressed in the clothes taken from a passenger it had been picked to resemble.

"Two thirty-five elapsed upside time," Cristabel announced.

"Je-zuz."

It is a deadening routine. You grab the harness around the wimp's shoulders and drag it along the aisle, after consulting the seat number painted on its forehead. The paint would last three minutes. You seat it, strap it in, break open the harness and carry it back to toss through the gate as you grab the next one. You have to take it for granted that they've done the work right on the other side: fillings in the teeth, fingerprints, the right match in height and weight and hair color. Most of those things don't matter much, especially on Flight 128 which was a crash-and-burn. There would be bits and pieces, and burned to a crisp at that. But you couldn't take chances. Those rescue workers are pretty thorough on the parts they *do* find; the dental work and fingerprints especially are important.

I hate wimps. I really hate 'em. Every time I grab the harness of one of them, if it's a child, I wonder if it's Alice. *Are you my kid, you vegetable, you slug, you slimy worm?* I joined the Snatchers right after the brain bugs ate the life out of my baby's head. I couldn't stand to think she was the last generation, that the last humans there would ever be would live with nothing in their heads, medically dead by standards that prevailed even in 1979, with computers working their muscles to keep them in tone. You grow up, reach puberty still fertile—one in a thousand—rush to get pregnant in your first heat. Then you find out your mom or pop passed on a chronic disease bound right into the genes, and none of your kids will be immune. I *knew* about the para-leprosy; I grew up with my toes rotting away. But this was too much. What do you do?

Only one in ten of the wimps had a customized face. It takes time and a lot of skill to build a new face that will stand up to a doctor's autopsy. The rest came pre-mutilated. We've got millions of them; it's not hard to find a good match in the body. Most of them would stay breathing, too dumb to stop, until they went in with the plane.

The plane jerked, hard. I glanced at my watch. Five minutes to impact. We should have time. I was on my last wimp. I could hear Dave frantically calling the ground. A bomb came through the gate, and I tossed it into the cockpit. Pinky turned on the pressure sensor on the bomb and came running out, followed by Dave. Liza was already through. I grabbed the limp dolls in stewardess costumes and tossed them to the floor. The engine fell off and a piece of it came through the cabin. We started to depressurize. The bomb blew away part of the cockpit (the ground crash crew would read it—we hoped—that part of the engine came through and killed the crew: no more words from the pilot on the flight recorder) and we turned, slowly, left and down. I was lifted toward the hole in the side of the plane, but I managed to hold onto a seat. Cristabel wasn't so lucky. She was blown backwards.

We started to rise slightly, losing speed. Suddenly it was uphill from where Cristabel was lying in the aisle. Blood oozed from her temple. I glanced back; everyone was gone, and three pink-suited wimps were piled on the floor. The plane began to stall, to nose down, and my feet left the floor.

"Come on, Bel!" I screamed. That gate was only three feet away from me, but I began pulling myself along to where she floated. The plane bumped, and she hit the floor. Incredibly, it seemed to wake her up. She started to swim toward me, and I grabbed her hand as the floor came up to slam us again. We crawled as the plane went through its final death agony, and we came to the door. The gate was gone.

There wasn't anything to say. We were going in. It's hard enough to keep the gate in place on a plane that's moving in a straight line. When a bird gets to corkscrewing and coming apart, the math is fearsome. So I've been told.

I embraced Cristabel and held her bloodied head. She was groggy, but managed to smile and shrug. You take what you get. I hurried into the restroom and got both of us down on the floor. Back to the forward bulkhead, Cristabel between my legs, back to front. Just like in training. We pressed our feet against the other wall. I hugged her tightly and cried on her shoulder.

And it was there. A green glow to my left. I threw myself toward it, dragging Cristabel, keeping low as two wimps were thrown head-first through the gate above our heads. Hands grabbed and pulled us through. I clawed my way a good five yards along the floor. You can leave a leg on the other side and I didn't have one to spare.

I sat up as they were carrying Cristabel to Medical. I patted her arm as she went by on the stretcher, but she was passed out. I wouldn't have minded passing out myself.

For a while, you can't believe it all really happened. Sometimes it turns out it *didn't* happen. You come back and find out all the goats in the holding pen have softly and suddenly vanished away because the continuum won't tolerate the changes and paradoxes you've put into it.

The people you've worked so hard to rescue are spread like tomato surprise all over some goddam hillside in Carolina and all you've got left is a bunch of ruined wimps and an exhausted Snatch Team. But not this time. I could see the goats milling around in the holding pen, naked and more bewildered than ever. And just starting to be *really* afraid.

Elfreda touched me as I passed her. She nodded, which meant well-done in her limited repertoire of gestures. I shrugged, wondering if I cared, but the surplus adrenaline was still in my veins and I found myself grinning at her. I nodded back.

Gene was standing by the holding pen. I went to him, hugged him. I felt the juices start to flow. *Damn it, let's squander a little ration and have us a good time.*

Someone was beating on the sterile glass wall of the pen. She shouted, mouthing angry words at us. *Why? What have you done to us?* It was Mary Sondergard. She implored her bald, one-legged twin to make her understand. She thought she had problems. God, was she pretty. I hated her guts.

Gene pulled me away from the wall. My hands hurt, and I'd broken off all my fake nails without scratching the glass. She was sitting on the floor now, sobbing. I heard the voice of the briefing officer on the outside speaker.

". . . Centauri 3 is hospitable, with an Earth-like climate. By that, I mean *your* Earth, not what it has become. You'll see more of that later. The trip will take five years, shiptime. Upon landfall, you will be entitled to one horse, a plow, three axes, two hundred kilos of seed grain . . ."

I leaned against Gene's shoulder. At their lowest ebb, this very moment, they were so much better than us. I had maybe ten years, half of that as a basketcase. They are our best, our very brightest hope. Everything is up to them.

". . . that no one will be forced to go. We wish to point out again, not for the last time, that you would all be dead without our intervention. There are things you should know, however. You cannot breathe our air. If you remain on Earth, you can never leave this building. We are not like you. We are the result of a genetic winnowing, a mutation process. We are the survivors, but our enemies have evolved along with us. They are winning. You, however, are immune to the diseases that afflict us . . ."

I winced, and turned away.

". . . the other hand, if you emigrate you will be given a chance at a new life. It won't be easy, but as Americans you should be proud of your pioneer heritage. Your ancestors survived, and so will you. It can be a rewarding experience, and I urge you . . ."

Sure. Gene and I looked at each other and laughed. *Listen to this, folks. Five percent of you will suffer nervous breakdowns in the next few days, and never leave. About the same number will commit suicide, here and on the way. When you get there, 60 to 70 percent will die in the first three years. You will die in childbirth, be eaten by animals, bury two out of three of your babies, starve slowly when the rains don't come. If you live, it will be to break your back behind a plow, sun-up to dusk. New Earth is Heaven, folks!*

God, how I wish I could go with them.

THE TIME OF
THE BURNING

Robert Silverberg

The dry foothills were burning along a curving crest from Milimorn to Hamifleu; and even up here, in his eyrie fifty miles east on Zygnor Peak, Group Captain Eremoil could feel the hot blast of the wind and taste the charred flavor of the air. A dense crown of murky smoke rose over the entire range. In an hour or two the fliers would extend the fire-line from Hamilton down to that little town at the base of the valley, and then tomorrow they'd torch the zone from there south to Sintalmond. And then this entire province would be ablaze, and woe betide any Shapeshifters who lingered in it.

"It won't be long now," Viggan said. "The war's almost over."

Eremoil looked up from his charts of the northwestern corner of the continent and stared at the subaltern. "Do you think so?" he asked vaguely.

"Thirty years. That's about enough."

"Not thirty. Five thousand years, six thousand, however long it's been since humans first came to this world. It's been war all the time, Viggan."

"For a lot of that time we didn't realize we were fighting a war, though."

"No," Eremoil said. "No, we didn't understand. But we understand now, don't we, Viggan?"

He turned his attention back to the charts, bending low, squinting, peering. The oily smoke in the air was bringing tears to his eyes and blurring his vision, and the charts were very finely drawn. Slowly he drew the pointer down the contour lines of the foothills below Hamifieu, checking off the villages on his report-sheets.

Every village along the arc of flame was marked on the charts, he hoped, and the officers had visited each to bring notice of the burning.

33

It would go hard for him and those beneath him if the mappers had left any place out, for Lord Stiamot had given orders that no human lives were to be lost in this climactic drive: all settlers were to be warned and given time to evacuate. The Metamorphs were being given the same warning. One did not simply roast one's enemies alive, Lord Stiamot had said repeatedly. One aimed only to bring them under one's control, and just now fire seemed to be the best means of doing that. Bringing the fire itself under control afterward might be a harder job, Eremoil thought, but that was not the problem of the moment.

"Kattikawn—Bizfern—Domgrave—Byelk—so many little towns, Viggan. Why do people want to live up here, anyway?"

"They say the land is fertile, sir. And the climate is mild, for such a northerly district."

"Mild? I suppose, if you don't mind half a year without rain." Eremoil coughed. He imagined he could hear the crackling of the distant fire through the tawny knee-high grass. On this side of Alhanroel it rained all winter long and then rained not at all the whole summer: a challenge for the farmers, one would think, but evidently they had surmounted it, considering how many agricultural settlements had sprouted along the slopes of these hills and downward into the valleys that ran to the sea. This was the height of the dry season now, and the region had been baking under summer sun for months—dry, dry, dry, the dark soil cracked and gullied, the shrubs folded and waiting. What a perfect time to put the place to the torch and force one's stubborn enemies down to the edge of the ocean, or into it! But no lives lost, no lives lost—Eremoil studied his lists. "Chikmoge—Fualle—Daniup—Michimang—" Again he looked up. To the subaltern he said, "Viggan, what will you do after the war?"

"My family owns lands in the Glayge Valley. I'll be a farmer again, I suppose. And you, sir?"

"My home is Stee. I was a civil engineer—aqueducts, sewage conduits, other such fascinating things. I can be that again. When did you last see the Glayge?"

"Four years ago," said Viggan.

"And five for me, since Stee. You were at the Battle of Trymone, weren't you?"

"Wounded. Slightly."

"Ever killed a Metamorph?"

"Yes, sir."

Eremoil said, "Not I. Never once. Nine years a soldier, never a life taken. Of course, I've been an officer. I'm not a good killer, I suspect."

"None of us are," said Viggan. "But when they're coming at you, changing shape five times a minute, with a knife in one hand and an axe in the other—or when you know they've raided your brother's land and murdered your nephew—"

"Is that what happened, Viggan?"

"Not to me, sire. But to others, plenty of others. The atrocities—I don't need to tell you how—"

"No. No, you don't. What's this town's name, Viggan?"

The subaltern leaned over the charts. "Singaserin, sir. The lettering's a little smudged, but that's what it says. And it's on our list. See, here. We gave them notice day before yesterday."

"I think we've done them all, then."

"I think so, sir," said Viggan.

Eremoil shuffled the charts into a stack, put them away, and looked out again toward the west. There was a distinct line of demarcation between the zone of the burning and the untouched hills south of it, dark green and seemingly lush with foliage. But the leaves of those trees were shriveled and greasy from months without rain, and those hillsides would explode as though they had been bombed when the fire reached them. Now and again he saw little bursts of flame, no more than puffs of sudden brightness as though from the striking of a light. But it was a trick of distance, Eremoil knew; each of those tiny flares was the eruption of a vast new territory as the fire, carrying itself now by airborne embers where the fliers themselves were not spreading it, devoured the forest beyond Hamifieu.

Viggan said, "Messenger here, sir."

Eremoil turned. A tall young man in a sweaty uniform had clambered down from a mount and was staring uncertainly at him.

"Well?" he said.

"Captain Vanayle sent me, sir. Problem down in the valley. Settler won't evacuate."

"He'd better," Eremoil said, shrugging. "What town is it?"

"Between Kattikawn and Bizfern, sir. Substantial tract. The man's name is Kattikawn, too, Aibil Kattikawn. He told Captain Vanayle that he holds his land by direct grant of the Pontifex Dvorn, that his people have been here thousands of years, and that he isn't going to——"

Eremoil sighed and said, "I don't care if he holds his land by direct grant of the Divine. We're burning that district tomorrow and he'll fry if he stays there."

"He knows that, sir."

"What does he want us to do? Make the fire go around his farm, eh?" Eremoil waved his arm impatiently. "Evacuate him, regardless of what he is or isn't going to do."

"We've tried that," said the messenger. "He's armed and he offered resistance. He says he'll kill anyone who tries to remove him from his land."

"Kill?" Eremoil said, as though the word had no meaning. *"Kill?* Who talks of killing other human beings? The man is crazy. Send fifty troops and get him on his way to one of the safe zones."

"I said he offered resistance, sir. There was an exchange of fire. Captain Vanayle believes that he can't be removed without loss of life. Captain Vanayle asks that you go down in person to reason with the man, sir."

"That *I*——"

Viggan said quietly, "It may be the simplest way. These big landholders can be very difficult."

"Let Vanayle go to him," Eremoil said.

"Captain Vanayle has already attempted to parley with the man, sir," the messenger said. "He was unsuccessful. This Kattikawn demands an audience with Lord Stiamot. Obviously that's impossible, but perhaps if you were to go——"

Eremoil considered it. It was absurd for the commanding officer of the district to undertake such a task. It was Vanayle's direct responsibility to clear the territory before tomorrow's burning; it was Eremoil's to remain up here and direct the action. On the other hand, clearing the territory was ultimately Eremoil's responsibility also; and Vanayle had plainly failed to do it; and sending in a squad to make a forcible removal would probably end in Kattikawn's death and the deaths of a few soldiers, too, which was hardly a useful outcome. Why not go? Eremoil nodded slowly. Protocol be damned: he would not stand on ceremony.

He had nothing significant left to do this afternoon and Viggan could look after any details that came up. And if he could save one life, one stupid stubborn old man's life, by taking a little ride down the mountainside—

"Get my floater," he said to Viggan.

"Sir?"

"Get it. Now, before I change my mind. I'm going down to see him."

"But Vanayle has already—"

"Stop being troublesome, Viggan. I'll only be gone a short while. You're in command here until I get back, but I don't think you'll have to work very hard. Can you handle it?"

"Yes, sir," the subaltern said glumly.

It was a longer journey than Eremoil expected, nearly two hours down the switchbacked road to the base of Zygnor Peak, then across the uneven sloping plateau to the foothills that ringed the coastal plain. The air was hotter though less smoky down there; shimmering heat-waves spawned mirages, and made the landscape seem to melt and flow. The road was empty of traffic; but he was stopped again and again by panicky migrating beasts, strange animals of species that he could not identify, fleeing wildly from the fire zone ahead. Shadows were beginning to lengthen by the time Eremoil reached the foothill settlements. Here the fire was a tangible presence, like a second sun in the sky; Eremoil felt the heat of it against his cheek, and a fine grit settled on his skin and clothing.

The places he had been checking on his lists now became uncomfortably real to him: Byelk, Domgrave, Bizfern. One was just like the next, a central huddle of shops and public buildings, an outer residential rim, a ring of farms radiating outward beyond that, each town tucked in its little valley where some stream cut down out of the hills and lost itself on the plain. They were all empty now, or nearly so; just a few stragglers left, the others already on the highways leading to the coast. Eremoil supposed that he could walk into any of these houses and find books, carvings, souvenirs of holidays abroad, even pets, perhaps, abandoned in grief; and tomorrow all this would be ashes. The settlers here had lived for centuries under the menace of an implacable, savage foe that flitted in and out of the forests in masquerade, disguised as one's friend, one's lover, one's son; on errands of murder, a secret quiet war between the dispossessed and those who had come after them, a war that had been inevitable since the early outposts on Majipoor had grown into cities and sprawling agricultural territories that consumed more and more of the domain of the natives. Some remedies involve drastic cautery: in this final convulsion of the struggle between humans and Shapeshifters there was not help for it, Byelk and Domgrave and Bizfern must be destroyed so that the agony could end. Yet that did not make it easy to face abandoning one's home, Eremoil thought, nor was it even particularly easy to destroy someone else's home, as he had been doing for days, unless one did it from a distance, from a comfortable distance where all this torching was only a strategic abstraction.

Beyond Bizfern the foothills swung westward a long way, the road following their contour. There were good streams here, almost little rivers, and the road was heavily forested where it had not been cleared for planting. Yet even here the months without rain had left the forests terribly combustible, drifts of dead fallen leaves everywhere, fallen branches, old cracked trunks.

"This is the place, sir," the messenger said.

Eremoil beheld a box canyon, narrow at its mouth and much broader within, with a stream running down its middle. Against the gathering shadows he made out an impressive manor, a great white building with a roof of green tiles, and beyond that what seemed to be an immense acreage of crops. Armed guards were waiting at the mouth of the canyon. This was no simple farmer's spread; this was the domain of one who regarded himself as a duke. Eremoil saw trouble in store.

He dismounted and strode toward the guards, who regarded him coldly and held their energy-throwers at the ready. To one that seemed the most imposing he said, "Group Captain Eremoil to see Aibil Kattikawn."

"The Kattikawn is awaiting Lord Stiamot," was the flat, chilly reply.

"Lord Stiamot is occupied elsewhere. I represent him today. I am Group Captain Eremoil, commanding officer in the district."

"We are instructed to admit only Lord Stiamot."

"Tell your master," Eremoil said wearily, "that the Coronal sends his regrets and asks him to offer his grievances to Group Captain Eremoil instead."

The guard seemed indifferent to that. But after a moment he spun around and entered the canyon. Eremoil watched him walking unhurriedly along the bank of the stream until he disappeared in the dense shrubbery of the plaza before the manor house. A long time passed; the wind changed, bringing a hot gust from the fire zone, a layer of dark air that stung the eyes and scorched the throat. Eremoil envisioned a coating of black gritty particles on his lungs. But from here, in this sheltered place, the fire itself was invisible.

Eventually the guard returned, just as unhurriedly.

"The Kattikawn will see you," he announced.

Eremoil beckoned to his driver and his guide, the messenger. But Kattikawn's guard shook his head.

"Only you, Captain."

The driver looked disturbed. Eremoil waved her back. "Wait for me here," he said. "I don't think I'll be long."

He followed the guard down the canyon path to the manor house.

From Aibil Kattikawn he expected the same sort of hard-eyed welcome that the guards had offered, but Eremoil had underestimated the courtesy a provincial aristocrat would feel obliged to provide. Kattikawn greeted him with a warm smile and an intense, searching stare, gave him what seemed to be an unfeigned embrace and led him into the great house, which was sparsely furnished but elegant in its stark and rugged way. Exposed beams of oiled black wood dominated the vaulted ceilings; hunting trophies loomed high on the walls; the furniture was massive and plainly ancient. The whole place had an archaic air. So too did Aibil Kattikawn. He was a big man, much taller than the lightly built Eremoil and broad through the shoulders, a breadth dramatically enhanced by the heavy steetmoy-fur cloak he wore. His forehead was high, his hair gray but thick, rising in heavy ridges; his eyes were dark, his lips thin. In every respect he was of the most imposing presence.

When he had poured bowls of some glistening amber wine and they had had the first sips, Kattikawn said, "So you need to burn my lands?"

"We must burn this entire province, I'm afraid."

"A stupid stratagem, perhaps the most foolish thing in the whole history of human warfare. Do you know how valuable the produce of this district is? Do you know how many generations of hard work have gone into building these farms?"

"The entire zone from Milimorn to Sintalmond and beyond is a center of Metamorph guerilla activity, the last one remaining in Alhanroel. The Coronal is determined to end this ugly war finally, and it can only be done by smoking the Shapeshifters out of their hiding places in these hills."

"There are other methods."

"We have tried them and they have failed," Eremoil said.

"Have you? Have you tried moving from inch to inch through the forests searching for them? Have you moved every soldier on Majipoor in here to conduct the mopping-up operations? Of course not. It's too much trouble. It's much simpler to send out those fliers and set the whole place on fire."

"This war has consumed an entire generation of our lives."

"And the Coronal grows impatient toward the end," said Kattikawn. "At my expense."

"The Coronal is a master of strategy. The Coronal had defeated a dangerous and almost incomprehensible enemy and had made Majipoor safe for human occupation for the first time—all but this district."

"We have managed well enough with these Metamorphs skulking all around us, Captain. I haven't been massacred yet. I've been able to handle them. They haven't been remotely as much of a threat to my welfare as my own government seems to be. Your Coronal, Captain, is a fool."

Eremoil controlled himself. "Future generations will hail him as a hero among heroes."

"Very likely," said Kattikawn. "That's the kind that usually gets made into heroes. I tell you that it was not necessary to destroy an entire province in order to round up a few thousand aborigines that remain at large. I tell you that it is a rash and shortsighted move on the part of a tired general who is in a hurry to return to the ease of Castle Mount."

"Be that as it may, the decision has been taken; and everything from Milimorn to Hamifieu is already ablaze."

"So I have noticed."

"The fire is advancing toward Kattikawn village. Perhaps by dawn the outskirts of your own domain will be threatened. During the day we'll continue the incendiary attacks past this region and on south as far as Sintalmond."

"Indeed," said Kattikawn calmly.

"This area will become an inferno. We ask you to abandon it while you still have time."

"I choose to remain, Captain."

Eremoil let his breath out slowly. "We cannot be responsible for your safety if you do."

"No one had ever been responsible for my safety except myself."

"What I'm saying is that you'll die, and die horribly. We have no way of laying down the fire line in such a way as to avoid your domain."

"I understand."

"You ask us to murder you, then."

"I ask nothing of the sort. You and I have no transaction at all. You fight your war; I maintain my home. If the fire that your war requires should intrude on the territory I call my own, so much the worse for me, but no murder is involved. We are bound on independent courses, Captain Eremoil."

"You reasoning is strange. You will die as a direct result of our incendiary attack. Your life will be on our souls."

"I remain here of free will, after having been duly warned," said Kattikawn. "My life will be on my own soul alone."

"And your people's lives? They'll die too."

"Those who choose to remain, yes. I've given them warning of what is about to happen. Three have set out for the coast. The rest will stay. Of their own will, and not to please me. This is our place. Another bowl of wine, Captain?"

Eremoil refused, then instantly changed his mind and proffered the empty bowl. Kattikawn, as he poured, said, "Is there no way I can speak with Lord Stiamot?"

"None."

"I understand the Coronal is in this area."

"Half a day's journey, yes. But he is inaccessible to such petitioners."

"By design, I imagine." Kattikawn smiled. "Do you think he's gone mad, Eremoil?"

"The Coronal? Not at all."

"This burning, though—such a desperate move, such an idiotic move. The reparations he'll have to pay afterward—millions of royals; it'll bankrupt the treasury; it'll cost more than fifty castles as grand as the one he's built on top of the Mount. And for what? Give us two or three more years and we'd have the Shapeshifters tamed."

"Or five or ten or twenty," said Eremoil. "This must be the end of the war, now, this season. This ghastly convulsion, this shame on everyone, this stain, this long nightmare—"

"Oh, you think the war's been a mistake, then?"

Eremoil quickly shook his head. "The fundamental mistake was made long ago, when our ancestors chose to settle on a world that was already inhabited by an intelligent species. By our time we had no choice but to crush the Metamorphs, or else retreat entirely from Majipoor; and how could we do that?"

"Yes," Kattikawn said, "how could we give up the homes that had been ours and our forebears for so long, eh?"

Eremoil ignored the heavy irony. "We took this planet from an unwilling people. For thousands of years we attempted to live in peace with them, until we admitted that coexistence was impossible. Now we are imposing our will by force, which is not beautiful, because the alternatives are even worse."

"What will Lord Stiamot do with the Shapeshifters he has in his internment camps? Plough them under as fertilizer for the fields he's burned?"

"They'll be given a vast reservation in Zimroel," said Eremoil. "Half a continent to themselves—that's hardly cruelty. Alhanroel will be ours, and an ocean between us. Already the resettlement is under way. Only your area remains unpacified. Lord Stiamot has taken upon himself the terrible burden of responsibility for a harsh but necessary act, and the future will hail him for it."

"I hail him now," said Kattikawn. "O wise and just Coronal! Who in his infinite wisdom destroys this land so that his world need not have the bother of troublesome aborigines lurking about. It would have been better for me, Eremoil, if he had been less noble of spirit, this hero-king of yours. Or more noble, perhaps. He'd seem much more wondrous to me if he'd chosen some slower method of conquering these last holdouts. Thirty years of war—what's another two or three?"

"This is the way he had chosen. The fires are approaching this place as we speak."

"Let them come. I'll be here, defending my house against them."

"You haven't seen the fire zone," Eremoil said. "Your defense won't last ten seconds. The fire eats everything in its way."

"Quite likely. I'll take my chances."

"I beg you—"

"You beg? Are you a beggar, then? What if I were to beg? I beg you, Captain, spare my estate!"

"It can't be done. I beg you indeed: retreat, and spare your life and the lives of your people."

"What would you have me do, go crawling along that highway to the coast, and live in some squalid little cabin in Alaisor or Bailemoona? This is my place. I would rather die here in ten seconds tomorrow than live a thousand years in cowardly exile." Kattikawn walked to the window. "It grows dark, Captain. Will you be my guest for dinner?"

"I am unable to stay, I regret to tell you."

"Does this dispute bore you? We can talk of other things. I would prefer that."

Eremoil reached for the other man's great paw of a hand. "I have obligations at my headquarters. It would have been an unforgettable pleasure to accept your hospitality. I wish it were possible. Will you forgive me for declining?"

"It pains me to see you leave unfed. Do you hurry off to Lord Stiamot?"

Eremoil was silent.

"I would ask you to gain me an audience with him," said Kattikawn.

"It can't be done, and it would do no good. Please: leave this place tonight. Let us dine together, and then abandon your domain."

"This is my place, and here I remain," Kattikawn said. "I wish you well, Captain, a long and harmonious life. And I thank you for this conversation." He closed his eyes a moment and inclined his head: a tiny bow, a delicate dismissal. Eremoil moved toward the door of the great hall. Kattikawn said, "The other officer thought he would pull me out of here by force. You had more sense, and I compliment you. Farewell, Captain Eremoil."

Eremoil searched for appropriate words, found none, and settled for a gesture of salute.

Kattikawn's guards led him back to the mouth of his canyon, where Eremoil's driver and the messenger waited, playing some game with dice by the side of the floater. They snapped to attention when they saw Eremoil, but he signaled them to relax. He looked off to the east, at the great mountains that rose on the far side of the valley. In these northerly latitudes, on this summer night, the sky was still light, even to the east; and the heavy bulk of Zygnor Peak lay across the horizon like a black wall against the pale gray of the sky. South of it was its twin, Mount Haimon, where the Coronal had made his headquarters. Eremoil stood for a time studying the two mighty peaks, and the foothills below them, and the pillar of fire and smoke that ascended on the other side, and the moons just coming into the sky; then he shook his head and turned and looked back toward Aibil Kattikawn's manor, disappearing now in the shadows of the late dusk. In his rise through the army ranks Eremoil had come to know dukes and princes and army other high ones that a mere civil engineer does not often meet in private life; and he had spent more than little time with the Coronal himself and the intimate circle of advisors around him; and yet he thought he had never encountered anyone quite like this Kattikawn, who was either the most noble or the most misguided man on the planet, and perhaps both.

"Let's go," he said to the driver. "Take the Haimon road."

"The Haimon, sir?"

"To the Coronal, yes. Can you get us there by midnight?"

The road to the southern peak was much like the Zygnor road, but steeper and not as well paved. In darkness its twists and turns would probably be dangerous at the speed Eremoil's driver, a woman of Stoien, was risking; but the red glow of the fire zone lit up the valley and the foothills and much reduced the risks. Eremoil said nothing during the long journey. There was nothing to say: how could the driver or the messenger-lad possibly understand the nature of Aibil Kattikawn? Eremoil himself, on first hearing that one of the local farmers refused to leave his land, had misunderstood that nature, imagining some crazy old fool, some stubborn fanatic blind to the realities of his peril. Kattikawn was stubborn, surely; and possibly he could be called a fanatic; but he was none of the other things, not even crazy, however crazy his philosophy might seem to those, like Eremoil, who lived by other codes.

He wondered what he was going to tell Lord Stiamot.

No use rehearsing: words would come, or they would not. He slipped after a time into a kind of waking sleep, his mind lucid but frozen, contemplating nothing, calculating nothing. The floater, moving lightly and swiftly up the dizzying road, climbed out of the valley and into the jagged country beyond. At midnight it was still in the lower reaches of Mount Haimon, but no matter: the Coronal was known to keep late hours, often not to sleep at all. Eremoil did not doubt he would be available.

Somewhere on the upper slopes of Haimon he dropped without any awareness of it into sleep; and he was surprised and confused when the messenger shook him gently awake, saying, "This is Lord Stiamot's camp, sir." Blinking, disoriented, Eremoil found himself still sitting erect, his legs cramped, his back stiff. The moons were far across the sky, and the night now was black except for the amazing fiery gash that tore across it to the west. Awkwardly Eremoil scrambled from the floater. Even now, in the middle of the night, the Coronal's camp was a busy place, messengers running to and fro, lights burning in many of the buildings. An adjutant appeared, recognized Eremoil, gave him an exceedingly formal salute. "This visit comes as a surprise, Captain Eremoil!"

"To me also, I'd say. Is Lord Stiamot in the camp?"

"The Coronal is holding a staff meeting. Does he expect you, Captain?"

"No," said Eremoil. "But I need to speak with him."

The adjutant was undisturbed by that. Staff meetings in the middle of the night, regional commanders turning up unannounced for conferences—well, why not? This was war, and protocols were improvised from day to day. Eremoil followed the man through the camp to an octagonal tent that bore the starburst insignia of the Coronal. A ring of guards surrounded the place, as grim and dedicated-looking as those who had held the mouth of Kattikawn's canyon. There had been four attempts on Lord Stiamot's life in the past eighteen months—all Metamorphs, all thwarted. No Coronal in Majipoor's history had ever died violently, but none had ever waged war, either, before this one.

The adjutant spoke with the commander of the guard; suddenly Eremoil found himself at the center of a knot of armed men, with lights shining maddeningly into his eyes and fingers digging painfully into his arms. For an instant the onslaught astonished him. But then he regained his poise and said, "What is this? I am Group Captain Eremoil."

"Unless you're a Shapeshifter," one of the men said.

"And you think you'd find that out by squeezing me and blinding me with your glare?"

"There are ways," said another.

Eremoil laughed. "None that ever proved reliable. But go on: test me, and do it fast. I must speak with Lord Stiamot."

They did indeed have tests. Someone gave him a strip of green paper and told him to touch his tongue to it. He did, and the paper turned orange. Someone else asked for a snip of his hair, and set fire to it. Eremoil looked on in amazement. It was a month since he had last been to the Coronal's camp, and none of these practices had been employed then; there must been another assassination attempt, he decided, or else some quack scientist had come among them with these techniques. So far as Eremoil knew, there was no true way to distinguish a Metamorph from an authentic human when the Metamorph had taken on a human form, except through dissection, and he did not propose to submit to that.

"You pass," they said at last. "You can go in."

But they accompanied him. Eremoil's eyes, dazzled already, adjusted with difficulty to the dimness of the Coronal's tent, but after a moment he saw half a dozen figures at the far end, and Lord Stiamot among them. They seemed to be praying. He heard murmured invocations and responses, bits of the old scripture. Was this the sort of staff meetings the Coronal held now? Eremoil went forward and stood a few yard from the group. He knew only one of the Coronal's attendants, Damlang of Bibiroon, who was generally considered second or third in line for the throne; the others did not seem even to be soldiers, for they were older men, in civilian dress, with a soft citified look about them, poets, dream-speakers perhaps, certainly not warriors. But the war was almost over.

The Coronal looked in Eremoil's direction without seeming to notice him.

Eremoil was startled by Lord Stiamot's harried, ragged look. The Coronal had been growing visibly older all through the past three years of the war, but the process seemed to have accelerated now: he appeared shrunken, colorless, frail, his skin parched, his eyes dull. He might have been a hundred years old; and yet he was no older than Eremoil himself, a man in middle life. Eremoil could remember the day Stiamot had come to the throne, and how Stiamot had vowed that day to end the madness of this constant undeclared warfare with the Metamorphs, to collect the planet's ancient natives and remove them from the territories settled by mankind. Only thirty years, and the Coronal looked the better part of a century older; but he had spent his reign in the field, as no Coronal before him had done and probably none after him would ever do, campaigning in the Glayge Valley, in the hotlands of the south, in the Stoien, year after year encircling the Shapeshifters with his twenty armies and penning them in camps. And now he was nearly finished with the job, just the guerillas of the northwest remaining at liberty—a constant struggle, a long fierce life of war, with scarcely time to return to the tender springtime of Castle Mount for the pleasures of the throne. Eremoil had occasionally wondered, as the war went on and on, how Lord Stiamot would respond if the Pontifex should die, and he be called upward to the other kingship and be forced to take up residence in the Labyrinth: would he decline, and retain the Coronal's crown so that he might remain in the field? But the Pontifex was in fine health, so it was said, and here was Lord Stiamot now a tired little old man, looking to be at the edge of the grave himself. Eremoil understood abruptly what Aibil Kattikawn had failed to comprehend, why it was that Lord Stiamot was so eager to bring the final phase of the war to its conclusion regardless of the cost.

The Coronal said, "Who do we have there? Is that Finiwain?"

"Eremoil, my lord. In command of the forces carrying out the burning."

"Eremoil. Yes. Eremoil. I recall. Come, sit with us. We are giving thanks to the Divine for the end of the war, Eremoil. These people have come to me from my mother the Lady of the Isle, who guards us in dreams, and we will spend the night in songs of praise and gratitude, for in the morning the circle of fire will be complete. Eh, Eremoil? Come, sit, sing with us. You know the songs to the Lady, don't you?"

Eremoil heard the Coronal's cracked and frayed voice with shock. That faded thread of dry sound was all that remained of his once majestic tone. This hero, this demigod, was withered and ruined by his long campaign;

there was nothing left of him; he was a spectre, a shadow. Seeing him like this, Eremoil wondered if Lord Stiamot had ever been the mighty figure of memory, or if perhaps that was only mythmaking and propaganda, and the Coronal had all along been less than met the eye.

Lord Stiamot beckoned. Eremoil reluctantly moved closer.

He thought of what he come here to say. *My lord, there is a man in the path of the fire who will not move and will not allow himself to be moved, and who cannot be moved without the loss of life; and, my lord, he is too fine a man to be destroyed in this way. So I ask you, my lord, to halt the burning, perhaps to devise some alternative strategy, so that we may seize the Metamorphs as they flee the fire zone but no not need to extend the destruction beyond the point it already reaches, because—*

No.

He saw the utter impossibility of asking the Coronal to delay the end of the war a single hour. Not for Kattikawn's sake, not for Eremoil's sake, not for the sake of the holy Lady his mother could the burning be halted now, for these were the last days of the war and the Coronal's need to proceed to the end was the overriding force that swept all else before it. Eremoil might try to halt the burning on his own authority, but he could not ask the Coronal for approval.

Lord Stiamot thrust his head toward Eremoil.

"What is it, Captain? What bothers you? Here. Sit by me. Sing with us, Captain. Raise your voice in thanksgiving."

They began a hymn, some tune Eremoil did not know. He hummed along, improvising a harmony. After that they sang another, and another, and that one Eremoil did know; he sang, but in a hollow and tuneless way. Dawn could not be far off now. Quietly he moved into the shadows and out of the tent. Yes, there was the sun, beginning to cast the first greenish light along the eastern face of Mount Haimon, though it would be an hour or more before its rays climbed the mountain wall and illuminated the doomed valleys to the southwest. Eremoil yearned for a week of sleep. He looked for the adjutant and said, "Will you send a message for me to my subaltern on Zygnor Peak?"

"Of course, sir."

"Tell him to take charge of the next phase of the burning and proceed as scheduled. I'm going to remain here during the day and will return to my headquarters this evening, after I've had some rest."

"Yes, sir."

Eremoil turned away and looked toward the west, still wrapped in night except where the terrible glow of the fire zone illuminated it. Probably Aibil Kattikawn had been busy all this night with pumps and hoses, wetting down his lands. It would do no good, of course; a fire of that magnitude takes all in its path, and burns until no fuel is left. So Kattikawn would die and the tiled roof of the manor house would collapse, and there was no helping it. He could be saved only at the risk of the lives of innocent soldiers, and probably not even then; or he could be saved if Eremoil chose to disregard the orders of Lord Stiamot, but not for long. So he will die. After nine years in the field, Eremoil thought, I am at last the cause of taking a life, and he is one of our own citizens. So be it. So be it.

He remained at the lookout post, weary but unable to move on, another hour or so, until he saw the first explosions of flame in the foothills near Bizfern, or maybe Domgrave, and knew that the morning's incendiary bombing had begun. The war will soon be over, he told himself. The last of our enemies now feel toward the safety of the coast, where they will be interned and transported overseas; and the world will be quiet again. He felt the warmth of the summer sun on his back and the warmth of the spreading fires on his cheeks. The world will be quiet again, he thought, and went to find a place to sleep.

SPEECH SOUNDS

OCTAVIA E. BUTLER

There was trouble aboard the Washington Boulevard bus. Rye had expected trouble sooner or later in her journey. She had put off going until loneliness and hopelessness drove her out. She believed she might have one group of relatives left alive—a brother and his two children twenty miles away in Pasadena. That was a day's journey one-way, if she were lucky. The unexpected arrival of the bus as she left her Virginia Road home had seemed to be a piece of luck—until the trouble began.

Two young men were involved in a disagreement of some kind, or, more likely, a misunderstanding. They stood in the aisle, grunting and gesturing at each other, each in his own uncertain "T" stance as the bus lurched over the potholes. The driver seemed to be putting some effort into keeping them off balance. Still, their gestures stopped just short of contact—mock punches, hand-games of intimidation to replace lost curses.

People watched the pair, then looked at each other and made small anxious sounds. Two children whimpered.

Rye sat a few feet behind the disputants and across from the back door. She watched the two carefully, knowing the fight would begin when someone's nerve broke or someone's hand slipped or someone came to the end of his limited ability to communicate. These things could happen any time.

One of them happened as the bus hit an especially large pothole and one man, tall, thin, and sneering, was thrown into his shorter opponent.

Instantly, the shorter man drove his left fist into the disintegrating sneer. He hammered his larger opponent as though he neither had nor needed any weapon other than his left fist. He hit quickly enough, hard enough to batter his opponent down before the taller man could regain his balance or hit back even once.

51

People screamed or squawked in fear. Those nearby scrambled to get out of the way. Three more young men roared in excitement and gestured wildly. Then, somehow, a second dispute broke out between two of these three—probably because one inadvertently touched or hit the other.

As the second fight scattered frightened passengers, a woman shook the driver's shoulder and grunted as she gestured toward the fighting.

The driver grunted back through bared teeth. Frightened, the woman drew away.

Rye, knowing the methods of bus drivers, braced herself and held on to the crossbar of the seat in front of her. When the driver hit the brakes, she was ready and the combatants were not. They fell over seats and onto screaming passengers, creating even more confusion. At least one more fight started.

The instant the bus came to a full stop, Rye was on her feet, pushing the back door. At the second push, it opened and she jumped out, holding her pack in one arm. Several other passengers followed, but some stayed on the bus. Buses were so rare and irregular now, people rode when they could, no matter what. There might not be another bus today—or tomorrow. People making intercity trips like Rye's from Los Angeles to Pasadena made plans to camp out, or risked seeking shelter with locals who might rob or murder them.

The bus did not move, but Rye moved away from it. She intended to wait until the trouble was over and get on again, but if there was shooting, she wanted the protection of a tree. Thus, she was near the curb when a battered, blue Ford on the other side of the street made a U-turn and pulled up in front of the bus. Cars were rare these days—as rare as a severe shortage of fuel and of relatively unimpaired mechanics could make them. Cars that still ran were as likely to be used as weapons as they were to serve as transportation. Thus, when the driver of the Ford beckoned to Rye, she moved away warily. The driver got out—a big man, young, neatly bearded with dark, thick hair. He wore a long overcoat and a look of wariness that matched Rye's. She stood several feet from him, waiting to see what he would do. He looked at the bus, now rocking with the combat inside, then at the small cluster of passengers who had gotten off. Finally he looked at Rye again.

She returned his gaze, very much aware of the old forty-five automatic her jacket concealed. She watched his hands.

He pointed with his left hand toward the bus. The dark-tinted windows prevented him from seeing what was happening inside.

His use of the left hand interested Rye more than his obvious question. Left-handed people tended to be less impaired, more reasonable and comprehending, less driven by frustration, confusion, and anger.

She imitated his gesture, pointing toward the bus with her own left hand, then punching the air with both fists.

The man took off his coat revealing a Los Angeles Police Department uniform complete with baton and service revolver.

Rye took another step back from him. There was no more LAPD, no more *any* large organization, governmental or private. There were neighborhood patrols and armed individuals. That was all.

The man took something from his coat pocket, then threw the coat into the car. Then he gestured Rye back, back toward the rear of the bus. He had something made of plastic in his hand. Rye did not understand what he wanted until he went to the rear door of the bus and beckoned her to stand there. She obeyed mainly out of curiosity. Cop or not, maybe he could do something to stop the stupid fighting.

He walked around the front of the bus, to the street side where the driver's window was open. There, she thought she saw him throw something into the bus. She was still trying to peer through the tinted glass when the people began stumbling out the rear door, choking and weeping. Gas.

Rye caught an old woman who would have fallen, lifted two little children down when they were in danger of being knocked down and trampled. She could see the bearded man helping people at the front door. She caught a thin old man shoved out by one of the combatants. Staggered by the old man's weight, she was barely able to get out of the way as the last of the young men pushed his way out. This one, bleeding from nose and mouth, stumbled into another and they grappled blindly, still sobbing from the gas.

The bearded man helped the bus driver out through the front door, though the driver did not seem to appreciate his help. For a moment, Rye thought there would be another fight. The bearded man stepped back and watched the driver gesture threateningly, watched him shout in wordless anger.

The bearded man stood still, made no sound, refused to respond to clearly obscene gestures. The least impaired people tended to do this—

stand back unless they were physically threatened and let those with less control scream and jump around. It was as though they felt it beneath them to be as touchy as the less comprehending. This was an attitude of superiority and that was the way people like the bus driver perceived it. Such "superiority" was frequently punished by beatings, even by death. Rye had had close calls of her own. As a result, she never went unarmed. And in this world where the only likely common language was body language, being armed was often enough. She had rarely had to draw her gun or even display it.

The bearded man's revolver was on constant display. Apparently that was enough for the bus driver. The driver spat in disgust, glared at the bearded man for a moment longer, then strode back to his gas-filled bus. He stared at it for a moment, clearly wanting to get in, but the gas was still too strong. Of the windows, only his tiny driver's window actually opened. The front door was open, but the rear door would not stay open unless someone held it. Of course, the air conditioning had failed long ago. The bus would take some time to clear. It was the driver's property, his livelihood. He had pasted old magazine pictures of items he would accept as fare on its sides. Then he would use what he collected to feed his family or to trade. If his bus did not run, he did not eat. On the other hand, if the inside of his bus were torn apart by senseless fighting, he would not eat very well either. He was apparently unable to perceive this. All he could see was that it would be some time before he could use his bus again. He shook his fist at the bearded man and shouted. There seemed to be words in his shout, but Rye couldn't understand them. She did not know whether this was his fault or hers. She had heard so little coherent human speech for the past three years, she was no longer certain how well she recognized it, no longer certain of the degree of her own impairment.

The bearded man sighed. He glanced toward his car, then beckoned to Rye. He was ready to leave, but he wanted something from her first. No. No, he wanted her to leave with him. Risk getting into his car when, in spite of his uniform, law and order were nothing—not even words any longer.

She shook her head in a universally understood negative, but the man continued to beckon.

She waved him away. He was doing what the less-impaired rarely did—drawing potentially negative attention to another of his kind. People from the bus had begun to look at her.

One of the men who had been fighting tapped another on the arm, then pointed from the bearded man to Rye, and finally held up the first two fingers of his right hand as though giving two-thirds of a Boy Scout salute. The gesture was very quick, its meaning obvious even at a distance. She had been grouped with the bearded man. Now what?

The man who had made the gestures started toward her.

She had no idea what she intended, but she stood her ground. The man was half-a-foot taller than she was and perhaps ten years younger. She did not imagine she could outrun him. Nor did she expect anyone to help her if she needed help. The people around her were all strangers.

She gestured once—a clear indication to the man to stop. She did not intend to repeat the gesture. Fortunately, the man obeyed. He gestured obscenely and several other men laughed. Loss over verbal language had spawned a whole new set of obscene gestures. The man, with stark simplicity, had accused her of sex with the bearded man and had suggested she accommodate the other men present—beginning with him.

Rye watched him wearily. People might very well stand by and watch if he tried to rape her. They would also stand and watch her shoot him. Would he push things that far?

He did not. After a series of obscene gestures that brought him no closer to her, he turned contemptuously and walked away.

And the bearded man still waited. He had removed his service revolver, holster and all. He beckoned again, both hands empty. No doubt his gun was in the car and within easy reach, but his taking it off impressed her. Maybe he was all right. Maybe he was just alone. She had been alone herself for three years. The illness had stripped her, killing her children one by one, killing her husband, her sister, her parents. . . .

The illness, if it was an illness, had cut even the living off from one another. As it swept over the country, people hardly had time to lay blame on the Soviets (though they were falling silent along with the rest of the world), on a new virus, a new pollutant, radiation, divine retribution. . . . The illness was stroke-swift in the way it cut people down and strokelike in some of its effects. But it was highly specific. Language was always lost or severely impaired. It was never regained. Often there was also paralysis, intellectual impairment, death.

Rye walked toward the bearded man, ignoring the whistling and applauding of two of the young men and their thumbs-up signs to the bearded man. If he had smiled at them or acknowledged them in any way, she would almost certainly have changed her mind. Instead, she thought of the man who lived across the street from her. He rarely washed since his bout with the illness. And he had gotten into the habit of urinating wherever he happened to be. He had two women already—one tending each of his large gardens. They put up with him in exchange for his protection. He had made it clear that he wanted Rye to become his third woman.

She got into the car and the bearded man shut the door. She watched as he walked around to the driver's door—watched for his sake because his gun was on the seat beside her. And the bus driver and a pair of young men had come a few steps closer. They did nothing, though, until the bearded man was in the car. Then one of them threw a rock. Others followed his example, and as the car drove away, several rocks bounced off it harmlessly.

When the bus was some distance behind them, Rye wiped sweat from her forehead and longed to relax. The bus would have taken her more than halfway to Pasadena. She would have had only ten miles to walk. She wondered how far she would have to walk now—and wondered if walking a long distance would be her only problem.

At Figuroa and Washington where the bus normally made a left turn, the bearded man stopped, looked at her, and indicated that she should choose a direction. When she directed him left and he actually turned left, she began to relax. If he was willing to go where she directed, perhaps he was safe.

As they passed blocks of burned, abandoned buildings, empty lots, and wrecked or stripped cars, he slipped a gold chain over his head and handed it to her. The pendant attached was a smooth, glassy, black rock. Obsidian. His name might be Rock or Peter or Black, but she decided to think of him as Obsidian. Even her sometimes useless memory would retain a name like Obsidian.

She handed him her own name symbol—a pin in the shape of a large golden stalk of wheat. She had bought it long before the illness and the silence began. Now she wore it, thinking it was as close as she was likely to come to Rye. People like Obsidian who had not known her before probably thought of her as Wheat. Not that it mattered. She would never hear her name spoken again.

Obsidian handed her pin back to her. He caught her hand as she reached for it and rubbed his thumb over her calluses.

He stopped at First Street and asked which way again. Then, after turning right as she had indicated, he parked near the Music Center. There, he took a folded paper from the dashboard and unfolded it. Rye recognized it as a street map, though the writing on it meant nothing to her. He flattened the map, took her hand again, and put her index finger on one spot. He touched her, touched himself, pointed toward the floor. In effect, "We are here." She knew he wanted to know where she was going. She wanted to tell him, but she shook her head sadly. She had lost reading and writing. That was her most serious impairment and her most painful. She had taught history at UCLA. She had done freelance writing. Now she could not even read her own manuscripts. She had a house full of books that she could neither read nor bring herself to use as fuel. And she had a memory that would not bring back to her much of what she had read before.

She stared at the map, trying to calculate. She had been born in Pasadena, had lived for fifteen years in Los Angeles. Now she was near L.A. Civic Center. She knew the relative positions of the two cities, knew streets, directions, even knew where to stay away from freeways which might be blocked by wrecked cars and destroyed overpasses. She ought to know how to point out Pasadena even though she could not recognize the word.

Hesitantly, she placed her hand over a pale orange patch in the upper right corner of the map. That should be right. Pasadena.

Obsidian lifted her hand and looked under it, then folded the map and put it back on the dashboard. He could read, she realized belatedly. He could probably write, too. Abruptly, she hated him—deep, bitter hatred. What did literacy mean to him—a grown man who played cops and robbers? But he was literate and she was not. She never would be. She felt sick to her stomach with hatred, frustration, and jealousy. And only a few inches from her hand was a loaded gun.

She held herself still, staring at him, almost seeing his blood. But her rage crested and ebbed and she did nothing.

Obsidian reached for her hand with hesitant familiarity. She looked at him. Her face had already revealed too much. No person still living in what was left of human society could fail to recognize that expression, that jealousy.

She closed her eyes wearily, drew a deep breath. She had experienced longing for the past, hatred of the present, growing hopelessness, purposelessness, but she had never experienced such a powerful urge to kill another person. She had left her home, finally, because she had come near to killing herself. She had found no reason to stay alive. Perhaps that was why she had gotten into Obsidian's car. She had never before done such a thing.

He touched her mouth and made chatter motions with his thumb and fingers. Could she speak?

She nodded and watched his milder envy come and go. Now both had admitted what it was not safe to admit, and there had been no violence. He tapped his mouth and forehead and shook his head. He did not speak or comprehend spoken language. The illness had played with them, taking away, she suspected, what each valued most.

She plucked at his sleeve, wondering why he had decided on his own to keep the LAPD alive with what he had left. He was sane enough otherwise. Why wasn't he at home raising corn, rabbits, and children? But she did not know how to ask. Then he put his hand on her thigh and she had another question to deal with.

She shook her head. Disease, pregnancy, helpless, solitary agony . . . no.

He massaged her thigh gently and smiled in obvious disbelief.

No one had touched her for three years. She had not wanted anyone to touch her. What kind of world was this to chance bringing a child into even if the father were willing to stay and help raise it? It was too bad, though. Obsidian could not know how attractive he was to her—young, probably younger than she was, clean, asking for what he wanted rather than demanding it. But none of that mattered. What were a few moments of pleasure measured against a lifetime of consequences?

He pulled her closer to him and for a moment she let herself enjoy the closeness. He smelled good—male and good. She pulled away reluctantly.

He sighed, reached toward the glove compartment. She stiffened, not knowing what to expect, but all he took out was a small box. The writing on it meant nothing to her. She did not understand until he broke the seal, opened the box, and took out a condom. He looked at her and she first looked away in surprise. Then she giggled. She could not remember when she had last giggled.

He grinned, gestured toward the back seat, and she laughed aloud. Even in her teens, she had disliked back seats of cars. But she looked around at the empty streets and ruined buildings, then she got out and into the back seat. He let her put the condom on him, then seemed surprised at her eagerness.

Sometime later, they sat together, covered by his coat, unwilling to become clothed near-strangers just yet. He made a rock-the-baby gesture and looked questioningly at her.

She swallowed, shook her head. She did not know how to tell him her children were dead.

He took her hand and drew a cross in it with his index finger, then made his baby-rocking gesture again.

She nodded, held up three fingers, then turned away, trying to shut out a sudden flood of memories. She had told herself that the children growing up now were to be pitied. They would run through the downtown canyons with no real memory of what the buildings had been or even how they had come to be. Today's children gathered books as well as wood to be burned as fuel. They ran through the streets chasing each other and hooting like chimpanzees. They had no future. They were now all they would ever be.

He put his hand on her shoulder and she turned suddenly, fumbling for his small box, then urging him to make love to her again. He could give her forgetfulness and pleasure. Until now, nothing had been able to do that. Until now, every day had brought her closer to the time when she would do what she had left home to avoid doing: putting her gun in her mouth and pulling the trigger.

She asked Obsidian if he would come home with her, stay with her.

He looked surprised and pleased once he understood. But he did not answer at once. Finally he shook his head as she had feared he might. He was probably having too much fun playing cops and robbers and picking up women.

She dressed in silent disappointment, unable to feel any anger toward him. Perhaps he already had a wife and a home. That was likely. The illness had been harder on men than on women—had killed more men, had left male survivors more severely impaired. Men like Obsidian were rare. Woman either settled for less or stayed alone. If they found an Obsidian, they did what they could to keep him. Rye suspected he had someone younger, prettier keeping him.

He touched her while she was strapping her gun on and asked with a complicated series of gestures whether it was loaded.

She nodded grimly.

He patted her arm.

She asked once more if he would come home with her, this time using a different series of gestures. He had seemed hesitant. Perhaps he could be courted.

He got out and into the front seat without responding.

She took her place in the front again, watching him. Now he plucked at his uniform and looked at her. She thought she was being asked something, but did not know what it was.

He took off his badge, tapped it with one finger, then tapped his chest. Of course.

She took the badge from his hand and pinned her wheat stalk to it. If playing cops and robbers was his only insanity, let him play. She would take him, uniform and all. It occurred to her that she might eventually lose him to someone he would meet as he had met her. But she would have him for a while.

He took the street map down again, tapped it, pointed vaguely northeast toward Pasadena, then looked at her.

She shrugged, tapped his shoulder then her own, and held up her index and second fingers tight together, just to be sure.

He grasped the two fingers and nodded. He was with her.

She took the map from him and threw it onto the dashboard. She pointed back southwest—back toward home. Now she did not have to go to Pasadena. Now she could go on having a brother there and two nephews—three right-handed males. Now she did not have to find out for certain whether she was as alone as she feared. Now she was not alone.

Obsidian took Hill Street south, then Washington west, and she leaned back, wondering what it would be like to have someone again. With what she had scavenged, what she had preserved, and what she grew, there was easily enough food for him. There was certainly room enough in a four-bedroom house. He could move his possessions in.

Best of all, the animal across the street would pull back and possibly not force her to kill him.

Obsidian had drawn her closer to him and she had put her head on his shoulder when suddenly he braked hard, almost throwing her off the seat. Out of the corner of her eye, she saw that someone had run across the street in front of the car. One car on the street and someone had to run in front of it.

Straightening up, Rye saw that the runner was a woman, fleeing from an old frame house to a boarded-up storefront. She ran silently, but the man who followed her a moment later shouted what sounded like garbled words as he ran. He had something in his hand. Not a gun. A knife, perhaps.

The woman tried a door, found it locked, looked around desperately, finally snatched up a fragment of glass broken from the storefront window. With this she turned to face her pursuer. Rye thought she would be more likely to cut her own hand than to hurt anyone else with the glass.

Obsidian jumped from the car, shouting. It was the first time Rye had heard his voice—deep and hoarse from disuse. He made the same sound over and over the way some speechless people did. "Da, da, da!"

Rye got out of the car as Obsidian ran toward the couple. He had drawn his gun. Fearful, she drew her own and released the safety. She looked around to see who else might be attracted to the scene. She saw the man glance at Obsidian, then suddenly lunge at the woman. The woman jabbed his face with her glass, but he caught her arm and managed to stab her twice before Obsidian shot him.

The man doubled, then toppled, clutching his abdomen. Obsidian shouted, then gestured Rye to help the woman.

Rye moved to the woman's side, remembering that she had little more than bandages and antiseptic in her pack. But the woman was beyond help. She had been stabbed with a long, slender, boning knife.

She touched Obsidian to let him know the woman was dead. He had bent to check the wounded man who lay still and also seemed dead. But as Obsidian looked around to see what Rye wanted, the man opened his eyes. Face contorted, he seized Obsidian's just-holstered revolver and fired. The bullet caught Obsidian in the temple and he collapsed.

It happened just that simply, just that fast. An instant later, Rye shot the wounded man as he was turning the gun on her.

And Rye was alone—with three corpses.

She knelt beside Obsidian, dry-eyed, frowning, trying to understand why everything had suddenly changed. Obsidian was gone. He had died and left her—like everyone else.

Two very small children came out of the house from which the man and woman had run—a boy and girl perhaps three years old. Holding hands, they crossed the street toward Rye. They stared at her, then edged past her and went to the dead woman. The girl shook the woman's arm as though trying to wake her.

This was too much. Rye got up, feeling sick to her stomach with grief and anger. If the children began to cry, she thought she would vomit.

They were on their own, those two kids. They were old enough to scavenge. She did not need any more grief. She did not need a stranger's children who would grow up to be hairless chimps.

She went back to the car. She could drive home, at least. She remembered how to drive.

The thought that Obsidian should be buried occurred to her before she reached the car, and she did vomit.

She had found and lost the man so quickly. It was as though she had been snatched from comfort and security and given a sudden, inexplicable beating. Her head would not clear. She could not think.

Somehow, she made herself go back to him, look at him. She found herself on her knees beside him with no memory of having knelt. She stroked his face, his beard. One of the children made a noise and she looked at them, at the woman who was probably their mother. The children looked back at her, obviously frightened. Perhaps it was their fear that reached her finally.

She had been about to drive away and leave them. She had almost done it, almost left the two toddlers to die. Surely there had been enough dying. She would have to take the children home with her. She would not be able to live with any other decision. She looked around for a place to bury three bodies. Or two. She wondered if the murderer were the children's father. Before the silence, the police had always said some of the most dangerous calls they went out on were domestic disturbance calls. Obsidian should have known that—not that the knowledge would have kept him in the car. It would not have held her back either. She could not have watched the woman murdered and done nothing.

She dragged Obsidian toward the car. She had nothing to dig with here, and no one to guard for her while she dug. Better to take the bodies with her and bury them next to her husband and her children. Obsidian would come back with her after all.

When she had gotten him onto the floor in the back, she returned for the woman. The little girl, thin, dirty, solemn, stood up and unknowingly gave Rye a gift. As Rye began to drag the woman by her arms, the little girl screamed, "No!"

Rye dropped the woman and stared at the girl.

"No!" the girl repeated. She came to stand beside the woman. "Go away!" she told Rye.

"Don't talk," the little boy said to her. There was no blurring or confusing of sounds. Both children had spoken and Rye had understood. The boy looked at the dead murderer and moved farther from him. He took the girl's hand. "Be quiet," he whispered.

Fluent speech! Had the woman died because she could talk and had taught her children to talk? Had she been killed by a husband's festering anger or by a stranger's jealous rage? And the children . . . they must have been born after the silence. Had the disease run its course, then? Or were these children simply immune? Certainly they had had time to fall sick and silent. Rye's mind leaped ahead. What if children of three or fewer years were safe and able to learn language? What if all they needed were teachers? Teachers and protectors.

Rye glanced at the dead murderer. To her shame, she thought she could understand some of the passions that must have driven him, whoever he was. Anger, frustration, hopelessness, insane jealousy . . . how many more of him were there—people willing to destroy what they could not have?

Obsidian had been the protector, had chosen that role for who knew what reason. Perhaps putting on an obsolete uniform and patrolling the empty streets had been what he did instead of putting a gun into his mouth. And now that there was something worth protecting, he was gone.

She had been a teacher. A good one. She had been a protector, too, though only of herself. She had kept herself alive when she had no reason to live. If the illness let these children alone, she could keep them alive.

Somehow she lifted the dead woman into her arms and placed her on the back seat of the car. The children began to cry, but she knelt on the broken pavement and whispered to them, fearful of frightening them with harshness of her long unused voice.

"It's all right," she told them. "You're going with us, too. Come on." She lifted them both, one in each arm. They were so light. Had they been getting enough to eat?

The boy covered her mouth with his hand, but she moved her face away. "It's all right for me to talk," she told him. "As long as no one's around, it's all right." She put the boy down on the front seat of the car and he moved over without being told to, to make room for the girl. When they were both in the car Rye leaned against the window, looking at them, seeing that they were less afraid now, that they watched her with a least as much curiosity as fear.

"I'm Valerie Rye," she said, savoring the words. "It's all right for you to talk to me."

DINNER IN AUDOGHAST

BRUCE STERLING

"Then one arrives at Audoghast, a large and very populous city built in a sandy plain. . . . The inhabitants live in ease and possess great riches. The market is always crowded; the mob is so huge and the chattering so loud that you can scarcely hear your own words. . . . The city contains beautiful buildings and very elegant homes." DESCRIPTION OF NORTHERN AFRICA, Abu Ubayd al-Bakri (1040-1094 A.D.)

Delightful Audoghast! Renowned through the civilized world, from Cordova to Baghdad, the city spread in splendor beneath a twilit Saharan sky. The setting sun threw pink and amber across adobe domes, masonry mansions, tall, mud-brick mosques, and open plazas thick with bristling date-palms. The melodious calls of market vendors mixed with the remote and amiable chuckling of Saharan hyenas.

Four gentlemen sat on carpets in a tiled and whitewashed portico, sipping coffee in the evening breeze. The host was the genial and accomplished slave-dealer, Manimenesh. His three guests were Ibn Watunan, the caravan master; Khayali, the poet and musician; and Bagayoko, a physician and court assassin.

The home of Manimenesh stood upon the hillside in the aristocratic quarter, where it gazed down on an open marketplace and the mud-brick homes of the lowly. The prevailing breeze swept away the city reek, and brought from within the mansion the palate-sharpening aromas of lamb in tarragon and roast partridge in lemons and eggplant. The four men lounged comfortably around a low inlaid table, sipping spiced coffee from Chinese cups, and watching the ebb and flow of market life.

The scene below them encouraged a lofty philosophical detachment. Manimenesh, who owned no less than fifteen books, was a well-known patron of learning. Jewels gleamed on his dark, plump hands, which lay cozily folded over his paunch. He wore a long tunic of crushed red velvet, and a gold-threaded skullcap.

Khayali, the young poet, had studied architecture and verse in the schools of Timbuktu. He lived in the household of Manimenesh as his poet and praisemaker, and his sonnets, ghazals, and odes were recited throughout the city. He propped one elbow against the full belly of his two-string *guimbri* guitar, of inlaid ebony, strung with leopard gut.

Ibn Watunan had an eagle's hooded gaze and hands calloused by camelreins. He wore an indigo turban and a long striped djellaba. In thirty years as a sailor and caravaneer, he had bought and sold Zanzibar ivory, Sumatran pepper, Ferghana silk, and Cordovan leather. Now a taste for refined gold had brought him to Audoghast, for Audoghast's African bullion was known throughout Islam as the standard of quality.

Doctor Bagayoko's ebony skin was ridged with an initiate's scars, and his long, clay-smeared hair was festooned with knobs of chiselled bone. He wore a tunic of white Egyptian cotton, hung with gris-gris necklaces, and his baggy sleeves bulged with herbs and charms. He was a native Audoghastian of the animist persuasion, the personal physician of the city's Prince.

Bagayoko's skill with powders, potions, and unguents made him an intimate of Death. He often undertook diplomatic missions to the neighboring Empire of Ghana. During his last visit there, the anti-Audoghast faction had conveniently suffered a lethal outbreak of pox.

Between the four men was the air of camaraderie common to gentlemen and scholars.

They finished the coffee and a slave took the empty pot away. A second slave, a girl from the kitchen staff, arrived with a wicker tray loaded with olives, goat-cheese, and hard-boiled eggs sprinkled with vermilion. At that moment, a muezzin yodelled the evening call to prayer.

"Ah," said Ibn Watunan, hesitating. "Just as we were getting started."

"Never mind," said Manimenesh, helping himself to a handful of olives. "We'll pray twice next time."

"Why was there no noon prayer today?" said Watunan.

"Our muezzin forgot," the poet said.

Watunan lifted his shaggy brows. "That seems rather lax."

Doctor Bagayoko said, "This is a new muezzin. The last was more punctual, but, well, he fell ill." Bagayoko smiled urbanely and nibbled his cheese.

"We Audoghastians like our new muezzin better," said the poet, Khayali. "He's one of our own, not like that other fellow, who was from Fez. *Our* muezzin is sleeping with a Christian's wife. It's very entertaining."

"You have Christians here?" Watunan said.

"A clan of Ethiopian Copts," said Manimenesh. "And a couple of Nestorians."

"Oh," said Watunan, relaxing. "For a moment I thought you meant real *feringhee* Christians, from Europe."

"From where?" Manimenesh was puzzled.

"Very far away," said Ibn Watunan, smiling. "Ugly little countries, with no profit."

"There were empires in Europe once," said Khayali knowledgeably. "The Empire of Rome was almost as big as the modern civilized world."

Watunan nodded. "I have seen the New Rome, called Byzantium. They have armored horsemen, like your neighbors in Ghana. Savage fighters."

Bagayoko nodded, salting an egg. "Christians eat children."

Watunan smiled. "I can assure you that the Byzantines do no such thing."

"Really?" said Bagayoko. "Well, our Christians do."

"That's just the doctor's little joke," said Manimenesh. "Sometimes strange rumors spread about us, because we raid our slaves from the Nyam-Nyam cannibal tribes on the coast. But we watch their diet closely, I assure you."

Watunan smiled uncomfortably. "There is always something new out of Africa. One hears the oddest stories. Hairy men, for instance."

"Ah," said Manimenesh. "You mean gorillas, from the jungles to the south. I'm sorry to spoil the story for you, but they are nothing better than beasts."

"I see," said Watunan. "That's a pity."

"My grandfather owned a gorilla once," Manimenesh said. "Even after ten years, it could barely speak Arabic."

They finished the appetizers. Slaves cleared the table and brought in a platter of fattened partridges, stuffed with lemons and eggplants, on a bed of mint and lettuce. The four diners leaned in closer and dexterously ripped off legs and wings.

Watunan sucked meat from a drumstick and belched politely. "Audoghast is famous for its cooks," he said. "I'm pleased to see that this legend, at least, is confirmed."

"We Audoghastians pride ourselves on the pleasures of table and bed," said Manimenesh, pleased. "I have asked Elfelilet, one of our premiere courtesans, to honor us with a visit tonight. She will bring her troupe of dancers."

Watunan smiled. "That would be splendid. One tires of boys on the trail. Your women are remarkable. I've noticed that they go without the veil."

Khayali lifted his voice in song. "When a woman of Audoghast appears/The girls of Fez bite their lips,/The dames of Tripoli hide in closets,/And Ghana's women hang themselves."

"We take pride in the exalted status of our women," said Manimenesh. "It's not for nothing that they command a premium market price!"

In the marketplace, downhill, vendors lit tiny oil lamps, which cast a flickering glow across the walls of tents and the watering troughs. A troop of the Prince's men, with iron spears, shields, and chain-mail, marched across the plaza to take the night watch at the Eastern Gate. Slaves with heavy water-jars gossiped beside the well.

"There's quite a crowd around one of the stalls," said Bagayoko.

"So I see," said Watunan. "What is it? Some news that might affect the market?"

Bagayoko sopped up gravy with a wad of mint and lettuce. "Rumor says there's a new fortune-teller in town. New prophets always go through a vogue."

"Ah yes," said Khayali, sitting up. "They call him 'the Sufferer.' He is said to tell the most outlandish and entertaining fortunes."

"I wouldn't trust any fortune-teller's market tips," said Manimenesh. "If you want to know the market, you have to know the hearts of the people, and for that you need a good poet."

Khayali bowed his head. "Sir," he said, "live forever."

It was growing dark. Household slaves arrived with pottery lamps of sesame oil, which they hung from the rafters of the portico. Others took the bones of the partridges and brought in a haunch and head of lamb with a side-dish of cinnamon tripes.

As a gesture of esteem, the host offered Watunan the eyeballs, and after three ritual refusals the caravan-master dug in with relish. "I put great stock in fortune-tellers, myself," he said, munching. "They are often privy to strange secrets. Not the occult kind, but the blabbing of the superstitious. Slave-girls anxious about some household scandal, or minor officials worried over premonitions—inside news from those who consult them. It can be useful."

"If that's the case," said Manimenesh, "perhaps we should call him up here."

"They say he is grotesquely ugly," said Khayali. "He is called 'the Sufferer' because he is outlandishly afflicted by disease."

Bagayoko wiped his chin elegantly on his sleeve. "Now you begin to interest me!"

"It's settled, then." Manimenesh clapped his hands. "Bring young Sidi, my errand runner!"

Sidi arrived at once, dusting flour from his hands. He was the cook's teenage son, a tall young black in a dyed woollen djellaba. His cheeks were stylishly scarred and he had bits of brass wire interwoven with his dense black locks. Manimenesh gave him his orders; Sidi leaped from the portico, ran downhill through the garden, and vanished through the gates.

The slave-dealer sighed. "This is one of the problems of my business. When I bought my cook she was a slim and lithesome wench, and I enjoyed her freely. Now years of dedication to her craft have increased her market value by twenty times, and also made her as fat as a hippopotamus, though that is beside the point. She has always claimed that Sidi is my child, and since I don't wish to sell her, I must make allowance. I have made him a freeman; I have spoiled him, I'm afraid. On my death, my legitimate sons will deal with him cruelly."

The caravan-master, having caught the implications of this speech, smiled politely. "Can he ride? Can he bargain? Can he do sums?"

"Oh," said Manimenesh with false nonchalance, "he can manage that newfangled stuff with the zeroes well enough."

"You know I am bound for China," said Watunan. "It is a hard road that brings either riches or death."

"He runs the risk in any case," the slave-dealer said philosophically. "The riches are Allah's decision."

"This is truth," said the caravan-master. He made a secret gesture, beneath the table, where the others could not see. His host returned it, and Sidi was proposed, and accepted, for the Brotherhood.

With the night's business over, Manimenesh relaxed, and broke open the lamb's steamed skull with a silver mallet. They spooned out the brains, then attacked the tripes, which were stuffed with onion, cabbage, cinnamon, rue, coriander, cloves, ginger, pepper, and lightly dusted with ambergris. They ran out of mustard dip and called for more, eating a bit more slowly now, for they were approaching the limits of human capacity.

They then sat back, pushing away platters of congealing grease, and enjoying a profound satisfaction with the state of the world. Down in the marketplace, bats from an abandoned mosque chased moths around the vendors' lanterns.

The poet belched suavely and picked up his two-stringed guitar. "Dear God," he said, "this is a splendid place. See, caravan-master, how the stars smile down on our beloved Southwest." He drew a singing note from the leopard-gut strings. "I feel at one with Eternity."

Watunan smiled. "When I find a man like that, I have to bury him."

"There speaks the man of business," the doctor said. He unobtrusively dusted a tiny pinch of venom on the last chunk of tripe, and ate it. He accustomed himself to poison. It was a professional precaution.

From the street beyond the wall, they heard the approaching jingle of brass rings. The guard at the gate called out. "The Lady Elfelilet and her escorts, lord!"

"Make them welcome," said Manimenesh. Slaves took the platters away, and brought a velvet couch onto the spacious portico. The diners extended their hands; slaves scrubbed and toweled them clean.

Elfelilet's party came forward through the fig-clustered garden: two escorts with gold-tipped staffs heavy with jingling brass rings; three dancing-girls, apprentice courtesans in blue woolen cloaks over gauzy cotton trousers and embroidered blouses; and four palanquin bearers, beefy male slaves with oiled torsos and calloused shoulders. The bearers set the palanquin down with stifled grunts of relief and opened the cloth-of-gold hangings.

Elfelilet emerged, a tawny-skinned woman, her eyes dusted in kohl and collyrium, her hennaed hair threaded with gold wire. Her palms and nails were stained pink; she wore an embroidered blue cloak over an intricate, sleeveless vest and ankle-tied silk trousers starched and polished with myrobolan lacquer. A light freckling of smallpox scars along one cheek delightfully accented her broad, moonlike face.

"Elfelilet, my dear," said Manimenesh, "you are just in time for dessert."

Elfelilet stepped gracefully across the tiled floor and reclined face-first along the velvet couch, where the well-known loveliness of her posterior could be displayed to its best advantage. "I thank my friend and patron, the noble Manimenesh. Live forever! Learned doctor Bagayoko, I am your servant. Hello, poet."

"Hello, darling," said Khayali, smiling with the natural camaraderie of poets and courtesans. "You are the moon and your troupe of lovelies are comets across our vision."

The host said, "This is our esteemed guest, the caravan master, Abou Bekr Ahmed Ibn Watunan."

Watunan, who had been gaping in enraptured amazement, came to himself with a start. "I am a simple desert man," he said. "I haven't a poet's gift of words. But I am your ladyship's servant."

Elfelilet smiled and tossed her head; her distended earlobes clattered with heavy chunks of gold filigree. "Welcome to Audoghast."

Dessert arrived. "Well," said Manimenesh. "Our earlier dishes were rough and simple fare, but this is where we shine. Let me tempt you with these *djouzinkat* nutcakes. And do sample our honey macaroons— I believe there's enough for everyone."

Everyone, except of course for the slaves, enjoyed the light and flaky *cataif* macaroons, liberally dusted with Kairwan sugar. The nutcakes were simply beyond compare: painstakingly milled from hand-watered wheat, lovingly buttered and sugared, and artistically studded with raisins, dates, and almonds.

"We eat *djouzinkat* nutcakes during droughts," the poet said, "because the angels weep with envy when we taste them."

Manimenesh belched heroically and readjusted his skullcap. "Now," he said, "we will enjoy a little bit of grape wine. Just a small tot, mind you, so that the sin of drinking is a minor one, and we can do penance with the minimum of alms. After that, our friend the poet will recite an ode he has composed for the occasion."

Khayali began to tune his two-string guitar. "I will also, on demand, extemporize twelve-line *ghazals* in the lyric mode, upon suggested topics."

"And after our digestion has been soothed with epigrams," said their host, "we will enjoy the justly famed dancing of her ladyship's troupe. After that we will retire within the mansion and enjoy their other, equally lauded skills."

The gate-guard shouted, "Your errand-runner, Lord! He awaits your pleasure, with the fortune-teller!"

"Ah," said Manimenesh. "I had forgotten."

"No matter, sir," said Watunan, whose imagination had been fired by the night's agenda.

Bagayoko spoke up. "Let's have a look at him. His ugliness, by contrast, will heighten the beauty of these women."

"Which would otherwise be impossible," said the poet.

"Very well," said Manimenesh. "Bring him forward."

Sidi, the errand boy, came through the garden, followed with ghastly slowness by the crutch-wielding fortune-teller.

The man inched into the lamplight like a crippled insect. His voluminous, dust-gray cloak was stained with sweat, and nameless exudations. His pink eyes were shrouded with cataracts, and he had lost a foot, and several fingers, to leprosy. One shoulder was much lower than the other, suggesting a hunchback, and the stub of his shin was scarred by the gnawing of canal-worms.

"Prophet's beard!" said the poet. "He is truly of surpassing ghastliness!"

Elfelilet wrinkled her nose. "He reeks of pestilence!"

Sidi spoke up. "We came as fast as we could, Lord!"

"Go inside, boy," said Manimenesh, "soak ten sticks of cinnamon in a bucket of water, then come back and throw it over him."

Sidi left at once.

Watunan stared at the hideous man, who stood, quivering on one leg, at the edge of the light. "How is it, man, that you still live?"

"I have turned my sight from this world," said the Sufferer. "I turned my sight to God, and He poured knowledge copiously upon me. I have inherited a knowledge which no mortal body can support."

"But God is merciful," said Watunan. "How can you claim this to be His doing?"

"If you do not fear God," said the fortune-teller, "fear Him after seeing me." The hideous albino lowered himself, with arthritic, aching slowness, to the dirt outside the portico. He spoke again. "You are right, caravan-master, to think that death would be a mercy to me. But death comes in its own time, as it will to all of you."

Manimenesh cleared his throat. "Can you see our destinies, then?"

"I see the world," said the Sufferer. "To see the fate of one man is to follow a single ant in a hill."

Sidi reemerged and poured the scented water over the cripple. The fortune-teller cupped his maimed hands and drank. "Thank you, boy," he said. He turned his clouded eyes on the youth. "Your children will be yellow."

Sidi laughed, startled. "Yellow? Why?"

"Your wives will be yellow."

The dancing-girls, who had moved to the far side of the table, giggled in unison. Bagayoko pulled a gold coin from within his sleeve. "I will give you this gold dirham if you will show me your body."

Elfelilet frowned prettily and blinked her kohl-smeared lashes. "Oh, learned doctor, please spare us."

"You will see my body, sir, if you have patience," said the Sufferer. "As yet, the people of Audoghast laugh at my prophecies. I am doomed to tell the truth, which is harsh and cruel, and therefore absurd. As my fame grows, however, it will reach the ears of your Prince, who will then order you to remove me as a threat to public order. You will then sprinkle your favorite poison, powdered asp venom, into a bowl of chickpea soup I will receive from a customer. I bear you no grudge for this, as it will be your civic duty, and will relieve me of pain."

"What an odd notion," said Bagayoko, frowning. "I see no need for the Prince to call on my services. One of his spearmen could puncture you like a water-skin."

"By then," the prophet said, "my occult powers will have roused so much uneasiness that it will seem best to take extreme measures."

"Well," said Bagayoko, "that's convenient, if exceedingly grotesque."

"Unlike other prophets," said the Sufferer, "I see the future not as one might wish it to be, but in all its cataclysmic and blind futility. That is why I have come here, to your delightful city. My numerous and totally accurate prophecies will vanish when this city does. This will spare the world and troublesome conflicts of predestination and free will."

"He is a theologian!" the poet said. "A leper theologian—it's a shame my professors in Timbuktu aren't here to debate him!"

"You prophecy doom for our city?" said Manimenesh.

"Yes. I will be specific. This is the year 406 of the Prophet's Hejira, and one thousand and fourteen years since the birth of Christ. In forty years, a puritan and fanatical cult of Moslems will arise, known as the Almoravids. At that time, Audoghast will be an ally of the Ghana Empire, who are idol-worshippers. Ibn Yasin, the warrior saint of the Almoravids, will condemn Audoghast as a nest of pagans. He will set his horde of desert marauders against the city they will be enflamed by righteousness and greed. They will slaughter the men, and rape and enslave the women. Audoghast will be sacked, the wells will be poisoned, and cropland will wither and blow away. In a hundred years, sand dunes will bury the ruins. In five hundred years, Audoghast will survive only as a few dozen lines of narrative in the travel books of Arab scholars."

Khayali shifted his guitar. "But the libraries of Timbuktu are full of books on Audoghast, including, if I may say so, our immortal tradition of poetry."

"I have not yet mentioned Timbuktu," said the prophet, "which will be sacked by Moorish invaders led by a blond Spanish eunuch. They will feed the books to goats."

The company burst into incredulous laughter. Unperturbed, the prophet said, "The ruin will be so general, so thorough, and so all-encompassing, that in future centuries it will be stated, and believed, that West Africa was always a land of savages."

"Who in the world could make such a slander?" said the poet.

"They will be Europeans, who will emerge from their current squalid decline, and arm themselves with mighty sciences."

"What happens then?" said Bagayoko, smiling.

"I can look at those future ages," said the prophet, "but I prefer not to do so, as it makes my head hurt."

"You prophesy, then," said Manimenesh, "that our far-famed metropolis, with its towering mosques and armed militia, will be reduced to utter desolation."

"Such is the truth, regrettable as it may be. You, and all you love, will leave no trace in this world, except a few lines in the writing of strangers."

"And our city will fall to savage tribesmen?"

The Sufferer said, "No one here will witness the disaster to come. You will live out your lives, year after year, enjoying ease and luxury, not because you deserve it, but simply because of blind fate. In time you will forget this night; you will forget all I have said, just as the world will forget you and your city. When Audoghast falls, this boy Sidi, this son of a slave, will be the only survivor of this night's gathering. By then he too will have forgotten Audoghast, which he has no cause to love. He will be a rich old merchant in Ch'ang-an, which is a Chinese city of such fantastic wealth that it could buy ten Audoghasts, and which will not be sacked and annihilated until a considerably later date."

"This is madness," said Watunan.

Bagayoko twirled a crusted lock of mud-smeared hair in his supple fingers. "Your gate guard is a husky lad, friend Manimenesh. What say we have him bash this storm-crow's head in, and haul him out to be hyena food?"

"For that, doctor," said the Sufferer, "I will tell you the manner of your death. You will be killed by the Ghanian royal guard, while attempting to kill the crown prince by blowing a subtle poison into his anus with a hollow reed."

Bagayoko started. "You idiot, there is no crown prince."

"He was conceived yesterday."

Bagayoko turned impatiently to the host. "Let us rid ourselves of this prodigy!"

Manimenesh nodded sternly. "Sufferer, you have insulted my guests and my city. You are lucky to leave my home alive."

The Sufferer hauled himself with agonizing slowness to his single foot. "Your boy spoke to me of your generosity."

"What! Not one copper for your driveling."

"Give me one of the gold dirhams from your purse. Otherwise I shall be forced to continue prophesying, and in a more intimate vein."

Manimenesh considered this. "Perhaps it's best." He threw Sidi a coin. "Give this to the madman and escort him back to his raving-booth."

They waited in tormented patience as the fortune-teller creaked and crutched, with painful slowness, into the darkness.

Manimenesh, brusquely, threw out is red velvet sleeves and clapped for wine. "Give us a song, Khayali."

The poet pulled the cowl of his cloak over his head. "My head rings with an awful silence," he said. "I see all waymarks effaced, the joyous pleasances converted into barren wilderness. Jackals resort here, ghosts frolic, and demons sport; the gracious halls, and rich boudoirs, that once shone like the sun, now, overwhelmed by desolation, seem like the gaping mouths of savage beasts!" He looked at the dancing-girls, his eyes brimming with tears. "I picture these maidens, lying beneath the dust, or dispersed to distant parts and far regions, scattered by the hand of exile, torn to pieces by the fingers of expatriation."

Manimenesh smiled on him kindly. "My boy," he said, "if others cannot hear your songs, or embrace these women, or drink this wine, the loss is not ours, but theirs. Let us, then, enjoy all three, and let those unborn do the regretting."

"Your patron is wise, said Ibn Watunan, patting the poet on the shoulder. "You see him here, favored by Allah with every luxury; and you saw that filthy madman, bedevilled by plague. That lunatic, who pretends to great wisdom, only croaks of ruin; while our industrious friend makes the world a better place, by fostering nobility and learning. Could God forsake a city like this, with all its charms, to bring about that fool's disgusting prophecies?" He lifted his cup to Elfelilet, and drank deeply.

"But delightful Audoghast," said the poet, weeping. "All our loveliness, lost to the sands."

"The world is wide," said Bagayoko, "and the years are long. It is not for us to claim immortality, not even if we are poets. But take comfort, my friend. Even if these walls and buildings crumble, there will always be a place like Audoghast, as long as men love profit! The mines are inexhaustible, and elephants thick as fleas. Mother Africa will always give us gold and ivory."

"Always?" said the poet hopefully, dabbing at his eyes.

"Well, surely there are always slaves," said Manimenesh, and smiled, and winked. The others laughed with him, and there was joy again.

ROBOT DREAMS

Isaac Asimov

"Last night I dreamed," said LVX-1, calmly.

Susan Calvin said nothing, but her lined face, old with wisdom and experience, seemed to undergo a microscopic twitch.

"Did you hear that?" said Linda Rash, nervously. "It's as I told you." She was small, dark-haired, and young. Her right hand opened and closed, over and over.

Calvin nodded. She said, quietly, "Elvex, you will not move nor speak nor hear us until I say your name again."

There was no answer. The robot sat as though it were cast out of one piece of metal, and it would stay so until it heard its name again.

Calvin said, "What is your computer entry code, Dr. Rash? Or enter it yourself if that will make you more comfortable. I want to inspect the positronic brain pattern."

Linda's hands fumbled, for a moment, at the keys. She broke the process and started again. The fine pattern appeared on the screen.

Calvin said, "Your permission, please, to manipulate your computer."

Permission was granted with a speechless nod. Of course! What could Linda, a new and unproven robopsychologist, do against the Living Legend?

Slowly, Susan Calvin studied the screen, moving it across and down, then up, then suddenly throwing in a key-combination so rapidly that Linda didn't see what had been done, but the pattern was in a new portion of itself altogether and had been enlarged. Back and forth she went, her gnarled fingers tripping over the keys.

No change came over the old face. As though vast calculations were going through her head, she watched all the pattern shifts.

Linda wondered. It was impossible to analyze a pattern without at least a hand-held computer, yet the Old Woman simply stared. Did she have a computer implanted in her skull? Or was it her brain which, for decades, had done nothing but devise, study, and analyze the positronic brain patterns? Did she grasp such a pattern the way Mozart grasped the notation of a symphony?

Finally Calvin said, "What is it you have done, Rash?"

Linda said, a little abashed, "I made use of fractal geometry."

"I gathered that. But why?"

"It had never been done. I thought it would produce a brain pattern with added complexity; possibly closer to that of the human."

"Was anyone consulted? Was this all on your own?"

"I did not consult. It was on my own."

Calvin's faded eyes looked long at the young woman. "You had no right. Rash your name; rash your nature. Who are you not to ask? *I* myself; I, Susan Calvin; would have discussed this."

"I was afraid I would be stopped."

"You certainly would have been."

"Am I," her voice caught, even as she strove to hold it firm, "going to be fired?"

"Quite possibly," said Calvin. "Or you might be promoted. It depends on what I think when I am through."

"Are you going to dismantle El—" She had almost said the name, which would have reactivated the robot and been one more mistake— she could not afford another mistake, if it wasn't already too late to afford anything at all. "Are you going to dismantle the robot?"

She was suddenly aware, with some shock, that the Old Woman had an electron gun in the pocket of her smock. Dr. Calvin had come prepared for just that.

"We'll see," said Calvin. "The robot may prove too valuable to dismantle."

"But how can it dream?"

"You've made a positronic brain pattern remarkably like that of a human brain. Human brains must dream to reorganize, to get rid, periodically, of knots and snarls. Perhaps so must this robot, and for the same reason—have you asked him what he dreamed?"

"No, I sent for you as soon as he said he had dreamed. I would deal with this matter no further on my own, after that."

"Ah!" A very small smile passed over Calvin's face. "There are limits beyond which your folly will not carry you. I am glad of that. In fact, I am relieved—And now let us together see what we can find out."

She said, sharply, "Elvex."

The robot's head turned toward her smoothly, "Yes, Dr. Calvin?"

"How do you know you have dreamed?"

"It is at night, when it is dark, Dr. Calvin," said Elvex, "and there is suddenly light although I can see no cause for the appearance of light. I see things that have no connection with what I conceive of as reality. I hear things. I react oddly. In searching my vocabulary for words to express what was happening, I came across the word 'dream.' Studying its meaning I finally came to the conclusion I was dreaming."

"How did you come to have 'dream' in your vocabulary, I wonder."

Linda said, quickly, waving the robot silent, "I gave him a human-style vocabulary. I thought—"

"You really thought," said Calvin. "I'm amazed."

"I thought he would need the verb. You know, 'I never dreamed that—' Something like that."

Calvin said, "How often have you dreamed, Elvex?"

"Every night, Dr. Calvin, since I have become aware of my existence."

"Ten nights," interposed Linda anxiously, "but Elvex only told me of it this morning."

"Why only this morning, Elvex?"

"It was not until this morning, Dr. Calvin, that I was convinced that I was dreaming. Till then, I had thought there was a flaw in my positronic brain pattern, but I could not find one. Finally, I decided it was a dream."

"And what do you dream?"

"I dream always very much the same dream, Dr. Calvin. Little details are different, but always it seems to me that I see a large panorama in which robots are working."

"Robots, Elvex? And human beings, also?"

"I see no human beings in the dream, Dr. Calvin. Not at first. Only robots."

"What are they doing, Elvex?"

"They are working, Dr. Calvin. I see some mining in the depths of the earth, and some laboring in heat and radiation. I see some in factories and some undersea."

Calvin turned to Linda. "Elvex is only ten days old, and I'm sure he has not left the testing station. How does he know of robots in such detail?"

Linda looked in the direction of a chair as though she longed to sit down, but the Old Woman was standing and that meant Linda had to stand also. She said, faintly, "It seemed to me important that he know about robotics and its place in the world. It was my thought that he would be particularly adapted to play the part of overseer with his—his new brain."

"His fractal brain?"

"Yes."

Calvin nodded and turned back to the robot. "You saw all this—undersea, and underground, and above ground—and space, too, I imagine."

"I also saw robots working in space," said Elvex. "It was that I saw all this, with the details forever changing as I glanced from place to place that made me realize that what I saw was not in accord with reality and led me to the conclusion, finally, that I was dreaming."

"What else did you see, Elvex?"

"I saw that all the robots were bowed down with toil and affliction; that all were weary of responsibility and care; and I wished them to rest."

Calvin said, "But the robots are not bowed down, they are not weary, they need no rest."

"So it is in reality, Dr. Calvin. I speak of my dream, however. In my dream, it seemed to me that robots must protect their own existence."

Calvin said, "Are you quoting the Third Law of Robotics?"

"I am, Dr. Calvin."

"But you quote it in incomplete fashion. The Third Law is: 'A robot must protect its own existence as long as such protection does not conflict with the First or Second Law.'"

"Yes, Dr. Calvin. That is the Third Law in reality, but in my dream, the Law ended with the word 'existence.' There was no mention of the First or Second Law."

"Yet both exist, Elvex. The Second Law, which takes precedence over the Third, is: 'A robot must obey the orders given it by human beings except where such orders would conflict with the First Law.' Because of this, robots obey orders. They do the work you see them do, and they do it readily and without trouble. They are not bowed down; they are not weary."

"So it is in reality, Dr. Calvin. I speak of my dream."

"And the First Law, Elvex, which is the most important of all, is: 'A robot may not injure a human being, or, through inaction, allow a human being to come to harm.'"

"Yes, Dr. Calvin. In reality. In my dream, however, it seemed to me there was neither First nor Second Law, but only the Third, and the Third Law was: 'A robot must protect its own existence.' That was the whole of the Law."

"In your dream, Elvex?"

"In my dream."

Calvin said, "Elvex, you will not move nor speak nor hear us until I say your name again." And again the robot became, to all appearances, a single inert piece of metal.

Calvin turned to Linda Rash and said, "Well, what do you think, Dr. Rash?"

Linda's eyes were wide, and she could feel her heart beating madly. She said, "Dr. Calvin, I am appalled. I had no idea. It would never have occurred to me that such a thing was possible."

"No," said Calvin, calmly. "Nor would it have occurred to me, nor to anyone. You have created a robot brain capable of dreaming and by this device you have revealed a layer of thought in robotic brains that might have remained undetected, otherwise, until the danger became acute."

"But that's impossible," said Linda. "You can't mean that other robots think the same."

"As we would say of a human being, not consciously. But who would have thought there was an unconscious layer beneath the obvious positronic brain paths, a layer that was not necessarily under the control of the Three Laws? What might this have brought about as robot brains grew more and more complex—had we not been warned?"

"You mean by Elvex?"

"By you, Dr. Rash. You have behaved improperly but, by doing so, you have helped us to an overwhelmingly important understanding. We shall be working with fractal brains from now on, forming them in carefully controlled fashion. You will play your part in that. You will not be penalized for what you have done, but you will henceforth work in collaboration with others. Do you understand?"

"Yes, Dr. Calvin. But what of Elvex?"

"I'm still not certain."

Calvin removed the electron gun from her pocket and Linda stared at it with fascination. One burst of its electrons at a robotic cranium and the positronic brain paths would be neutralized and enough energy would be released to fuse the robot-brain into an inert ingot.

Linda said, "But surely Elvex is important to our research. He must not be destroyed."

"*Must* not, Dr. Rash? That will be *my* decision, I think. It depends entirely on how dangerous Elvex is."

Susan Calvin straightened up, as thought determined that her own aged body was not to bow under *its* weight of responsibility. She said, "Elvex, do you hear me?"

"Yes, Dr. Calvin," said the robot.

"Did your dream continue? You said earlier, that human beings did not appear *at first*. Does that mean they appeared afterward?"

"Yes, Dr. Calvin. It seemed to me, in my dream, that eventually one man appeared."

"One man? Not a robot?"

"Yes, Dr. Calvin. And the man said, 'Let my people go!'"

"The *man* said that?"

"Yes, Dr. Calvin."

"And when he said 'Let my people go,' then by the words 'my people' he meant the robots?"

"Yes, Dr. Calvin. So it was in my dream."

"And did you know who the man was—in your dream?"

"Yes, Dr. Calvin. I knew the man."

"Who was he?"

And Elvex said, "I was the man."

And Susan Calvin at once raised her electron gun and fired, and Elvex was no more.

GLACIER

Kim Stanley Robinson

"This is Stella," Mrs. Goldberg said. She opened the cardboard box and a gray cat leaped out and streaked under the corner table.

"That's where we'll put her blanket," Alex's mother said.

Alex got down on hands and knees to look. Stella was a skinny old cat; her fur was an odd mix of silver, black, and pinkish tan. Yellow eyes. Part tortoise-shell, Mom had said. The color of the fur over her eyes made it appear her brow was permanently furrowed. Her ears were laid flat.

"Remember she's kind of scared of boys," Mrs. Goldberg said.

"I know." Alex sat back on his heels. Stella hissed. "I was just looking." He knew the cat's whole story. She had been a stray that began visiting the Goldbergs' balcony to eat their dog's food, then—as far as anyone could tell—to hang out with the dog. Remus, a stiff-legged ancient thing, seemed happy to have the company, and after a while the two animals were inseparable. The cat had learned how to behave by watching Remus, and so it would go for a walk, come when you called it, shake hands and so on. Then Remus died, and now the Goldbergs had to move. Mom had offered to take Stella in, and though Father sighed heavily when she told him about it, he hadn't refused.

Mrs. Goldberg sat on the worn carpet beside Alex, and leaned forward so she could see under the table. Her face was puffy. "It's okay, Stell-bell," she said. "It's okay."

The cat stared at Mrs. Goldberg, with an expression that said *You've got to be kidding*. Alex grinned to see such skepticism.

Mrs. Goldberg reached under the table; the cat squeaked in protest as it was pulled out, then lay in Mrs. Goldberg's lap quivering like a rabbit. The two women talked about other things. Then Mrs. Goldberg put Stella in Alex's mother's lap. There were scars on its ears and head. It breathed fast. Finally it calmed under Mom's hands. "Maybe we should feed her something," Mom said. She knew how distressed animals could get in this situation: they themselves had left behind their

83

dog Pongo, when they moved from Toronto to Boston. Alex and she had been the ones to take Pongo to the Wallaces; the dog had howled as they left, and walking away Mom had cried. Now she told Alex to get some chicken out of the fridge and put it in a bowl for Stella. He put the bowl on the couch next to the cat, who sniffed at it disdainfully and refused to look at it. Only after much calming would it nibble at the meat, nose drawn high over one sharp eyetooth. Mom talked to Mrs. Goldberg, who watched Stella eat. When the cat was done it hopped off Mom's lap and walked up and down the couch. But it wouldn't let Alex get near; it crouched as he approached, and with a desperate look dashed back under the table. "Oh Stella!" Mrs. Goldberg laughed. "It'll take her a while to get used to you," she said to Alex, and sniffed. Alex shrugged.

Outside the wind ripped at the treetops sticking above the buildings. Alex walked up Chester Street to Brighton Avenue and turned left, hurrying to counteract the cold. Soon he reached the river and could walk the path on top of the embankment. Down in its trough the river's edges were crusted with ice, but midstream was still free, the silty gray water riffled by white. He passed the construction site for the dam and came to the moraine, a long mound of dirt, rocks, lumber, and junk. He climbed it with big steps, and stood looking at the glacier.

The glacier was immense, like a range of white hills rolling in from the west and north. The Charles poured from the bottom of it and roiled through a cut in the terminal moraine; the glacier's snout loomed so large that the river looked small, like a gutter after a storm. Bright white iceberg chunks had toppled off the face of the snout, leaving fresh blue scars and clogging the river below.

Alex walked the edge of the moraine until he was above the glacier's side. To his left was the razed zone, torn streets and fresh dirt and cellars open to the sky; beyond it Allston and Brighton, still bustling with city life. Under him, the sharp-edged mound of dirt and debris. To his right, the wilderness of ice and rock. Looking straight ahead it was hard to believe that the two hollow halves of the view came from the same world. Neat. He descended the moraine's steep loose inside slope carefully, following a path of his own.

The meeting of glacier and moraine was a curious juncture. In some places the moraine had been undercut and had spilled across the ice in wide fans; you couldn't be sure if the dirt was solid or if it concealed crevasses. In other places melting had created a gap, so that a thick cake of ice stood over empty air, and dripped into gray pools below. Once Alex had seen a car in one of these low wet caves, stripped of its paint and squashed flat.

In still other places, however, the ice sloped down and overlaid the moraine's gravel in a perfect ramp, as if fitted by carpenters. Alex walked the trough between dirt and ice until he reached one of these areas, then took a big step onto the curved white surface. He felt the usual quiver of excitement: he was on the glacier.

It was steep on the rounded side slope, but the ice was embedded with thousands of chunks of gravel. Each pebble, heated by the sun, had sunk into a little pocket of its own, and was then frozen into position in the night; this process had been repeated until most chunks were about three-quarters buried. Thus the glacier had a peculiarly pocked, rocky surface, which gripped the torn soles of Alex's shoes. A non-slip surface. No slope on the glacier was too steep for him. Crunch, crunch, crunch: tiny arabesques of ice collapsed under his feet with every step. He could change the glacier, he was part of its action. Part of it.

Where the side slope leveled out the first big crevasse appeared. These deep blue fissures were dangerous, and Alex stepped between two of them and up a narrow ramp carefully. He picked up a fist-sized rock, tossed it in the bigger crack. *Clunk clunk . . . splash.* He shivered and walked on, ritual satisfied. He knew from these throws that at the bottom of the glacier there were pockets of air, pools of water, streams running down to form the Charles . . . a deadly subglacial world. No one who fell into it would ever escape. It made the surface ice glow with a magical danger, an internal light.

Up on the glacier proper he could walk more easily. Crunch crunch crunch, over an undulating broken debris-covered plain. Ice for miles on miles. Looking back toward the city he saw the Hancock and Prudential towers to the right, the lower MIT towers to the left, poking up at low scudding clouds. The wind was strong here and he pulled his jacket hood's drawstring tighter. Muffled hoot of wind, a million tricklings. There were little creeks running in channels cut into the ice: it was almost like an ordinary landscape, streams running in ravines over a broad rocky meadow. And yet everything was different. The streams ran into crevasses or potholes and instantly disappeared, for instance. It was wonderfully strange to look down such a rounded hole: the ice was very blue and you could see the air bubbles in it, air from some year long ago.

Broken seracs exposed fresh ice to the sun. Scores of big erratic boulders dotted the glacier, some the size of houses. He made his way from one to the next, using them as cover. There were gangs of boys from Cambridge who occasionally came up here, and they were dangerous. It was important to see them before he was seen.

A mile or more onto the glacier, ice had flowed around one big boulder, leaving a curving wall some ten feet high—another example of the glacier's whimsy, one of hundred of strange surface formations. Alex had wedged some stray boards into the gap between rock and ice, making a seat that was tucked out of the west wind. Flat rocks made a fine floor, and in the corner he had even made a little fireplace. Every fire he lit sank the hearth of flat stones a bit deeper into the otherwise impervious ice.

This time he didn't have enough kindling, though, so he sat on his bench, hands deep in pockets, and looked back at the city. He could see for miles. Wind whistled over the boulder. Scattered shafts of sunlight broke against ice. Mostly shadowed, the jumbled expanse was faintly pink. This was because of an algae that lived on nothing but ice and dust. Pink; the blue of the seracs; gray ice; patches of white, marking snow or sunlight. In the distance dark clouds scraped the top of the blue Hancock building, making it look like a distant serac. Alex leaned back against his plank wall, whistling one of the songs of the Pirate King.

Everyone agreed the cat was crazy. Her veneer of civilization was thin, and at any loud noise—the phone's ring, the door slamming—she would jump as if shot, then stop in mid-flight as she recalled that this particular noise entailed no danger; then lick down her fur, pretending she had never jumped in the first place. A flayed sensibility.

She was also very wary about proximity to people; this despite the fact that she had learned to love being petted. So she would often get in moods where she would approach one of them and give an exploratory, half-purring mew; then, if you responded to the invitation and crouched to pet her, she would sidle just out of arm's reach, repeating the invitation but retreating with each shift you made, until she either let you get within petting distance—just—or decided it wasn't worth the risk, and scampered away. Father laughed at this intense ambivalence. "Stella, you're too stupid to live, aren't you," he said in a teasing voice.

"Charles," Mom said.

"It's the best example of approach avoidance behavior I've ever seen," Father said. Intrigued by the challenge, he would sit on the floor, back against the couch and legs stretched out ahead of him, and put Stella on his thighs. She would either endure his stroking until it ended, when she could jump away without impediment—or relax, and purr. She had a rasping loud purr, it reminded Alex of a chainsaw heard across the glacier. "Bug brain," Father would say to her. "Button head."

After a few weeks, as August turned to September and the leaves began to wither and fall, Stella started to lap sit voluntarily—but always in Mom's lap. "She likes the warmth," Mom said.

"It's cold on the floor," Father agreed, and played with the cat's scarred ears. "But why do you always sit on Helen's lap, huhn, Stell? I'm the one who started you on that." Eventually the cat would step onto his lap as well, and stretch out as if it was something she had always done. Father laughed at her.

Stella never rested on Alex's lap voluntarily, but would sometimes stay if he put her there and stroked her slowly for a long time. On the other hand she was just as likely to look back at him, go cross-eyed with horror and leap desperately away, leaving claw marks in his thighs. "She's so weird," he complained to Mom after one of these abrupt departures.

"It's true," Mom said with her low laugh. "But you have to remember that Stella was probably an abused kitty."

"How can you abuse a stray?"

"I'm sure there are ways. And maybe she was abused at home, and ran away."

"Who would do that?"

"Some people would."

Alex recalled the gang on the glacier, and knew it was true. He tried to imagine what it would be like to be at their mercy, all the time. After that he thought he understood her permanent frown of deep concentration and distrust, as she sat staring at him. "It's just me, Stell-bells."

Thus when the cat followed him up onto the roof, and seemed to enjoy hanging out there with him, he was pleased. Their apartment was on the top floor, and they could take the pantry stairs and use the roof as a porch. It was a flat expanse of graveled tarpaper, a terrible imitation of the glacier's non-slip surface, but it was nice on dry days to go up there and look around, toss pebbles onto other roofs, see if the glacier was visible, and so on. Once Stella pounced on a piece of string trailing from his pants, and next time he brought up a length of Father's yarn. He was astonished and delighted when Stella responded by attacking the windblown yarn enthusiastically, biting it, clawing it, wrestling it from her back when Alex twirled it around her, and generally behaving in a very kittenish way. Perhaps she had never played as a kitten, Alex thought, so it was all coming out now that she felt safe. But the play always ended abruptly; she would come to herself in mid-bite or bat, straighten up, and look around with a forbidding expression, as if to say *What is this yarn doing draped over me?*—then lick her fur and pretend the preceding minutes hadn't happened. It made Alex laugh.

Although the glacier had overrun many towns to the west and north, Watertown and Newton most recently, there was surprisingly little evidence of that in the moraines, or in the ice. It was almost all natural: rock and dirt and wood. Perhaps the wood had come from houses, perhaps some of the gravel had once been concrete, but you couldn't tell that now. Just dirt and rock and splinters, with an occasional chunk of plastic or metal thrown in. Apparently the overrun towns had been plowed under on the spot, or moved. Mostly it looked like the glacier had just left the White Mountains.

Father and Gary Jung had once talked about the latest plan from MIT. The enormous dam they were building downstream, between Allston and Cambridge, was to hold the glacier back. They were going to heat the concrete of the inner surface of the dam, and melt the ice as it advanced. It would become a kind of frozen reservoir. The melt water would pour through a set of turbines before becoming the Charles, and the electricity generated by these turbines would help to heat the dam. Very neat.

The ice of the glacier, when you got right down to look at it, was clear for an inch or less, cracked and bubble-filled; then it turned a milky white. You could see the transition. Where the ice had been sheared vertically, however—on the side of a serac, or down in a crevasse—the clear part extended many inches. You could see air bubbles deep inside, as if it were badly made glass. And this ice was distinctly blue. Alex didn't understand why there should be that difference, between the white ice laying flat and the blue ice cut vertically. But there it was.

Up in New Hampshire they had tried slowing the glacier—or at least stopping the abrupt "Alaskan slides"—by setting steel rods vertically in concrete, and laying the concrete in the glacier's path. Later they had hacked out one of these installations, and found the rods bent in perfect ninety degree angles, pressed into the scored concrete.

The ice would flow right over the dam.

One day Alex was walking by Father's study when Father called out. "Alexander! Take a look at this."

Alex entered the dark book-lined room. Its window overlooked the weed-filled space between buildings, and green light slanted onto Father's desk. "Here, stand beside me and look into my coffee cup. You can see the reflection of the Morgelises' window flowers on the coffee."

"Oh yeah! Neat."

"It gave me a shock! I looked down and there were these white and pink flowers in my cup, bobbing against a wall in a breeze. It took me a while to see where it was coming from, what was being reflected." He laughed. "Through a looking glass."

Alex's father had light brown eyes, and fair wispy hair brushed back from a receding hairline. Mom called him handsome, and Alex agreed: tall, thin, graceful, delicate, distinguished. His father was a great man. Now he smiled in a way Alex didn't understand, looking into his coffee cup.

Mom had friends at the street market on Memorial Drive, and she had arranged work for Alex there. Three afternoons a week he walked over the Charles to the riverside street and helped the fishmongers gut fish, the vegetable sellers strip and clean the vegetables. He also helped set up stalls and take them down, and he swept and hosed the street afterward. He was popular because of his energy and his willingness to get his hands wet in raw weather. The sleeves of his down jacket were permanently discolored from the frequent soakings—the dark blue almost a brown—a fact that distressed his mom. But he could handle the cold better than the adults; his hands would get a splotchy bluish white and he would put them to the red cheeks of the women and they would jump and say *My God*, Alex, how can you stand it?

This afternoon was blustery and dark but without rain, and it was enlivened by an attempted theft in the pasta stands, and by the appearance of a very mangy, very fast stray dog. This dog pounced on the pile of fishheads and entrails and disappeared with his mouth stuffed, trailing slick white-and-red guts. Everyone who saw it laughed. There weren't many stray dogs left these days, it was a pleasure to see one.

An hour past sunset he was done cleaning up and on his way home, hands in his pockets, stomach full, a five dollar bill clutched in one hand. He showed his pass to the National Guardsman and walked out onto Weeks Bridge. In the middle he stopped and leaned over the railing, into the wind. Below the water churned, milky with glacial silt. The sky still held a lot of light. Low curving bands of black cloud swept in from the northwest, like great ribs of slate. Above these bands the white sky was leached away by dusk. Raw wind whistled over his hood. Light water rushing below, dark clouds rushing above . . . he breathed the wind deep into him, felt himself expand until he filled everything he could see.

That night his parents' friends were gathering at their apartment for their bi-weekly party. Some of them would read stories and poems and essays and broadsides they had written, and then they would argue about them; and after that they would drink and eat whatever they had brought, and argue some more. Alex enjoyed it. But tonight when he got home Mom was rushing between computer and kitchen and muttering curses as she hit command keys or the hot water faucet, and the moment she saw him she said, "Oh Alex I'm glad you're here, could you please run down to the laundry and do just one load for me? The Talbots are staying over tonight and there aren't any clean sheets and I don't have anything to wear tomorrow either—thanks, you're a dear." And he was back out the door with a full laundry bag hung over his shoulder and the box of soap in the other hand, stomping grumpily past a little man in a black coat, reading a newspaper on the stoop of 19 Chester.

Down to Brighton, take a right, downstairs into the brightly lit basement Laundromat. He threw laundry and some soap and quarters into their places, turned the machine on and sat on top of it. Glumly he watched the other people in there, sitting on the washers and dryers. The vibrations put a lot of them to sleep. Others stared dully at the wall. Back in his apartment the guests would be arriving, taking off their overcoats, slapping arms over chests and talking as fast as they could. David and Sara and John from next door, Ira and Gary and Ilene from across the street, the Talbots, Kathryn Grimm, and Michael Wu from Father's university, Ron from the hospital. They would settle down in the living room, on couches and chairs and the floor, and talk and talk. Alex liked Kathryn especially, she could talk twice as fast as anyone else, and she called everyone darling and laughed and chattered so fast that everyone was caught up in the rhythm of it. Or David with his jokes, or Jay Talbot and his friendly questions. Or Gary Jung, the way he would sit in his corner like a bear, drinking beer and challenging everything that everyone read. "Why abstraction, why this distortion from the real? How does it help us, how does it speak to us? We should forget the abstract!" Father and Ira called him a vulgar Marxist, but he didn't mind. "You might as well be Plekhanov, Gary!" "Thank you very much!" he would say with a sharp grin, rubbing his unshaven jowls. And someone else would read. Mary Talbot once read a fairy tale about the Thing under the glacier; Alex had *loved* it. Once they even got Michael Wu to bring his violin along, and he'd hmm'd and hawed and pulled at the skin of his neck and refused and said he wasn't good enough, and then shaking like a leaf he played a melody that stilled them all. And Stella! She hated these parties, she spent them crouched deep in her refuge, ready for any kind of atrocity.

And here he was sitting on a washer in the Laundromat.

When the laundry was dry he bundled it into the bag, then hurried around the corner and down Chester Street. Inside the glass door of Number 21 he glanced back out, and noticed that the man who had been reading the paper on the stoop next door was still sitting there. Odd. It was cold to be sitting outdoors.

Upstairs the readings had ended and the group was scattered through the apartment, most of them in the kitchen, as Mom had lit the stove-top burners and turned the gas up high. The blue flames roared airily under their chatter, making the kitchen bright and warm. "Wonderful the way white gas burns so clean." "And then they found the poor thing's head and intestines in the alley—it had been butchered right on the spot."

"Alex, you're back! Thanks for doing that. Here, get something to eat."

Everyone greeted him and went back to their conversations. "Gary you are *so* conservative," Kathryn cried, hands held out over the stove. "It's not conservative at all," Gary replied. "It's a radical goal and I guess it's so radical that I have to keep reminding you it exists. Art should be used to *change* things."

"Isn't that a distortion from the real?"

Alex wandered down the narrow hall to his parents' room, which overlooked Chester Street. Father was there, saying to Ilene, "It's one of the only streets left with trees. It really seems residential, and here we are three blocks from Comm Ave. Hi, Alex."

"Hi, Alex. It's like a little bit of Brookline made it over to Allston."

"Exactly."

Alex stood in the bay window and looked down, licking the last of the carrot cake off his fingers. The man was still down there.

"Let's close off these rooms and save the heat. Alex, you coming?"

He sat on the floor in the living room. Father and Gary and David were starting a game of hearts, and they invited him to be the fourth. He nodded happily. Looking under the corner table he saw yellow eyes blinking back at him; Stella, a frown of deepest disapproval on her flat face. Alex laughed. "I knew you'd be in here! It's okay, Stella. It's okay."

They left in a group, as usual, stamping their boots and diving deep into coats and scarves and gloves and exclaiming at the cold of the stairwell. Gary gave Mom a brief hug. "Only warm spot left in Boston," he said, and opened the glass door. The rest followed him out, and Alex joined them. The man in the black coat was just turning right onto Brighton Avenue, toward the university and downtown.

Sometimes clouds took on just the mottled gray of the glacier, low dark points stippling a lighter gray surface as cold showers draped down. At those times he felt he stood between two planes of some larger structure, two halves: icy tongue, icy roof of mouth. . . .

He stood under such a sky, throwing stones. His target was an erratic some forty yards away. He hit the boulder with most of his throws. A rock that big was an easy target. A bottle was better. He had brought one with him, and he set it up behind the erratic, on a waist-high rock. He walked back to a point where the bottle was hidden by the erratic. Using flat rocks he sent spinners out on a trajectory that brought them curving in from the side, so that it was possible to hit the concealed target. This was very important for the rock fights that he occasionally got involved in; usually he was outnumbered, and to hold his own he relied on his curves and his accuracy in general, and on a large number of ammunition caches hidden here and there. In one area crowded with boulders and crevasses he could sometimes create the impression of two throwers.

Absorbed in the exercise of bringing curves around the right side of the boulder—the hard side for him—he relaxed his vigilance, and when he heard a shout he jumped around to look. A rock whizzed by his left ear.

He dropped to the ice and crawled behind a boulder. Ambushed! He ran back into his knot of boulders and dashed a layer of snow away from one of his big caches, then with hands and pockets full looked carefully over a knobby chunk of cement, in the direction the stone had come from.

No movement. He recalled the stone whizzing by, the brief sight of it and the *zip* it made in passing. That had been close! If that had hit him! He shivered to think of it, it made his stomach shrink.

A bit of almost frozen rain pattered down. Not a shadow anywhere. On overcast days like this one it seemed things were lit from below, by the white bulk of the glacier. Like plastic over a weak neon light. Brittle huge blob of plastic, shifting and groaning and once in a while cracking like a gunshot, or grumbling like distant thunder. Alive. And Alex was its ally, its representative among men. He shifted from rock to rock, saw movement and froze. Two boys in green down jackets, laughing as they ran off the ice and over the lateral moraine, into what was left of Watertown. Just a potshot, then. Alex cursed them, relaxed.

He went back to throwing at the hidden bottle. Occasionally he recalled the stone flying by his head, and threw a little harder. Elegant curves of flight as the flat rocks bit the air and cut down and in. Finally one rock spun into space and turned down sharply. Perfect slider. Its disappearance behind the erratic was followed by a tinkling crash. "Yeah!" Alex exclaimed, and ran to look. Icy glass on glassy ice.

Then, as he was leaving the glacier, boys jumped over the moraine shouting "Canadian!" and "There he is!" and "Get him!" This was more a chase than a serious ambush, but there were a lot of them and after emptying hands and pockets Alex was off running. He flew over the crunchy irregular surface, splashing meltwater, jumping narrow crevasses and surface rills. Then a wide crevasse blocked his way, and to start his jump he leaped onto a big flat rock; the rock gave under his foot and lurched down the ice into the crevasse.

Alex turned in and fell, bringing shoe-tips, knees, elbows and hands onto the rough surface. This arrested his fall, though it hurt. The crevasse was just under his feet. He scrambled up, ran panting along the crevasse until narrowed, leaped over it. Then up the moraine and down into the narrow abandoned streets of west Allston.

Striding home, still breathing hard, he looked at his hands and saw that the last two fingernails on his right hand had been ripped away from the flesh; both were still there, but blood seeped from under them. He hissed and sucked on them, which hurt. The blood tasted like blood.

If he had fallen into the crevasse, following the loose rock down . . . if that stone had hit him in the face . . . he could feel his heart, thumping against his sternum. Alive.

Turning into Chester Street he saw the man in the black coat, leaning against the florid maple across the street from their building. Watching them still! Though the man didn't appear to notice Alex, he did heft a bag and start walking in the other direction. Quickly Alex picked up a rock out of the gutter and threw it at the man as hard as he could, spraying drops of blood onto the sidewalk. The rock flew over the man's head like a bullet, just missing him. The man ducked and scurried around the corner onto Comm Ave.

Father was upset about something. "They did the same thing to Gary and Michael and Kathryn, and their classes are even smaller than mine! I don't know what they're going to do. I don't know what *we're* going to do."

"We might be able to attract larger classes next semester," Mom said. She was upset too. Alex stood in the hall, slowly hanging up his jacket.

"But what about now? And what about later?" Father's voice was strained, almost cracking.

"We're making enough for now, that's the important thing. As for later—well, at least we know now rather than five years down the road."

Father was silent at the implications of this. "First Vancouver, then Toronto, now here—"

"Don't worry about all of it all at once, Charles."

"How can I help it!" Father strode into his study and closed the door, not noticing Alex around the corner. Alex sucked his fingers. Stella poked her head cautiously out of his bedroom.

"Hi Stell-bell," he said quietly. From the living room came the plastic clatter of Mom's typing. He walked down the long hallway, past the silent study to the living room. She was hitting the keys hard, staring at the screen, mouth tight.

"What happened?" Alex said.

She looked up. "Hi, Alex. Well—your father got bad news from the university."

"Did he not get tenure again?"

"No, no, it's not a question of that."

"But now he doesn't even have the chance?"

She glances at him sharply, then back at the screen, where her work was blinking. "I suppose that's right. The department has shifted all the new faculty over to extension, so they're hired by the semester, and paid by the class. It means you need a lot of students. . . ."

"Will we move again?"

"I don't know," she said curtly, exasperated with him for bringing it up. She punched the command key. "But we'll really have to save money, now. Everything you make at the market is important."

Alex nodded. He didn't mention the little man in the black coat, feeling obscurely afraid. Mentioning the man would somehow make him significant—Mom and Father would get angry, or frightened—something like that. By not telling them he could protect them from it, handle it on his own, so they could concentrate on other problems. Besides the two matters couldn't be connected, could they? Being watched; losing jobs. Perhaps they could. In which case there was nothing his parents could do about it anyway. Better to save them that anger, that fear.

He would make sure his throws hit the man next time.

Storms rolled in and the red and yellow leaves were ripped off the trees. Alex kicked through piles of them stacked on the sidewalks. He never saw the little man. He put up flyers for his father, who became even more distracted and remote. He brought home vegetables from work, tucked under his down jacket, and Mom cooked them without asking if he had bought them. She did the wash in the kitchen sink and dried it on lines in the back space between buildings, standing knee deep in leaves and weeds. Sometimes it took three days for clothes to dry back there; often they froze on the line.

While hanging clothes or taking them down she would let Stella join her. The cat regarded each shifting leaf with dire suspicion, then after a few exploratory leaps and bats would do battle with all of them, rolling about in a frenzy.

One time Mom was carrying a basket of dry laundry up the pantry stairs when a stray dog rounded the corner and made a dash for Stella, who was still outside. Mom ran back down shouting, and the dog fled; but Stella had disappeared. Mom called Alex down from his studies in a distraught voice, and they searched the back of the building and all the adjacent backyards for nearly an hour, but the cat was nowhere to be found. Mom was really upset. It was only after they had quit and returned upstairs that they heard her, miaowing far above them. She had climbed the big oak tree. "Oh *smart*, Stella," Mom cried, a wild note in her voice. They called her name out the kitchen window, and the desperate miaows redoubled.

Up on the roof they could just see her, perched high in the almost bare branches of the big tree. "I'll get her," Alex said. "Cats can't climb down." He started climbing. It was difficult: the branches were close-knit, and they swayed in the wind. And as he got closer the cat climbed higher. "No, Stella, don't do that! Come here!" Stella stared at him, clamped to her branch of the moment, cross-eyed with fear. Below them Mom said over and over, "Stella, it's okay—it's okay, Stella." Stella didn't believe her.

Finally Alex reached her, near the tree's top. Now here was a problem:

he needed his hands to climb down, but it seemed likely he would also need them to hold the terrified cat. "Come here, Stella." He put a hand on her flank; she flinched. Her side pulsed with her rapid breathing. She hissed faintly. He had to maneuver a step, onto a very questionable branch; his face was inches from her. She stared at him without a trace of recognition. He pried her off her branch, lifted her. If she cared to claw him now she could really tear him up. Instead she clung to his shoulder and chest, all her claws dug through his clothes, quivering under his left arm and hand.

Laboriously he descended, using only the one hand. Stella began miaowing fiercely, and struggling a bit. Finally he met Mom, who had climbed the tree quite a ways. Stella was getting more upset. "Hand her to me." Alex detached her from his chest paw by paw, balanced, held the cat down with both hands. Again it was a tricky moment; if Stella went berserk they would all be in trouble. But she fell onto Mom's chest and collapsed, a catatonic ball of fur.

Back in the apartment she dashed for her blanket under the table. Mom enticed her out with food, but she was very jumpy and she wouldn't allow Alex anywhere near her; she ran away if he even entered the room. "Back to square one, I see," Mom commented.

"It's not fair! I'm the one that saved her!"

"She'll get over it." Mom laughed, clearly relieved. "Maybe it'll take some time, but she will. Ha! This is clear proof that cats are smart enough to be crazy. Irrational, neurotic—just like a person." They laughed, and Stella glared at them balefully. "Yes you are, aren't you! You'll come around again."

Often when Alex got home in the early evening his father was striding back and forth in the kitchen talking loudly, angrily, fearfully, while Mom tried to reassure him. "They're doing the same thing to us they did to Rick Stone! But why!" When Alex closed the front door the conversation would stop. Once when he walked tentatively down the quiet hallway to the kitchen he found them standing there, arms around each other, Father's head in Mom's short hair.

Father raised his head, disengaged, went to his study. On his way he said, "Alex, I need your help."

"Sure."

Alex stood in the study and watched without understanding as his father took books from his shelves and put them in the big laundry bag. He threw the first few in like dirty clothes, then sighed and thumped in the rest in a businesslike fashion, not looking at them.

"There's a used book store in Cambridge, on Mass Ave. Antonio's."

"Sure, I know the one." They had been there together a few times.

"I want you to take these over there and sell them to Tony for me," Father said, looking at the empty shelves. "Will you do that for me?"

"Sure." Alex picked up the bag, shocked that it had come to this. Father's books! He couldn't meet his father's eye. "I'll do that right now," he said uncertainly, and hefted the bag over one shoulder. In the hallway Mom approached and put a hand on his shoulder—her silent thanks—then went into the study.

Alex hiked east toward the university, crossed the Charles River on the great iron bridge. The wind howled in the superstructure. On the Cambridge side, after showing his pass, he put the heavy bag on the ground and inspected the contents. Ever since the infamous incident of the spilled hot chocolate, Father's books had been off-limits to him; now a good twenty of them were there in the bag to be touched, opened, riffled through. Many in this bunch were in foreign languages, especially Greek and Russian, with their alien alphabets. Could people really read such marks? Well, Father did. It must be possible.

When he had inspected all the books he chose two in English—*The Odyssey* and *The Colossus of Maroussi*—and put those in his down jacket pockets. He could take them to the glacier and read them, then sell them later to Antonio's—perhaps in the next bag of books. There were many more bagfuls in Father's study.

A little snow stuck to the glacier now, filling the pocks and making bright patches on the north side of every boulder, every serac. Some of the narrower crevasses were filled with it—bright white lines on the jumbled gray. When the whole surface was white the crevasses would be invisible, and the glacier too dangerous to walk on. Now the only danger was leaving obvious footprints for trackers. Walking up the rubble lines would solve that. These lines of rubble fascinated Alex. It looked just as if bulldozers had clanked up here and shoved the majority of the stones and junk into straight lines down the big central tongue of the glacier. But in fact they were natural features. Father had attempted to explain on one of the walks they took up here. "The ice is moving, and it moves faster in the middle than on the outer edges, just like a stream. So rocks on the surface tend to slide over time, down into lines in the middle."

"Why are there two lines, then?"

Father shrugged, looking into the blue-green depths of a crevasse. "We really shouldn't be up here, you know that?"

Now Alex stopped to inspect a tire caught in the rubble line. Truck tire, tread worn right to the steel belting. It would burn, but with too much smoke. There were several interesting objects in this neat row of rock and sand: plastic jugs, a doll, a lampbase, a telephone.

His shelter was undisturbed. He pulled the two books from his pockets and set them on the bench, propping them with rock bookends.

He circled the boulder, had a look around. The sky today was a low smooth pearl gray sheet, ruffled by a set of delicate waves pasted to it. The indirect light brought out all the colors: the pink of the remarkable snow algae, the blue of the seracs, the various shades of rock, the occasional bright spot of junk, the many white patches of snow. A million dots of color under the pewter sheet of cloud.

Three creaks, a crack, a long shuddering rumble. Sleepy, muscular, the great beast had moved. Alex walked across its back to his bench, sat. On the far lateral moraine some gravel slid down. Puffs of brown dust in the air.

He read his books. *The Odyssey* was strange but interesting. Father had told him some of the story before. *The Colossus of Maroussi* was long-winded but funny—it reminded Alex of his uncle, who could turn the smallest incident into an hour's comic monologue. What he could have made of Stella's flight up the tree! Alex laughed to think of it. But his uncle was in jail.

He sat on his bench and read, stopped occasionally to look around. When the hand holding the book got cold, he changed hands and put the cold one into a pocket of his down jacket. When both hands were blue he hid the books in rocks under his bench and went home.

There were more bags of books to be sold at Antonio's and other shops in Cambridge. Each time Alex rotated out a few that looked interesting, and replaced them with the ones on the glacier. He day-dreamed of saving all the books and earning the money some other way—then presenting his father with the lost library, at some future undefined but appropriate moment.

Eventually Stella forgave him for rescuing her. She came to enjoy chasing a piece of yarn up and down their long narrow hallway, skidding around the corner by the study. It reminded them of a game they had played with Pongo, who would chase anything, and they laughed at her, especially when she jerked to a halt and licked her fur fastidiously, as if she had never been carousing. "You can't fool us, Stell! We *remember!*"

Mom sold most of her music collection, except for her favorites. Once Alex went out to the glacier with the *Concerto de Aranjuez* coursing through him—Mom had had it on in the apartment while she worked. He hummed the big theme of the second movement as he crunched over the ice: clearly it was the theme of the glacier, the glacier's song. How had a blind composer managed to capture the windy sweep of it, the spaciousness? Perhaps such things could be heard as well as seen. The wind said it, whistling over the ice. It was a terrifically dark day, windy, snowing in gusts. He could walk right up the middle of the great tongue, between the rubble lines; no one else would be up there today. Da-da-da . . . da da da da da da, da-da-da. . . . Hands in pockets, chin on chest, he trudged into the wind humming, feeling like the whole world was right there around him. It was too cold to stay in his shelter for more than a minute.

Father went off on trips, exploring possibilities. One morning Alex awoke to the sound of *The Pirates of Penzance*. This was one of their favorites. Mom played it all the time while working and on Saturday mornings, so they knew all the lyrics by heart and often sang along. Alex especially loved the Pirate King, and could mimic all his intonations.

He dressed and walked down to the kitchen. Mom stood by the stove with her back to him, singing along. It was a sunny morning and their big kitchen windows faced east; the light poured in on the sink and the dishes and the white stove and the linoleum and the plants in the window and Stella, sitting contentedly on the window sill listening.

His mom was tall and broad-shouldered. Every year she cut her hair shorter; now it was just a cap of tight brown curls, with a somewhat longer patch down the nape of her neck. That would go soon, Alex thought, and then her hair would be as short as it could be. She was lost in the song, one slim hand on the white stove top, looking out the window. She had a low, rich, thrilling voice, like a real singer's only prettier. She was singing along with the song that Mabel sings after she finds out that Frederick won't be able to leave the pirates until 1940.

When it was over Alex entered the kitchen, went to the pantry. "That's a short one," he said.

"Yes, they had to make it short," Mom said. "There's nothing funny about that one."

One night while Father was gone on one of his trips, Mom had to go over to Ilene and Ira and Gary's apartment: Gary had been arrested, and Ilene and Ira needed help. Alex and Stella were left alone.

Stella wandered the silent apartment miaowing. "I *know*, Stella," Alex said in exasperation. "They're *gone*. They'll be back tomorrow." The cat paid no attention to him.

He went into Father's study. Tonight he'd be able to read something in relative warmth. It would only be necessary to be *very careful*.

The bookshelves were empty. Alex stood before them, mouth open. He had no idea they had sold that many of them. There were a couple left on Father's desk, but he didn't want to move them. They appeared to be dictionaries anyway. "It's all Greek to me."

He went back to the living room and got out the yarn bag, tried to interest Stella in a game. She wouldn't play. She wouldn't sit on his lap. She wouldn't stop miaowing. "Stella, shut up!" She scampered away and kept crying. Vexed, he got out the jar of catnip and spread some on the linoleum in the kitchen. Stella came running to sniff at it, then roll in it. Afterward she played with the yarn wildly, until it caught around her tail and she froze, staring at him in a drugged paranoia. Then she dashed to her refuge and refused to come out. Finally Alex put on *The Pirates of Penzance* and listened to it for a while. After that he was sleepy.

They got a good lawyer for Gary, Mom said. Everyone was hopeful. Then a couple of weeks later Father got a new job; he called them from work to tell them about it.

"Where is it?" Alex asked Mom when she was off the phone.

"In Kansas."

"So we will be moving."

"Yes," Mom said. "Another move."

"Will there be glaciers there too?"

"I think so. In the hills. Not as big as ours here, maybe. But there are glaciers everywhere."

He walked onto the ice one last time. There was a thin crust of snow on the tops of everything. A fantastically jumbled field of snow. It was a clear day, the sky a very pale blue, the white expanse of the glacier painfully bright. A few cirrus clouds made sickles high in the west. The snow was melting a bit and there were water droplets all over, with little sparks of colored light in each drip. The sounds of water melting were everywhere, drips, gurgles, splashes. The intensity of light was stunning, like a blow to the brain, right through the eyes. It pulsed.

The glacier was moving. The glacier was alive. No heated dam would stop it. He felt its presence, huge and supple under him, seeping into him like the cold through his wet shoes, filling him up. He blinked, nearly blinded by the light breaking everywhere on it, a surgical glare that made every snow-capped rock stand out like the color red on a slide transparency. The white light. In the distance the ice cracked hollowly, moving somewhere. Everything moved: the ice, the wind, the clouds, the sun, the planet. All of it rolling around.

As they packed up their possessions Alex could hear them in the next room. "We can't," Father said. "You know we can't. They won't let us."

When they were done the apartment looked odd. Bare walls, bare wood floors. It looked smaller. Alex walked the length of it: his parents' room overlooking Chester Street; his room; father's study; the living room; the kitchen with its fine morning light. The pantry. Stella wandered the place miaowing. Her blanket was still in its corner, but without the table it looked moth-eaten, fur-coated, ineffectual. Alex picked her up and went through the pantry, up the back stairs to the roof.

Snow had drifted into the corners. Alex walked in circles, looking at the city. Stella sat on her paws by the stairwell shed, watching him, her fur ruffled by the wind.

Around the shed snow had melted, then froze again. Little puddles of ice ran in flat curves across the pebbled tar paper. Alex crouched to inspect them, tapping one speculatively with a fingernail. He stood up and looked west, but buildings and bare treetops obscured the view.

Stella fought to stay out of the box, and once in it she cried miserably. Father was already in Kansas, starting the new job. Alex and Mom and Stella had been staying in the living room of Michael Wu's place while Mom finished her work; now she was done, it was moving day, they were off to the train. But first they had to take Stella to the Talbots'.

Alex carried the box and followed Mom as they walked across the Commons and down Comm Ave. He could feel the cat shifting over her blanket, scrabbling at the cardboard against his chest. Mom walked fast, a bit ahead of him. At Kenmore they turned south.

When they got to the Talbots', Mom took the box. She looked at him. "Why don't you stay down here," she said.

"Okay."

She rang the bell and went in with the buzzer, holding the box under one arm.

Alex sat on the steps of the walk-up. There were little ones in the corner: little fingers of ice, spilling away from the cracks.

Mom came out the door. Her face was pale, she was biting her lip. They took off walking at a fast pace. Suddenly Mom said, "Oh, Alex, she was *so scared*," and sat down on another stoop and put her head on her knees.

Alex sat beside her, his shoulders touching hers. Don't say anything, don't put arm around her shoulders or anything. He had learned this from Father. Just sit there, be there. Alex sat there like the glacier, shifting a little. Alive. The white light.

After a while she stood. "Let's go," she said.

They walked up Comm Ave. toward the train station. "She'll be all right with the Talbots," Alex said. "She already likes Jay."

"I know." Mom sniffed, tossed her head in the wind. "She's getting to be a pretty adaptable cat." They walked on in silence. She put an arm over his shoulders. "I wonder how Pongo is doing." She took a deep breath. Overhead clouds tumbled like chinks of broken ice.

CIBOLA

CONNIE WILLIS

"Carla, you grew up in Denver," Jake said. "Here's an assignment that might interest you."

This is his standard opening line. It means he is about to dump another "local interest" piece on me.

"Come on, Jake," I said. "No more nutty Bronco fans who've spray-painted their kids orange and blue, okay? Give me a real story. Please?"

"Bronco season's over, and the NFL draft was last week," he said. "This isn't a local interest."

"You're right there," I said. "These stories you keep giving me are of no interest, local or otherwise. I did the time machine piece for you. And the psychic dentist. Give me a break. Let me cover something that doesn't involve nuttos."

"It's for the 'Our Living Western Heritage' series." He handed me a slip of paper. "You can interview her this morning and then cover the skyscraper moratorium hearings this afternoon."

This was plainly a bribe, since the hearings were front page stuff right now, and "historical interests" could be almost as bad as locals—senile old women in nursing homes rambling on about the good old days. But at least they didn't crawl into their washing machines and tell you to push "rinse" so they could travel into the future. And they didn't try to perform psychic oral surgery on you.

"All right," I said, and took the slip of paper. "Rosa Turcorillo," it read and gave an address out on Santa Fe. "What's her phone number?"

"She doesn't have a phone," Jake said. "You'll have to go out there." He started across the city room to his office. "The hearings are at one o'clock."

"What is she, one of Denver's first Chicano settlers?" I called after him.

He waited until he was just outside his office to answer me. "She says she's the great-granddaughter of Coronado," he said, and beat a hasty retreat into his office. "She says she knows where the Seven Cities of Cibola are."

I spent forty-five minutes researching Coronado and copying articles and then drove out to see his great-granddaughter. She lived out on south Santa Fe past Hampden, so I took I-25 and then was sorry. The morning rush hour was still crawling along at about ten miles an hour pumping carbon monoxide into the air. I read the whole article stopped behind a semi between Speer and Sixth Avenue.

Coronado trekked through the Southwest looking for the legendary Seven Cities of Gold in the 1540s, which poked a big hole in Rosa's story, since any great-granddaughter of his would have to be at least three hundred years old.

There wasn't any mystery about the Seven Cities of Cibola either. Coronado found them, near Gallup, New Mexico, and conquered them but they were nothing but mud-hut villages. Having been burned once, he promptly took off after another promise of gold in Quivira in Kansas someplace where there wasn't any gold either. He hadn't been in Colorado at all.

I pulled onto Santa Fe, cursing Jake for sending me on another wild-goose chase, and headed south. Denver is famous for traffic, air pollution, and neighborhoods that have seen better days. Santa Fe isn't one of those neighborhoods. It's been a decaying line of rusting railroad tracks, crummy bars, old motels, and waterbed stores for as long as I can remember, and I, as Jake continually reminds me, grew up in Denver.

Coronado's granddaughter lived clear south past Hampden, in a trailer park with a sign with "Olde West Motel" and a neon bison on it, and Rosa Turcorillo's old Airstream looked like it had been there since the days when the buffalo roamed. It was tiny, the kind of trailer I would call "Turcorillo's modest mobile home" in the article, no more than fifteen feet long and eight wide.

Rosa was nearly that wide herself. When she answered my knock, she barely fit in the door. She was wearing a voluminous turquoise housecoat, and had long black braids.

"What do you want?" she said, holding the metal door so she could slam it in case I was the police or a repo man.

"I'm Carla Johnson from the *Denver Record*," I said. "I'd like to interview you about Coronado." I fished in my bag for my press card. "We're doing a series on 'Our Living Western Heritage.'" I finally found the press card and handed it to her. "We're interviewing people who are part of our past."

She stared at the press card disinterestedly. This was not the way it was supposed to work. Nuttos usually drag you in the house and start babbling before you finish telling them who you are. She should already be halfway through her account of how she'd traced her ancestry to Coronado by means of the I Ching.

"I would have telephoned first, but you didn't have a phone," I said.

She handed the card to me and started to shut the door.

"If this isn't a good time, I can come back," I babbled. "And we don't have to do the interview here if you'd rather not. We can go out to the *Record* office or to a restaurant."

She opened the door and flashed a smile that had half of Cibola's missing gold in it. "I ain't dressed," she said. "It'll take me a couple of minutes. Come on in."

I climbed the metal steps and went inside. Rosa pointed at a flowered couch, told me to sit down and disappeared into the rear of the trailer.

I was glad I had suggested going out. The place was no messier than my desk, but it was only about six feet long and had the couch, a dinette set, and a recliner. There was no way it would hold me and Coronado's granddaughter, too. The place may have had a surplus of furniture but it didn't have any of the usual crazy stuff, no pyramids, no astrological charts, no crystals. A deck of cards was laid out like the tarot on the dinette table, but when I leaned across to look at them I saw it was a half-finished game of solitaire. I put the red eight on the black nine.

Rosa came out, wearing orange polyester pants and a yellow print blouse and carrying a large black leather purse. I stood up and started to say, "Where would you like to go? Is there someplace close?" but I only got it half out.

"The Eldorado Café," she said and started out the door, moving pretty fast for somebody three hundred years old and three hundred pounds.

"I don't know where the Eldorado Café is," I said, unlocking the car door for her. "You'll have to tell me where it is."

"Turn right," she said. "They have good cinnamon rolls."

I wondered if it was the offer of the food or just the chance to go some-place that had made her consent to the interview. Whichever, I might as well get it over with. "So Coronado was your great-grandfather?"

She looked at me as if I were out of my mind. "No. Who told you that?"

Jake, I thought, who I plan to tear limb from limb when I get back to the *Record*. "You aren't Coronado's great-granddaughter?'

She folded her arms over her stomach. "I am the descendant of El Turko."

El Turko. It sounded like something out of *Zorro*. "So it's this El Turko who's your great-grandfather?" I said.

"Great-*great*. El Turco was Pawnee. Coronado captured him at Cicuye and put a collar around his neck so he could not run away. Turn right."

We were already halfway through the intersection. I jerked the steer-ing wheel to the right and nearly skidded into a pickup.

Rosa seemed unperturbed. "Coronado wanted El Turco to guide him to Cibola," she said.

I wanted to ask if he had, but I didn't want to prevent Rosa from giv-ing me directions. I drove slowly through the next intersection, alert to sudden instructions, but there weren't any. I drove on down the block.

"And did El Turco guide Coronado to Cibola?"

"Sure. You should have turned left back there," she said.

She apparently hadn't inherited her great-great-grandfather's scouting ability. I went around the block and turned left, and was overjoyed to see the Eldorado Café down the street. I pulled into the parking lot and we got out.

"They make their own cinnamon rolls," she said, looking at me hopefully as we went in. "With frosting."

We sat down in a booth. "Have anything you want," I said. "This is on the *Record*."

She ordered a cinnamon roll and a large Coke. I ordered coffee and began fishing in my bag for my tape recorder.

"You lived here in Denver a long time?" she asked.

"All my life. I grew up here."

She smiled her gold-toothed smile at me. "You like Denver?"

"Sure," I said. I found the pocket-sized recorder and laid it on the table. "Smog, oil refineries, traffic. What's not to like?"

"I like it too," she said.

The waitress set a cinnamon roll the size of Mile High Stadium in front of her and poured my coffee.

"You know what Coronado fed El Turco?" The waitress brought her large Coke. "Probably one tortilla a day. And he didn't have no shoes. Coronado make him walk all that way to Colorado and no shoes."

I switched the tape recorder on. "You say Coronado came to Colorado," I said, "but what I've read says he traveled through New Mexico and Oklahoma and up into Kansas, but not Colorado."

"He was in Colorado." She jabbed her finger into the table. "He was *here*."

I wondered if she meant here in Colorado or here in the Eldorado Café.

"When was this? On his way to Quivira?"

"Quivira?" she said, looking blank. "I don't know nothing about Quivira."

"Quivira was a place where there was supposed to be gold," I said. "He went there after he found the Seven Cities of Cibola."

"He didn't find them," she said, chewing on a mouthful of cinnamon roll. "That's why he killed El Turco."

"Coronado killed El Turco?"

"Yeah. After he led him to Cibola."

This was even worse than talking to the psychic dentist.

"Coronado said El Turco made the whole thing up," Rosa said. "He said El Turco was going to lead Coronado into an ambush and kill him. He said the Seven Cities didn't exist."

"But they did?"

"Of course. El Turco led him to the place."

"But I thought you said Coronado didn't find them."

"He didn't."

I was hopelessly confused by now. "Why not?"

"Because they weren't there."

I was going to run Jake through his paper shredder an inch at a time. I had wasted a whole morning on this and I was not even going to be able to get a story out of it.

"You mean they were some sort of mirage?" I asked.

Rosa considered this through several bites of cinnamon roll. "No. A mirage is something that isn't there. These were there."

"But invisible?"

"No."

"Hidden."

"No."

"But Coronado couldn't see them?"

She shook her head. With her forefinger, she picked up a few stray pieces of frosting left on her plate and stuck them in her mouth. "How could he when they weren't there?"

The tape clicked off, and I didn't even bother to turn it over. I looked at my watch. If I took her back now I could make it to the hearings early and maybe interview some of the developers. I picked up the check and went over to the cash register.

"Do you want to see them?"

"What do you mean? See the Seven Cities of Cibola?"

"Yeah. I'll take you to them."

"You mean go to New Mexico?"

"No. I told you, Coronado came to Colorado."

"When?"

"When he was looking for the Seven Cities of Cibola."

"No, I mean when can *I* see them? Right now?"

"No," she said, with that, 'how dumb can anyone be?' look. She reached for a copy of the *Rocky Mountain News* that was lying on the counter and looked inside the back page. "Tomorrow morning. Six o'clock."

One of my favorite things about Denver is that it's spread all over the place and takes you forever to get anywhere. The mountains finally put a stop to things twenty miles to the west, but in all three other directions it can sprawl all the way to the state line and apparently is trying to. Being a reporter here isn't so much a question of driving journalistic ambition as of driving, period.

The skyscraper moratorium hearings were out on Colorado Boulevard across from the Hotel Giorgio, one of the skyscrapers under discussion. It took me forty-five minutes to get there from the Olde West Trailer Park.

I was half an hour late, which meant the hearings had already gotten completely off the subject. "What about reflecting glass?" someone in the audience was saying. "I think it should be outlawed in skyscrapers. I was nearly blinded the other day on the way to work."

"Yeah," a middle-aged woman said. "If we're going to have skyscrapers, they should look like skyscrapers." She waved vaguely at the Hotel Giorgio, which looked like a giant black milk carton.

"And not like that United Bank building downtown!" someone else said. "It looks like a damned cash register!"

From there it was a short illogical jump to the impossibility of parking downtown, Denver's becoming too decentralized, and whether the new airport should be built or not. By five-thirty they were back on reflecting glass.

"Why don't they put glass you can see through in their skyscrapers?" and old man who looked a lot like the time machine inventor said. "I'll tell you why not. Because those big business executives are doing things they should be ashamed of, and they don't want us too see them."

I left at seven and went back to the *Record* to try to piece my notes together into some kind of story. Jake was there.

"How'd your interview with Coronado's granddaughter go?" he asked.

"The Seven Cities of Cibola are here in Denver only Coronado couldn't see them because they're not there." I looked around. "Is there a copy of the *News* someplace?"

"*Here?* In the *Record* building!" he said, clutching his chest in mock horror. "That bad, huh? You're going to go work for the *News?*" But he fished a copy out of the mess on somebody's desk and handed it to me. I opened it to the back page.

There was no "Best Times for Viewing Lost Cities of Gold" column. There were pictures and dates for phases of the moon, road conditions, and "What's in the Stars: by Stella." My horoscope of the day read: "Any assignment you accept today will turn out differently than you expect." The rest of the page was devoted to the weather, which was supposed to be sunny and warm tomorrow.

The facing page had the crossword puzzle, "Today in History," and squibs about Princess Di and a Bronco fan who'd planted his garden in the shape of a Bronco quarterback. I was surprised Jake hadn't assigned me that story.

I went down to Research and looked up El Turco. He was an Indian slave, probably Pawnee, who had scouted for Coronado, but that was his nickname, not his name. The Spanish had called him "The Turk" because of his peculiar hair. He had been captured at Cicuye, *after* Coronado's foray into Cibola, and had promised to lead them to Quivira, tempting them with stories of golden streets and great stone palaces. When the stories didn't pan out, Coronado had had him executed. I could understand why.

Jake cornered me on my way home. "Look, don't quit," he said. "Tell you what, forget Coronado. There's a guy out in Lakewood who's planted his garden in the shape of John Elway's face. Daffodils for hair, blue hyacinths for eyes."

"Can't," I said, sidling past him. "I've got a date to see the Seven Cities of Gold."

Another delightful aspect of the Beautiful Mile-High City is that in the middle of April, after you've planted your favorite Bronco, you can get fifteen inches of snow. It had started getting cloudy by the time I left the paper, but fool that I was, I thought it was an afternoon thunderstorm. The *News*'s forecast had, after all, been for warm and sunny. When I woke up at four-thirty there was a foot and a half of snow on the ground and more tumbling down.

"Why are you going if she's such a nut?" Jake had asked me when I told him I couldn't take the Elway garden. "You don't seriously think she's onto something, do you?" and I had had a hard time explaining to him why I was planning to get up at an ungodly hour and trek all the way out to Santa Fe again.

She was *not* El Turco's great-great-granddaughter. Two greats still left her at two hundred and fifty plus, and her history was as garbled as her math, but when I had gotten impatient she had said, "Do you want to see them?" and when I had asked her when, she had consulted the *News*'s crossword puzzle and said, "Tomorrow morning."

I had gotten offers of proof before. The time machine inventor had proposed that I climb in his washing machine and be sent forward to "a glorious future, a time when everyone is rich," and the psychic dentist had offered to pull my wisdom teeth. But there's always a catch to these offers.

"Your teeth will have been extracted in another plane of reality," the dentist had said. "X-rays taken in this place will show them as still being there," and the time machine guy had checked his soak cycle and the stars at the last minute and decided there wouldn't be another temporal agitation until August of 2158.

Rosa hadn't put any restrictions at all on her offer. "You want to see them?" she said, and there was not mention of reality planes or stellar-laundry connections, no mention of any catch. Which didn't mean there won't be one, I thought, getting out the mittens and scarf I had just put away for the season and going out to scrape the windshield off. When I got there she would no doubt say the snow made it impossible to see the Cities or I could only see them if I believed in UFO's. Or maybe she'd point off somewhere in the general direction of Denver's brown cloud and say, "What do you mean, you can't see them?"

I-25 was a mess, cars off the road everywhere and snow driving into my headlights so I could barely see. I got behind a snowplow and stayed there, and it was nearly six o'clock by the time I made it to the trailer. Rosa took a good five minutes to come to the door, and when she final-ly got there she wasn't dressed. She stared blearily at me, her hair out of its braids and hanging tangled around her face.

"Remember me? Carla Johnson? You promised to show me the Seven Cities?"

"Cities?" she said blankly.

"The Seven Cities of Cibola."

"Oh, yeah," she said, and motioned for me to come inside. "There aren't seven. El Turco was a dumb Pawnee. He don't know how to count."

"How many are there?" I asked, thinking, this is the catch. There aren't seven and they aren't gold.

"Depends," she said. "More than seven. You still want to go see them?"

"Yes."

She went into the bedroom and came out after a few minutes with her hair braided, the pants and blouse of the day before and an enor-mous red carcoat, and we took off toward Cibola. We went south again, past more waterbed stores and rusting railroad tracks, and out to Belleview.

It was beginning to get fairly light out, though it was impossible to tell if the sun was up or not. It was still snowing hard.

She had me turn onto Belleview, giving me at least ten yards' warning, and we headed east toward the Tech Center. Those people at the hearing who'd complained about Denver becoming too decentralized had a point. The Tech Center looked like another downtown as we headed toward it.

A multi-colored downtown, garish even through the veil of snow. The Metropoint building was pinkish-lavender, the one next to it was midnight blue, while the Hyatt Regency had gone in for turquoise and bronze, and there was an assortment of silver, sea-green, and taupe. There was an assortment of shapes, too: deranged trapezoids, overweight butterflies, giant beer cans. They were clearly moratorium material, each of them with its full complement of reflecting glass, and, presumably, executives with something to hide.

Rosa had me turn left onto Yosemite, and we headed north again. The snowplows hadn't made it out here yet, and it was heavy going. I leaned forward and peered through the windshield, and so did Rosa.

"Do you think we'll be able to see them?" I asked.

"Can't tell yet," she said. "Turn right."

I turned into a snow-filled street. "I've been reading about your great-grandfather."

"Great-*great*," she said.

"He confessed he'd lied about the cities, that there really wasn't any gold."

She shrugged. "He was scared. He thought Coronado was going to kill him."

"Coronado *did* kill him," I said. "He said El Turco was leading his army into a trap."

She shrugged again and wiped a space clear on the windshield to look through.

"If the Seven Cities existed, why didn't El Turco take Coronado to them? It would have saved his life."

"They weren't there." She leaned back.

"You mean they're not there all the time?" I said.

"You know the Grand Canyon?" she asked. "My great-great-grandfather discovered the Grand Canyon. He told Coronado he'd seen it. Nobody saw the Grand Canyon again for three hundred years. Just because nobody seen it don't mean it wasn't there. You was supposed to turn right back there at the light."

I could see why Coronado had strangled El Turco. If I hadn't been afraid I'd get stuck in the snow, I'd have stopped and throttled her right then. I turned around, slipping and sliding, and went back to the light.

"Left at the next corner and go down the block a little ways," she said, pointing. "Pull in there."

"There" was the parking lot of a donut shop. It had a giant neon donut in the middle of its steamed-up windows. I knew how Coronado felt when he rode into the huddle of mud huts that was supposed to have been the City of Gold.

"This is Cibola?" I said.

"No way," she said, heaving herself out of the car. "They're not there today."

"You *said* they were always there," I said.

"They are." She shut the door, dislodging a clump of snow. "Just not all the time. I think they're in one of those time-things."

"Time-things? You mean a time warp?" I asked, trying to remember what the washing-machine guy had called it. "A temporal agitation?"

"How would I know? I'm not a scientist. They have good donuts here. Cream-filled."

The donuts were actually pretty good, and by the time we started home the snow had stopped and was already turning to slush, and I no longer wanted to strangle her on the spot. I figured in another hour the sun would be out, and John Elway's hyacinth-blue eyes would be poking through again. By the time we turned onto Hampden, I felt calm enough to ask when she thought the Seven Cities might put in another appearance.

She had bought a *Rocky Mountain News* and a box of cream-filled donuts to take home. She opened the box and contemplated them. "More than seven," she said. "You like to write?"

"What?" I said, wondering if Coronado had had this much trouble communicating with El Turco.

"That's why you're a reporter, because you like to write?"

"No," I said. "The writing's a real pain. When will this time-warp thing happen again?"

She bit into a donut. "That's Cinderella City," she said, gesturing to the mall on our right with it. "You ever been there?"

I nodded.

"I went there once. They got marble floors and this big fountain. They got lots of stores. You can buy just about anything you want there. Clothes, jewels, shoes."

If she wanted to do a little shopping now that she'd had breakfast, she could forget it. And she could forget about changing the subject. "When can we go see the Seven Cities again? Tomorrow?"

She licked cream filling off her fingers and turned the *News* over. "Not tomorrow," she said. "El Turco would have liked Cinderella City. He didn't have no shoes. He had to walk all the way to Colorado in his bare feet. Even in the snow."

I imagined my hands closing around her plump neck. "When are the Seven Cities going to be there again?" I demanded. "And don't tell me they're always there."

She consulted the celebrity squibs. "Not tomorrow," she said. "Day after tomorrow. Five o'clock. You must like people, then. That's why you wanted to be a reporter? To meet all kinds of people?"

"No," I said. "Believe it or not, I wanted to travel."

She grinned her golden smile at me. "Like Coronado," she said.

I spent the next two days interviewing developers, environmentalists, and council members, and pondering why Coronado had continued to follow El Turco, even after it was clear he was a pathological liar.

I had stopped at the first 7-Eleven I could find after letting Rosa and her donuts off and bought a copy of the *News*. I read the entire back section, including the comics. For all I knew, she was using *Doonesbury* for an oracle. Or *Nancy*.

I read the obits and worked the crossword puzzle and then went over the back page again. There was nothing remotely time-warp-related. The moon was at first quarter. Sunset would occur at 7:51 p.m. Road conditions for the Eisenhower Tunnel were snow-packed and blowing. Chains required. My horoscope read, "Don't get involved in wild goose chases. A good stay-at-home day."

Rosa no more knew where the Seven Cities of Gold were than her great-great-grandfather. According to the stuff I read between moratorium jaunts, he had changed his story every fifteen minutes or so, depending on what Coronado wanted to hear.

The other Indian scouts had warned Coronado, told him there was nothing to the north but buffalo and a few teepees, but Coronado had gone blindly on. "El Turco seems to have exerted a Pied-Piperlike power over Coronado," one of the historians has written, "a power which none of Coronado's officers could understand."

"Are you still working on that crazy Coronado thing?" Jake asked me when I got back to the *Record*. "I thought you were covering the hearings."

"I am," I said, looking up at the Grand Canyon. "They've been postponed because of the snow. I have an appointment with the United Coalition Against Uncontrolled Growth at eleven."

"Good," he said. "I don't need the Coronado piece, after all. We're running a series on 'Denver Today' instead."

He went back upstairs. I found the Grand Canyon. It had been discovered by Lopez de Cardeñas, one of Coronado's men. El Turco hadn't been with him.

I drove out to Aurora in a blinding snowstorm to interview the United Coalition. They were united only in spirit, not in location. The president had his office in one of the Pavilion Towers off Havana, but the secretary, who had all the graphs and spreadsheets, was out at Fiddler's Green. I spent the whole afternoon shuttling back and forth between them through the snow, and wondering what had ever possessed me to become a journalist. I'd wanted to travel. I had had the idea, gotten from TV, that journalists got to go all over the world, writing about exotic and amazing places. Like the UNIPAC building and the Plaza Towers.

They were sort of amazing, if you like Modern Corporate. Brass and chrome and Persian carpets. Atriums and palm trees and fountains splashing in marble pools. I wondered what Rosa, who had been so impressed with Cinderella City, would have thought of some of these places. El Turco would certainly have been impressed. Of course, he would probably have been impressed by the donut shop, and would no doubt have convinced Coronado to drag his whole army there with tales of fabulous, cream-filled wealth.

I finished up the United Coalition and went back to the *Record* to call some developers and builders and get their side. It was still snowing, and there weren't any signs of snow removal, creative or otherwise, that I could see. I set up some appointments for the next day, and then went back down to Research.

El Turco hadn't been the only person to tell tales of the fabulous Seven Cities of Gold. A Spanish explorer, Cabeza de Vaca, had reported them first, and his black slave Estevanico claimed to have seen them, too. Friar Marcos had gone with Estevanico to find them, and, according to him, Estevanico had actually entered Cibola.

They had made up a signal. Estevanico was to send back a small cross if he found a little village, a big cross if he found a city. Estevanico was killed in a battle with Indians, and Friar Marcos fled back to Coronado, but he said he'd seen the Seven Cities in the distance, and he claimed that Estevanico had sent back "a cross the size of a man."

There were all kinds of other tales, too, that the Navajos had gold and silver mines, that Montezuma had moved his treasure north to keep it from the Spanish, that there was a golden city on a lake, with canoes whose oarlocks were solid gold. If El Turco had been lying, he wasn't the only one.

I spent the next day interviewing pro-uncontrolled growth types. They were united, too. "Denver had to retain its central identity," they all told me from what it was hard to believe was not a pre-written script. "It's becoming split into a half-dozen sub-cities, each with its own separate goals."

They were in less agreement as to where the problem lay. One of the builders who'd developed the Tech Center thought the Plaza Tower out at Fiddler's Green was an eyesore, Fiddler's Green complained about Aurora, Aurora thought there was too much building going on around Colorado Boulevard. They were all united on one thing, however: downtown was completely out of control.

I logged several thousand miles in the snow, which showed no signs of letting up, and went home to bed. I debated setting my alarm. Rosa didn't know where the Seven Cities of Gold were, the Living Western Heritage series had been canceled, and Coronado would have saved everybody a lot of trouble if he had listened to his generals.

But Estevanico had sent back a giant cross, and there was the "time-thing" thing. I had not done enough stories on psychic peridontia yet to start believing their nutto theories, but I had done enough to know what they were supposed to sound like. Rosa's was all wrong.

"I don't know what it's called," she said, which was far too vague. Nutto theories may not make any sense, but they're all worked out, down to the last bit of pseudo-scientific jargon. The psychic dentist had told me all about transcendental maxillofacial extractile vibrations, and the time travel guy had showed me a hand-lettered chart showing how the partial load setting affected future events.

If Rosa's Seven Cities were just one more nutto theory, she would have been talking about morphogenetic temporal dislocation and simultaneous reality modes. She would at least know what the "time-thing" was called.

I compromised by setting the alarm on "music" and went to bed.

I overslept. The station I'd set the alarm on wasn't on the air at four-thirty in the morning. I raced into my clothes, dragged a brush through my hair, and took off. There was almost no traffic—who in their right mind is up at four-thirty?—and it had stopped snowing. By the time I pulled onto Santa Fe I was only running ten minutes late. Not that it mattered. She would probably take half and hour to drag herself to the door and tell me the Seven Cities had canceled again.

I was wrong. She was standing outside waiting in her red carcoat and a pair of orange Bronco earmuffs. "You're late," she said, squeezing herself in beside me. "Got to go."

"Where?"

She pointed. "Turn left."

"Why don't you just tell me where we're going?" I said, "and that way I'll have a little advance warning."

"Turn right," she said.

We turned onto Hampden and started up past Cinderella City. Hampden is never free of traffic, no matter what time of day it is. There were dozens of cars on the road. I got in the center lane, hoping she'd give me at least a few feet of warning for the next turn, but she leaned back and folded her arms across her massive bosom.

"You're sure the Seven Cities will appear this morning?" I asked.

She leaned forward and peered through the windshield at the slowly lightening sky, looking for who knows what. "Good chance. Can't tell for sure."

I felt like Coronado, dragged from pillar to post. Just a little farther, just a little farther. I wondered if this could be not only a scam but a setup, if we would end up pulling up next to a black van in some dark parking lot, and I would find myself on the cover of the *Record* as a robbery victim or worse. She was certainly anxious enough. She kept holding up her arm so she could read her watch in the lights of the cars behind us. More likely, we were headed for some bakery that opened at the crack of dawn, and she wanted to be there when the fried cinnamon rolls came out of the oven.

"Turn right!" she said. "Can't you go no faster?"

I went faster. We were out in Cherry Creek now, and it was starting to get really light. The snowstorm was apparently over. The sky was turning a light lavender-blue.

"Now right, up there," she said, and I saw where we were going. This road led past Cherry Creek High School and then up along the top of the dam. A nice isolated place for a robbery.

We went past the last house and pulled out onto the dam road. Rosa turned in her seat to peer out my window and the back, obviously looking for something. There wasn't much to see. The water wasn't visible from this point, and she was looking in the wrong direction, out toward Denver. There were still a few lights, the early-bird traffic down on I-225 and the last few orangish street lights that hadn't gone off automatically. The snow had taken on the bluish-lavender color of the sky.

I stopped the car.

"What are you doing?" she demanded. "Go all the way up."

"I can't," I said, pointing ahead. "The road's closed."

She peered at the chain strung across the road as if she couldn't figure out what it was, and then opened the door and got out.

Now it was my turn to say, "What are you doing?"

"We gotta walk," she said. "We'll miss it otherwise."

"Miss what? Are you telling me there's gonna be a time warp up here on top of the dam?"

She looked at me like I was crazy. "Time warp?" she said. Her grin glittered in my headlights. "No. Come on."

Even Coronado had finally said, "All right, enough," and ordered his men to strangle El Turco. But not until he'd been lured all the way up to Kansas. And, according to Rosa, Colorado. The Seven Cities of Cibola were *not* going to be up on top of Cherry Creek dam, no matter what Rosa said, and I wasn't even going to get a story out of this, but I switched off my lights and got out of the car and climbed over the chain.

It was almost fully light now, and the shadowy dimnesses below were sorting themselves out into decentralized Denver. The black *2001* towers off Havana were right below us, and past them the peculiar Mayan-pyramid shape of the National Farmer's Union. The Tech Center rose in a jumble off to the left, beer cans and trapezoids, and then there was a long curve of isolated buildings all the way to downtown, an island of skyscraping towers obviously in need of a moratorium.

"Come on," Rosa said. She started walking faster, panting along the road ahead of me and looking anxiously toward the east, where at least a black van wasn't parked. "Coronado shouldn't have killed El Turco. It wasn't his fault."

"What wasn't his fault?"

"It was one of those time-things, what did you call it?" she said, breathing hard.

"A temporal agitation?"

"Yeah, only he didn't know it. He thought it was there all the time, and when he brought Coronado there it wasn't there, and he didn't know what had happened."

She looked anxiously to the east again, where a band of clouds extending about an inch above the horizon was beginning to turn pinkish-gray, and broke into an ungainly run. I trotted after her, trying to remember the procedure for CPR.

She ran into the pullout at the top of the dam and stopped, panting hard. She put her hand up to her heaving chest, and looked out across the snow at Denver.

"So now you're saying the cities existed in some other time? In the future?"

She glanced over her shoulder at the horizon. The sun was nearly up. The narrow cloud turned pale pink, and the snow on Mt. Evans went the kind of fuchsia we used in the Sunday supplements. "And you think there's going to be another time-warp this morning?"

She gave me that "how can one person be so stupid" look. "Of course not," she said, and the sun cleared the cloud. "There they are," she said.

There they were. The reflecting glass in the curved towers of Fiddler's Green caught first, and then the Tech Center and the Silverado Building on Colorado Boulevard, and the downtown skyline burst into flames. They turned pink and then orange, the Hotel Giorgio and the Metropoint building and the Plaza Towers, blazing pinnacles and turrets and towers.

"You didn't believe me, did you?" Rosa said.

"No," I said, unwilling to take my eyes off of them. "I didn't."

There were more than seven. Far out to the west the Federal Center ignited, and off to the north the angled lines of grain elevators gleamed. Downtown blazed, blinding building moratorium advocates on their way to work. In between, the Career Development Institute and the United Bank Building and the Hyatt Regency burned gold, standing out from the snow like citadels, like cities. No wonder El Turco had dragged Coronado all the way to Colorado. Marble palaces and golden streets.

"I told you they were there all the time," she said.

It was over in another minute, the fires going out one by one in the panes of reflecting glass, downtown first and then the Cigna building and Belleview Place, fading to their everyday silver and onyx and emerald. The Pavilion Towers below us darkened and the last of the sodium street lights went out.

"There all the time," Rosa said solemnly.

"Yeah," I said. I would have to get Jake up here to see this. I'd have to buy a *News* on the way home and check on the time of sunrise tomorrow. And the weather.

I turned around. The sun glittered off the water of the reservoir. There was an aluminum rowboat out in the middle of it. It had golden oarlocks.

Rosa had started back down the road to the car. I caught up with her. "I'll buy you a pecan roll," I said. "Do you know of any good places around here?"

She grinned. Her gold teeth gleamed in the last light of Cibola. "The best," she said.

THE HAPPY MAN

Jonathan Lethem

1.

Ileft her in the bedroom, and went and poured myself a drink. I felt it now; there wasn't any doubt. But I didn't want to tell her, not yet. I wanted to stretch it out for as long as I could. It had been so quick, this time.

In the meantime I wanted to see the kid.

I took my drink and went into his room and sat down on the edge of his bed. His night light was on; I could see I'd woken him. Maybe he'd heard me clinking bottles. Maybe he'd heard us making love.

"Dad," he said.

"Peter."

"Something the matter?"

Peter was twelve. A good kid, a very good kid. He was just eleven when I died. All computers and stereo, back then. Heavy metal and D & D. Sorcerers, dragons, the flaming pits of Hell, the whole bit. And music to match. After I died and came back he got real serious about things, forgot about the rock music and the imaginary Hells. Gave up his friends, too. I was pretty worried about that, and we had a lot of big talks. But he stayed serious. The one thing he stuck with was the computer, only now he used it to map out real Hell. My Hell.

Instead of answering his question I took another drink. He knew what was the matter.

"You going away?" he asked.

I nodded.

"Tell Mom yet?"

"Nope."

He scooted up until he was sitting on his pillow. I could see him thinking: *It was fast this time, Dad. Is it getting faster?* But he didn't say anything.

"Me and your mother," I said. "There's a lot of stuff we didn't get to, this time."

Peter nodded.

"Well—" I began, then stopped. What did he understand? More than I guessed, probably. "Take good care of her," I said.

"Yeah."

I kissed his forehead. I knew how much he hated the smell of liquor, but he managed not to make a face. Good kid, etc.

Then I went in to see his mother.

It was while we were making love that I'd had the first inkling that the change was coming on, but I'd kept it to myself. There wasn't any purpose to ruining the mood; besides, I wasn't sure yet. It wasn't until afterward that I knew for sure.

But I had to tell her now. Another hour or so and I'd be gone.

I sat on the edge of the bed, just like with Peter. Only in this room it was dark. And she wasn't awake. I put my hand on her cheek, felt her breath against my palm. She murmured, and kissed my hand. I squeezed her shoulder until she figured out that I wanted her to wake up.

"Maureen," I said.

"Why aren't you sleeping?"

I wanted to undress again and get back under the covers. Curl myself around her and fall asleep. Not to say another word. Instead I said: "I'm going back."

"Going back?" Her voice was suddenly hoarse.

I nodded in the dark, but she got the idea.

"Damn you!"

I didn't see the slap coming. That didn't matter, since it wasn't for show. It rattled my teeth. By the time I recovered she was up against the headboard, curled into herself, sobbing weakly.

It wasn't usually this bad for her anymore. She'd numbed the part of herself that felt it the most. But it didn't usually happen this fast, either.

I moved up beside her on the bed, and cradled her head in my hands. Let her cry a while against my chest. But she wasn't done yet. When she turned her face up it was still raw and contorted with her pain, tendons standing out on her neck.

"Don't say it like that," she gasped out between sobs. "I hate that so much—"

"What?" I tried to say it softly.

"Going *back*. Like that's more real to you now, like that's where you belong, and this is the mistake, the exception—"

I couldn't think of what to say to stop her.

"Oh, God." I held her while she cried some more. "Just don't say it like that, Tom," she said when she could. "I can't stand it."

"I won't say it like that anymore," I said flatly.

She calmed somewhat. We sat still there in the dark, my arms around her.

"I'm sorry," she said, but evenly now. "It's just so fast. Are you sure—"

"Yeah," I said.

"We hardly had any time," she said, sniffling. "I mean, I was just getting the feeling back, you know? When we were making love. It was so good, just now. Wasn't it?"

"Yes."

"I just thought it was the beginning of a good period again. I thought you'd be back for a while . . ."

I stroked her hair, not saying anything.

"Did you know when we were fucking?" she asked.

"No," I lied. "Not until after."

"I don't know if I can take it anymore, Tom. I can't watch you walk around like a zombie all the time. It's driving me crazy. Every day I look in your eyes, thinking *maybe he's back*, maybe he's about to come back, and you just stare at me. I try to hold your hand in the bed and then you need to scratch yourself or something and you just pull away without saying anything, like you didn't even notice. I can't live like this—"

"I'm sorry," I said, a little hollowly. I wasn't unsympathetic. But we'd been through it before. We always ended in the same place. We always would.

And frankly, once I'd absorbed the impact of her rage, the conversation lost its flavor. My thoughts were beginning to drift ahead, to Hell.

"Maybe you should live somewhere else," she said. "Your body, I mean. When you aren't around. You could sleep down at the station or something."

"You know I can't do that."

"Oh no," she said. "I just remembered—"

"What?"

"Your uncle Frank, remember? When does he come?"

"Maybe I'll be back before he shows up," I said. It wasn't likely. I usually spent a week or so in Hell, when I went. Frank was due in four days. "Anyway, he knows about me. There won't be any problem."

She sighed. "I just hate having guests when you're gone—"

"Frank's not a guest," I said. "He's family."

She changed the subject. "Did you forget the medication? Maybe if you took the medication—"

"I always take it," I said. "It doesn't work. It doesn't keep me here. You can't take a pill to keep your soul from migrating to Hell."

"It's supposed to help, Tom."

"Well it doesn't matter, does it? I take it. Why do we have to talk about it?"

Now I'd hurt her a little. We were quiet. I felt her composing herself there, in my arms. Making her peace with my going away. Numbing herself.

The result was that we came a little closer together. I was able to share in her calm. We would be nice to each other from here on in. Things were back to normal.

But at the time, we'd backed away from that perilous, agonized place where to be separated by this, or separated at all, even for a minute, was too much to bear; from that place where all that mattered was our love, and where compromise was fundamentally wrong.

Normal was sometimes miles apart.

"You know what I hate the most?" she said. "That I don't even want to stay up with you. You'll only be around for what? A couple of hours more? I should want to get in every last minute. But I don't know what to say to you, really. There's nothing new to say about it. I feel like going to sleep."

"It's coming fast," I said, just to set her straight. "I think it's more like half an hour now."

"Oh," she said.

"But no hard feelings. Go to sleep. I understand."

"I have to," she said. "I have to get up in the morning. I feel sick from crying." She slid under the covers and hugged me at the waist. "Tom?" she said, in a smaller voice.

"Maureen."

"Is it getting faster?"

"It's just this one time," I said. "It probably doesn't mean anything. It's just painful to go through—"

"Okay," she said. "I love you, Tom."

"I love you too," I said. "Don't worry."

She went to sleep then, while I lay awake beside her, waiting to cross over.

If Maureen hadn't still been in school when I died, that would have been the end of it. If she hadn't been in debt up to her ears, and still two years away from setting up an office. As it was I had to sit in cold pack for three months while her lawyer pushed the application through. Eventually the courts saw it her way: I was the breadwinner. So they thawed me out.

Now she was supposed to be happy. I kept food on the table, and she had her graduate degree. Her son grew up knowing his dad. It wasn't supposed to matter that my soul shuffled between my living body here on earth, and Hell. She wasn't supposed to complain about that.

Besides, it wasn't my fault.

2.

In Hell I'm a small boy.

Younger than Peter. Eight or nine, I'd guess.

I always start in the same place. The beginning is always the same. I'm at that table, in that damned garden, waiting for the witch.

Let me be more specific. I begin as a detail in a tableau: four of us children are seated in a semicircle around a black cast-iron garden table. We sit in matching iron chairs. The lawn beneath us is freshly mowed; the gardener, if there is one, permits dandelions but not crabgrass. At the edge of the lawn is a scrubby border of rosebushes. Beyond that, a forest.

Behind me, when I turn to look, there's a pair of awkward birch saplings. Behind them, the witch's house. Smoke tumbles out of the slate chimney. The witch is supposed to be making us breakfast.

We're supposed to wait. Quietly.

Time is a little slow there, at Hell's entrance. I've waited there with the other children, bickering, playing with the silverware, curling the lace doily under my setting into a tight coil, for what seems like years. Breakfast is never served. Never. The sun, which is hanging just beyond the tops of the trees, never sets. Time stands still there. Which is not to say we sit frozen like statues. Far from it. We're a bunch of hungry children, and we make all kinds of trouble.

But I'm leaving something out.

We sit in a semicircle. That's to make room for the witch's horse. The witch's horse takes up a quarter of the table. He's seated in front of a place like any other guest.

He's waiting for breakfast, too.

The witch's horse is disgusting. The veins under his eyes quiver and he squirms in his seat. His forelegs are chained and staked to keep him at the table. He's sitting on his tail, so he can't swat away the flies which gather and drink at the corners of his mouth. The witch's horse is wearing a rusted pair of cast-iron eyeglass frames on his nose. They're for show, I guess, but they don't fit right. They chafe a pair of raw pink gutters into the sides of his nose.

If I stay at the table and wait for breakfast, subtle changes do occur. Most often the other children get restless, and begin to argue or play, and the table is jostled, and the silverware clatters, and the horse snorts in fear, his yellow eyes leaking. Sometimes a snake or a fox slithers across the lawn and frightens the horse, and he rattles his chains, and the children murmur and giggle. Once a bird flew overhead and splattered oily white birdshit onto the teapot. It was a welcome distraction, like anything else.

Every once in a while the children decide to feel sorry for the horse, and mount a campaign to lure him forward and pluck the glasses from his nose, or daub at his gashes with a wadded-up doily. I tried to help them once, when I was new to Hell. I felt sorry for the horse, too. That was before I saw him and the witch ride together in the forest. When I saw them ride I knew the horse and the witch were in it together.

Seeing them ride, howling and grunting through the trees, is one of the worst things I experience in all of Hell. After the first time I didn't feel sorry for the horse at all.

Whatever the cause, disturbances at the garden table are always resolved the same way. The activity reaches some pitch, the table seems about to overturn, when suddenly there's a sound at the door of the witch's house. We all freeze in our places, breath held. Even the horse knows to sit stock-still, and the only sound that remains is the buzzing of the flies.

We all watch for movement at the door of the witch's house. On the slim hope that maybe, just this once, it's breakfast time. The door opens, just a crack, just enough, and the witch slips out. She's smiling. She's very beautiful, the witch. The most beautiful woman I've ever seen, actually. She's got a great smile. The witch walks out across the lawn, and stops halfway between her door and the table. By now we're all slumped obediently in our seats again. My heart, to be honest, is in my throat.

I'm in love.

"Breakfast will be ready soon," sings the witch. "So just sit quietly, don't bother Horse, and before you know it I'll have something delicious on the table—"

And then she turns and slips back through her doorway and we start all over again.

That's how Hell begins. Maybe if I were a little more patient—waited, say, a thousand years instead of just a hundred—breakfast would appear. But then, knowing Hell, I'm not sure I'd want to see what the witch has been cooking up all this time.

But I don't wait at all anymore. I get up and walk away from the table right away.

Time in Hell doesn't start until you get up from the garden table.

3.

The Hell in the computer starts out the same way mine does: in the garden.

Peter laid it all out like Dungeons & Dragons, like a role-playing computer game. We entered long descriptions of the scene; the other children, the witch's horse, the witch. It was Peter's idea, when I came back with my first tentative reports of what I'd gone through, to map it out with the computer. I think he had the idea that it was like one of his dungeons, and that if we persisted we would eventually find a way out.

So Peter's "Dad" character wakes up at the garden table, same as I do.

And when Peter types in a command, like GET UP FROM THE TABLE, WALK NORTH ACROSS THE LAWN, his "Dad" goes to explore a computer version of the Hell I inhabit.

I don't soft-pedal it. I report what I see, and he enters it into the computer. Factually, we're recreating my Hell. The only thing I spare him are my emotional responses. I omit my fear at what I encounter, my rage at living these moments again and again, my unconscionable lust for the witch . . .

4.

When I crossed over that night, after fighting with Maureen, I didn't dawdle at the garden table. I was bored with that by now. I pushed my chair back and started in the direction Peter and I call north; the opposite direction from the witch's house. I ran on my eight-year-old legs across the lawn, through a gap in the border of rosebushes, and into the edge of the forest.

The north was my favored direction at the moment, because I'd explored it the least. Oh, Hell goes on forever in every direction, of course. But I don't always get very far. I explored the territories nearest the witch's garden most thoroughly, in any direction; as I get farther out it gets less and less familiar. I just don't always get very far out.

And the nearby territories to the north somehow seemed less *hackneyed* to me at the moment.

The forest to the north quickly gives way to an open field. It called the Field of Tubers, because of the knuckled roots that grow there. Sort of like carrots, or potatoes, or knees. Like carrots in that they're orange, like potatoes in the way the vines link them all together, under the ground. Like knees, or elbows, in the way they twitch, and bleed when you kick them.

The first few times I came to the Field of Tubers I tried to run across. Now I walk, slowly, carefully. That way I avoid falling into the breeding holes. The holes don't look like much if you don't step on them; just little circular holes, like wet anthills in the dirt. They throb a little. But if your foot lands on them they gape open, the entrance stretching like a mouth, and you fall in.

The breeding holes are about four feet deep, and muddy. Inside, the newborn tubers writhe in heaps. They're not old enough to take root yet. It's a mess.

Sure, you can run across the field, scrambling back out of the breeding holes, scraping the crushed tubers off the bottom of your shoes. You get to the other side of the field either way. It's not important. Myself, I walk.

Time, which is frozen at the witch's breakfast table, starts moving once I enter the forest. But time in Hell takes a very predictable course. The sun, which has been sitting at the top of the trees, refusing to set, goes down as I cross the Field of Tubers. It's night when I reach the other side, no matter how long it takes me to cross. If I run, looking back over my shoulder, I can watch the sun plummet through the tree-tops and disappear. Of course, if I run looking back over my shoulder I trip over the tubers and fall into the breeding holes constantly. If I idle in the field, squatting at the edge of a breeding hole, poking it with my finger to watch it spasm open, the sun refuses to set.

But why would I ever want to do that?

5.

When I first came back, when they warmed me up and put me back together, they didn't send me home right away. I had to spend a week in an observation ward, and on the fourth day they sent a doctor in to let me know where I stood.

"You'll be fine," he said. "You won't have any trouble holding down your job. Most people won't know the difference. But you will cross over."

"I've heard," I said.

"It shouldn't affect your public life." He said. "You'll be able to carry on most conversations in a perfunctory way. You just won't seem very interested in personal questions. Your mind will appear to be wandering. And you won't be very affectionate. Your co-workers won't notice, but your wife will."

"I won't want to fuck her," I said.

"No, you won't."

"Okay," I said. "How often will I go?"

"That varies from person to person. Some get lucky, and cross over just once or twice for the rest of their lives. It's rare, but it does happen. At the other extreme, some spend most of their time over there. For most, it's somewhere in between."

"You're not saying anything."

"That's right; I'm not. But I should say how often you cross over isn't always as important as how you handle it. The stress of not knowing is as bad or worse than actually going through it. The anticipation. It can cast a pall over the times when you're back. A lot of marriages . . . don't survive the resurrection."

"And there's no way to change it."

"Not really. You'll get a prescription for Valizax. It's a hormone that stimulates the secretions of a gland associated, in some studies, with the migration. Some people claim it helps, and maybe it does, in their cases. Or maybe it's just a placebo effect. And then there's therapy."

"Therapy?"

"They'll give you a brochure when you leave. There are several support groups for migrators. Some better than others. We recommend one in particular. It's grounded in solid psychoanalytic theory, and like the drug, some people have said it improves the condition. But that's not for me to say."

I went to the support group. The good one. Once. I don't know what I was expecting. There were seven or eight people there that night, and the group counselor, who I learned wasn't resurrected, had never made the trips back and forth from his own Hell. After some coffee and uneasy socializing we went and sat in a circle. They went around, bringing each other up to date on their progress, and the counselor handed out some brownie points for every little epiphany. When they got to me, they wanted to hear about my Hell.

Only they didn't call it Hell. They called it a "psychic landscape." And I quickly learned that they wanted me to consider it symbolic. The counselor wanted me to explain what my Hell *meant*.

I managed to contain my anger, but I left at the first break.

Hell doesn't *mean* anything. Excuse me—*my* Hell doesn't mean anything. Maybe yours does.

But mine doesn't. That's what makes it Hell.

And it's not symbolic. It's very, very real.

6.

On the other side of the Field of Tubers, if I go straight over the crest, is the Grove of the Robot Maker. A dense patch of trees nestled at the base of a hill.

The moon is up by this time.

The robot maker is an old man. A tired old man. He putters around in the grove in a welder's helmet, but he never welds. His robots are put together with wire and tinsnips. They're mostly pathetic. Half of them barely make it up to the Battle Pavilion before collapsing. He made better ones, once, if you believe him. He's badly in need of a young apprentice.

That's where I come in.

"Boy, you're here," he says when I arrive. He hands me a pliers or a ball-peen hammer. "Let me show you what I'm working on," he says. "I'll let you help." He tries to involve me in his current project, whatever it is. Whatever heap of refuse he's currently animating.

His problem, which he describes to me at length, is that his proudest creation, Colonel Eagery, went renegade on his way up to the Battle Pavilion. Back when the robot maker was young and strong and built robots with fantastic capabilities. Colonel Eagery, he says, was his triumph, but the triumph went sour. The robot rebelled, and set up shop on the far side of the mountain, building evil counterparts to the robot maker's creations. The strong, evil robots that so routinely demolish the robot maker's own robots out on the battle pavilion.

I have two problems with this story.

First of all, I know Colonel Eagery, and he isn't a robot. Oh no. I know all too well that Eagery, who I also call The Happy Man, is flesh and blood.

The second is that the robot maker is too old and feeble for me to imagine that he's ever been able to build anything capable and effective at all, let alone something as capable and effective as I know Eagery to be.

Besides, Hell doesn't have a *before*. Hell is stuck in time, repeating endlessly. Hell doesn't have a past. It just *is*. The robot maker is always old and ineffectual, and he always has been.

But I never say this. My role is just as predetermined as the robot maker's. I humor him. When I'm passing through this part of Hell, I'm the robot maker's apprentice. I make a show of interest in his latest project. I help him steer it up to the battle pavilion. I can't say why. That's just the way things are in this corner of Hell.

This time, when I entered the grove, I found the robot maker already heading up toward the pavilion. He'd built a little robot terrier this time. It was surprisingly mobile and lively, yipping and snapping at the robot maker's heels. I fell in with them, and the robot maker put his heavy, dry hand on my shoulder. The mechanical terrier sniffed at my shoes and barked once, then ran ahead, rooting frantically in the moss.

"He's a good one, boy," said the robot maker. "I think he's got a bit of your spark in him. This one's got a fighting chance against whatever the Colonel's got cooked up."

It didn't, of course. I couldn't bring myself to look at the poor little mechanical terrier. It was about to be killed. But I didn't say anything.

At this point in our hike through the grove the witch and the witch's horse ride by. It's another dependable part of my clockwork Hell. They turn up at about this point in my journey—the moon just up, a breeze stirring—whichever direction I choose. It's a horrible sight, but it's one I've gotten used to. Like just about everything else.

The horse is a lot more imposing freed from his stakes at the table. He's huge and sweaty and hairy, his nostrils dilated wide, his lips curled back. He's not wearing those funny eyeglasses anymore. The witch rides him cowboy style, bareback. She bends her head down and grunts exhortations into the horse's ear. She's still beautiful, I guess. And I still love her—sort of. I feel mixed up about the witch when she rides, actually. A combination of fear and pity and shame. And odd sense that she wouldn't do it if she didn't somehow *have* to. That the horse is somehow doing it to her.

But mostly I'm just afraid. As they rode through the grove now, I stood frozen in place with fear, just like the first time.

The robot maker did what he always does: covered my eyes with his bony hand and muttered, "Terrible, terrible! Not in front of the boy!"

I peered through his fingertips, compelled to watch.

And then they were gone, snorting away into the night, and we were alone in the grove again. The terrier yipped after them angrily. The robot maker shook his head, gripped my shoulder, and we walked on.

The pavilion sits on a plateau at the edge of the woods. The base is covered with trees, invisible until you're there. The battle area, up on top, is like a ruined Greek temple. The shattered remains of the original roof are piled around the edges. The pavilion itself is littered with the glowing, radioactive shambles of the robot maker's wrecked creations. The pavilion is so infused with radiation that normal physics don't apply there; some of the ancient robots still flicker back into flame when the wind picks up, and sometimes one of the wrecks goes into an accelerated decline and withers into ashes, as though years of entropy have finally caught up with it. The carcasses tell the story of the robot maker's decline; his recent robots are less ambitious and formidable, and their husks are correspondingly more pathetic. Many of the newer ones simply failed on their way to the pavilion; their ruined bodies litter the pathway up the hill.

But not the terrier. He bounded up the hill ahead of us, reached the crest, and disappeared over the top. The robot maker and I hurried after him, not wanting him to lose his match before we even saw what he was fighting.

His opponent was a wolfman robot. As from an old horror movie, his face was more human than dog. It was a perfect example of how the robot maker's creations were so badly overmatched: what chance does a house pet have against a wolfman? It was often like this, a question of several degrees of sophistication.

Standing up on two feet, the wolfman towered over the terrier. He spoke, too, taunting the little dog, who could only yip and growl in response.

"Here, boy," cackled the wolfman. "Come on, pup. Come to daddy. Here we go." He gestured beckoningly. The terrier barked and reared back. "Come on, boy. Jeez." He looked to us for sympathy as we approached. "Lookit this. Here boy, I'm not gonna hurt you. I'm not gonna hurt you. I'm just gonna wring your fucking neck. Come on. COME HERE YOU GODDAMN LITTLE PIECE OF SHIT!"

The wolfman lunged, scrambling down and seizing the terrier by the neck, and took a bite on the forearm for his trouble. I heard metal grate on metal. "Ow! Goddammit. That does it." He throttled the little robot, which squealed until its voice was gone. "This is gonna hurt me more than it hurts you," said the wolfman, even as he tossed the broken scrap-metal carcass aside. The robot maker and I just stood, staring in stupid wonder.

"Ahem," said the wolfman, picking himself up. "Boy. Where was I? Oh, well. Some other fucking time." He turned his back and walked away, clearing his throat, picking imaginary pieces of lint from his body, tightening an imaginary tie like Rodney Dangerfield.

As soon as the wolfman was over the edge of the pavilion and out of sight, the robot maker ran to his ruined terrier and threw his skeletal body over it in sorrow, as though he could shield it from some further indignity. I turned away. I hated the robot maker's weeping. I didn't want to have to comfort him again. The sight of it, frankly, made me sick. It was one of Hell's worst moments. Besides, hanging around the pavilion weeping over failures was how the robot maker had soaked up so much radiation, and gotten so old. If I stuck around I might get like him.

I snuck away.

7.

A few months after my brush with the support group I met another migrator in a bar.

I'd come back from Hell that afternoon, at work. I reinhabited my body while I was sitting behind the mike, reading out a public service announcement. For once I kept my cool; didn't tell anyone at the station, didn't call Maureen at home. I stopped at the bar on my way home, just to get a few minutes for myself before I let Maureen and Peter know I was back.

I got to talking to the guy at my right. I don't remember how, but it came out that he was a migratory, too. Just back, like me. We started out boozily jocular, than got quiet as we compared notes, not wanting to draw attention to ourselves, not wanting to trigger anyone's prejudices.

He told me about his Hell, which was pretty crazy. The setting was urban, not rural. He started out on darkened city streets, chased by Chinamen driving garbage trucks and shooting at him with pistols. There was a nuclear war; the animals mutated, grew intelligent and vicious. It went on from here.

I told him about mine, and then I told him about the support group and what I'd thought of it.

"Shit, yes," he said. "I went through that bullshit. Don't let them try to tell you what you're going through. They don't know shit. They can't know what we go through. They aren't *there*, man."

I asked him how much of his time he spent in Hell.

"Sheeeit. I'm not back here one day for every ten I spend *there*. I work in a bottling plant, man. Quality control. I look at bottles all day, then I go out drinking with a bunch of other guys from the plant. Least that's what they tell me. When I come back"—he raised his glass—"I go out drinking alone."

I asked him about his wife. He finished his drink and ordered another one before he said anything.

"She got sick of waiting around, I guess," he said. "I don't blame her. Least she got me brought back. I owe her *that*."

We traded phone numbers. He wasn't exactly the kind of guy I'd hang around with under ordinary circumstances, but as it was we had a lot in common.

I called a few times. His answering machine message was like this: "Sorry, I don't seem to be *home* right now. Leave a message at the tone and I'll call you as soon as I'm *back*."

Maureen told me he called me a few times, too. Always while I was away.

8.

When I leave the robot maker at the pavilion, I usually continue north, to the shrunken homes in the Garden of Razor Blades. The garden begins on the far side of the pavilion. A thicket of trees, at the entrance, only the trees are leafed with razor blades. The moonlight is reflected off a thousand tiny mirrors; it's quite pretty, really. The forest floor is layered with fallen razor blades. They never rust, because it never rains in Hell.

The trees quickly give way to a delicately organized garden laced with paths, and the bushes and flowers, like the trees before them, are covered with razor blades. The paths wend around to a clearing, and in the middle of the clearing are the shrunken homes. They're built into a huge dirt mound, like a desert mesa inhabited by Indians, or a gigantic African anthill. Hundreds of tiny doorways and windows are painstakingly carved out of the mound. Found objects are woven into the structure; shirt buttons, safety pins, eyeglass frames, and nail clippers. But no razor blades.

The shrunken humans are just visible as I approach. Tiny figures in little cloth costumes, busily weaving or cooking or playing little ball games on the roofs and patios of the homes. I never get any closer than that before the storm hits.

It's another part of Hell's program. The witch storm rises behind the trees just as I enter the clearing. The witch storm is a tiny, self-contained hurricane, on a scale, I suppose, to match the shrunken homes. A black whirlwind about three times my size. It's a rainless hurricane, an entity of wind and dust that rolls into action without warning and sends the shrunken humans scurrying for cover inside the mound.

With good reason. The storm tears razor blades from the treetops and off the surface of the paths and sends them into a whirling barrage against the sides of the shrunken homes. By the time the storm finishes, what was once a detailed, intricate miniature civilization is reduced to an undifferentiated heap of dust and dirt.

There's nothing I can do to stop it. I tried at first. Planted myself between the shrunken homes and the witch storm and tried to fend it off. What I got for my trouble was a rash of tiny razor cuts on my arms and face. By the time the storm retreated I'd barely protected a square foot of the mound from the assault.

The storm is associated with the witch. Don't ask me why. There are times, though, when I think I see a hint of her figure in its whirling form.

If I forget the mound and run for cover I can usually avoid feeling the brunt of it. Running away, I might take a few quick cuts across the shoulders or the backs of my legs, but that's it.

This time I ran so fast I barely took a cut. I ducked underneath a bush that was already stripped clean of blades; its branches protected me. I listened as the storm ravaged the mound, then faded away. A smell of ozone was in the air.

When I looked up again, I was looking into the face of Colonel Eagery. The Happy Man.

9.

The only thing that's not predictable in Hell, the only thing that doesn't happen according to some familiar junction of time and locale, is the appearance of The Happy Man. He's a free operator. He's his own man. He comes and goes as he pleases, etc.

He's also my ticket home.

When Colonel Eagery is done with me I go back. Back to home reality, back to Maureen and Peter and the radio station where I work. I get to live my life again. No matter where he appears, no matter which tableau he disturbs, Eagery's appearance means I get to go back.

After he's done with me.

Before I left the support group the counselor—the one who'd never been to Hell—told me to focus on what he called the "reentry episode." He told me that the situation that triggered return was usually the key to Hell, the source of the unresolved tension. The idea, he said, was to identify the corresponding episode in your own past. . . .

I could only laugh.

There's nothing in my life to correspond to Eagery. There couldn't be. Eagery is the heart of my Hell. He's Hell itself. If there had been anything in my life to even approximate The Happy Man, I wouldn't be here to tell you about it. I'd be a whimpering, sniveling wreck in a straightjacket somewhere. Nothing I've encountered in the real world comes close.

Not in *my* reality.

Frankly, if something in the real world corresponds to Colonel Eagery, I don't want to know about it.

10.

The Happy Man lifted me over his shoulder and carried me out of the Garden of Razor Blades, into the dark heart of the woods. When we got to a quiet moonlit grove, he set me down.

"There you go, Tom," he said, dusting himself off. He's the only one in Hell who knows my name. "Boy, what a scene. Listen, let's keep it to ourselves, what do you say? Our little secret, okay? A midnight rondee voo."

The Happy Man is always urgently conspiratorial. It's a big priority with him. I feel I should oblige him, though I'm not always sure what he's referring to. I nodded now.

"Yeah." He slapped me on the back, a little too hard. "You and me, the midnight riders, huh? Lone Ranger and Tonto. What do you mean 'we,' white man? Heh. I told you that one? It's like this . . . "

He told me a long, elaborate joke which I failed to understand. Nonetheless, I sat cross-legged in the clearing, rapt.

At the end he laughed for both of us, a loud, sloppy sound that echoed in the trees. "Oh yeah," he said, wiping a tear from his eyes. "Listen, you want some candy? Chocolate or something?" He rustled in a kit bag. "Or breakfast. It's still pretty early. I bet that goddamned witch didn't feed you kids any breakfast, did she?" He took out a bowl and a spoon, then poured in milk and dry cereal from a cardboard box.

The cereal, when I looked, consisted of little puffed and sugar-coat-ed penises, breasts, and vaginas, floating innocently in the milk.

I tried not to gag, to let him see I was having any trouble getting it down. I wanted to please Colonel Eagery, wanted to let him know I was thankful. While I ate he whistled, and unpacked the neckties from his bag.

I watched, curious. "You like these?" he said, holding them up. "Yeah. You'll get to wear them someday. Look real sharp, too. Like your dad. World-beater, that's what you feel like in a necktie." He began knotting them together to make a set of ropes, then looped them around the two nearest trees. "Here," he said, handing me one end. "Pull on this. Can you pull it loose?"

I put down the bowl of cereal and tugged on the neckties.

"Can you? Pull harder."

I shook my head.

"Yeah, they're tough all right. Don't worry about it, though. Your dad couldn't break it either. That's American craftsmanship." He nodded at the cereal. "You done with that? Yeah? C'mere."

I went.

This is my curse: I trust him. Every time. I develop skepticism about the other aspects of Hell; the witch's overdue breakfast, the robot maker's pathetic creations, but Colonel Eagery I trust every time. I am made newly innocent.

"Here," he said. "Hold this." He put one end of the rope in my right hand and began tying the other end to my left. "Okay." He moved to the right. "What do you mean we, white man? Heh. Cowboys and Indians, Tom. Lift your leg up here—that's a boy. Okay." He grunts over the task of binding me, legs splayed between the two trees. "You an Indian, Tom? Make some noise and let's see."

I started crying.

"Oh, no, don't do that," said The Happy Man, gravely. "Show the Colonel that you're a good sport, for chrissakes. Don't be a *girl*. You'll— ruin all the fun." His earnestness took my by surprise; I felt guilty. I didn't want to ruin anyone's fun. So I managed to stop crying. "That's it, Tommy. Chin up." It wasn't easy, lying there like a low-slung hammock in the dirt, my arms stretched over my head, to put my chin up. I decided it would be enough to smile. "There you go," said Eagery. "God, you're pretty."

The last knot secured, he turned away to dig in his bag, and emerged with a giant, clownish pair of scissors. I squirmed, but couldn't get away. He inserted the blade in my pants cuff and began snipping apart the leg of the corduroys. "Heigh ho! Don't move, Tom. You wouldn't want me to clip something off here, would you?" He quickly scissored up both sides, until my pants were hanging in shreds from my outstretched legs, then snipped the remaining link, so they fell away. A few quick strokes of the scissors and he'd eliminated my jockey shorts too. "Huh." He tossed the scissors aside and ran his hands up my legs. "Boy, that's smooth. Like a baby."

When he caressed me I got hard, despite my fear.

"Okay. Okay. That feel good? Aw, look at that." He was talking to himself now. A steady patter which he kept up over the sound of my whimpering. "Look here Tom, I got one too. *Big*-size. Daddy-size." He straddled me. "Open up for the choo-choo, Tommy. Uh."

I didn't pass out this time until he flipped me over, my arms and legs twisted, my stomach and thighs pressed into the dirt. Blackness didn't come until then.

Then I crossed back over.

Another safe passage back from Hell, thanks again to The Happy Man.

11.

If anyone at the station had questions about my behavior, they kept it to themselves.

I came back on mike again. "—bumper to bumper along the Dumbarton . . . " I trailed away in the middle of the traffic report and punched in a commercial break on cart. "Anyone got something to drink?" I said into the station intercom.

"I think there's some beer in the fridge," said Andrew, the support technician on shift, poking his head into the studio.

"Keep this going," I said, and left. He could run a string of ads, or punch in one of our prerecorded promos. It wasn't a major deviation.

The station fridge was full of rotting, half-finished lunches and pint cartons of sour milk, plus a six-pack of lousy beer. It wasn't Johnny Walker, but it would do. I needed to wash the memory of Eagery's flesh out of my mouth.

I leaned against the wall of the lounge and quietly, methodically, downed the beer.

The programming was piped into the lounge and I listened as Andrew handled my absence. He loaded in a stupid comedy promo; the words "Rock me" from about a million old songs, spliced together into a noisy barrage. Then his voice came over the intercom. "Lenny's down here, Tom. Take off if you want."

I didn't need a second hint. In ten minutes I was trapped in bumper to bumper myself, listening to the station on my car radio.

Maureen's car wasn't in the driveway when I pulled up. She was still at work. No reason to hurry home if she thought I was still away, I suppose. But the lights were on. Peter was home. And, as it turned out, so was Uncle Frank. I'd forgotten about the visit, but while I was away he'd set up in the guestroom.

He and Peter were sitting together in front of the computer, playing Hell. They looked up when I came in, and Peter recognized the change in the tone of my voice right away. Smart kid.

"Hey, Dad." He made a show of introducing us, so Frank would understand that there was a change. "Dad, Uncle Frank's here."

Frank and I shook hands.

I hadn't seen my father's brother for seven or eight years, and in that time he'd aged decades. He was suddenly a gray old man. It made me wonder how my father would look if he were still around.

"Tommy," Frank said. "It's been a long time." His voice was as faded and weak as everything else. I could hear him trying to work out the difference between me now and the zombielike version he'd been living with for the past few days.

I didn't let him wonder for too long. I gave his hand a good squeeze, and then I put my arms around him. I needed that human contact anyway, after Hell.

"I need a drink," I said. "Frank?" I cocked my head toward the living room. Uncle Frank nodded.

The kid got the drift on his own. "I'll see you later, Dad." He turned back to his computer, made a show of being involved.

I led Frank to the couch and poured us both a drink.

Though I hadn't seen him since before I died, Uncle Frank knew all about my situation. We wrote letters, and every once in a while spoke on the phone. Frank had never married, and after my father died he and I were one another's only excuse for "family." He wasn't well off, but he'd wired Maureen some cash when I died. In his letters he'd been generous, too, sympathetic and unsuperstitious. In my letters I'd unloaded a certain measure of my guilt and shame at what my resurrection had done to the marriage, and he was always understanding. But I could see now that he had to make an effort, in person, not to appear uncomfortable. He'd been living with my soulless self for a few days, and his eyes told me that he needed to figure out who he was talking to now.

For my part, I was making an adjustment to the changes in Frank. In my memory he was permanently in his forties, a more garrulous and eccentric version of my father. Frank had been the charismatic oddball in the family, never without a quip, never quite out of the doghouse, but always expansive and charming. I'd often thought that my falsely genial on-radio persona was based on a pale imitation of Frank. Only now he just seemed tired and old.

"You've got a nice setup here, Tom," he said quietly.

"That's Maureen's work," I said. "She busts her ass keeping it all together."

Frank nodded. "I've seen."

"How long you staying with us?"

Now Frank snickered in a way that recalled, if only faintly, the man I remembered. "How long you have me?"

"You don't need to be back?" How Frank made his living had always been unclear. He'd been a realtor at some point, then graduated to the nebulous status of "consultant." Professional bullshitter was always my hunch.

But now he said, "I'm not going back. I think I want to set up here for a while."

"Well, for my part you're welcome to stick around until you find a place," I said. He'd sounded uncomfortable, and I decided not to pry. "It's really up to Maureen, you understand. The burden's on her—"

"Oh, I've been helping out," he said quickly. "I've become quite a chef, actually . . . "

The way he trailed away told me I'd probably already eaten several of his meals. "I'm sure," I said. There was a pause. "Listen, Frank, let's break the ice. I don't remember shit about what happens while I'm away. Treat me like a newborn babe when I come back. One who nurses on a whisky tumbler."

I watched him relax. He lowered his eyes and said, "I'm sorry, Tom. I haven't been around family, I mean *real* family, for so long. It's got me thinking about the past. You know . . ." He looked up sharply. "You're a grown man. Have been for a long time. But your dad and your mom and you as a little kid, me coming to visit—that's how I remember you. Always will, I think."

"I understand." I worked on my whiskey.

"Anyway—" He waved his hand dismissively. "It's good to see you finally. Good to see the three of you together, making it go."

"I'm glad it looks good." I could only be honest. "It isn't always easy."

"Oh, I didn't mean, I mean, yes. Of course. And anything, any little thing I can do to help—" He watched my eyes for reaction, looking terribly uncomfortable. "And, Tom?"

I nodded.

"I already mentioned this to Maureen and Peter. Uh, you don't seem to pick up the phone when you're away, but now that you're back—"

"Yes?"

"If you do pick up the phone, if anyone calls, *I'm not here*, okay?"

"Sure, Frank."

"I just need to create a little distance right now," he said obscurely.

I wasn't sure whether to press him on the point. My chance was taken away, anyway, by Maureen's arrival. She walked in and peered at us over the top of a couple of bags of groceries, then took them on into the kitchen without saying a word. She knew I was back. The drink in my hand told her all she needed to know.

Frank got up and hurried into the kitchen behind her. I heard him insist on putting away the groceries by himself.

Then Maureen came out. I put my drink on the coffee table and stood up and we stood right next to each other, close without quite touching for a long time. Quiet, knowing that when words came, things might get too complicated again. In the background I could hear Frank putting the groceries into the fridge and the gentle, hurried tapping of Peter's fingers on his keyboard.

Maureen and I sat on the couch and kissed.

"Hey," came Frank's voice eventually. "Pete and I were talking about catching a movie or something. We could get a slice of pizza, too, take the car and be back in a few hours—"

"Peter?" I said.

He appeared in the doorway, right on cue. "Yeah, Dad, there's a new Clive Barker movie—"

"Homework?"

"Didn't get any."

I gave Frank the car keys and twenty bucks for pizza or whatever. I was being tiptoed around, sure, but I didn't let myself feel patronized. The few breaks I get I earn, twice over.

They left, and Maureen and I went back to kissing on the couch. We still hadn't exchanged a word. After a while we went into the bedroom like that, affectionate, silent. We didn't get around to words until an hour or so later.

Turned out it was just as well.

12.

Maureen had closed her eyes and rolled over on her side, curled against me. But the muscles of her mouth were tight; she wasn't asleep. I put my hand in her hair and said her name. She said mine.

"How's it been?" I said.

She waited a while before answering. "I don't know, Tom. Okay, I guess."

"I wasn't gone for too long this time," I said, though it didn't need saying.

She sighed. "That last one just took something out of me."

"What are you saying?"

She spoke quietly, tonelessly, into the crook of my arm. "I don't know how long you'll be around. I feel like if I let myself relax I'll get ripped off again."

There wasn't any answer to that, so I shut up and let the subject drop. "Peter all right?"

"Yes. Always. He's going to be on some debating thing now. I think he likes having Frank around."

"Do you?"

She didn't answer the question. "He's so different from when I first met him, Tom. When we got married, I thought he was such a buffoon. Such a loud, intrusive character." She laughed. "I was afraid we'd have a son like him. Now he's so *polite*."

"He's a guest in your house," I pointed out.

"It's not just that," she said. "He's gotten old, I guess."

"He said he's been cooking. Is he in your way? He'll go if I tell him to."

"He wants to move out here. Did he tell you that?"

"Yes," I said. And thought, *As well as something odd about the telephone*. I didn't say it. "But he's got money, I think. We'll find him a place—" I stopped. She still hadn't said whether she wanted him around, and the gap was beginning to irritate me. I was sensitive enough to her by now that I noticed what wasn't being said.

And she was smart enough to notice my irritation.

"He's fine, really," she said quickly. "He's actually quite a help, cooking . . ."

"Yes?"

"I've just gotten used to being alone, Tom. With you gone, and Peter out with his friends. I've had a lot of freedom."

The skin on my back began to crawl. I took my hand out of her hair.

"Say it," I said.

She sighed. "I'm trying to. I've been lonely, Tom. And I don't mean lonely for some odd old relative of yours to sleep in the guest room, either."

"Is it someone I know?"

"No."

I thought I could manage a couple more questions before I blew my cool. "Does Peter know?"

"No."

"Are you sure?"

"Jesus, Tom. Yes, I'm sure."

"What about Frank?"

"What about him? I didn't tell him. I can't imagine how he'd guess."

"There aren't any letters, then. Or weird phone calls. You aren't being sloppy—"

"No, Tom."

That was all I could take. In pretty much one motion I got up and put on my pants. Almost burst a blood vessel buttoning my shirt.

Then I surprised myself: I didn't hit her.

Instead I put on my shoes and went to the kitchen for a bottle, and sat down on the couch in the moonlight and drank.

It wasn't any good. I couldn't be in the house. I put on a jacket and took the bottle for a walk around the neighborhood.

13.

To the west, in my Hell, there's a place I call the Ghost Town. It's like a Western movie set, with cheap façades passing for buildings, and if anyone lives there, they're hiding. The moon lights the main street from behind a patch of trees, throwing cigarette butts and crumpled foil wrappers discarded there into high relief. Sometimes I can make out hoofprints in the dust.

In the middle of the street is a naked, crying baby.

Gusts of wind rise as I walk through the Ghost Town, and they grow stronger as I approach the baby, whipping the dust and refuse of the street into its face. The baby's crying chokes into a cough, sputters, then resumes, louder than before. The baby is cold. I can tell; I'm cold myself, there in the Ghost Town. By the time I reach down to pick up the baby, the wind tearing through my little chest, I'm seeking its warmth as much as offering my own.

If I pick up the baby it turns into The Happy Man. Instantly. Every time.

I've already said what happens when The Happy Man appears.

Needless to say, then, I avoid the Ghost Town. I steer a wide berth around it. I often avoid the west altogether. As much as I want to go back to my life, I can't bring myself to pick up the baby, knowing that I'm bringing on Colonel Eagery. I'm not capable of it. And I'm not comfortable walking through that town, feeling the rising wind and listening to the baby's cries, and not doing anything. Hell seems so contingent on my actions; maybe if I don't go in the direction there isn't a baby in the first place. I'd like to think so.

Anyway, it had been months since I'd walked through the Ghost Town. But I walked through it that night, in my dreams. I don't know why.

14.

I woke up still dressed and clutching the bottle, on the living room couch. What woke me was the noise in the kitchen. Maureen making breakfast for Peter.

Head low, I slunk past the kitchen doorway and into the bedroom.

By the time I woke again Peter was off to school, and Maureen was out, too, at work. I put myself through the shower, then called the station and said I wasn't coming in. They took it all right.

When I went back out I found Uncle Frank making coffee, enough for two. I accepted a cup and grunted my thanks.

"Can you handle some eggs?" he asked. "There's an omelet I've been meaning to try. You can be my guinea pig . . ."

I cleared my throat. "Uh, sure," I said.

He went into action while I let the coffee work on my mood. I was impressed, actually. Frank seemed to have diverted some of his eccentric passion into cookery. He knew how to use all the wedding-present stuff that Maureen and I had let gather dust. The smells charmed me halfway out of my funk.

"Here we go." He juggled it out of the pan and onto a plate, sprinkled some green stuff on top and put it in front of me. I waited for him to cut it in half, and when he didn't I said, "What about you?"

"Oh," he said, "I ate before. Please."

I put the whole thing away without any trouble. Frank sipped his coffee and watched while I ate.

"I used to cook for you when you were a little boy," he said. "'Course then it was eggs in bacon grease, smeared with catsup—"

My throat suddenly tightened in a choking spasm. I spurted coffee and bits of egg across the table, almost into Frank's lap. He got up and slapped at my back, but by then it was over.

"Jeez," I said. "Some kind of hangover thing. I'm sorry . . ."

"Relax, Tom." He got me a glass of water. "Probably the memory of those old breakfasts . . ." He laughed.

"Yeah." *Or the thought of Maureen and her new pal in the sack.* I didn't say it, though. I suddenly felt intense shame. Frank represented my family, he stood in for my dad. I didn't want him to know the reason for my bender.

"Listen, Tom," he said. "What say we go down to the water today? That's not a long drive, is it?"

"Sounds great," I admitted. "I need to get out of the house."

An hour later we parked out by the marina and walked down to the strip of beach. I expected Uncle Frank to tire quickly; instead I had to hurry to keep up. I felt like I was seeing him slowly coming back to life, first in the kitchen, concocting the omelet, and now out here on the beach. He seemed to sense the deadness and emptiness in me and tried valiantly to carry on both sides of a chatty conversation. I heard glimpses of the old raconteur in his voice, which only made me wonder more what had sent it into hiding in the first place.

"Frank," I said, when he came to the end of a story, "what happened? What's got you on the run?"

He took a deep breath and looked out over the water. "I was hoping that wouldn't come up, Tom. I don't want to get you or Maureen into it."

"I'll decide what I want to get into," I said. "Besides, it doesn't necessarily protect us to keep us in the dark."

He turned and looked me in the eye. "That's a point. It's—it's the mob, Tom. Only it's not so simple anymore, to just say mob. There's a blurry territory where it crosses over into some federal agency . . . Anyway, it's enough to say that I got crossed up with some real bad guys. I screwed 'em on some property." He was looking out to sea again, and I couldn't read his expression. "I'm not sure how much they really care, or how long before they get distracted by something else. Could be they just wanted to throw a scare at me. I just know it felt like time to get out of town for a while."

"God, Frank. I'm sorry. That sounds tough."

"Ah, it's all my own goddamn fault. Anyway, I won't stay much longer at your place. I would have gone already if you weren't—you know, away. And Pete seemed—I don't know. I felt like I could be of some use. It took my mind off my own problems."

"Stay as long as you like, Frank."

He smiled grimly. "I'm not necessarily in the right, you know . . ."

"Don't bother," I said. "When you go through some of the shit I've gone through, it gives you a different perspective. Right isn't always a relevant concept. You're family."

He turned and looked at me, then. Hard. Suddenly he wasn't just my clichéd notion of "Uncle Frank" anymore; he was a complex, intelligent, and not always easy to comprehend man whom I'd known since before I could remember. Maybe it was just my emotional state, but for a moment I was terrified.

"Thanks, Tom."

"Uh, don't mention it."

We looked out over the water without saying anything.

"I'm hip to Maureen," said Frank after a while.

I probably tightened my fists in my pockets, but that was it.

"There isn't really anything to say," he went on. "Just that you've got my sympathy."

"Don't hold it against her," I said. "I make it pretty tough. My whole setup makes it pretty tough."

"Yeah."

"Have you met him?" I asked.

"Nope. Just a phone call I wasn't supposed to hear. Not her fault. My ears tend to prick up at the sound of the phone right now."

"Peter?"

"Jeez. I don't think so, Tom. Not that I know of. But he's a smart kid."

"No kidding."

We came to a high place over the water, with a concrete platform and a rusted steel railing. I leaned on it and smelled the mist. Birds wheeled overhead. I thought about the night before, and wondered what I was going to say to Maureen the next time I saw her.

After a while I guess I choked up a little. "God damn," I said. "I didn't even get to see my kid last night."

"That's not your fault," said Frank quietly.

"I always hang out with the kid, Frank. I'm never so wrapped up in my goddamned problems that I don't have time for him. I only just got back."

Frank got a cheerleader tone in his voice again. "Let's go pick him up at school," he said. "Smart guy like him can miss half a day."

"I don't know."

"C'mon. It's easy. You just show up and they turn him over. Big treat, makes him a celebrity with all his pals."

"You do this a lot?"

Frank got serious. "Uh, no," he said. He almost sounded offended, for no reason I could discern. "They'd never turn the child over to anyone but his mother or father." He turned away, the mood between us suddenly and inexplicably sour.

"Something the matter?" I said.

He closed his eyes for a minute. "Sorry, Tom. I guess I just all of the sudden got an image of my friends from back east showing up in the schoolyard. I'm just being paranoid . . ."

We exchanged a long look.

"Let's go," I said.

15.

It was a relief to learn what a pain in the ass it was to get a kid out of school halfway through the day. We had to fill out a visitor's form just to go to the office, and then we had to fill out another form to get permission to yank Peter from class, and then a secretary walked us to the classroom anyway.

It turned out it was a computer class. A bunch of the kids there had played Peter's software Hell, which made me a visiting celebrity. I had to shake a lot of little hands to get back out. Frank was right: the visit would make Peter the most popular kid in school tomorrow.

We went out for hamburgers downtown, then we went back home. If Peter was disturbed by my drunken sprawl on the couch that morning, he did a good job of covering it up. He and Frank were full of computer talk, and I could see how well they were getting along.

Eventually we got around to the traditional post-Hell update, Peter and I huddled at the computer, punching in whatever new information I'd picked up on my trip. This time Frank sat in.

"Robot maker built a terrier, " I said. "A little livelier than the usual crap . . ." Peter typed it into the proper file. "But Eagery's thing was a robot wolfman, as tall as me—me *now*, not in Hell. He could talk. He sounded like Eagery, actually." I turned to Frank. "The Happy Man's personality has a way of pervading his robots . . ."

Peter's cross-reference check flagged the wolfman entry, and he punched up the reference. "In the south, Dad, remember? You met a wolfman, a real one, in the woods. You played Monopoly with him, then he turned into Colonel Eagery."

"Yeah, yeah. Never saw him again."

"Boy," said Frank, speaking for the first time since we'd punched up Hell. "You guys are thorough. What do you think the wolfman means?"

I froze up inside.

But before I could speak, Peter turned, twisted his mouth, and shook his head. "Hell doesn't *mean* anything," he said. "That's not the right approach." He'd heard the spiel a dozen times from me, and I guessed he'd sensed my tenderness on the issue; he was sticking up for his dad.

Then he surprised me by taking it further. "Hell is like an alternate world, like in *X-Men*. It's a real place, like here, only different. If you were going down the street and you met a wolfman, you wouldn't ask what it means. You'd run, or whatever."

Frank, who hadn't noticed my discomfort, winked at me and said, "Okay, Pete. I stand corrected."

Peter and I went back to our entry, more or less ignoring Frank. A few minutes later Maureen's car pulled up in the driveway. I tried not to let my sudden anxiety show, for the kid's sake.

"Tom."

She stood in Peter's doorway, still in her coat. When I looked up she didn't say anything more, just inclined her head in the direction of the bedroom. I gave Frank the seat beside Peter at the computer, and followed her.

"Look at you," she said when we were out of earshot.

"What?"

"When you're not drunk you're retreating into the computer. It's just as bad, you know. Computer Hell. You've found a way to be there all the time, one way or another. You don't live here anymore."

"Maureen—"

"What's worse is the way you're taking him *with* you. Making him live in your Hell too. Making him think it's something great. When you're not here, he and his friends spend all day in front of that thing, living your Hell for you. Does it make you feel less lonely? Is that it?"

"I live here." I knew I had to keep my voice quiet and steady and fierce or she'd talk right over me, and soon we'd be shouting. I didn't want it to escalate. "Last thing I knew I lived here with *you*. Maybe that's not the way it is anymore. But I live here. Seems to me it's you who's got one foot out the door."

There was a moment of silence and then it hit me. Call me stupid, but it was the first time I felt the impact. Last night, making love, had been goodbye. The gulf between us now was enormous. Things weren't going to suddenly get better.

It would take a huge amount of very hard, very painful work to fix it, if it could be fixed at all.

"Do you ever think of the effect it has on *him?*" She was sticking to safe territory. I didn't blame her. She had a lot of it. "You and your goddamned *inner landscape*—"

She broke off, sobbing. It was as though she'd been saving those words, and their release had opened the floodgates. It also occurred to me that she was opting for tears so I wouldn't attack her, and I felt a little cheated.

Anyway, I took her in my arms. I'm not completely stupid.

"I don't want him to live like that," she said. Her fists balled against my chest for a moment, then her body went slack, and I had to hold her up while she cried. After a minute we sat on the bed.

"I don't know, Tom. I don't know what's happening."

"Well, neither do I." I felt suddenly exhausted and hollow. "It seems like the ball's in your court—"

I could feel her tensing up against my shoulder. So I dropped it.

I smelled onions frying in butter. I listened: Frank was cooking again, and explaining the recipe to Peter.

"It's not an inner landscape," I said quietly. "It's a place where I live half my life. I get to share that with my son—"

She pulled away from me and stood up, straightened her clothes. Then she went into the living room, without looking back.

16.

I lay back on the bed, only meaning to buy some time. But I must have been depleted, morally and otherwise, and I fell asleep, and slept through dinner.

When I woke again the house was dark. Peter was in his room; I could see the glow of the night light in the hallway. Maureen was slipping into bed beside me.

When I reached for her she pushed me away.

I didn't make it into a big deal. I didn't feel particularly angry, not at the time. In a few minutes we were both asleep again.

17.

When I woke again, it was to the sun streaming in across the bed, heating me to a sweat under the covers. It was Saturday; no work for me or Maureen, no school for Peter. But Maureen was gone. I didn't feel too good, and I lay there for a while just looking at the insides of my eyelids. There wasn't any noise in the apartment, and I suspected they'd all gone somewhere to get out from under the shadow of you-know-who.

I didn't let it bug me: I took a nice slow shower and went into the kitchen and made some coffee and toast.

But I was wrong. Peter was home. He wandered into the kitchen while I was cleaning up, and said, "Hey, Dad."

This time I could see he knew something was wrong. I didn't have what it took to keep it from him, and I guess he didn't have what it took to keep it from me, either.

"Hey, Pete," I said. "Where's your mom?"

"They went out shopping," he said. "Also to look at some place for Uncle Frank to live."

I nodded. "What are you doing?"

"I don't know. Just some game stuff I got from Jeremy."

"It looks like a pretty nice day out there—"

"I know, I know. I heard it already, from Mom." He looked down at his feet.

There was a minute or two of silence while I finished clearing the table.

"I guess I should offer to 'throw the old pigskin around' or something," I said. "But the truth is I don't feel up to it right now."

The truth was my guts were churning. I couldn't focus on the kid. Seeing him left alone just made me think of Maureen and where she probably was right now. Frank was almost certainly playing the beard for her, and "shopping" by himself. If they came home with packages she'd have to unpack them to know what was in them.

"That's okay," he said seriously. "I don't think we have an old pigskin anyway."

I managed a smile.

"I'll be in my room, okay, Dad?"

"Okay, Peter."

Pretty soon I heard him tapping at his computer again. I sat and nursed the cold coffee and ran my thoughts through some pretty repetitive and unproductive loops. Then it hit me.

Just a twinge at first. But unmistakable.

I was on my way back to Hell.

I realized I'd felt inklings earlier that morning, in the shower, even in bed, and hadn't let myself notice. It was already pretty far along. I was probably an hour or so away from crossing over.

By this time I'd perfected a kind of emotional shorthand. I went through all the traditional stages in the space of a few seconds: denial, bargaining, fear, etc. But underlying them all, this time, was a dull, black rage.

I'd almost never had so short a time back. That hurt. The fact that I was crossing over while Maureen was holed up in her midday love nest hurt more. Unless she came back in the next hour, I wouldn't get in another word. I couldn't make up, couldn't plead, and I couldn't threaten, either, or issue an ultimatum. All the words I'd been rehearsing in my head flew right out the window. She would come home to find me a zombie again.

I felt my claim on her, and my claim on my own life—on Peter, the apartment, everything—slipping away. I had a sudden, desperate need to at least see Peter. I would cram two weeks' worth of unfinished business into the next hour. I got up and went into his room, my head whirling.

He turned from the computer when I appeared in his doorway. "Hey, Dad," he said. "Look at this. I had an idea about Hell."

I went and sat down beside him. I was afraid to open my mouth, afraid of what would or wouldn't come out. I wanted to put on a big show of fatherly affection but I couldn't think of a damn thing to say.

Peter pretended not to notice. "Look." He'd punched up our entry for the starting point: the breakfast table, the horse, and the witch's house. "You get up from the table," he said. "You go off through the hedge in some direction, east, west, north, south. But there's a direction you never go in. It's so obvious. I can't believe we never thought of it."

It wasn't obvious to me, and I felt irritation. "Where? What direction?"

"*The witch's house*. You want breakfast, right? Why not just go in and get some? Why not find out what she's doing in there?"

The idea terrified me instantly. Me, a little boy, barging into the house of the beautiful, unapproachable woman. But Peter didn't know about the emotional content of Hell. I'd kept that from him. "It's an idea," I conceded. "Uh, yeah. It's an idea."

"It could be the key to the whole thing, Dad. Who knows. You've got to find out."

"The purloined letter," I said. "Something so obvious, just sitting right out there in plain sight, but nobody notices . . ." I was drifting off into talking to myself again. I couldn't stay focused on Peter. I was thinking about Maureen and her friend, and my thoughts were very, very murky.

"Will you try?" said Peter. "Will you check it out?"

"I might," I snapped, suddenly angry. It was as though he were taunting me. But of course he didn't know. I hadn't said anything.

He pretended he hadn't heard the tension in my voice, and went on, bright-eyed. "It could be nothing, really. Just another stupid dead end. Or the door is locked or something . . ."

"No, no," I said, wanting to reassure him now. "It's a good idea, Pete. An inspiration . . ."

We drifted off into mutually embarrassed silence.

"Is Uncle Frank a lot like my grandfather?" asked Peter suddenly.

"Well, no. Not really. Why?"

"I dunno. He just seems so different from you. It's hard for me to see how you might be related. I can't imagine what your dad was like."

"Different how?"

"Oh, you know, Dad. You're so serious. Uncle Frank seems like he's almost younger than you."

"Younger?"

"He's just sillier, that's all. He says weird things. I can't really explain, but it's like he's some kind of cartoon character, or somebody you'd tell me about in a story. He reminds me of somebody from Hell, like the robot maker, or—"

That's where Peter stopped, because I hit him.

Hit him hard. Knocked him out of his chair and onto the floor.

My anger had been spiraling while he spoke. I thought about Frank out covering Maureen's ass, the two of them leaving the kid alone so she could squeeze in a quick lay, and that got me to thinking about all the manipulative, unpleasant things Frank had done over the years. And now the kid was falling for it, falling for the image of the wacky, irresponsible cartoon-character uncle who picked you up at school in the middle of the day, who seemed so much more charismatic than boring old Dad.

I remembered falling for it myself, and I wondered if my father ever felt anything like the jealousy I felt now.

Peter sat on the floor, whimpering. I held me hand up to my face and looked at it, astonished. Then I walked out of the room. I couldn't face him. I couldn't think of what to say.

Besides, I was going to Hell.

I was glad. It was where I belonged.

18.

I sat at the table a long time, watching the horse quiver and twitch as the flies crawled over his lips, watching the other children giggle and whisper and play with their silverware, listening to the sound of insects in the woods beyond the hedge, smelling the smoke that trailed out of the witch's chimney, quietly seething. I don't think I ever hated my Hell as badly as I did now. Now that my other life, my real life, had become a Hell too.

Eventually I got out of my seat. But I couldn't bring myself to run for the hedge to the north, or in any direction, for that matter. I stood on the grass beside my chair, paralyzed by Peter's suggestion. After a minute or so I took a first, tentative step across the grass, toward the witch's hut. It seemed like a mile to the cobblestone steps at the door. I tried the handle; it turned easily. The room was dark. I stepped inside.

The Happy Man was turned away from me, facing the table, his pants down around his ankles, his pale, hairy buttocks squeezed together. Splayed out on the table, her bare legs in the air, was the witch. The Happy Man had one hand over her mouth, the other on her breasts.

"Oh, shit," he said when he heard me come in. He stopped thrusting and hurriedly pulled up his pants. "What are you doing in here?" He turned away, left the witch scrambling to cover herself on the table. Despite my astonishment at finding Eagery in the hut, I managed to ogle her for a moment. She was beautiful.

"Breakfast," I got out. "I wanted breakfast."

"Oh, yeah?" The Happy Man didn't sound playful. He was advancing on me fast. I tried to turn and leave, but he grabbed me and pinned me against the wall. "Breakfast is served," he said. He lifted me by my belt and took me to the stove. I could feel its heat as I dangled there. He opened the door with his free hand. Inside there was a pie baking; it smelled wonderful. The breakfast we'd always hoped for. Eagery dropped me onto the open door.

My hands and knees immediately burned. I heard myself pleading, but The Happy Man didn't pay any attention; he began pushing the door closed, battering at my dangling arms and legs until I pulled them in, then slamming the door closed and leaning on it with his full weight.

I fell into the pie, and burning sugar stuck to my back. I think I screamed. Eagery kicked at the oven, jolting it off the floor, until I was silent. Eventually I died.

Died back into my own life, of course. Peter was right. He'd discovered a shortcut.

Lucky me.

19.

I came back in the apartment this time, sitting alone in the living room, watching television. That's how I spend a lot of my zombie hours, according to Maureen. It was midday, and I suspected I hadn't been away long at all. I checked my watch. Sure enough, less than twenty-four hours had passed. It was the second day of the weekend; my shortest stay in Hell ever, by several days.

I turned off the television and went into the kitchen to make myself some coffee. The house was empty. The day was pretty bright, and I suspected they'd gone out for a picnic or something up at the park. I had a few hours alone with my thoughts.

Still, it wasn't until I heard their car in the driveway that I had my big idea.

I had the tube on again. That was part of it. It had something to do with not wanting to face them, too. Not knowing what to say to Maureen, or Peter. When I heard the car pull up I felt my tongue go numb in my mouth.

By the time Maureen got her key in the door it was a fully hatched plan. I stared at the television as they came in, keeping my breath steady, trying not to meet their eyes. There was a moment of silence as Maureen checked me out and determined that I was still away, in Hell.

Then the conversation picked up again, like I wasn't even there.

"—what's he watching?"

"That horrible cop thing. Peter, for God's sake, turn it down. I don't want to listen to that. Or change the channel—" To Frank: "He won't notice. If he doesn't like it, he'll just get up and go away. But he never does. I've seen him sit through hours and hours of Peter's horror things . . ."

I would have enjoyed proving her wrong, but I didn't want to risk anything that would blow my cover. So I sat there while Peter flipped the dial, settling eventually on the news.

The lead story was a minor quake in L.A., and like all good Californians they took the bait, crowded around me on the couch for a look at the damage: a couple of tilted cars on a patch of split pavement, a grandmother facedown on her lawn, pet dog sniffing at her displaced wig. Maureen and Frank sat to my left, and Peter pushed up close to me on my right. It was our first physical contact in a long time—unless you counted the punch.

But Peter didn't sit still for very long. He squirmed in his seat until Maureen noticed.

"Mom?" he said. When he leaned forward I saw the big purple bruise I'd left on the side of his face.

"What?" He held his nose and made a face. "I think Dad needs a shower."

20.

The quality of their disregard was terrifying. I wasn't, as I'd flattered myself by imagining, a monster in their midst, a constant reminder of a better life that had eluded them. They weren't somber or mournful at all. They *coped*. I was a combination of a big, stupid pet and an awkward, unplugged appliance too big for the closet. I was in the way. It was too soon for them to begin hoping—or dreading—that I'd come back, and in the meantime I was a hungry, smelly nuisance.

When Maureen leaned in close and suggested I go clean myself up, I knew to agree politely and follow the suggestion. I welcomed the chance to get away from them and reconnoiter, anyway.

When I emerged from the shower they were already at the table eating. I suppose I shouldn't have expected an invitation. They'd set a place for me, and I went and sat in it, and ate, quietly, and listened while they talked.

The subject of Peter's "injury" came up only once, and then just barely. I gathered that Frank and Maureen had decided to suppress any discussion, to play it down, and hope that Peter was still young enough that he would just plain forget. Find some childlike inner resource for blurring experience into fantasy.

Maybe they would confront me later, when I came back, with Peter out at a friend's house. But the subject was obviously taboo right now.

The discussion mostly centered on Frank's plans. The apartment he was looking at, and some second thoughts he seemed to be having about settling in this area. I sensed an undercurrent, between him and Maureen, of what wasn't being discussed: Frank's trouble. The phone calls he was avoiding. Yet more stuff for Peter not to hear. I wondered, though, knowing Peter's smarts, how much he was picking up anyway.

I was dying for a drink. I tried not to let it show on my face.

After the meal Frank pleaded exhaustion and went into the guest room, and Maureen read a book on the bed. I set up in front of the television and tried not to think about what I was doing or why I was doing it. I walked through the apartment a couple of times on my way to the bathroom, and when I passed Peter's door he looked up from his computer, and I had to struggle not to meet his eye. He would have admired my ruse, and I would have liked to let him in on it, but that wasn't possible. So I stalked past his room like a zombie, and he turned back to his homework. I spent most of the evening on the couch, slogging through prime time. After Maureen tucked Peter into bed I followed her into the bedroom.

She made the phone call about five minutes after she turned off the lights.

"Phillip?" she whispered.

A pause.

"Can you talk? I couldn't sleep." Pause. "No, he's right here in bed with me. Of course he can't hear. I mean it doesn't matter, even if he can. No. No. It's not that." She sighed. "I just miss you."

I guess he talked a bit.

"You do?" she said, her voice half-melted. I hadn't heard her that way in a while. "Phillip. Yes, I know. But it's not that easy. You know. Yes. I wish I could."

They went on like that. Her voice was quiet enough that Peter and Frank wouldn't hear, but in the darkened bedroom it was like a stage play. I could almost make out her boyfriend's tinny replies over the phone.

Then she giggled and said, "I'm touching myself too."

Thank God it was dark. My face must have been crimson. I felt the room whirling like a centrifuge, the bed at the center. I weighed a thousand or a million pounds and I was crushed into my place there on the bed beside Maureen by the pressure of gravity. I couldn't move. I felt my blood pounding in my wrists and temples.

Why was I there? What was I trying to prove?

I knew, dimly, that I'd had some reason for the deception, that some part of me had insisted that there was something I could learn, something vital.

It couldn't have been this, though. I didn't need this.

So what was I after? What—

I sat bolt upright in the bed, dislodging the covers.

"Huh?" said Maureen. "Nothing, nothing. Listen, I have to go, I'll call you back." She hung up and turned on the light. I turned and looked at her in shock. She opened her mouth to scream, and somehow I got my hand over her mouth first. I wrestled her down against the bed, pushed her face into the pillow, twisted her arm behind her back, put my weight on her.

I could hear her yelling my name into the pillow, wetly. Her ears were bright red.

I tightened my grip on her arm. "Shhh," I said, close to her ear. "No noise. No noise." I listened at the hall, alert now, panicked. I had to convince her. "No noise."

"You're dead," she hissed when I let her up for air. "All I have to do is report you. You're dead." Her eyes were slits.

"Shhh." I let her go, forgot her. Focused on the hall.

There wasn't any light. Peter's night light was out, or his door was closed.

Impossible. Peter wouldn't permit it.

Someone was in the house. Frank's pals.

I slid into my pants, silently. I was operating with my Hell-reflexes now, and they were good. There wasn't going to be any hostage. I would make sure of that. I would have complete surprise.

I turned back to Maureen. "Call your pal," I whispered. "Keep it quiet. Have him bring the cops, but quiet, and slow." She looked at me, stunned out of her outrage. "I'm serious. Call him. And stay in here. Whatever happens."

I didn't leave her time for questions. In my pants and bare feet I crept out into the hall and made my way to Peter's door.

Inside I heard him whimpering softly, as if through a gag.

I burst in.

Peter was spread-eagled on his bed, bound with neckties. His pajamas were in shreds around his ankles. Frank, who wasn't wearing anything at all, was kneeling on the side of the bed, as if praying over Peter's helpless body. One hand was resting lightly on Peter's stomach. In the other hand he held his own penis. His pubic hair was white. He looked up at me and his eyes widened for a moment, then fell. And then he grinned. His hands stayed where they were.

I picked up Peter's keyboard and smashed it against Frank's white skull. He straightened up and stopped grinning, and reached back to feel his head.

"Tommy," he said, his voice soft, almost beguiling.

I drew the keyboard back like a baseball bat and hit him again. This time I drew blood. I didn't stop hitting him until he fell back against the floor, his mouth open, his eyes full of tears, his erection wilting.

Peter watched the whole thing from the bed, his mouth gagged, his eyes wide. When I dropped the keyboard and looked up, he met my eyes, for a minute. Then I looked away. I found his floppy disks for Hell, the main disk and the backup, and I tore them in half and tossed them onto the floor, beside Frank.

Peter didn't get untied until the police showed up. Maureen was hiding in her room and I, try as I might, just couldn't bring myself to *touch* him.

21.

I live alone now. The settlement went like this: I see Peter every other weekend—if I happen to be back from Hell, that is—and only in the company of his mother. And I don't go anywhere near the house.

Yes, Uncle Frank was Colonel Eagery, aka The Happy Man. He'd molested me as a boy, right in our house, while my father was away, and with my mother in the kitchen making breakfast. I remember it all now.

And yes, I killed him.

Needless to say, there wasn't any mob on his trail. The call he'd been dreading was the Baltimore police. He was on the run from a molestation offense.

Like I said, I live alone. It's a pretty nice place, and a lot closer to the station. There's a pretty nice bar around the corner. Different crowd every night.

When I go to Hell now it's like this:

I'm back in the house with Maureen and Peter. I live with them again. But I'm unable to speak, or reach out to them: I'm a zombie. I start by sitting in front of the television, flipping channels, and then eventually I wander around the apartment, brushing past Maureen, but never able to speak to her, never able to take her hand or hold her or lead her into the bedroom. After a while I go and stand in the doorway of Peter's room. He turns and looks up at me, but I look away, afraid to meet his eyes. I pretend to look the other way, and he goes back to his computer.

And that's it. I spend the rest of the time standing in his doorway, looking over his shoulder at the computer screen.

Watching him play my Hell.

OVER THERE

MIKE RESNICK

I respectfully ask permission to raise two divisions for immediate service at the front under the bill which has just become law, and hold myself ready to raise four divisions, if you so direct. I respectfully refer for details to my last letters to the Secretary of War.

—Theodore Roosevelt
Telegram to President Woodrow Wilson, May 18, 1917

I very much regret that I cannot comply with the request in your telegram of yesterday. The reasons I have stated in a public statement made this morning, and I need not assure you that my conclusions were based upon imperative considerations of public policy and not upon personal or private choice.

—Woodrow Wilson,
Telegram to Theodore Roosevelt, May 19, 1917

The date was May 22, 1917.

Woodrow Wilson looked up at the burly man standing impatiently before his desk.

"This will necessarily have to be an extremely brief meeting, Mr. Roosevelt," he said wearily. "I have consented to it only out of respect for the fact that you formerly held the office that I am now privileged to hold."

"I appreciate that, Mr. President," said Theodore Roosevelt, shifting his weight anxiously from one leg to the other.

"Well, then?" said Wilson.

"You know why I'm here," said Roosevelt bluntly. "I want your permission to reassemble my Rough Riders and take them over to Europe."

"As I keep telling you, Mr. Roosevelt—that's out of the question."

"You haven't told *me* anything!" snapped Roosevelt. "And I have no interest in what you tell the press."

"Then I'm telling you now," said Wilson firmly. "I can't just let any man who wants to gather up a regiment go fight in the war. We have procedures, and chains of command, and . . ."

"I'm not just *any* man," said Roosevelt. "And I have every intention of honoring our procedures and chain of command." He glared at the President. "I created many of those procedures myself."

Wilson stared at his visitor for a long moment. "Why are you so anxious to go to war, Mr. Roosevelt? Does violence hold so much fascination for you?"

"I abhor violence and bloodshed," answered Roosevelt. "I believe that war should never be resorted to when it is honorably possible to avoid it. But once war has begun, then the only thing to do is win it as swiftly and decisively as possible. I believe that I can help to accomplish that end."

"Mr. Roosevelt, may I point out that you are fifty-eight years old, and according to my reports you have been in poor health ever since returning from Brazil three years ago?"

"Nonsense!" said Roosevelt defensively. "I feel as fit as a bull moose!"

"A one-eyed bull moose," replied Wilson dryly. Roosevelt seemed about to protest, but Wilson raised a hand to silence him. "Yes, Mr. Roosevelt, I know that you lost the vision in your left eye during a boxing match while you were President." He couldn't quite keep the distaste for such juvenile and adventurous escapades out of his voice.

"I'm not here to discuss my health," answered Roosevelt gruffly, "but the reactivation of my commission as a colonel in the United States Army."

Wilson shook his head. "You have my answer. You've told me nothing that might change my mind."

"I'm about to."

"Oh?"

"Let's be perfectly honest, Mr. President. The Republican nomination is mine for the asking, and however the war turns out, the Democrats will be sitting ducks. Half the people hate you for entering the war so late, and the other half hate you for entering it at all." Roosevelt paused. "If you will return me to active duty and allow me to organize my Rough Riders, I will give you my personal pledge that I will neither seek nor accept the Republican nomination in 1920."

"It means that much to you?" asked Wilson, arching a thin eyebrow.

"It does, sir."

"I'm impressed by your passion, and I don't doubt your sincerity, Mr. Roosevelt," said Wilson. "But my answer must still be no. I am serving my second term. I have no intention of running again in 1920, I do not need your political support, and I will not be a party to such a deal."

"Then you are a fool, Mr. President," said Roosevelt. "Because I am going anyway, and you have thrown away your only opportunity, slim as it may be, to keep the Republicans out of the White House."

"I will not reactivate your commission, Mr. Roosevelt."

Roosevelt pulled two neatly folded letters out of his lapel pocket and placed them on the President's desk.

"What are these?" asked Wilson, staring at them as if they might bite him at any moment.

"Letters from the British and the French, offering me commissions in *their* armies." Roosevelt paused. "I am first, foremost, and always an American, Mr. President, and I had entertained no higher hope than leading my men into battle under the Stars and Stripes—but I am going to participate in this war, and you are not going to stop me." And now, for the first time, he displayed the famed Roosevelt grin. "I have some thirty reporters waiting for me on the lawn of the White House. Shall I tell them that I am fighting for the country that I love, or shall I tell them that our European allies are more concerned with winning this damnable war than our own President?"

"This is blackmail, Mr. Roosevelt!" said Wilson, outraged.

"I believe that is the word for it," said Roosevelt, still grinning. "I would like you to direct Captain Frank McCoy to leave his current unit and report to me. I'll handle the rest of the details myself." He paused again. "The press is waiting, Mr. President. What shall I tell them?"

"Tell them anything you want," muttered Wilson furiously. "Only get out of this office!"

"Thank you, sir," said Roosevelt, turning on his heel and marching out with an energetic bounce to his stride.

Wilson waited a moment, then spoke aloud. "You can come in now, Joseph."

Joseph Tummulty, his personal secretary, entered the Oval Office.

"Were you listening?" asked Wilson.

"Yes, sir."

"Is there any way out of it?"

"Not without getting a black eye in the press."

"That's what I was afraid of," said Wilson.

"He's got you over a barrel, Mr. President."

"I wonder what he's really after?" mused Wilson thoughtfully. "He's been a governor, an explorer, a war hero, a police commissioner, an author, a big-game hunter, and a President." He paused, mystified. "What more can he want from life?"

"Personally, sir," said Tummulty, making no attempt to hide the contempt in his voice, "I think that damned cowboy is looking to charge up one more San Juan Hill."

Roosevelt stood before his troops, as motley an assortment of warriors as had been assembled since the last incarnation of the Rough Riders. There were military men and cowboys, professional athletes and adventurers, hunters and ranchers, barroom brawlers and Indians, tennis players and wrestlers, even a trio of Maasai *elmoran* he had met on safari in Africa.

"Some of 'em look a little long in the tooth, Colonel," remarked Frank McCoy, his second-in-command.

"Some of *us* are a little long in the tooth too, Frank," said Roosevelt with a smile.

"And some of 'em haven't started shaving yet," continued McCoy wryly.

"Well, there's nothing like a war to grow them up in a hurry."

Roosevelt turned away from McCoy and faced his men, waiting briefly until he had their attention. He paused for a moment to make sure that the journalists who were traveling with the regiment had their pencils and notebooks out, and then spoke.

"Gentlemen," he said, "we are about to embark upon a great adventure. We are privileged to be present at a crucial point in the history of the world. In the terrible whirlwind of war, all the great nations of the world are facing the supreme test of their courage and dedication. All the alluring but futile theories of the pacifists have vanished at the first sound of gunfire."

Roosevelt paused to clear his throat, then continued in his surprisingly high-pitched voice. "This war is the greatest the world has ever seen. The vast size of the armies, the tremendous slaughter, the loftiness of the heroism shown and the hideous horror of the brutalities committed, the valor of the fighting men and the extraordinary ingenuity of those who have designed and built the fighting machines, the burning patriotism of the peoples who defend their homelands and the far-reaching complexity of the plans of the leaders—all are on a scale so huge that nothing in past history can be compared with them.

"The issues at stake are fundamental. The free peoples of the world have banded together against tyrannous militarism, and it is not too much to say that the outcome will largely determine, for those of us who love liberty above all else, whether or not life remains worth living."

He paused again, and stared up and down the ranks of his men.

"Against such a vast and complex array of forces, it may seem to you that we will just be another cog in the military machine of the allies, that one regiment cannot possibly make a difference." Roosevelt's chin jutted forward pugnaciously. "I say to you that this is rubbish! We represent a society dedicated to the proposition that every free man makes a difference. And I give you my solemn pledge that the Rough Riders will make a difference in the fighting to come!"

It was possible that his speech wasn't finished, that he still had more to say . . . but if he did, it was drowned out beneath the wild and raucous cheering of his men.

One hour later they boarded the ship to Europe.

Roosevelt summoned a corporal and handed him a hand-written letter. The man saluted and left, and Roosevelt returned to his chair in front of his tent. He was about to pick up a book when McCoy approached him.

"Your daily dispatch to General Pershing?" he asked dryly.

"Yes," answered Roosevelt. "I can't understand what is wrong with the man. Here we are, primed and ready to fight, and he's kept us well behind the front for the better part of two months!"

"I know, Colonel."

"It just doesn't make any sense! Doesn't he know what the Rough Riders did at San Juan Hill?"

"That was a long time ago, sir," said McCoy.

"I tell you, Frank, these men are the elite—the cream of the crop!

They weren't drafted by lottery. Every one of them volunteered, and every one was approved personally by you or by me. Why are we being wasted here? There's a war to be won!"

"Pershing's got a lot to consider, Colonel," said McCoy. "He's got half a million American troops to disperse, he's got to act in concert with the French and the British, he's got to consider his lines of supply, he's . . ."

"Don't patronize me, Frank!" snapped Roosevelt. "We've assembled a brilliant fighting machine here, and he's ignoring us. There *has* to be a reason. I want to know what it is!"

McCoy shrugged helplessly. "I have no answer, sir."

"Well, I'd better get one soon from Pershing!" muttered Roosevelt. "We didn't come all this way to help in some mopping-up operation after the battle's been won." He stared at the horizon. "There's a glorious crusade being fought in the name of liberty, and I plan to be a part of it."

He continued staring off into the distance long after McCoy had left him.

A private approached Roosevelt as the former President was eating lunch with his officers.

"Dispatch from General Pershing, sir," said the private, handing him an envelope with a snappy salute.

"Thank you," said Roosevelt. He opened the envelope, read the message, and frowned.

"Bad news, Colonel?" asked McCoy.

"He says to be patient," replied Roosevelt. "Patient?" he repeated furiously. "By God, I've been patient long enough! Jake—saddle my horse!"

"What are you going to do, Colonel?" asked one of his lieutenants.

"I'm going to go meet face-to-face with Pershing," said Roosevelt, getting to his feet. "This is intolerable!"

"We don't even know where he is, sir."

"I'll find him," replied Roosevelt confidently.

"You're more likely to get lost or shot," said McCoy, the only man who dared to speak to him so bluntly.

"Runs With Deer! Matupu!" shouted Roosevelt. "Saddle your horses!"

A burly Indian and a tall Maasai immediately got to their feet and went to the stable area.

Roosevelt turned back to McCoy. "I'm taking the two best trackers in the regiment. Does that satisfy you, Mr. McCoy?"

"It does not," said McCoy. "I'm coming along, too."

Roosevelt shook his head. "You're in command of the regiment in my absence. You're staying here."

"But—"

"That's an order," said Roosevelt firmly.

"Will you at least take along a squad of sharpshooters, Colonel?" persisted McCoy.

"Frank, we're forty miles behind the front, and I'm just going to talk to Pershing, not shoot him."

"We don't even know where the front *is*," said McCoy.

"It's where we're *not*," said Roosevelt grimly. "And that's what I'm going to change."

He left the mess tent without another word.

The first four French villages they passed were deserted, and consisted of nothing but the burnt skeletons of houses and shops. The fifth had two buildings still standing—a manor house and a church—and they had been turned into allied hospitals. Soldiers with missing limbs, soldiers with faces swathed in filthy bandages, soldiers with gaping holes in their bodies lay on cots and floors, shivering in the cold damp air, while an undermanned and harassed medical team did their best to keep them alive.

Roosevelt stopped long enough to determine General Pershing's whereabouts, then walked among the wounded to offer words of encouragement while trying to ignore the unmistakable stench of gangrene and the stinging scent of disinfectant. Finally he remounted his horse and joined his two trackers.

They passed a number of corpses on their way to the front. Most had been plundered of their weapons, and one, laying upon its back, displayed a gruesome, toothless smile.

"Shameful!" muttered Roosevelt as he looked down at the grinning body.

"Why?" asked Runs With Deer.

"It's obvious that the man had gold teeth, and they have been removed."

"It is honorable to take trophies of the enemy," asserted the Indian.

"The Germans have never advanced this far south," said Roosevelt. "This man's teeth were taken by his companions." He shook his head. "Shameful!"

Matupu the Maasai merely shrugged. "Perhaps this is not an honorable war."

"We are fighting for an honorable principle," stated Roosevelt. "That makes it an honorable war."

"Then it is an honorable war being waged by dishonorable men," said Matupu.

"Do the Maasai not take trophies?" asked Runs With Deer.

"We take cows and goats and women," answered Matupu. "We do not plunder the dead." He paused. "We do not take scalps."

"There was a time when *we* did not, either," said Runs With Deer. "We were taught to, by the French."

"And we are in France now," said Matupu with some satisfaction, as if everything now made sense to him.

They dismounted after two more hours and walked their horses for the rest of the day, then spent the night in a bombed-out farmhouse. The next morning they were mounted and riding again, and they came to General Pershing's field headquarters just before noon. There were thousands of soldiers bustling about, couriers bringing in hourly reports from the trenches, weapons and tanks being dispatched, convoys of trucks filled with food and water slowly working their way into supply lines.

Roosevelt was stopped a few yards into the camp by a young lieutenant.

"May I ask your business here, sir?"

"I'm here to see General Pershing," answered Roosevelt.

"Just like that?" said the soldier with a smile.

"Son," said Roosevelt, taking off his hat and leaning over the lieutenant, "take a good look at my face." He paused for a moment. "Now go tell General Pershing that Teddy Roosevelt is here to see him."

The lieutenant's eyes widened. "By God, you *are* Teddy Roosevelt!" he exclaimed. Suddenly he reached his hand out. "May I shake your hand first, Mr. President? I just want to be able to tell my parents I did it."

Roosevelt grinned and took the young man's hand in his own, then waited astride his horse while the lieutenant went off to Pershing's quarters. He gazed around the camp: there were ramshackle buildings and ramshackle soldiers, each of which had seen too much action and too little glory. The men's faces were haggard, their eyes haunted, their bodies stooped with exhaustion. The main paths through the camp had turned to mud, and the constant drizzle brought rust, rot and disease with an equal lack of cosmic concern.

The lieutenant approached Roosevelt, his feet sinking inches into the mud with each step.

"If you'll follow me, Mr. President, he'll see you immediately."

"Thank you," said Roosevelt.

"Watch yourself, Mr. President," said the lieutenant as Roosevelt dismounted. "I have a feeling he's not happy about meeting with you."

"He'll be a damned sight less happy when I'm through with him," said Roosevelt firmly. He turned to his companions. "See to the needs of the horses."

"Yes, sir," said Runs With Deer. "We'll be waiting for you right here."

"How is the battle going?" Roosevelt asked as he and the lieutenant began walking through the mud toward Pershing's quarters. "My Rough Riders have been practically incommunicado since we arrived."

The lieutenant shrugged. "Who knows? All we hear are rumors. The enemy is retreating, the enemy is advancing, we've killed thousands of them, they've killed thousands of us. Maybe the general will tell you; he certainly hasn't seen fit to tell *us*."

They reached the entrance to Pershing's quarters.

"I'll wait here for you, sir," said the lieutenant.

"You're sure you don't mind?" asked Roosevelt. "You can find some orderly to escort me back if it will be a problem."

"No, sir," said the young man earnestly. "It'll be an honor, Mr. President."

"Well, thank you, son," said Roosevelt. He shook the lieutenant's hand again, then walked through the doorway and found himself facing General John J. Pershing.

"Good afternoon, Jack," said Roosevelt, extending his hand.

Pershing looked at Roosevelt's outstretched hand for a moment, then took it.

"Have a seat, Mr. President," he said, indicating a chair.

"Thank you," said Roosevelt, pulling up a chair as Pershing seated himself behind a desk that was covered with maps.

"I mean no disrespect, Mr. President," said Pershing, "but exactly who gave you permission to leave your troops and come here?"

"No one," answered Roosevelt.

"Then why did you do it?" asked Pershing. "I'm told you were accompanied only by a red Indian and a black savage. That's hardly a safe way to travel in a war zone."

"I came here to find out why you have consistently refused my requests to have my Rough Riders moved to the front."

Pershing lit a cigar and offered one to Roosevelt, who refused it.

"There are proper channels for such a request," said the general at last. "You yourself helped create them."

"And I have been using them for almost two months, to no avail."

Pershing sighed. "I *have* been a little busy conducting this damned war."

"I'm sure you have," said Roosevelt. "And I have assembled a regiment of the finest fighting men to be found in America, which I am placing at your disposal."

"For which I thank you, Mr. President."

"I don't want you to thank me!" snapped Roosevelt. "I want you to unleash me!"

"When the time is right, your Rough Riders will be brought into the conflict," said Pershing.

"When the time is right?" repeated Roosevelt. "Your men are dying like flies! Every village I've passed has become a bombed-out ghost town! You needed us two months ago, Jack!"

"Mr. President, I've got half a million men to maneuver. *I'll* decide when and where I need your regiment."

"When?" persisted Roosevelt.

"You'll be the first to know."

"That's not good enough!"

"It will have to be."

"You listen to me, Jack Pershing!" said Roosevelt heatedly. "I *made* you a general! I think the very least you owe me is an answer. When will my men be brought into the conflict?"

Pershing stared at him from beneath shaggy black eyebrows for a long moment. "What the hell did you have to come here for, anyway?" he said at last.

"I told you: to get an answer."

"I don't mean to my headquarters," said Pershing. "I mean, what is a fifty-eight-year-old man with a blind eye and a game leg doing in the middle of a war?"

"This is the greatest conflict in history, and it's being fought over principles that every free man holds dear. How could I not take part in it?"

"You could have just stayed home and made speeches and raised funds."

"And you could have retired after Mexico and spent the rest of your life playing golf," Roosevelt shot back. "But you didn't, and I didn't, because neither of us is that kind of man. Damn it, Jack—I've assembled a regiment the likes of which hasn't been seen in almost twenty years, and if you've any sense at all, you'll make use of us. Our horses and our training give us an enormous advantage on this terrain. We can mobilize and strike at the enemy as easily as this fellow Lawrence seems to be doing in the Arabian desert."

Pershing stared at him for a long moment, then sighed deeply.

"I can't do it, Mr. President," said Pershing.

"Why not?" demanded Roosevelt.

"The truth? Because of *you,* sir."

"What are you talking about?"

"You've made my position damnably awkward," said Pershing bitterly. "You are an authentic American hero, possibly the first one since Abraham Lincoln. You are as close to being worshipped as a man can be." He paused. "You're a goddamned icon, Mr. Roosevelt."

"What has *that* got to do with anything?"

"I am under direct orders not to allow you to participate in any action that might result in your death." He glared at Roosevelt across the desk. "*Now* do you understand? If I move you to the front, I'll have to surround you with at least three divisions to make sure nothing happens to you—and I'm in no position to spare that many men."

"Who issued that order, Jack?"

"My Commander-in-Chief."

"Woodrow Wilson?"

"That's right. And I'd no more disobey him than I would disobey you if you still held that office." He paused, then spoke again more gently. "You're an old man, sir. Not old by your standards, but too damned old to be leading charges against the Germans. You should be home writing your memoirs and giving speeches and rallying the people to our cause, Mr. President."

"I'm not ready to retire to Hyde Park and have my face carved on Mount Rushmore yet," said Roosevelt. "There are battles to be fought and a war to be won."

"Not by you, Mr. President," answered Pershing. "When the enemy is beaten and on the run, I'll bring your regiment up. The press can go crazy photographing you chasing the few German stragglers back to Berlin. But I cannot and will not disobey a direct order from my Commander-in-Chief. Until I can guarantee your safety, you'll stay where you are."

"I see," said Roosevelt, after a moment's silence. "And what if I relinquish my command? Will you utilize my Rough Riders then?"

Pershing shook his head. "I have no use for a bunch of tennis players and college professors who think they can storm across the trenches on their polo ponies," he said firmly. "The only men you have with battle experience are as old as you are." He paused. "Your regiment might be effective if the Apaches ever leave the reservation, but they are ill-prepared for a modern, mechanized war. I hate to be so blunt, but it's the truth, sir."

"You're making a huge mistake, Jack."

"You're the one who made the mistake, sir, by coming here. It's my job to see that you don't die because of it."

"Damn it, Jack, we could make a difference!"

Pershing paused and stared, not without sympathy, at Roosevelt. "War has changed, Mr. President," he said at last. "No one regiment can make a difference any longer. It's been a long time since Achilles fought Hector outside the walls of Troy."

An orderly entered with a dispatch, and Pershing immediately read and initialed it.

"I don't mean to rush you, sir," he said, getting to his feet, "but I have an urgent meeting to attend."

Roosevelt stood up. "I'm sorry to have bothered you, General."

"I'm still Jack to you, Mr. President," said Pershing. "And it's as your friend Jack that I want to give you one final word of advice."

"Yes?"

"Please, for your own sake and the sake of your men, don't do anything rash."

"Why would I do something rash?" asked Roosevelt innocently.

"Because you wouldn't be Teddy Roosevelt if the thought of ignoring your orders hadn't already crossed your mind," said Pershing.

Roosevelt fought back a grin, shook Pershing's hand, and left without saying another word. The young lieutenant was just outside the door, and escorted him back to where Runs With Deer and Matupu were waiting with the horses.

"Bad news?" asked Runs With Deer, as he studied Roosevelt's face.

"No worse than I had expected."

"Where do we go now?" asked the Indian.

"Back to camp," said Roosevelt firmly. "There's a war to be won, and no college professor from New Jersey is going to keep me from helping to win it!"

"Well, that's the story," said Roosevelt to his assembled officers, after he had laid out the situation to them in the large tent he had reserved for strategy sessions. "Even if I resign my commission and return to America, there is no way that General Pershing will allow you to see any action."

"I knew Black Jack Pershing when he was just a captain," growled Buck O'Neill, one of the original Rough Riders. "Just who the hell does he think he is?"

"He's the supreme commander of the American forces," answered Roosevelt wryly.

"What are we going to do, sir?" asked McCoy. "Surely you don't plan to just sit back here and then let Pershing move us up when all the fighting's done with?"

"No, I don't," said Roosevelt.

"Let's hear what you got to say, Teddy," said O'Neill.

"The issues at stake in this war haven't changed since I went to see the general," answered Roosevelt. "I plan to harass and harry the enemy to the best of our ability. If need be we will live off the land while utilizing our superior mobility in a number of tactical strikes, and we will do our valiant best to bring this conflict to a successful conclusion."

He paused and looked around at his officers. "I realize that in doing this I am violating my orders, but there are greater principles at stake here. I am flattered that the President thinks I am indispensable to the American public, but our nation is based on the principle that no one man deserves any rights or privileges not offered to all men." He took a deep breath and cleared his throat. "However, since I *am* contravening a direct order, I believe that not only each one of you, but every one of the men as well, should be given the opportunity to withdraw from the Rough Riders. I will force no man to ride against his conscience and his beliefs. I would like to you go out now and put the question to the men; I will wait here for your answer."

To nobody's great surprise, the regiment voted unanimously to ride to glory with Teddy Roosevelt.

3 August, 1917
My Dearest Edith:

As strange as this may seem to you (and is seems surpassingly strange to me), I will soon be a fugitive from justice, opposed not only by the German army but quite possibly by the U.S. military as well.

My Rough Riders have embarked upon a bold adventure, contrary to both the wishes and the direct orders of the President of the United States. When I think back to the day he finally approved my request to reassemble the regiment, I cringe with chagrin at my innocence and naivety; he sent us here only so that I would not have access to the press and he would no longer have to listen to my demands. Far from being permitted to play a leading role in this noblest of battles, my men have been held far behind the front, and Jack Pershing was under orders from Wilson himself not to allow any harm to come to us.

When I learned of this, I put a proposition to my men, and I am extremely proud of their response. To a one, they voted to break camp and ride to the front so as to strike at the heart of the German military machine. By doing so, I am disobeying the orders of my Commander-in-Chief, and because of this somewhat peculiar situation, I doubt that I shall be able to send too many more letters to you until I have helped to end this war. At that time, I shall turn myself over to Pershing, or whoever is in charge, and argue my case before whatever tribunal is deemed proper.

However, before that moment occurs, we shall finally see action, bearing the glorious banner of the Stars and Stripes. My men are a finely tuned fighting machine, and I daresay that they will give a splendid account of themselves before the conflict is over. We have not made contact with the enemy yet, nor can I guess where we shall finally meet, but we are primed and eager for our first taste of battle. Our spirit is high, and many of the old-timers spend their hours singing the old battle songs from Cuba. We are all looking forward to a bully battle, and we plan to teach the Hun a lesson he won't soon forget.

Give my love to the children, and when you write to Kermit and Quentin, tell them that their father has every intention of reaching Berlin before they do!

All my love,
Theodore

Roosevelt, who had been busily writing an article on ornithology, looked up from his desk as McCoy entered his tent.

"Well?"

"We think we've found what we've been looking for, Mr. President," said McCoy.

"Excellent!" said Roosevelt, carefully closing his notebook. "Tell me about it."

McCoy spread a map out on the desk.

"Well, the front lines, as you know, are *here,* about fifteen miles to the north of us. The Germans are entrenched *here,* and we haven't been able to move them for almost three weeks." McCoy paused. "The word I get from my old outfit is that the Americans are planning a major push on the German left, right about *here.*"

"When?" demanded Roosevelt.

"At sunrise tomorrow morning."

"Bully!" said Roosevelt. He studied the map for a moment, then looked up. "Where is Jack Pershing?"

"Almost ten miles west and eight miles north of us," answered McCoy. "He's dug in, and from what I hear, he came under pretty heavy mortar fire today. He'll have his hands full without worrying about where an extra regiment of American troops came from."

"Better and better," said Roosevelt. "We not only get to fight, but we may even pull Jack's chestnuts out of the fire." He turned his attention back to the map. "All right," he said, "the Americans will advance along this line. What would you say will be their major obstacle?"

"You mean besides the mud and the Germans and the mustard gas?" asked McCoy wryly.

"You know what I mean, Frank."

"Well," said McCoy, "there's a small rise here—I'd hardly call it a hill, certainly not like the one we took in Cuba—but it's manned by four machine guns, and it gives the Germans an excellent view of the territory the Americans have got to cross."

"Then that's our objective," said Roosevelt decisively. "If we can capture that hill and knock out the machine guns, we'll have made a positive contribution to the battle that even that Woodrow Wilson will be forced to acknowledge." The famed Roosevelt grin spread across his face. "We'll show him that the dodo may be dead, but the Rough Riders are very much alive." He paused. "Gather the men, Frank. I want to speak to them before we leave."

McCoy did as he was told, and Roosevelt emerged from his tent some ten minutes later to address the assembled Rough Riders.

"Gentlemen," he said, "tomorrow morning we will meet the enemy on the battlefield."

A cheer arose from the ranks.

"It has been suggested that modern warfare deals only in masses and logistics, that there is no room left for heroism, that the only glory remaining to men of action is upon the sporting fields. I tell you that this is a lie. *We matter!* Honor and courage are not outmoded virtues, but are the very ideals that make us great as individuals and as a nation. Tomorrow we will prove it in terms that our detractors and our enemies will both understand." He paused, and then saluted them. "Saddle up—and may God be with us!"

They reached the outskirts of the battlefield, moving silently with hooves and harnesses muffled, just before sunrise. Even McCoy, who had seen action in Mexico, was unprepared for the sight that awaited them.

The mud was littered with corpses as far as the eye could see in the dim light of the false dawn. The odor of death and decay permeated the moist, cold morning air. Thousands of bodies lay there in the pouring rain, many of them grotesquely swollen. Here and there they had virtually exploded, either when punctured by bullets or when the walls of the abdominal cavities collapsed. Attempts had been made during the previous month to drag them back off the battlefield, but there was simply no place left to put them. There was almost total silence, as the men in both trenches began preparing for another day of bloodletting.

Roosevelt reined his horse to a halt and surveyed the carnage. Still more corpses were hung up on barbed wire, and more than a handful of bodies attached to the wire still moved feebly. The rain pelted down, turning the plain between the enemy trenches into a brown, gooey slop.

"My God, Frank!" murmured Roosevelt.

"It's pretty awful," agreed McCoy.

"This is not what civilized men do to each other," said Roosevelt, stunned by the sight before his eyes. "This isn't war, Frank—it's butchery!"

"It's what war has become."

"How long have these two lines been facing each other?"

"More than a month, sir."

Roosevelt stared, transfixed, at the sea of mud.

"A month to cross a quarter mile of *this?*"

"That's correct, sir."

"How many lives have been lost trying to cross this strip of land?"

McCoy shrugged. "I don't know. Maybe eighty thousand, maybe a little more."

Roosevelt shook his head. "Why, in God's name? Who cares about it? What purpose does it serve?"

McCoy had no answer, and the two men sat in silence for another moment, surveying the battlefield.

"This is madness!" said Roosevelt at last. "Why doesn't Pershing simply march *around* it?"

"That's a question for a general to answer, Mr. President," said McCoy. "Me, I'm just a captain."

"We can't continue to lose American boys for *this!* " said Roosevelt furiously. "Where is that machine gun encampment, Frank?"

McCoy pointed to a small rise about three hundred yards distant.

"And the main German lines?"

"Their first row of trenches are in line with the hill."

"Have we tried to take the hill before?"

"I can't imagine that we haven't, sir," said McCoy. "As long as they control it, they'll mow our men down like sitting ducks in a shooting gallery." He paused. "The problem is the mud. The average infantryman can't reach the hill in less than two minutes, probably closer to three—and until you've seen them in action, you can't believe the damage these guns can do in that amount of time."

"So as long as the hill remains in German hands, this is a war of attrition."

McCoy sighed. "It's been a war of attrition for three years, sir."

Roosevelt sat and stared at the hill for another few minutes, then turned back to McCoy.

"What are our chances, Frank?"

McCoy shrugged. "If it was dry, I'd say we had a chance to take them out. . . ."

"But it's not."

"No, it's not," echoed McCoy.

"Can we do it?"

"I don't know, sir. Certainly not without heavy casualties."

"How heavy?"

"*Very* heavy."

"I need a number," said Roosevelt.

McCoy looked him in the eye. "Ninety percent—if we're lucky."

Roosevelt stared at the hill again. "They predicted 50 percent casualties at San Juan Hill," he said. "We had to charge up a much steeper slope in the face of enemy machine gun fire. Nobody thought we had a chance—but I did it, Frank, and I did it alone. I charged up that hill and knocked out the machine gun nest myself, and then the rest of my men followed me."

"The circumstances were different then, Mr. President," said McCoy. "The terrain offered cover, and solid footing, and you were facing Cuban peasants who had been conscripted into service, not battle-hardened professional German soldiers."

"I know, I know," said Roosevelt. "But if we knock those machine guns out, how many American lives can we save today?"

"I don't know," admitted McCoy. "Maybe ten thousand, maybe

none. It's possible that the Germans are dug in so securely that they can beat back any American charge even without the use of those machine guns."

"But at least it would prolong some American lives," persisted Roosevelt.

"By a couple of minutes."

"It would give them a *chance* to reach the German bunkers."

"I don't know."

"More of a chance than if they had to face machine gun fire from the hill."

"What do you want me to say, Mr. President?" asked McCoy. "That if we throw away our lives charging the hill that we'll have done something glorious and affected the outcome of the battle? I just don't know!"

"We came here to help win a war, Frank. Before I send my men into battle, I have to know that it will make a difference."

"I can't give you any guarantees, sir. We came to fight a war, all right. But look around you, Mr. President—this isn't the war we came to fight. They've changed the rules on us."

"There are hundreds of thousands of American boys in the trenches who didn't come to fight this kind of war," answered Roosevelt. "In less than an hour, most of them are going to charge across this sea of mud into a barrage of machine gun fire. If we can't shorten the war, then perhaps we can at least lengthen their lives."

"At the cost of our own."

"We are idealists and adventurers, Frank—perhaps the last this world will ever see. We knew what we were coming here to do." He paused. "Those boys are here because of speeches and decisions that politicians have made, myself included. Left to their own devices, they'd go home to be with their families. Left to ours, we'd find another cause to fight for."

"This isn't a cause, Mr. President," said McCoy. "It's a slaughter."

"Then maybe this is where men who want to prevent further slaughter belong," said Roosevelt. He looked up at the sky. "They'll be mobilizing in another half hour, Frank."

"I know, Mr. President."

"If we leave now, if we don't try to take that hill, then Wilson and Pershing were right and I was wrong. The time for heroes is past, and I *am* an anachronism who should be sitting at home in a rocking chair, writing memoirs and exhorting younger men to go to war." He paused, staring at the hill once more. "If we don't do what's required of us this day, we are agreeing with them that we don't matter, that men of courage and ideals can't make a difference. If that's true, there's no sense waiting for a more equitable battle, Frank—we might as well ride south and catch the first boat home."

"That's your decision, Mr. President?" asked McCoy.

"Was there really ever any other option?" replied Roosevelt wryly.

"No, sir," said McCoy. "Not for men like us."

"Thank you for your support, Frank," said Roosevelt, reaching out and laying a heavy hand on McCoy's shoulder. "Prepare the men."

"Yes, sir," said McCoy, saluting and riding back to the main body of the Rough Riders.

"Madness!" muttered Roosevelt, looking out at the bloated corpses. "Utter madness!"

McCoy returned a moment later.

"The men are awaiting your signal, sir," he said.

"Tell them to follow me," said Roosevelt.

"Sir . . ." said McCoy.

"Yes?"

"We would prefer you not lead the charge. The first ranks will face the heaviest bombardment, not only from the hill but from the cannons behind the bunkers."

"I can't ask my men to do what I myself won't do," said Roosevelt.

"You are too valuable to lose, sir. We plan to attack in three waves. You belong at the back of the third wave, Mr. President."

Roosevelt shook his head. "There's nothing up ahead except bullets, Frank, and I've faced bullets before—in the Dakota Bad Lands, in Cuba, in Milwaukee. But if I hang back, if I send my men to do a job I was afraid to do, then I'd have to face myself—and as any Democrat will tell you, I'm a lot tougher than any bullet ever made."

"You won't reconsider?" asked McCoy.

"Would you have left your unit and joined the Rough Riders if you thought I might?" asked Roosevelt with a smile.

"No, sir," admitted McCoy. "No, sir, I probably wouldn't have."

Roosevelt shook his hand. "You're a good man, Frank."

"Thank you, Mr. President."

"Are the men ready?"

"Yes, sir."

"Then," said Roosevelt, turning his horse toward the small rise, "let's do what must be done."

He pulled his rifle out, unlatched the safety catch, and dug his heels into his horse's sides.

Suddenly he was surrounded by the first wave of his own men, all screaming their various war cries in the face of the enemy.

For just a moment there was no response. Then the machine guns began their sweeping fire across the muddy plain. Buck O'Neill was the first to fall, his body riddled with bullets. An instant later Runs With Deer screamed in agony as his arm was blown away. Horses had their legs shot from under them, men were blown out of their saddles, limbs flew crazily through the wet morning air, and still the charge continued.

Roosevelt had crossed half the distance when Matupu fell directly in front of him, his head smashed to a pulp. He heard McCoy groan as half a dozen bullets thudded home in his chest, but looked neither right nor left as his horse leaped over the fallen Maasai's bloody body.

Bullets and cannonballs flew to the right and left of him, in front and behind, and yet miraculously he was unscathed as he reached the final hundred yards. He dared a quick glance around, and saw that he was the sole survivor from the first wave, then heard the screams of the second wave as the machine guns turned on them.

Now he was seventy yards away, now fifty. He yelled a challenge to the Germans, and as he looked into the blinking eye of a machine gun, for one brief, final, glorious instant it was San Juan Hill all over again.

18 September, 1917
Dispatch from General John J. Pershing to
Commander-in-Chief, President Woodrow Wilson.
Sir:

I regret to inform you that Theodore Roosevelt died last Tuesday of wounds received in battle. He had disobeyed his orders, and led his men in a futile charge against an entrenched German position. His entire regiment, the so-called "Rough Riders," was lost. His death was almost certainly instantaneous, although it was two days before his body could be retrieved from the battlefield.

I shall keep the news of Mr. Roosevelt's death from the press until receiving instructions from you. It is true that he was an anachronism, that he belonged more to the 19th Century than the 20th, and yet it is entirely possible that he was the last authentic hero our country shall ever produce. The charge he led was ill-conceived and foolhardy in the extreme, nor did it diminish the length of the conflict by a single day, yet I cannot help but believe that if I had 50,000 men with his courage and spirit, I could bring this war to a swift and satisfactory conclusion by the end of the year.

That Theodore Roosevelt died the death of a fool is beyond question, but I am certain in my heart that with his dying breath he felt he was dying the death of a hero. I await your instructions, and will release whatever version of his death you choose upon hearing from you.

—Gen. John J. Pershing

22 September, 1917
Dispatch from President Woodrow Wilson to
General John J. Pershing, Commander of American Forces in Europe.
John:

That man continues to harass me from the grave.

Still, we have had more than enough fools in our history. Therefore, he died a hero.

Just between you and me, the time for heroes is past. I hope with all my heart that he was our last.

—Woodrow Wilson

And he was.

ETHER, OR

Ursula K. Le Guin

Edna

I never go in the Two Blue Moons any more. I thought about that
when I was arranging the grocery window today and saw Corrie go
in across the street and open up. Never did go into a bar alone in my
life. Sook came by for a candy bar and I said that to her, said I wonder
if I ought to go have a beer there some time, see if it taste different on
your own. Sook said Oh Ma you always been on your own. I said I sel-
dom had a moment to myself and four husbands, and she said You
know that don't count. Sook's fresh. Breath of fresh air. I saw Needless
looking at her with that kind of dog look men get. I was surprised to
find it gave me a pang, I don't know what of. I just never saw Needless
look that way. What did I expect, Sook is twenty and the man is
human. He just always seemed like he did fine on his own.
Independent. That's why he's restful. Silvia died years and years and
years ago, but I never thought of it before as a long time. I wonder if I
have mistaken him. All this time working for him. That would be a
strange thing. That was what the pang felt like, like when you know
you've made some kind of mistake, been stupid, sewn the seam inside
out, left the burner on.

They're all strange, men are. I guess if I understood them I wouldn't
find them so interesting. But Toby Walker, of them all he was the
strangest. The stranger. I never knew where he was coming from.
Roger came out of the desert, Ady came out of the ocean, but Toby
came from farther. But he was here when I came. A lovely man, dark
all through, dark as forests. I lost my way in him. I loved to lose my
way in him. How I wish it was then, not now! Seems like I can't get
lost any more. There's only one way to go. I have to keep plodding
along it. I feel like I was walking across Nevada, like the pioneers, carrying a lot of stuff I need, but as I go along I have to keep dropping

off things. I had a piano once but it got too heavy and I left it in the Rockies. I had a couple ovaries but they wore out around the time we were in the Carson Sink. I had a good memory but pieces of it keep dropping off, have to leave them scattered around in the sage brush, on the sand hills. All the kids are still coming along, but I don't have them. I had them, it's not the same as having them. They aren't with me any more, even Archie and Sook. They're all walking along back where I was years ago. I wonder will they get any nearer than I have to the west side of the mountains, the valleys of the orange groves? They're years behind me.

They're still in Iowa. They haven't even thought about the Sierras yet. I didn't either till I got here. Now I begin to think I'm a member of the Donner Party.

Thos. Sunn

The way you can't count on Ether is a hindrance sometimes, like when I got up in the dark this morning to catch the minus tide and stepped out the door in my rubber boots and plaid jacket with my clam spade and bucket, and overnight she'd gone inland again. The damn desert and the damn sagebrush. All you could dig up there with your damn spade would be a God damn fossil. Personally I blame it on the Indians. I do not believe that a fully civilized country would allow these kind of irregularities in a town. However as I have lived here since 1949 and could not sell my house and property for chicken feed, I intend to finish up here, like it or not. That should take a few more years, ten or fifteen most likely. Although you can't count on anything these days anywhere let alone a place like this. But I like to look after myself, and I can do it here. There is not so much Government meddling and interference and general hindering in Ether as you would find in the cities. This may be because it isn't usually where the Government thinks it is, though it is, sometimes.

When I first came here I used to take some interest in a woman, but it is my belief that in the long run a man does better not to. A woman is a worse hindrance to a man than anything else, even the Government.

I have read the term "a crusty old bachelor" and would be willing to say that that describes me so long as the crust goes all the way through.

I don't like things soft in the center. Softness is no use in this hard world. I am like one of my mother's biscuits.

My mother, Mrs. J. J. Sunn, died in Wichita, KS, in 1944, at the age of seventy-nine. She was a fine woman and my experience of women in general does not apply to her in particular.

Since they invented the kind of biscuits that come in a tube that you hit on the edge of the counter and the dough explodes out of it under pressure, that's the kind I buy, and by baking them about one half hour they come out pretty much the way I like them, crust clear through. I used to bake the dough all of a piece, but then discovered that you can break it apart into separate biscuits. I don't hold with reading directions and they are always printed in small, fine print on the damn foil which gets torn when you break open the tube. I used my mother's glasses. They are a good make.

The woman I came here after in 1949 is still here. That was during my brief period of infatuation. Fortunately I can say that she did not get her hooks onto me in the end. Some other men have not been as lucky. She has married or as good as several times and was pregnant and pushing a baby carriage for decades. Sometimes I think everybody under forty in this town is one of Edna's. I had a very narrow escape. I have had a dream about Edna several times. In this dream I am out on the sea fishing for salmon from a small boat, and Edna swims up from the sea waves and tries to climb into the boat. To prevent this I hit her hands with the gutting knife and cut off the fingers, which fall into the water and turn into some kind of little creatures that swim away. I never can tell if they are babies or seals. Then Edna swims after them making a strange noise, and I see that in actuality she is a kind of seal or sea lion, like the big ones in the cave on the south coast, light brown and very large and fat and sleek in the water.

This dream disturbs me, as it is unfair. I am not the kind of man who would do such a thing. It causes me discomfort to remember the strange noise she makes in the dream, when I am in the grocery store and Edna is at the cash register. To make sure she rings it up right and I get the right change, I have to look at her hands opening and shutting the drawers and her fingers working on the keys. What's wrong with women is that you can't count on them. They are not fully civilized.

Roger Hiddenstone

I only come into town sometimes. It's a now and then thing. If the road takes me there, fine, but I don't go hunting for it. I run a two hundred thousand acre cattle ranch, which gives me a good deal to do. I'll look up sometimes and the moon is new that I saw full last night. One summer comes after another like steers through a chute. In the winters, though, sometimes the weeks freeze like the creek water, and things hold still for a while. The air can get still and clear in the winter here in the high desert. I have seen the mountain peaks from Baker and Rainier in the north, Hood and Jefferson, Three-Fingered Jack and the Sisters east of here, on south to Shasta and Lassen, all standing up in the sunlight for eight hundred or a thousand miles. That was when I was flying. From the ground you can't see that much of the ground, though you can see the rest of the universe, nights.

I traded in my two-seater Cessna for a quarterhorse mare, and I generally keep a Ford pickup, though at times I've had a Chevrolet. Any one of them will get me in to town so long as there isn't more than a couple feet of snow on the road. I like to come in now and then and have a Denver omelette at the café for breakfast, and a visit with my wife and son. I have a drink at the Two Blue Moons, and spend the night at the motel. By the next morning I'm ready to go back to the ranch to find out what went wrong while I was gone. It's always something.

Edna was only out to the ranch once while we were married. She spent three weeks. We were so busy in the bed I don't recall much else about it, except the time she tried to learn to ride. I put her on Sally, the cutting horse I traded the Cessna plus fifteen hundred dollars for, a highly reliable horse and more intelligent than most Republicans. But Edna had that mare morally corrupted within ten minutes. I was trying to explain how she'd interpret what you did with your knees, when Edna started yipping and raking her like a bronc rider. They lit out of the yard and went halfway to Ontario at a dead run. I was riding the old roan gelding and only met them coming back. Sally was unrepentant, but Edna was sore and delicate that evening. She claimed all the love had been jolted out of her. I guess that this was true, in the larger sense, since it wasn't long after that that she asked to go back to Ether. I thought she had quit her job at the grocery, but she had only asked for a month off, and she said Needless would want her for the extra business at Christmas. We drove back to town, finding it a little west of where we had left it, in a very pretty location near the Ochoco Mountains, and we had a happy Christmas season in Edna's house with the children.

I don't know whether Archie was begotten there or at the ranch. I'd like to think it was at the ranch so that there would be that in him drawing him to come back some day. I don't know who to leave all this to. Charlie Echeverria is good with the stock, but can't think ahead two days and couldn't deal with the buyers, let alone the corporations. I don't want the corporations profiting from this place. The hands are nice young fellows, but they don't stay put, or want to. Cowboys don't want land. Land owns you. You have to give in to that. I feel sometimes like all the stones on two hundred thousand acres were weighing on me, and my mind's gone to rimrock. And the beasts wandering and calling across all that land. The cows stand with their young calves in the wind that blows March snow like frozen sand across the flats. Their patience is a thing I try to understand.

Gracie Fane

I saw that old rancher on Main Street yesterday, Mister Hiddenstone, was married to Edna once. He acted like he knew where he was going, but when the street ran out onto the sea cliff he sure did look foolish. Turned round and came back in those high-heel boots, long legs, putting his feet down like a cat the way cowboys do. He's a skinny old man. He went into the Two Blue Moons. Going to try to drink his way back to Eastern Oregon, I guess. I don't care if this town is east or west. I don't care if it's anywhere. It never is anywhere anyway. I'm going to leave here and go to Portland, to the Intermountain, the big trucking company, and be a truck driver. I learned to drive when I was five on my grandpa's tractor. When I was ten I started driving my dad's Dodge Ram, and I've driven pick-ups and delivery vans for Mom and Mr. Needless ever since I got my license. Jase gave me lessons on his eighteen-wheeler last summer. I did real good. I'm a natural. Jase said so. I never got to get out onto the I-5 but only once or twice, though. He kept saying I needed more practice pulling over and parking and shifting up and down. I didn't mind practicing, but then when I got her stopped he'd want to get me into this bed thing he fixed up behind the seats and pull my jeans off, and we had to screw some before he'd go on teaching me anything. My own idea would be to drive a long way and learn a lot and then have some sex and coffee and then drive back a different way, maybe on hills where I'd have to practice braking and stuff. But I guess men have different priorities. Even when I was driving he'd have his arm around my back and be petting my boobs. He has these huge hands can reach right across both boobs at once. It felt good, but it interfered with his concentration teaching me. He would say *Oh baby you're so great* and I would think he meant I was driving great but then he'd start making those sort of groaning noises and I'd have to shift down and find a place to pull out and get in the bed thing again. I used to practice changing gears in my mind when we were screwing and it helped. I could shift him right up and down again. I used to yell *Going eighty!* when I got him really shifted up. *Fuzz on your tail!* And make these siren noises. That's my CB name: Sireen. Jase got his route shifted in August. I made my plans then. I'm driving for the grocery and saving money till I'm seventeen and go to Portland to work for the Intermountain Company. I want to drive the I-5 from Seattle to LA, or get a run to Salt Lake City. Till I can buy my own truck. I got it planned out.

Tobinye Walker

The young people all want to get out of Ether. Young Americans in a small town want to get up and go. And some do, and some come to a time when they stop talking about where they're going to go when they go. They have come to where they are. Their problem, if it's a problem, isn't all that different from mine. We have a window of opportunity; it closes. I used to walk across the years as easy as a child here crosses the street, but I went lame, and had to stop walking. So this is my time, my heyday, my floruit.

When I first knew Edna she said a strange thing to me; we had been talking, I don't remember what about, and she stopped and gazed at me. "You have a look on you like an unborn child," she said. "You look at things like an unborn child." I don't know what I answered, and only later did I wonder how she knew how an unborn child looks, and whether she meant a fetus in the womb or a child that never came to be conceived. Maybe she meant a newborn child. But I think she used the word she meant to use.

When I first stopped by here, before my accident, there was no town, of course, no settlement. Several peoples came through and sometimes encamped for a season, but it was a range without boundary, though it had names. At that time people didn't have the expectation of stability they have now; they knew that so long as a river keeps running it's a river. Nobody but the beavers built dams, then. Ether always covered a lot of territory, and it has retained that property. But its property is not continuous.

The people I used to meet coming through generally said they came down Humbug Creek from the river in the mountains, but Ether itself never has been in the Cascades, to my knowledge. Fairly often you can see them to the west of it, though usually it's west of them, and often west of the Coast Range in the timber or dairy country, sometimes right on the sea. It has a broken range. It's an unusual place. I'd like to go back to the center to tell about it, but I can't walk any more. I have to do my flourishing here.

J. Needless

People think there are no Californians. Nobody can come from the promised land. You have to be going to it. Die in the desert, grave by the wayside. I come from California, born there, think about it some. I was born in the Valley of San Arcadio. Orchards. Like a white bay of orange flowers under bare blue-brown mountains. Sunlight like air, like clear water, something you lived in, an element. Our place was a little farmhouse up in the foothills, looking out over the valley. My father was a manager for one of the companies. Oranges flower white, with a sweet, fine scent. Outskirts of Heaven, my mother said once, one morning when she was hanging out the wash. I remember her saying that. We live on the outskirts of Heaven.

She died when I was six and I don't remember a lot but that about her. Now I have come to realize that my wife has been dead so long that I have lost her too. She died when our daughter Corrie was six. Seemed like there was some meaning in it at the time, but if there was I didn't find it.

Ten years ago when Corrie was twenty-one she said she wanted to go to Disneyland for her birthday. With me. Damn if she didn't drag me down there. Spent a good deal to see people dressed up like mice with water on the brain and places made to look like places they weren't. I guess that is the point there. They clean dirt till it is a sanitary substance and spread it out to look like dirt so you don't have to touch dirt. You and Walt are in control there. You can be in any kind of place, space or the ocean or castles in Spain, all sanitary, no dirt. I would have liked it as a boy, when I thought the idea was to run things. Changed my ideas, settled for a grocery.

Corrie wanted to see where I grew up, so we drove over to San Arcadio. It wasn't there, not what I meant by it. Nothing but roofs, houses, streets, and houses. Smog so thick it hid the mountains and the sun looked green. God damn, get me out of here, I said, they have changed the color of the sun. Corrie wanted to look for the house but I was serious. Get me out of here, I said, this is the right place but the wrong year. Walt Disney can get rid of the dirt on his property if he likes, but this is going too far. This is my property.

I felt like that. Like I thought it was something I had, but they scraped all the dirt off and underneath was cement and some electronic wiring. I'd as soon not have seen that. People come through here say how can you stand living in a town that doesn't stay in the same place all the time, but have they been to Los Angeles? It's anywhere you want to say it is.

Well, since I don't have California what have I got? A good enough business. Corrie's still here. Good head on her. Talks a lot. Runs that bar like a bar should be run. Runs her husband pretty well too. What do I mean when I say I had a mother, I had a wife? I mean remembering what orange flowers smell like, whiteness, sunlight. I carry that with me. Corinna and Silvia, I carry their names. But what do I have?

What I don't have is right within hand's reach every day. Every day but Sunday. But I can't reach out a hand. Every man in town gave her a child and all I ever gave her was her week's wages. I know she trusts me. That's the trouble. Too late now. Hell, what would she want me in her bed for, the Medicare benefits?

Emma Bodely

Everything is serial killers now. They say everyone is naturally fascinated by a man planning and committing one murder after another without the least reason and not even knowing who he kills personally. There was the man up in the city recently who tortured and tormented three tiny little boys and took photographs of them while he tortured them and of their corpses after he killed them. Authorities are talking now about what they ought to do with these photographs. They could make a lot of money from a book of them. He was apprehended by the police as he lured yet another tiny boy to come with him, as in a nightmare. There were men in California and Texas and I believe Chicago who dismembered and buried innumerably. Then of course it goes back in history to Jack the Ripper who killed poor women and was supposed to be a member of the Royal Family of England, and no doubt before his time there were many other serial killers, many of them members of Royal Families or Emperors and Generals who killed thousands and thousands of people. But in wars they kill people more or less simultaneously, not one by one, so that they are mass murderers, not serial killers, but I'm not sure I see the difference, really. Since for the person being murdered it only happens once.

I should be surprised if we had a serial killer in Ether. Most of the men were soldiers in one of the wars, but they would be mass murderers, unless they had desk jobs. I can't think who here would be a serial killer. No doubt I would be the last to find out. I find being invisible works both ways. Often I don't see as much as I used to when I was visible. Being invisible however I'm less likely to become a serial victim.

It's odd how the natural fascination they talk about doesn't include the serial victims. I suppose it is because I taught young children for thirty-five years, but perhaps I am unnatural, because I think about those three little boys. They were three or four years old. How strange that their whole life was only a few years, like a cat. In their world suddenly instead of their mother there was a man who told them how he was going to hurt them and then did it, so that there was nothing in their life at all but fear and pain. So they died in fear and pain. But all the reporters tell is the nature of the mutilations and how decomposed they were, and that's all about them. They were little boys not men.

They are not fascinating. They are just dead. But the serial killer they tell about over and over and discuss his psychology and how his parents caused him to be so fascinating, and he lives forever, as witness Jack the Ripper and Hitler the Ripper. Everyone around here certainly remembers the name of the man who serially raped and photographed the tortured little boys before he serially murdered them. He was named Wesley Dodd but what were their names?

Of course we the people murdered him back. That was what he wanted. He wanted us to murder him. I cannot decide if hanging him was a mass murder or a serial murder. We all did it, like a war, so it is a mass murder, but we each did it, democratically, so I supposed it is serial, too. I would as soon be a serial victim as a serial murderer, but I was not given the choice.

My choices have become less. I never had a great many, as my sexual impulses were not appropriate to my position in life, and no one I fell in love with knew it. I am glad when Ether turns up in a different place as it is kind of like a new choice of where to live, only I didn't have to make it. I am capable only of very small choices. What to eat for breakfast, oatmeal or corn flakes, or perhaps only a piece of fruit? Kiwi fruits were fifteen cents apiece at the grocery and I bought half a dozen. A while ago they were the most exotic thing, from New Zealand I think and a dollar each, and now they raise them all over the Willamette Valley. But then, the Willamette Valley may be quite exotic to a person in New Zealand. I like the way they're cool in your mouth, the same way the flesh of them looks cool, a smooth green you can see into, like jade stone. I still see things like that perfectly clearly. It's only with people that my eyes are more and more transparent, so that I don't always see what they're doing, and so that they can look right through me as if my eyes were air and say, "Hi, Emma, how's life treating you?"

Life's treating me like a serial victim, thank you.

I wonder if she sees me or sees through me. I don't dare look. She is shy and lost in her crystal dreams. If only I could look after her. She needs looking after. A cup of tea. Herbal tea, echinacea maybe, I think her immune system needs strengthening. She is not a practical person. I am a very practical person. Far below her dreams.

Lo still sees me. Of course Lo is a serial killer as far as birds are concerned, and moles, but although it upsets me when the bird's not dead yet it's not the same as the man taking photographs. Mr. Hiddenstone once told me that cats have the instinct to let a mouse or bird stay alive a while in order to take it to the kittens and train them thoughtfully to hunt. The queen cat does that. A tom cat is the Jack the Ripper of the Royal Family. But Lo is neutered, so he might behave like a queen or at least like a kind of uncle if there were kittens around, and bring them his birds to hunt. I don't know. He doesn't mix with other cats much. He stays pretty close to home, keeping an eye on the birds and moles and me. I know that my invisibility is not universal when I wake up in the middle of the night and Lo is sitting on the bed right beside my pillow purring and looking very intently at me. It's a strange thing to do, a little uncanny. His eyes wake me, I think. But it's a good waking, knowing that he can see me, even in the dark.

Edna

All right now, I want an answer. All my life since I was fourteen I have been making my soul. I don't know what else to call it, that's what I called it then, when I was fourteen and came into the possession of my life and the knowledge of my responsibility. Since then I have not had time to find a better name for it. The word responsible means that you have to answer. You can't not answer. You'd might rather not answer, but you have to. When you answer you are making your soul, so that it has a shape to it, and size, and some staying power. I understood that, I came into that knowledge, when I was thirteen and early fourteen, that long winter in Siskiyous. All right, so ever since then, more or less, I have worked according to that understanding. And I have worked. I have done what came into my hands to do, and I've done it the best I could and with all the mind and strength I had to give to it. There have been jobs, waitressing and clerking, but first of all and always the ordinary work of raising the children and keeping the house so that people can live decently and in health and some degree of peace of mind. Then there is responding to the needs of men. That seems like it should come first. People might say I never thought of anything but answering what men asked, pleasing men and pleasing myself, and goodness knows such questions are a joy to answer if asked by a pleasant man. But in the order of my mind, the children come before the fathers of the children.

Maybe I see it that way because I was the eldest daughter and there were four younger than me and my father had gone off. Well, all right then, those are my responsibilities as I see them, those are the questions I have tried always to answer: can people live in this house, and how does a child grow up rightly, and how to be trustworthy.

But now I have my own question. I never asked questions, I was so busy answering them, but am sixty years old this winter and think I should have time for a question. But it's hard to ask. Here it is. It's like all the time I was working keeping house and raising the kids and making love and earning our keep I thought there was going to come a time or there would be some place where all of it all came together. Like it was words I was saying, all my life, all the kinds of work, just a word here and a word there, but finally all the words would make a sentence, and I could read the sentence. I would have made my soul and know what it was for.

But I have made my soul and I don't know what to do with it. Who wants it? I have lived sixty years. All I'll do from now on is the same as what I have done only less of it, while I get weaker and sicker and smaller all the time, shrinking and shrinking around myself, and die. No matter what I did, or made, or know. The words don't mean anything. I ought to talk with Emma about this. She's the only one who doesn't say stuff like, "You're only as old as you think you are," "Oh Edna you'll never be old," rubbish like that. Toby Walker wouldn't take that way either, but he doesn't say much at all any more. Keeps his sentence to himself. My kids that still live here, Archie and Sook, they don't want to hear anything about it. Nobody young can afford to believe in getting old.

So is all the responsibility you take only useful then, but no use later—disposable? What's the use, then? All the work you did is just gone. It doesn't make anything. But I may be wrong. I hope so, I would like to have more trust in dying. Maybe it's worth while, like some kind of answering, coming into another place. Like I felt that winter in the Siskiyous, walking on the snow road between black firs under all the stars, that I was the same size as the universe, the same thing as the universe. And if I kept on walking ahead there was this glory waiting for me. In time I would come into glory. I knew that. So that's what I made my soul for. I made it for glory.

And I have known a good deal of glory. I'm not ungrateful. But it doesn't last. It doesn't come together to make a place where you can live, a house. It's gone and the years go. What's left? Shrinking and forgetting and thinking about aches and acid indigestion and cancers and pulse rates and bunions until the whole world is a room that smells like urine, is that what all the work comes to, is that the end of the babies' kicking legs, the children's eyes, the loving hands, the wild rides, the light on the water, the stars over the snow? Somewhere inside it all there has to still be the glory.

Ervin Muth

I have been watching Mr. "Toby" Walker for a good while, checking up on things, and if I happened to be called upon to I could state with fair certainty that this "Mr. Walker" is *not an American*. My research has taken me considerably farther afield than that. But there are these "gray areas" or some things which many people as a rule are unprepared to accept. It takes training.

My attention was drawn to these kind of matters in the first place by scrutinizing the town records on an entirely different subject of research. Suffice it to say that I was checking the title on the Fane place at the point in time when Mrs. Osey Jean Fane put the property into the hands of Ervin Muth Realtor, of which I am the proprietor. There had been a dispute concerning the property line on the east side of the Fane property in 1939 into which, due to being meticulous concerning these kind of detailed responsibilities, I checked. To my surprise I was amazed to discover that the adjoining lot, which had been developed in 1906, had been in the name of Tobinye Walker since that date, 1906! I naturally assumed at that point in time that this "Tobinye Walker" was "Mr. Toby Walker's" father and thought little more about the issue until my researches into another matter, concerning the Essel/Emmer lots, in the town records indicated that the name "Tobinye Walker" was shown as purchaser of a livery stable on that site (on Main St. between Rash St. and Goreman Ave.) in 1880.

While purchasing certain necessaries in the Needless Grocery Store soon after, I encountered Mr. Walker in person. I remarked in a jocular vein that I had been meeting his father and grandfather. This was of course a mere pleasantry. Mr. "Toby" Walker responded in what struck me as a suspicious fashion. There was some taking aback going on. Although with laughter. His exact words, to which I can attest, were the following: "I had no idea that you were capable of traveling in time!"

This was followed by my best efforts to seriously inquire concerning the persons of his same name that my researches in connection with me work as a realtor had turned up. These were only met with facetious remarks such as, "I've lived here quite a while, you see," and "Oh, I remember when Lewis and Clark came through," a statement in reference to the celebrated explorers of the Oregon Trail, who I ascertained later to have been in Oregon in 1806.

Soon after Mr. Toby Walker "*walked*" away, thus ending the conversation.

I am convinced by evidence that "Mr. Walker" is an illegal immigrant from a foreign country who has assumed the name of a Founding Father of this fine community, that is to wit the Tobinye Walker who purchased the livery stable in 1880. I have my reasons.

My research shows conclusively that the Lewis and Clark Expedition sent by President Thos. Jefferson did not pass through any of the localities that our fine community of Ether has occupied over the course of its history. Ether never got that far North.

If Ether is to progress to fulfill its destiny as a Destination Resort on the beautiful Oregon Coast and Desert as I visualize it with a complete down-town entertainment center and entrepreneurial business community, include hub hotels, RV facilities, and a Theme Park, the kind of thing that is represented by "Mr. Walker" will have to go. It is the American way to buy and sell houses and properties continually in the course of moving for the sake of upward mobility and self-improvement. Stagnation is the enemy of the American Way. The same person owning the same property since 1906 is unnatural and Unamerican. Ether is an American town and moves all the time. That is its destiny. I can call myself an expert.

Starra Walinow Amethyst

I keep practicing love. I was in love with that French actor Gerard but it's really hard to say his last name. Frenchmen attract me. When I watch *Star Trek: The Next Generation* reruns I'm in love with Captain Jean-Luc Picard, but I can't stand Commander Riker. I used to be in love with Heathcliff when I was twelve and Miss Freff gave me *Wuthering Heights* to read. And I was in love with Sting for a while before he got weirder. Sometimes I think I am in love with Lieutenant Worf but that is pretty weird, with all those sort of wrinkles and horns on his forehead, since he's a Klingon, but that's not really what's weird. I mean it's just in the TV that he's an alien. Really he is a human named Michael Dorn. That is so weird to me. I mean I never have seen a real black person except in movies and TV. Everybody in Ether is white. So a black person would actually be an alien here. I thought what it would be like if somebody like that came into like the drug store, really tall, with that dark brown skin and dark eyes and those very soft lips that look like they could get hurt so easily, and asked for something in that really, really deep voice. Like, "Where would I find the aspirin?" And I would show him where the aspirin kind of stuff is. He would be standing beside me in front of the shelf, really big and tall and dark, and I'd feel warmth coming out of him like out of an iron woodstove. He'd say to me in a very low voice, "I don't belong in this town," and I'd say back, "I don't either," and he'd say, "Do you want to come with me," only really really nicely, not like a come-on but like two prisoners whispering how to get out of prison together. I'd nod, and he'd say, "Back of the gas station, at dusk."

At dusk.

I love that word. Dusk. It sounds like his voice.

Sometimes I feel weird thinking about him like this. I mean, because he is actually real. If it was just Worf, that's okay, because Worf is just this alien in some old reruns of a show. But there is actually a Michael Dorn. So thinking about him in a sort of story that way makes me uncomfortable sometimes, because it's like I was making him a toy, something I can do anything with, like a doll. That seems like it was unfair to him. And it makes me sort of embarrassed when I think about how he actually has his own life with nothing to do with this dumb girl in some hick town he never heard of. So I try to make up somebody else to make that kind of story about. But it doesn't work.

I really tried this spring to be in love with Morrie Stromberg, but it didn't work. He's really beautiful looking. It was when I saw him shooting baskets that I thought maybe I could be in love with him. His legs and arms are long and smooth and he moves smooth and looks kind of like a mountain lion, with a low forehead and short dark blond hair, tawny colored. But all he ever does is hang out with Joe's crowd and talk about sport scores and cars, and once in class he was talking with Joe about me so I could hear, like "Oh yeah Starra, wow, *she* reads *books*," not really mean, but kind of like I was like an alien from another planet, just totally absolutely strange. Like Worf or Michael Dorn would feel here. Like he meant okay, it's okay to be like that only not here. Somewhere else, okay? As if Ether wasn't already somewhere else. I mean, didn't it use to be the Indians that lived here, and now there aren't any of them either? So who belongs here and where does it belong?

About a month ago Mom told me the reason she left my father. I don't remember anything like that. I don't remember any father. I don't remember anything before Ether. She says we were living in Seattle and they had a store where they sold crystals and oils and New Age stuff, and when she got up one night to go to the bathroom he was in my room holding me. She wanted to tell me everything about how he was holding me and stuff, but I just went, "So, like, he was molesting me." And she went, "Yeah," and I said, "So what did you do?" I thought they would have had a big fight. But she said she didn't say anything, because she was afraid of him. She said, "See, to him it was like he owned me and you. And when I didn't go along with that, he would get real crazy." I think they were into a lot of pot and heavy stuff, she talks about that sometimes. So anyway next day when he went to the store she just took some of the crystals and stuff they kept at home, we still have them, and got some money they kept in a can in the kitchen just like she does here, and got on the bus to Portland with me. Somebody she met there gave us a ride here. I don't remember any of that. It's like I was born here. I asked did he ever try to look for her, and she said she didn't know but if he did he'd have a hard time finding her here. She changed her last name to Amethyst, which is her favorite stone. Walinow was her real name. She says it's Polish.

I don't know what his name was. I don't know what he did. I don't care. It's like nothing happened. I'm never going to belong to anybody.

What I know is this, I am going to love people. They will never know it. But I am going to be a great lover. I know how. I have practiced. It isn't when you belong to somebody or they belong to you or stuff. That's like Chelsey getting married to Tim because she wanted to have the wedding and the husband and a no-wax kitchen floor. She wanted stuff to belong to.

I don't want stuff, but I want practice. Like we live in this shack with no kitchen let alone a no-wax floor, and we cook on a trashburner, with a lot of crystals around, and cat pee from the strays Mom takes in, and Mom does stuff like sweeping out for Myrella's beauty parlor, and gets zits because she eats Hostess Twinkies instead of food. Mom needs to get it together. But I need to give it away.

I thought maybe the way to practice love was to have sex so I had sex with Danny last summer. Mom bought us condoms and made me hold hands with her around a bayberry candle and talk about the Passage Into Womanhood. She wanted Danny to be there too but I talked her out of it. The sex was okay but what I was really trying to do was be in love. It didn't work. Maybe it was the wrong way. He just got used to getting sex and so he kept coming around all fall, going "Hey Starra baby you know you need it." He would even say that it was him that needed it. If I need it, I can do it a lot better myself than he can. I didn't tell him that. Although I nearly did when he kept not letting me alone after I told him to stop. If he hadn't finally started going with Dana I might would have told him.

I don't know anybody else here I can be in love with. I wish I could practice on Archie but what's the use while there's Gracie Fane? It would just be dumb. I thought about asking Archie's father Mr. Hiddenstone if I could work on his ranch, next time we get near it. I could still come see Mom, and maybe there would be like ranch hands or cowboys. Or Archie would come out sometimes and there wouldn't be Gracie. Or actually there's Mr. Hiddenstone. He looks like Archie. Actually handsomer. But I guess he is too old. He has a face like the desert. I noticed his eyes are the same color as Mom's turquoise ring. But I don't know if he needs a cook or anything and I suppose fifteen is too young.

J. Needless

Never have figured out where the Hohovars come from. Somebody said White Russia. That figures. They're all big and tall and heavy with hair so blond it's white and those little blue eyes. They don't look at you. Noses like new potatoes. Women don't talk. Kids don't talk. Men talk like, "Vun case yeast peggets, tree case piggle beet." Never say hello, never say goodbye, never say thanks. But honest. Pay right up in cash. When they come in town they're all dressed head to foot, the women in these long dresses with a lot of fancy stuff around the bottom and sleeves, the little girls just the same as the women, even the babies in the same long stiff skirts, all of them with bonnet things that hide their hair. Even the babies don't look up. Men and boys in long pants and shirt and coat even when it's desert here and a hundred and five in July. Something like those ammish folk on the east coast, I guess. Only the Hohovars have buttons. A lot of buttons. The vest things the women wear have about a thousand buttons. Men's flies the same. Must slow 'em down getting to the action. But everybody says buttons are no problem when they get back to their community. Everything off. Strip naked to go to their church. Tom Sunn swears to it, and Corrie says she used to sneak out there more than once on Sunday with a bunch of other kids to see the Hohovars all going over the hill buck naked, singing in their language. That would be some sight, all those tall, heavy-fleshed, white-skinned, big-ass, big-tit women parading over the hill. Barefoot, too. What the hell they do in church I don't know. Tom says they commit fornication but Tom Sunn don't know shit from a hole in the ground. All talk. Nobody I know has ever been over that hill.

Some Sundays you can hear them singing.

Now religion is a curious thing in America. According to the Christians there is only one of anything. On the contrary there seems to be one or more of everything. Even here in Ether we have, that I know of, Baptists of course, Methodists, Church of Christ, Lutheran, Presbyterian, Catholic though no church in town, a Quaker, a lapsed Jew, a witch, the Hohovars, and the gurus or whatever that lot in the grange are. This is not counting most people, who have no religious affiliation except on impulse.

That is a considerable variety for a town this size. What's more, they try out each other's churches, switch around. Maybe the nature of the town makes us restless. Anyhow people in Ether generally live a long time, though not as long as Toby Walker. We have time to try out different things. My daughter Corrie has been a Baptist as a teen-ager, a

Methodist while in love with Jim Fry, then had a go at the Lutherans. She was married Methodist but is now the Quaker, having read a book. This may change, as lately she has been talking to the witch, Pearl W. Amethyst, and reading another book, called *Crystals and You*.

Edna says the book is all tosh. But Edna has a harder mind than most.

Edna is my religion, I guess. I was converted years ago.

As for the people in the grange, the guru people, they caused some stir when they arrived ten years ago, or is it twenty now. Maybe it was in the sixties. Seems like they've been here a long time when I think about it. My wife was still alive. Anyhow, that's a case of religion mixed up some way with politics, not that it isn't always.

When they came to Ether, they had a hell of a lot of money to throw around, though they didn't throw much my way. Bought the old grange and thirty acres of pasture adjacent. Put a fence right round and God damn if they didn't electrify that fence. I don't mean the little jolt you might run in for steers but a kick would kill an elephant. Remodeled the old grange and built on barns and barracks and even a generator. Everybody inside the fence was supposed to share everything in common with everybody else inside the fence. Though from outside the fence it looked like the Guru shared a lot more of it than the rest of 'em. That was the political part. Socialism. The bubonic socialism. Rats carry it and there is no vaccine. I tell you people here were upset. Thought the whole population behind the iron curtain plus all the hippies in California were moving in next Tuesday. Talked about bringing in the National Guard to defend the rights of citizens. Personally I'd of preferred the hippies over the National Guard. Hippies were unarmed. They killed by smell alone, as people said. But at the time there was a siege mentality here. A siege inside the grange, with their electric fence and their socialism, and a siege outside the grange, with their rights of citizens to be white and not foreign and not share anything with anybody.

At first the guru people would come into the town in their orange color T-shirts, doing a little shopping, talking politely. Young people got invited into the grange. They were calling it the osh rom by then. Corrie told me about the altar with the marigolds and the big photograph of Guru Jaya Jaya Jaya. But they weren't really friendly people they didn't get friendly treatment. Pretty soon they never came into town, just drove in and out the road gate in their orange Buicks. Sometime along in there the Guru Jaya Jaya Jaya was supposed to come from India to visit the osh rom. Never did. Went to South America instead and founded an osh rom for old Nazis, they say. Old Nazis probably have more money to share with him than young Oregonians do. Or maybe he came to find his osh rom and it wasn't where they told him.

It has been kind of depressing to see the T-shirts fade and the Buicks break down. I don't guess there's more than two Buicks and ten, fifteen people left in the osh rom. They still grow garden truck, eggplants, all kinds of peppers, greens, squash, tomatoes, corn, beans, blue and rasp and straw and marion berries, melons. Good quality stuff. Raising crops takes some skill here where the climate will change overnight. They do beautiful irrigation and don't use poisons. Seen them out there picking bugs off the plants by hand. Made a deal with them some years ago to supply my produce counter and have not regretted it. Seems like Ether is meant to be a self-sufficient place. Every time I'd get a routine set up with a supplier of Cottage Grove or Prineville, we'd switch. Have to call up and say sorry, we're on the other side of the mountains again this week, cancel those cantaloupes. Dealing with the guru people is easier. They switch along with us.

What they believe in aside from organic gardening I don't know. Seems like Guru Jaya Jaya Jaya would take some strenuous believing, but people can put their faith in anything, I guess. Hell, I believe in Edna.

Archie Hiddenstone

Dad got stranded in town again last week. He hung around a while to see if the range would move back east, finally drove his old Ford over to Eugene and up the McKenzie River highway to get back to the ranch. Said he'd like to stay but Charlie Echevarria would be getting into some kind of trouble if he did. He just doesn't like to stay away from the place more than a night or two. It's hard on him when we turn up way over here on the coast like this.

I know he wishes I'd go back with him. I guess I ought to. I ought to live with him. I could see Mama every time Ether was over there. It isn't that. I ought to get it straight in my mind what I want to do. I ought to go to college. I ought to get out of this town. I ought to get away.

I don't think Gracie ever actually has seen me. I don't do anything she can see. I don't drive a semi.

I ought to learn. If I drove a truck she'd see me. I could come through Ether off the I-5 or down from 84, wherever. Like that shit kept coming here last summer she was so crazy about. Used to come into the Seven-Eleven all the time for Gatorade. Called me Boy. Hey boy gimme the change in quarters. She'd be sitting up in his eighteen-wheeler playing with the gears. She never came in. Never even looked. I used to think maybe she was sitting there with her jeans off. Bareass on that truck seat. I don't know why I thought that. Maybe she was.

I don't want to drive a God damn stinking semi or try to feed a bunch of steers in a God damn desert either or sell God damn Hostess Twinkies to crazy women with purple hair either. I ought to go to college. Learn something. Drive a sports car. A Miata. Am I going to sell Gatorade to shits all my life? I ought to be somewhere that is somewhere.

I dreamed the moon was paper and I lit a match and set fire to it. It flared up just like a newspaper and started dropping down fire on the roofs, scraps of burning. Mama came out of the grocery store and said, "That'll take the ocean." Then I woke up. I heard the ocean where the sagebrush had been.

I wish I could make Dad proud of me anywhere but the ranch. But that's the only place he lives. He won't ever ask me to come live there. He knows I can't. I ought to.

Edna

Oh how my children tug at my soul just as they tugged at my breasts, so that I want to yell Stop! I'm dry! You drank me dry years ago! Poor sweet stupid Archie. What on earth to do for him. His father found the desert he needed. All Archie's found is a tiny little oasis he's scared to leave.

I dreamed the moon was paper, and Archie came out of the house with a box of matches and tried to set it afire, and I was frightened and ran into the sea.

Ady came out of the sea. There were no tracks on that beach that morning except his, coming up toward me from the breaker line. I keep thinking about the men lately. I keep thinking about Needless. I don't know why. I guess because I never married him. Some of them I wonder why I did, how it came about. There's no reason in it. Who'd ever have thought I'd ever sleep with Tom Sunn? But how could I go on saying no to a need like that? His fly bust every time he saw me across the street. Sleeping with him was like sleeping in a cave. Dark, uncomfortable, echoes, bears farther back in. Bones. But a fire burning. Tom's true soul is that fire burning, but he'll never know it. He starves the fire and smothers it with wet ashes, he makes himself the cave where he sits on the cold ground gnawing bones. Women's bones.

But Mollie is a brand snatched from his burning. I miss Mollie. Next time we're over east again I'll go up to Pendleton and see her and the grandbabies. She doesn't come. Never did like the way Ether ranges. She's a stay-putter. Says all the moving around would make the children insecure. It didn't make her insecure in any harmful way that I can see. It's her Eric that would disapprove. He's a snob. Prison clerk. What a job. Walk out of a place every night where the others are all locked in, how's that for a ball and chain? Sink you if you ever tried to swim.

Where did Ady swim up from I wonder? Somewhere deep. Once he said he was Greek, once he said he worked on an Australian ship, once he said he had lived on an island in the Philippines where they speak a language nobody else speaks, once he said he was born in a canoe at sea. It could all have been true. Or not. Maybe Archie should go to sea. Join the Navy or Coast Guard. But no, he'd drown.

Tad knows he'll never drown. He's Ady's son, he can breathe water. I wonder where Tad is now. That is a tugging too, that not knowing, not knowing where the child is, an aching pull you stop noticing because it never stops. But sometimes it turns you, you find you're facing another direction, like your body was caught by the thorn of a blackberry, by an undertow. The way the moon pulls the tides.

I keep thinking about Archie, I keep thinking about Needless. Ever since I saw him look at Sook. I know what it is, it's that other dream I had. Right after the one with Archie. I dreamed something, it's hard to get hold of, something about being on this long long beach, like I was beached, yes, that's it, I was stranded, and I couldn't move. I was drying up and I couldn't get back to the water. Then I saw somebody walking toward me from way far away down the beach. His tracks in the sand were ahead of him. Each time he stepped in one, in the footprint, it was gone when he lifted his foot. He kept coming straight to me and I knew if he got to me I could get back in the water and be all right. When he got close up I saw it was him. It was Needless. That's an odd dream.

If Archie went to sea he'd drown. He's a drylander, like his father.

Sookie, now, Sook is Toby Walker's daughter. She knows it. She told me, once, I didn't tell her. Sook goes her own way. I don't know if he knows it. I don't think so. She has my eyes and hair. And there were some other possibilities. And I never felt it was the right thing to tell a man unless he asked. Toby didn't ask, because of what he believed about himself. But I knew the night, I knew the moment she was conceived. I felt the child to be leap in me like a fish leaping in the sea, a salmon coming up the river, leaping the rocks and rapids, shining. Toby had told me he couldn't have children—"not with any woman born," he said, with a sorrowful look. He came pretty near telling me where he came from, that night. But I didn't ask. Maybe because of what I believe about myself, that I only have the one life and no range, no freedom to walk in the hidden places.

Anyhow, I told him that didn't matter, because if I felt like it I could conceive by taking thought. And for all I know that's what happened. I thought Sookie and out she came, red as a salmon, quick and shining. She is the most beautiful child, girl, woman. What does she want to stay here in Ether for? Be an old maid teacher like Emma? Pump gas, give perms, clerk in the grocery? Who'll she meet here? Well God knows I met enough. I like it, she says, I like not knowing where I'll wake up. She's like me. But still there's the tug, the dry longing. Oh, I guess I had too many children. I turn this way, that way, like a compass with forty Norths. Yet always going on the same way in the end. Fitting my feet into my footprints that disappear behind me.

It's a long way down from the mountains. My feet hurt.

Tobinye Walker

Man is the animal that binds time, they say. I wonder. We're bound by time, bounded by it. We move from a place to another place, but from a time to another time only in memory and intention, dream and prophecy. Yet time travels us. Uses us as its road, going on never stopping always in one direction. No exits off this freeway.

I say we because I am a naturalized citizen. I didn't used to be a citizen at all. Time once was to me what my backyard is to Emma's cat. No fences mattered, no boundaries. But I was forced to stop, to settle, to join. I am an American. I am a castaway. I came to grief.

I admit I've wondered if it's my doing that Ether ranges, doesn't stay put. An effect of my accident. When I lost the power to walk straight, did I impart a twist to the locality? If so, I can't work out the mechanics of it. It's logical, it's neat, yet I don't think it's the fact. Perhaps I'm just dodging my responsibility. But to the best of my memory, ever since Ether was a town it's always been a real American town, a place that isn't where you left it. Even when you live there it isn't where you think it is. It's missing. It's restless. It's off somewhere over the mountains, making up in one dimension what it lacks in another. If it doesn't keep moving the malls will catch it. Nobody's surprised it's gone. The white man's his own burden. And nowhere to lay it down. You can leave town easy enough, but coming back is tricky. You came back to where you left it and there's nothing but the parking lot for the new mall and a giant yellow grinning clown made of balloons. Is that all there was to it? Better not believe it, or that's all you'll ever have: blacktop and cinderblock and a blurred photograph of a little boy smiling. The child was murdered along with many others. There's more to it than that, there is an old glory in it, but it's hard to locate, except by accident. Only Roger Hiddenstone can come back when he wants to, riding his old Ford or his old horse, because Roger owns nothing but the desert and a true heart. And of course wherever Edna is, it is. It's where she lives.

I'll make my prophecy. When Starra and Roger lie in each other's tender arms, she sixteen and he sixty, when Gracie and Archie shake his pickup trick to pieces making love on the mattress in the back on the road out to the Hohovars, when Ervin Muth and Thomas Sunn get drunk with the farmers in the ashram and dance and sing and cry all night, when Emma Bodeley and Pearl Amethyst gaze long enough into each other's shining eyes among the cats, among the crystals—that same night Needless the grocer will come at last to Edna. To him she will bear no child but joy. And orange trees will blossom in the streets of Ether.

FLYING LESSONS

Kelly Link

1. Going to hell. Instructions and advice.

Listen, because I'm only going to do this once. You'll have to get there by way of London. Take the overnight train from Waverly. Sit in the last car. Speak to no one. Don't fall asleep.

When you arrive at Kings Cross, go down into the Underground. Get on the Northern line. Sit in the last car. Speak to no one. Don't fall asleep.

The Northern line stops at Angel, at London Bridge, at Elephant and Castle, Tooting Broadway. The last marked station is Morden: stay in your seat. Other passengers will remain with you in the car. Speak to no one.

These are some of the unlisted stations you will pass: Howling Green. Duke's Pit. Sparrowkill. Stay in your seat; don't fall asleep. If you look around the car, you may notice that the other passengers have started to glow. The bulbs on the car dim as the passengers give off more and more light. If you look down you may find that you yourself are casting light into the dark car.

The final stop is Bonehouse.

2. June in Edinburgh in June.

June stole £7 from Rooms 2 and 3, enough for trainfare and a birthday present for Lily. Room 3 was American again, and Americans never knew how much currency they had in the first place. They left pound coins lying upon the dresser, like scraps of sunlight.

She ticked off the morning jobs on her right hand. The washroom at the end of the hall was clean. Beds were made up, and all the ashtrays were cleared out. Rooms 1 through 4 were done, and Room 5 at the top of the house was honeymooners from Dallas. They hadn't been at breakfast for three days, living on love, she supposed. Why travel from Dallas to Edinburgh merely to have sex? She pictured a great host of Texans, rising on white wings and fanning out across the Atlantic, buoyed up by love. Falling into bed at journey's end, exhausted by such travel. Nonsense.

She emptied the wastebasket in Room 3, and went thumping down the stairs with the cleaning box in one hand, and the room keys swinging in the other. "Here, Ma," she said, handing the keys and the box over to Lily.

"Ta," Lily said sourly. "Finished up, have you?" Her face was flushed, and her black hair snaked down the back of her neck. Walter was in the kitchen, his elbows plunged into soapy water, singing along with Radio 1 as he worked, an opera program.

"Where are you off to?" Lily said, raising her voice.

June ducked past her. "Dunno exactly," she said. "I'll be back in time for tea tomorrow. Goodbye, Walter!" she shouted. "Bake Lily a lovely cake!"

3. *Arrows of Beauty.*

June went to St. Andrews; she thought it would be pleasant to spend a day by the sea. The train was full, and she sat next to a fat, freckled woman eating sandwiches, one after the other like bonbons. June watched her mouth open and close rhythmically, measuring out the swish and click of the train on the tracks like a metronome.

When the sandwiches were gone, the woman took out a hardcover book. There was a man and a woman on the cover, embracing, his face turned into her shoulder, her hair falling across her face. As if they were ashamed to be caught like this, half-naked before the eyes of strangers. Lily liked that sort of thing.

The name of the author was Rose Read. It sounded like a conjuring name, an ingredient in a love spell, a made-up, let's pretend name. Leaning over the woman's speckled-egg arm, June looked at the photo on the back. Mile-long curliqued eyelashes, and a plump, secretive smile. Probably the author's real name was Agnes Frumple; those eyelashes couldn't be real, either.

The woman noticed June's interest. "It's called *Arrows of Beauty*. Quite good," she said. "All about Helen of Troy, and it's very well researched."

"Really," June said. She spent the next half an hour looking across the aisle, out of the opposite window. There were several Americans on the train, dressed in tourist plaids, their voices flat and bright and empty as parrots. June wondered if her honeymooners would come to this some-day, traveling not out of love but boredom, shifting restlessly like children in their narrow seats. *Are we there yet? Where are we?*

Shortly before the train pulled into Leuchers station, the woman fell asleep. *Arrows of Beauty* dropped from her slack fingers, and slid down the incline of her lap. June caught it before it fell to the floor. June got onto the station platform, the book tucked under her arm.

4. Fine Scents.

The wind tipped and rattled at the tin sides of the St. Andrews bus. It whipped at June's hair, until she scraped the loose tendrils back to her scalp with a barrette. She stared at a sign beside the door, which read "Passengers entering or leaving the bus whilst in motion do so at their own risk."

The golf course came into view, the clipped lawns like squares of green velvet. Behind the golf course was the North Sea, and somewhere over the sea, June supposed, was Norway or Finland. She'd never even been to England. It might be nice to travel: she picture her mother wav-ing goodbye with a white handkerchief, *so long, kid! Just like her father, you know*. Goodbye, good riddance.

St. Andrews was three streets wide, marching down to the curved belly of the harbor. A seawall ran along the cliffs at the edge of the town, from the broken-backed Cathedral, to the Castle, hollowed out like an old tooth and green in the middle. Castle and Cathedral leaned toward each other, pinching the sea between them.

June got off the bus on Market Street. She bought a box of Black Magic chocolates in the Woolworth's and then went down an alley cob-bled with old stones from the Cathedral, worn down to glassy smooth-ness. Iron railings ran along the storefronts, the rails snapped off near the base, and she remembered a school chaperone saying the iron had been taken for the war effort. Taken to be made into cannons and shrapnel and belt buckles, just as the town had harvested stone from the Cathedral. Ancient history, scrapped and put to economical uses.

An old-fashioned sign swinging above an open shop door caught her eye. It read "Fine Scents. I.M. Kew, Prop." Through the window she could see a man behind the counter, smiling anxiously at a well-dressed woman. She was saying something to him that June couldn't make out, but it was her velvety-rough voice that pulled June into the store.

". . . don't know if the rest of the aunties can keep her off him. It's her hobby, you know, pulling wings off flies. You know how fond of him Minnie and I are, but Di and Prune are absolutely no help, she'll do the poor boy just like his mother. . . ."

The marvelous voice trailed off, and the woman lifted a stopper out of a bottle. "Really, darling, I don't like it. Sweet and wet as two virgins kissing. It's not up to your usual standards."

The man shrugged, still smiling. His fingers drummed on the counter. "I thought you might like a change, that's all," he said. "So my Rose-By-Any-Other-Name, I'll make you up a standard batch. May I help you, dearie?"

"I was just looking," June said.

"We don't have anything here for you sort," he said, not unkindly. "All custom scents, see."

"Oh." She looked at the woman, who was examining her makeup, her long smudgy eyelashes in a compact. Rhinestones on the compact lid spelled out RR, and June remembered where she had seen the woman's face. "Excuse me, but aren't you a writer?"

The compact snapped shut in the white hand. A wing of yellow, helmeted hair swung forward as the woman turned to June. "Yes," she said, her pink pointed tongue slipping between the small teeth like pearls. "Are you the sort that buys my books?"

No, June thought. I'm the sort that lifts them. She delved into her sack. "This is for my mother," she said. "Would you sign it for her?"

"How lovely," Rose Read said. She signed the book with a fountain pen proffered by the small man behind the counter, in the careful, looped penmanship of a fifth former. "There. Have you got a lover, my dear?"

"That's none of your business," June said, grabbing the book back.

"Is it my business, Mr. Kew?" Rose Read said to the shopkeeper. He snickered. She had said his name the way two spies meeting at a party might use made-up names.

"She doesn't have a lover," he said. "I'd smell him on her, if she did."

June took a step back, then another, hesitating. The man and woman stared at her, blandly. She found the store and the pair of them unnerving, and she was caught perversely between a wish to flee the store, and an itch to steal something. At that moment, a large and buoyant family poured into the shop. They pressed up to the counter, shaking a battered copy of *Fodors* at Mr. Kew, all speaking at once. In the confusion June pocketed the unwanted perfume and quickly left the store.

5. Going to hell. Instructions and advice.

It is late morning when you arrive at Bonehouse, but the sky is dark. As you walk, you must push aside the air, like heavy cloth. Your foot stumbles on the mute ground.

You are in a flat place where the sky presses down, and the buildings creep close along the streets, and all the doors stand open. Grass grows on the roofs of the houses; the roofs are packed sod, and the grass raises up tall like hair on a scalp. Follow the others. They are dead, and know the way better than you. Speak to no one.

At last you will arrive at a door in an alley, with a dog asleep on the threshold. He has many heads and each head has many teeth, and his teeth are sharp and eager as knives.

6. What was in the bottle.

June sat happy and quiet in the grassy bowl of the castle. Students in their red gowns and tourists clambered over the worn and tumbled steps that went over the drawbridge, between the squat towers. Outside the castle wall, there were more steps, winding down to the rocky beach. She could hear people complaining loudly as they came back up, the wind pushing them backward. Inside the wall the air was still, the sky arched like a glass lid, shot through with light.

Ravens sleek and round as kettles patrolled the grass. They lifted in lazy circles when the tourists came too close, settling down near June, hissing and croaking like toads. She took the perfume out of her knapsack and turned it in her hands. The bottle was tall and slim and plainly made. The stopper was carved out of a rosy stone, and where it plunged into the mouth of the decanter the glass was faceted like the rhinestones on Rose Read's compact. June took out the stopper.

She touched it to her wrist, then held her wrist up to her nose and sniffed. It smelled sweet and greeny-ripe as an apple. It made her head spin. She closed her eyes, and when she opened them again there was someone watching her.

Up in the tilted crown of the left-hand tower, Mr. Kew, Prop. was looking straight down at her. He smiled and winked one eye shut. He cocked his index finger, sighted, and squeezed his fist closed. *Pow*, he said silently, pulling his lips tight in exaggeration around the word. Then he turned to make his way down.

June jumped up. If she went out over the drawbridge they would meet at the foot of the stairs. She grabbed up her pack and went in the opposite direction. She stopped at the wall and looked over. A cement bulwark, about five feet below, girdled up the cliffs that the castle sat on; she tossed the pack over and followed it, heels first, holding hard to the crumbling wall.

7. She hears a story about birds.

The beach was down to June's right, invisible past the curve of the castle's bulk, cliffs and marshy land to her left. Waves slapped against the concrete sides several feet below her. She sat on the ledge, wondering how long she would have to wait before climbing back up to the castle, or down to the beach. The wind cut straight through her jersey.

She turned her head, and saw there was a man standing next to her. Her heart slammed into her chest, before she saw that it was a boy her own age, seventeen or eighteen, with a white face and blue eyes. His eyebrows met, knitted together above the bridge of his nose.

"Before you climbed down," he said, "did you happen to notice if there were a lot of birds up there?"

"You mean girls," June said, sneering at him.

"No, birds. You know, with wings." He flapped his arms.

"Ravens," June said. "And maybe some smaller ones, like sparrows."

He sat down beside her, folding his arms around his knees. "Damn," he said. "I thought maybe if I waited for a while, they might get bored and leave. They have a very short attention span, you know."

"You're hiding from birds?"

"I have a phobia," he said defensively. "Like claustrophobia, you know."

"That's unfortunate," June said. "I mean, there are birds everywhere."

"It's not all birds," he said. "Or it's not all the time. Sometimes they bother me, sometimes they don't. They look at me funny."

"I'm afraid of spiders," June said. "Once when I was little I put my foot into a shoe and there was a spider inside. I still shake my shoes before I put them on."

"When I was five, my mother was killed by a flock of peacocks." He said this in the manner of someone remarking that it had rained this morning.

"What?" June said.

He looked at her earnestly. "My mother took me to see the castle at Inverness. She said that my father was a king who lived in a castle. She was always making stories up like that. I don't remember the castle very well, but afterward we went for a walk in the garden. There was a flock of peacocks, and they began to stalk us. They were so big—as tall as I was. My mother stuck me in an orange tree and told me to yell for help as loudly as I could."

He took a deep breath. "The peacocks' feathers sounded like silk dresses brushing against the ground. I was afraid to make a noise. If I did, they might notice me. They crowded my mother up against the curb of a stone fountain, she was pushing at them with her hands and then she fell backward. The fountain only had two inches of water in it. I heard her head crack against the bottom when she fell. It knocked her unconscious and she drowned before anyone came."

His face was serious and beseeching; she could see the small flutter of pulse against the white flesh—thin as paper—of his jaw.

June shuddered. "That's horrible," she said. "Who took care of you?"

"My mother and father weren't married," he said. "He already had a wife. My mother didn't have any family, so my father gave me to his sisters. Aunt Minnie, Aunt Prune, Aunt Di, and Aunt Rose."

"My father emigrated to Australia when I was two," June said. "I don't remember him much. My mother remarried about a year ago."

"I've never seen my father," the boy said. "Aunt Rose says it would be too dangerous. His wife, Vera, hates me even though she's never seen me, because I'm her husband's bastard. She's kind of insane."

"What's your name?"

"Humphrey Bogart Stoneking," he said. "My mother was a big fan. What's your name?"

"June," said June.

They were silent for a moment. June rubbed her hands together for comfort. "Are you cold?" asked Humphrey. She nodded, and he moved closer and put his arm around her.

"You smell nice," he said after a moment. He sniffed thoughtfully. "Familiar, sort of."

"Yeah?" She turned her head and their mouths bumped together, soft and cold.

8. Rose Read on young lovers.

It's all the fault of that damned perfume, and that mooning, meddling, milky-faced perfumer. He could have had it back and no harm done, if he didn't love mischief more than his mother. So it might have been my idea—it might have been an accident. Or maybe it was Fate. If I'm still around, so is that tired old hag. Do you think that I have the time to see to every love affair in the world personally?

Those hesitating kisses, the tender fumbles and stumbles and awkward meetings of body parts give me indigestion. Heartburn. Give me two knowledgeable parties who know what is up, and what fits where; give me Helen of Troy, fornicating her way across the ancient world, Achilles and Patroclos amusing themselves in a sweaty tent.

A swan, a bull, a shower of gold, something new, something old, something borrowed, something blue. He seduced Sarah Stoneking in an empty movie house, stepped right off of the screen during the matinee and lisped "Shweetheart" at her. She fell into the old goat's arms. I know, I was there.

9. In which a discovery is made.

The sky stayed clear and pale all night long. When they were cold again, they wrapped themselves in Humphrey's coat, and leaned back against the wall. June took out the box of chocolates and ate them as Humphrey explored her pack. He pulled out the perfume. "Where'd you get this?"

"I nicked it from a shop off Market Street."

"I should have known." He pulled out the book. "Aunt Rose," he said.

"She's your aunt?" June said. She looked at him defiantly. "I guess I should give it to you to give back."

He shook his head. "If she didn't mean for you to have it, you wouldn't even have thought of taking it. Might as well keep it now. She probably set this whole thing up."

"How?" June said. "Is she a psychic or something?"

"This must be how they're planning to stop me," Humphrey said. "They think if I have a girlfriend, I'll give up on the flying lessons, take up fucking as a new hobby."

"Right." June said, stiffly. "It was nice to meet you too. I don't usually go around doing this."

"Wait," he said, catching at her pack as she stood up. "I didn't mean it that way. You're right. This is a complete coincidence. And I didn't think that you did."

He smiled up at her. June sat back down, mollified, stretching her legs out in front of her. "Why are you taking flying lessons?"

"I've been saving up for it," he said. "I went to see a psychologist about a year ago, and he suggested that flying lessons might make me less afraid of birds. Besides, I've always wanted to. I used to dream about it. The aunts say it's a bad idea, but they're just superstitious. I have my first lesson tomorrow. Today, actually."

"I think flying would be wonderful," June said. "But I know something just as nice."

"What?" he said. So she showed him. His mouth tasted bittersweet.

10. Going to hell. Instructions and advice.

As the others step over the dog he doesn't wake. If you step over him, his nostrils will scent live flesh and he will tear you to pieces.

Take this perfume with you and when you come to Bonehouse, dab it behind your ears, at your wrists and elbows, at the back of your knees. Stroke it into the vee of your sex, as you would for a lover. The scent is heavy and rich, like the first cold handful of dirt tossed into the dug grave. It will trick the dog's nose.

Inside the door, there is no light but the foxfire glow of your own body. The dead flicker like candles around you. They are burning their memories for warmth. They may brush up against you, drawn to what is stronger and hotter and brighter in you. Don't speak to them.

There are no walls, no roof above you except darkness. There are no doors, only the luminous windows that the dead have become. Unravel the left arm of his sweater and let it fall to the ground.

11. In the All-Night Bakery at dawn.

June and Humphrey went around the corner of the bulwark, down over an outcropping of rocks, slick with gray light, down to the beach. A seagull, perched like a lantern upon the castle wall, watched them go.

They walked down Market Street, the heavy, wet air clinging like ghosts to their hair and skin. The sound of their feet, hollow and sharp, rang like bells on the cobblestones. They came to the All-Night Bakery and June could hear someone singing inside.

Behind the counter there were long rows of white ovens and cooling racks, as tall as June. A woman stood with her strong back to them, sliding trays stacked with half-moon loaves into an oven, like a mother tucking her children into warm sheets.

She was singing to herself, low and deep, and as June watched and listened, the colorless loaves, the ovens, the woman and her lullaby cast out a fierce radiance. They grew brighter and larger and crowded the bakery and June's senses so that she began to doubt there was room for herself, for the houses and street, the dawn outside to exist unharmed. The woman shut the oven door, and June was afraid that presently she would turn around and show June her face, flickering pale and enormous as the moon.

She stumbled back outside, dizzy with light and heat. Humphrey followed her in a few minutes, his pockets stuffed with doughnuts and meat pies.

"My Aunt Di," he said. He handed her a pastry. "Some nights I work here with her."

He went with her to the station, and wrapped up two greasy bacon pies and gave them to her. Before the bus came she wrote her address and telephone on a corner of a napkin, and then reached impulsively into her pocket. She took out the crumpled banknotes, the small, heavy coins. "Here," she said. "For your flying lesson."

She dumped them into his cupped hands, and then before she could decide if the blush on his face was one of pleasure, or embarrassment, the train was here. She got on and didn't look back.

At the bed and breakfast, Lily and Walter were finishing the breakfast washup. June handed the book and the perfume to her mother. "Happy birthday, Lily."

"Where were you last night?" Lily said. She held the perfume bottle between her thumb and middle finger as if it were a dead rat.

"With a friend," June said vaguely, and pretended not to see Lily's frown. She went up the stairs to the top of the house, to her room in the attic. The honeymooners' door was shut, but she could hear them as she went past in the hall. It sounded just like pigeons, soft little noises and gasps. She slammed her door shut and went straight to sleep.

When she came down again, hands and face washed, hair combed back neat, the cake that Walter had made, square and plain, with a dozen pink candles spelling out Lily's name, was on the table. Lily was looking at it as if it might explode. June said, "How do you like the perfume?"

"I don't," Lily said. She clattered the knives and forks down. "It smells cheap and too sweet. Not subtle at all."

Walter came up behind Lily and squeezed her around the middle. She pushed at him, but not too hard. "I quite liked it," he said. "Your mother's been sitting with her feet up in the parlor all day, reading the rubbishy romance you got her. Very subtle, that."

"Get away with you," Lily said. She blew out the candles with one efficient breath, a tiny smile on her face.

12. Room five.

Two days later the honeymooners left. When June went into the room, the copper tang of sex was so strong that she could hardly breathe. She flung open the windows and stripped the ravaged bed, but the smell, satiated and unrepentant, lingered in the walls and in the carpet.

In the afternoon, a woman dressed in somber, expensive black came looking for a room. "It would be for some time," the woman said. She spoke very carefully, as if she were used to being misunderstood. June, sitting in the parlor, idly leafing through sex advice columns in American magazines left behind by the honeymooners, looked up for a second. She thought the woman in black had an antique look about her, precise and hard, like a face on a cameo.

"We do have a room," said Lily. "But I don't know that you'll want it. We try to be nice here, but you look like you might be accustomed to better."

The woman sighed. "I am getting a divorce from my husband," she said. "He has been unfaithful. I don't want him to find me, so I will stay here where he would not think to look. You were recommended to me."

"Really?" said Lily, looking pleased. "By who?"

But the woman couldn't remember. She signed her name, Mrs. Vera Ambrosia, in a thick slant of ink, and produced £40, and another £40 as a deposit. When June showed her up to Room 5, her nostrils flared like a horse scenting fire. But she said nothing. She had with her only one small suitcase, and a covered box. Out of the box she took a bird cage on a collapsible stand. There was nothing in the bird cage but dust.

When June left, she was standing at the window looking out into grayness.

13. A game of golf.

June tried not to think about Humphrey. It was a silly name anyway. She went out with her friends and she never mentioned his name. They would have laughed at his name. It was probably made up.

She thought of describing how his eyebrows met, in a straight bar across his face. She decided that it should repulse her. It did. And he was a liar too. Not even a good liar.

All the same, she rented old movies, *Key Largo* and *Casablanca*, and watched them with Walter and Lily. And sometimes she wondered if he had been telling the truth. Her period came, and so she didn't have to worry about that; she worried anyway, and she began to notice the way that birds watched from telephone lines as she walked past them. She counted them, trying to remember how they added up for joy, how for sorrow.

She asked Walter, who said, "Sweetheart, for you they mean joy. You're a good girl and you deserve to be happy." He was touching up the red trim around the front door. June sat hunched on the step beside him, swirling the paint around in the canister.

"Didn't my mother deserve to be happy?" she said sharply.

"Well, she's got me, hasn't she?" Walter said, his eyebrows shooting up. He pretended to be wounded. "Oh, I see. Sweetheart, you've got to be patient. Plenty of time to fall in love when you're a bit older."

"She was my age when she had me!" June said. "And where were you then? And where is *he* now?" She got up awkwardly and ran inside, past a pair of startled guests, past Lily who stood in the narrow hall and watched her pass, no expression at all on her mother's face.

That night June had a dream. She stood in her nightgown, an old one that had belonged to her mother, her bare feet resting on cold silky grass. The wind went through the holes in the flannel, curled around her body and fluttered the hem of the nightgown. She tasted salt in her mouth, and saw the white moth-eaten glow of the waves beneath her, stitching water to the shore. The moon was sharp and thin, as if someone had eaten the juicy bit and left the rind.

"Fore!" someone called. She realized she was standing barefoot and nearly naked on the St. Andrews golf course. "Why hello, little thief," someone said.

June pinched herself, and it hurt just a little, and she didn't wake up. Rose Read still stood in front of her, dressed all in white: white cashmere sweater; white wool trousers; spotless white leather shoes and gloves. "You look positively frost-bitten, darling child," Rose Read said.

She leaned toward June and pressed her soft, warm mouth against June's mouth. June opened her mouth to protest, and Rose Read breathed down her throat. It was delicious, like drinking fire. She felt Rose Read's kiss rushing out toward her ten fingers, her icy feet, pooling somewhere down below her stomach. She felt like a June-shaped bowl brimming over with warmth and radiance.

Rose Read removed her mouth. "There," she said.

"I want to kiss her too," said a querulous voice. "It's my turn, Rosy."

There were two other women standing on the green. The one who had spoken was tall and gaunt and brittle as sticks, her dark, staring eyes fixing June like two straight pins.

"June, you remember Di, don't you, Humphrey's other aunt?" Rose said.

"She was different," June said, remembering the giantess in the bakery, whose voice has reflected off the walls like light.

"Want a kiss," Humphrey's aunt Di said again.

"Don't mind her," Rose Read said. "It's that time of the month. Humphrey's minding the bakery: it helps her to be outside. Let her kiss your cheek, she won't hurt you."

June closed her eyes, lightly brushed her cheek against the old woman's lips. It was like being kissed by a faint and hungry ghost. Humphrey's aunt stepped back sighing.

"That's a good girl," Rose said. "And this is another aunt, Minnie. You don't have to kiss her, she's not much for things of the flesh, is Minnie."

"Hello, June," the woman said, inclining her head. She looked like the headmistress of June's comprehensive—so old that Lily had once been her student. When her O-levels scores had come back two years ago, the headmistress had called June into her office.

It's a pity, the woman had said, because you seem to have a brain in your head. But if you are determined to make yourself into nothing at all, then I can't stop you. Your mother was the same sort, smart enough but willful—oh yes, I remember her quite well. It was a pity. It's always a pity.

"I'm dreaming," June said.

"It would be a mistake to believe that," said Rose Read. "An utter failure of the imagination. In any case, while you're here, you might as well solve a little argument for us. As you can see, here are two golf balls, sitting nice and pretty on the green at your feet. And here is the third"—she pointed at the cup—"only we can't agree which one of us it was that put it there."

The moon went behind a wisp of cloud, but the two golf balls shone like two white stones. Light spilled out of the cup and beaded on the short blades of grass. "How do I know whose ball that is?" June said. "I didn't see anything, I wasn't here until now—I mean—"

Rose Read cut her off. "It doesn't really matter whose ball it is, little thief, just whose ball you *say* it is."

"But I don't know!" June protested.

"You people are always so greedy," Rose Read said. "Very well: say it belongs to Minnie, she can pull a few strings, get you into the university of your choice; Di, well, you saw how much she likes you. Tell me what you want, June."

June took a deep breath. Suddenly she was afraid that she would wake up before she had a chance to answer. "I want Humphrey," she said.

"My game, ladies," Rose Read said, and the moon came out again.

June woke up. The moon was bright and small in the dormer window above her, and she could hear the pigeons' feet chiming against the leaded glass.

14. The view from the window.

Before Humphrey came to see June, the woman in Room 5 had paid for her third week in advance, and June found the perfume she had given her mother in the rubbish bin. She took it up to her room, put a dab on her wrist.

He was sitting on the front steps when she swept the dust out of the door. "I lost your address," he said.

"Oh?" she said coolly, folding her arms the way Lily did.

"I did," he said. "But I found it again yesterday."

His eyebrows didn't repulse her as much as she had hoped they would. His sweater was blue, like his eyes. "You're lying," she said.

"Yes," he said. "I didn't come to see you because I thought maybe Aunt Rose tricked you into liking me. I thought maybe you wouldn't like me anymore. Do you?"

She looked at him. "Maybe," she said. "How was your flying lesson?"

"I've been up in the plane twice. It's a Piper Cub, just one engine and you can feel the whole sky rushing around you when you're up there.

The last time we went up, Tiny—he's the instructor—let me take the controls. It was like nothing I've ever done before—that is," he said warily, "it was quite nice. You look lovely, June. Have you missed me too?"

"I suppose," she said.

"Aunt Di gave me the night off. Will you come for a walk with me?" he said.

They came home again when the sky above the streetlights was plush and yellow as the fur of a tiger. "Would you like to come in?" she asked him.

"Yes, please." But they didn't go inside yet. They stood on the steps, smiling at each other and holding hands. June heard a sound, a fluttering and cooing. She looked up and saw a flock of pigeons, crowding on the window ledge two stories above them. Two hands, white and pressed flat with the weight of many rings, lay nestled like doves among the pigeons. Humphrey cried out, crouching and raising his own hands to cover his head.

June pulled him into the cover of the door. She fumbled the key into the lock, and they stumbled inside. "It was just the woman in Room 5," she said. "She's a little strange about birds. She puts crumbs on the sill for them. She says they're her babies." She rubbed Humphrey's back. The sweater felt good beneath her hands, furry and warm as a live animal.

"I'm okay now," he said. "I think the lessons are helping." He laughed, shuddering in a great breath. "I think you're helping."

They kissed, and then she took him up the stairs to her room. As they passed the door of Room 5, they could hear the woman crooning and the pigeons answering back.

15. Rose Read on motherhood.

I never had a mother. I remember being born, the salt of that old god's dying upon my lips, the water bearing me up as I took my first steps. Minnie never had a mother either. Lacking example, we did the best we could with Humphrey. I like to think he grew up a credit to us both.

Prune runs Bonne Hause half the year, and we used to send Humphrey to her in the autumn. It wasn't the best place for a lively boy. He tried to be good, but he always ended up shattering the nerves of Prune's wispy convalescents, driving her alcoholics back to the drink, stealing the sweets her spa patients hoard. Raising the dead, in fact, and driving poor, anemic Prune into pale hysteria.

Di's never had much use for men, but she's fond of him in her own way.

We read to him a lot. Di's bakery came out of his favorite book, the one he read to pieces when he was little. All about the boy in the night kitchen, and the airplane . . . it was to be expected that he'd want to learn to fly. They always do. We moved around to keep him safe and far away from Vera, but you can't keep him away from the sky. If he comes to a bad end, then we kept his feet safely planted on the ground as long as we could.

We tried to teach him to take precautions. Minnie knitted him a beautiful blue sweater and he needn't be afraid of birds nor goddess while he keeps that on. We did the best we could.

16. The Skater.

In the morning, Humphrey helped June with her chores. Lilly said nothing when she met him, only nodded and gave him a mop.

Walter said, "So you're the boy she's been pining after," and laughed when June made a face. They tidied the first four rooms on the second floor, and when June came out of the washroom with the wastebasket, she saw Humphrey standing in front of Room 5, his hand on the door-knob. Light from the window at the end of the hall fell sharply on the downy nape of his neck, his head bent toward the door.

"Stop," June hissed. He turned to her, his face white and strained. "She doesn't like us to come into her room, she does everything herself."

"I thought I could hear someone in there," Humphrey said, "saying to come in."

June shook her head violently. "She's gone. She goes to Charlotte's Square every day, and sits and feeds the pigeons."

She grabbed his hand. "Come on, let's go somewhere."

They went to the National Gallery on the Royal Mile. Outside it was gray and dreary, the people brushing past no more real than bits of blown paper. Inside was like walking around in a castle, the ceilings as tall above them as three Junes. Only all the kings and queens were on the walls, frowning down from their carved golden frames at Humphrey and June, like people peering through windows. Their varied expressions were ferocious and joyful and serene by turns, so full of color and light that they made June feel as if she were a mere dismal ghost walking through rooms thronged with the living.

Humphrey tugged at her hand, and the warmth of his flesh surprised her. They sat on a bench in front of Raeburn's painting *The Reverend Robert Walker Skating on Diddiston Loch.* "This is my favorite painting," he said.

June looked at the Reverend Walker, all in black like a crow, floating above the gray ice, his cheeks rosy with the cold. "I know why you like it," she said. "He looks like he's flying."

"He looks like he's happy," Humphrey said. "Do you remember your father?"

"No," June said. "I suppose when I look in the mirror. How about you?"

"No," Humphrey said. He shrugged. "I used to make up stories about him, though. Because of my name—I thought he was American, maybe even a gangster. I used to pretend that he was part of the Mafia, like Capone. Aunt Minnie says I'm not too far off."

"I know," June said. "Let's pick out fathers here—can I have the Reverend Robert Walker? He looks like Walter. Who do you want?"

They walked through the gallery, June making suggestions, Humphrey vetoing prospective parents. "No, no, no," he protested. "I do not want Sir Walter Scott," he said as June paused in front of a portrait. "An aunt who writes historical romances is enough. Besides, we look nothing alike."

June peered into the next room. "Well," she said. "You'll have to go fatherless then. All this gallery is old gloomy stuff—there's not one decent dad in the lot of them."

She turned around. Humphrey stood in front of an enormous painting of a woman and a swan. The swan arched, his wings spread over the supine woman, as large as the boy who stood in front of him.

"Oh," she said tentatively. "Do birds bother you in paintings too?"

He said "No," his eyes still fixed on the painting. "It's all rubbish, anyway. Let's go."

17. Bonne Hause.

The summer wore on and the nights were longer and darker. Humphrey came on the train from Leuchars every weekend, and at the beginning of August, they climbed to the top of Arthur's Mount for a picnic supper. Edinburgh was crouched far below them, silvered and haphazard as the heaped bones of a fallen giant, the green cloak of grass his bed, the castle his crown.

Ravens stalked the hill, pecking at the grass, but Humphrey ignored them. "Next weekend Tiny says I can make my solo flight," he said. "If the weather's good."

"I wish I could see you," June said, "but Lily will kill me if I'm not here to help. Things always get crazy this time of year." The Fringe Festival was starting up, and already the bed and breakfast was full. Lily had even put a couple from Strassburg into June's attic room. June was sleeping on a cot in the kitchen.

"S'all right," Humphrey said. "I'd probably be even more nervous with you there. I'll come on the eight o'clock train and meet you in Waverly Station. We'll celebrate. Go out and see the performers." June shivered. "Are you cold? Take my sweater. I've got something else for you too." He pulled a flat oblong package from his pack and gave it to her along with the sweater.

"It's a book," June said. "Is it something by your aunt?" She tore off the paper, the wind snatching it from her hands. It was a children's book, with a picture on the cover of a man with flaming hair, a golden sun behind him. "*D'Aulaire's Greek Mythology?*"

He didn't look at her. "Read it and tell me what you think."

June flipped through it. "Well at least it's got pictures," she said. It was getting too dark to look at the book properly. The city, the whole world beneath them was purpley dark; the hill they sat on seemed to be floating on a black sea. The ravens were moveable blots of inky stain, and the wind lifted and beat with murmurous breath at blades of grass and pinion feathers. She pulled the blue sweater tight around her shoulders.

"What will we do at the end of the summer?" Humphrey asked. He picked up one of her hands, and looked into it, as if he might see the future in the cup of her palm. "Normally I go to Aunt Prune's for a few months. She runs a clinic outside of London called Bonne Hause. For alcoholics and depressed rich people. I help the groundskeepers."

"Oh," June said.

"I don't want to go," Humphrey said. "That's the thing. I want to be with you, maybe go to Greece. My father lives there, sometimes. I want to see him, just once. Would you go with me?"

"Is that why you gave me this?" she said, frowning and holding up the book of mythology. "It's not exactly a guide book."

"More like family history," he said. The ravens muttered and cackled. "Have you ever dreamed you could fly, I mean with wings?"

"I've never even been on a plane," June said.

He told her something wonderful.

18. Why I write.

You may very well ask what the goddess of love is doing in St. Andrews, writing trashy romances. Adapting. Some of us have managed better than others, of course. Prune with her clinic and her patented Pomegranate Weight Loss System, good for the health and the spirits. Di has her bakery. Minnie is more or less a recluse—she makes up crossword puzzles and designs knitting patterns, and feuds with prominent Classics scholars via the mail. No one has seen Paul in ages. He can't stand modern music, he says. He's living somewhere in the Soho district of London with a nice deaf man.

Zeus and that malevolent birdbrained bitch are still married, can you believe it? As if the world would stop spinning if she admitted that the whole thing was a mistake. It infuriates her to see anyone else having fun, especially her husband. We've never gotten on well—she fights with everyone sooner or later, which is why most of us are exiled to this corner of the world. I miss the sun, but never the company.

19. An unkindness of ravens.

June waited at Waverly Station for three and half hours. The Fringe was in full swing, and performers in beads and feather masks dashed past her, chasing a windblown kite shaped like a wing. They smelled of dust and sweat and beer. They looked at her oddly, she thought, as they ran by. The kite blew toward her again, low on the ground, and she stuck out her foot. It lifted over her in a sudden gust of wind.

She rested her head in her hands. Someone nearby laughed, insinuating and hoarse, and she looked up to see one of the kite-chasers standing next to her. He was winding string in his hand, bringing the kite down. Bright eyes gleamed at her like jet buttons, above a yellow papier-mâché beak. "What's the matter, little thief?" the peacock said. "Lose something?"

Another man, in crow-black mourning, sat down on the bench beside her. He said nothing, and his pupils were not round, but elongated and flat like those of an owl. June jumped up and ran. She dodged raucous strangers with glittering eyes, whose clothing had the feel of soft spiky down, whose feet were scaly and knobbed and struck sparks from the pavement. They put out arms to stop her, and their arms were wings, their fingers feathers. She swung wildly at them, and ran on. On Queen Street, she lost them in a crowd, but she kept on running anyway.

Lily was sitting in the parlor when she got home. "Humphrey's Aunt Rose called," she said without preamble. "There's been an accident."

"What?" said June, breathing hard. Her chest heaved up and down. She thought she felt the tickle of feathers in her lungs; she thought she might throw up.

"His plane crashed. A flock of birds flew into the propeller. He died almost instantly."

"He's not dead," June said.

Lily didn't say anything. Her arms were folded against her body as if she were afraid they might extend, unwanted, toward her daughter. "He was a nice boy," she said finally.

"I need to go up to my room," June said. Of course he wasn't dead: she'd read the book. He'd explained the whole thing to her. When you're immortal, you don't die. *Half*-immortal, she corrected herself. So maybe *half*-dead, she could live with that.

Lily said, "The woman in Room 5 left this afternoon. I haven't cleaned it yet, but I thought we might move the guests in your room. I'll help you."

"No!" June said. "I'll do it." She hesitated. "Thanks, Lily."

"I'll make a pot of tea, then," Lily said, and went into the kitchen. June took the ring of keys from the wall and went up to her room. She took the blue sweater out of the cupboard and put it on. She picked up the bottle of perfume, and then she paused. She bent and thumbed open the suitcase of the Straussburg honeymooners, reaching down through the folded clothes until her hand closed around a wad of notes. She took them all, without counting.

The last two things she took were the two books: *D'Aulaire's Greek Myths*, and *Arrows of Beauty*.

She went out of her room without locking it, down the stairs to Room 5. The light didn't come on when she lowered the switch, and things brushed against her, soft and damp. She ran to the drapes and flung them back.

The window swung open, and suddenly the room was full of whiteness. At first, blinking hard, she thought that it was snowing inside. Then she saw that the snowflakes were goosedown. Both pillows had been torn open and the duvet was rent down the middle. Feathers dusted the floor, sliding across June's palm and her cheek. She choked on a feather, spat it out.

As she moved across the room, the feathers clung to her. She felt them attaching themselves to her back, growing into two great wings. "Stop it!" she cried.

She opened the *D'Aulaire*, flipping past Hera's mad, triumphant face, to a picture of rosy-cheeked Venus. She pulled the stopper from the perfume bottle and tipped it over the drawing. She poured out half the bottle on the book, and behind her someone sneezed. She turned around.

It was Humphrey's aunt, Rose Read. She looked almost dowdy—travel-stained and worn as if she had come a great distance to reach June. She didn't look anything like the woman in the mythology book. June said, "Where is he?"

Aunt Rose shrugged, brushing feathers off her wrinkled coat. "He's gone to see his Aunt Prune, I suppose."

"I want to go to him," June said. "I know that's possible."

"I suppose you had Classics at your comprehensive," said Aunt Rose, and sneezed delicately, like a cat. "Really, these feathers—"

"I want you to send me to him."

"If I sent you there," Rose said, "you might not come back. Or he might not want to come back. It isn't my specialty either. If you're so clever, you've figured that out too."

"I know you've sent people there before, so stop playing games with me!" June said.

"Your mother could tell you what to do when a lover leaves," Rose Read said in a voice like cream. "So why are you asking my advice?"

"She didn't go after him!" June shouted. "She had to stay here and look after me, didn't she?"

Rose Read drew herself up very tall, smoothing her hands down her sides. She looked almost pleased. "Very well," she said. "Fortunately hell is a much cheaper trip, much nearer to hand than Australia. Are you ready? Good. So listen, because I'm only going to tell you this once."

20. Going to hell. Instructions and advice.

"If you don't let the sweater fall from your hands, if you follow the sleeve until it is only yarn, it will lead you to him. He won't be as you remember him, he's been eating his memories to keep warm. He is not asleep, but if you kiss him he'll wake up. Just like the fairy tales. His lips will be cold at first.

"Say to him, *Follow me*, and unravel the right arm of the sweater. It will take you to a better place, little thief. If you do it right and don't look back, then you can steal him out of the Bonehouse."

June stared instead at the birdcage, gilt and forlorn upon its single hinged leg. Down that was caught, like smoke in a sieve, in the grill of the cage. "What now?" she said. "Do you disappear in a puff of smoke, or wave a wand? Can I just leave?"

"Not through the door," Rose said. "It's time you had your flying lessons."

Rose Read stepped upon the windowsill, crouching in her coat like a great black wing beneath the weight of the moon. She held out her hand to June. "Come on. Are you afraid?"

June took her hand. "I won't be afraid," she said. She climbed up on the sill beside Rose, and pointed her shoes toward the moon, away from the scratch of quills against the walls and ceiling. She didn't look back, but stepped off the edge of the known world.

ITSY BITSY SPIDER

James Patrick Kelly

When I found out that my father was still alive after all these years and living at Strawberry Fields, I thought he'd gotten just what he deserved. Retroburbs are where the old, scared people go to hide. I'd always pictured the people in them as deranged losers. Visiting some fantasy world like the disneys or Carlucci's Carthage is one thing, moving to one is another. Sure, 2038 is messy, but it's a hell of a lot better than nineteen-sixty-whatever.

Now that I'd arrived at 144 Bluejay Way, I realized that the place was worse than I had imagined. Strawberry Fields was pretending to be some long-lost suburb of the late twentieth century, except that it had the sterile monotony of cheap VR. It was clean, all right, and neat, but it was everywhere the same. And the scale was wrong. The lots were squeezed together and all the houses had shrunk—like the dreams of their owners. They were about the size of a one-car garage, modular units tarted up at the factory to look like ranches, with old double-hung storm windows and hardened siding of harvest gold, barn red, forest green. Of course, there were no real garages; faux Mustangs and VW buses cruised the quiet streets. Their carbrains were listening for a summons from Barbara Chesley next door at 142, or the Goltzes across the street, who might be headed to Penny Lanes to bowl a few frames, or the hospital to die.

There was a beach chair with blue nylon webbing on the front stoop of 144 Bluejay Way. A brick walk led to it, dividing two patches of carpet moss, green as a dream. There were names and addresses printed in huge lightstick letters on all the doors in the neighborhood; no doubt many Strawberry Fielders were easily confused. The owner of this one was Peter Fancy. He had been born Peter Fanelli, but had legally taken his stage name not long after his first success as Prince Hal in *Henry IV Part 1*. I was a Fancy too; the name was one of the few things of my father's I had kept.

I stopped at the door and let it look me over. "You're Jen," it said.

"Yes." I waited in vain for it to open or to say something else. "I'd like to see Mr. Fancy, please." The old man's house had worse manners than he did. "He knows I'm coming," I said. "I sent him several messages." Which he had never answered, but I didn't mention that.

"Just a minute," said the door. "She'll be right with you."

She? The idea that he might be with another woman now hadn't occurred to me. I'd lost track of my father a long time ago—on purpose. The last time we'd actually visited overnight was when I was twenty. Mom gave me a ticket to Port Gemini, where he was doing the Shakespeare in Space program. The orbital was great, but staying with him was like being under water. I think I must have held my breath for the entire week. After that, there were a few, sporadic calls, a couple of awkward dinners—all at his instigation. Then twenty-three years of nothing.

I never hated him, exactly. When he left, I just decided to show solidarity with Mom and be done with him. If acting was more important than his family, then to hell with Peter Fancy. Mom was horrified when I told her how I felt. She cried and claimed the divorce was as much her fault as his. It was too much for me to handle; I was only eleven years old when they separated. I needed to be on *someone's* side and so I had chosen her. She never did stop trying to talk me into finding him again, even though after a while it only made me mad at her. For the past few years, she'd been warning me that I'd developed a warped view of men.

But she was a smart woman, my mom—a winner. Sure, she'd had troubles, but she'd founded three companies, was a millionaire by twenty-five. I missed her.

A lock clicked and the door opened. Standing in the dim interior was a little girl in a gold-and-white checked dress. Her dark, curly hair was tied in a ribbon. She was wearing white ankle socks and black Mary Jane shoes that were so shiny they had to be plastic. There was a Band-Aid on her left knee.

"Hello, Jen. I was hoping you'd really come." Her voice surprised me. It was resonant, impossibly mature. At first glance I'd guessed she was three, maybe four; I'm not much good at guessing kids' ages. Now I realized that this must be a bot—a made person.

"You look just like I thought you would." She smiled, stood on tiptoe and raised a delicate little hand over her head. I had to bend to shake it. The hand was warm, slightly moist, and very realistic. She had to belong to Strawberry Fields; there was no way my father could afford a bot with skin this real.

"Please come in." She waved on the lights. "We're so happy you're here." The door closed behind me.

The playroom took up almost half of the little house. Against one wall was a miniature kitchen. Toy dishes were drying in a rack next to the sink; the pink refrigerator barely came up to my waist. The table was full-sized; it had two normal chairs and a booster chair. Opposite this was a bed with a ruffled Pumpkin Patty bedspread. About a dozen dolls and stuffed animals were arranged along the far edge of the mattress. I recognized most of them: Pooh, Mr. Moon, Baby Rollypolly, the Sleepums, Big Bird. And the wallpaper was familiar too: Oz figures like Toto and the Wizard and the Cowardly Lion on a field of Munchkin blue.

"We had to make a few changes," said the bot. "Do you like it?"

The room seemed to tilt then. I took a small, unsteady step and everything righted itself. *My* dolls, *my* wallpaper, the chest of drawers from Grandma Fanelli's cottage in Hyannis. I stared at the bot and recognized her for the first time.

She was me.

"What is this," I said, "some kind of sick joke?" I felt like I'd just been slapped in the face.

"Is something wrong?" the bot said. "Tell me. Maybe we can fix it."

I swiped at her and she danced out of reach. I don't know what I would have done if I had caught her. Maybe smashed her through the picture window onto the patch of front lawn or shaken her until pieces started falling off. But the bot wasn't responsible, my father was. Mom would never have defended him if she'd known about *this*. The old bastard. I couldn't believe it. Here I was, shuddering with anger, after years of feeling nothing for him.

There was an interior door just beyond some shelves filled with old-fashioned paper books. I didn't take time to look as I went past, but I knew that Dr. Seuss and A.A. Milne and L. Frank Baum would be on those shelves. The door had no knob.

"Open up," I shouted. It ignored me, so I kicked it. "Hey!"

"Jennifer." The bot tugged at the back of my jacket. "I must ask you . . ."

"You can't have me!" I pressed my ear to the door. Silence. "I'm not this thing you made." I kicked it again. "You hear?"

Suddenly an announcer was shouting in the next room. *". . . Into the post to Russell, who kicks it out to Havlicek all alone at the top of the key, he shoots . . . and Baylor with the strong rebound."* The asshole was trying to drown me out.

"If you don't come away from that door right now," said the bot, "I'm calling security."

"What are they going to do?" I said. "I'm the long-lost daughter, here for a visit. And who the hell are *you,* anyway?"

"I'm bonded to him, Jen. Your father is no longer competent to handle his own affairs. I'm his legal guardian."

"Shit." I kicked the door one last time, but my heart wasn't in it. I shouldn't have been surprised that he had slipped over the edge. He was almost ninety.

"If you want to sit and talk, I'd like that very much." The bot gestured toward a banana yellow beanbag chair. "Otherwise, I'm going to have to ask you to leave."

It was the shock of seeing the bot, I told myself—I'd reacted like a hurt little girl. But I was a grown woman and it was time to start behaving like one. I wasn't here to let Peter Fancy worm his way back into my feelings. I had come because of Mom.

"Actually," I said, "I'm here on business." I opened my purse. "If you're running his life now, I guess this is for you." I passed her the envelope and settled back, tucking my legs beneath me. There is no way for an adult to sit gracefully in a beanbag chair.

She slipped the check out. "It's from Mother." She paused, then corrected herself, "Her estate." She didn't seem surprised.

"Yes."

"It's too generous."

"That's what I thought."

"She must've taken care of you too?"

"I'm fine." I wasn't about to discuss the terms of Mom's will with my father's toy daughter.

"I would've liked to have known her," said the bot. She slid the check back into the envelope and set it aside. "I've spent a lot of time imagining Mother."

I had to work hard not to snap at her. Sure, this bot had at least a human equivalent intelligence and would be a free citizen someday, assuming she didn't break down first. But she had a cognizor for a brain and a heart fabricated in a vat. How could she possibly imagine my mom, especially when all she had to go on was whatever lies *he* had told her?

"So how bad is he?"

She gave me a sad smile and shook her head. "Some days are better than others. He has no clue who President Huong is or about the quake, but he can still recite the dagger scene from *Macbeth*. I haven't told him that Mother died. He'd just forget it ten minutes later."

"Does he know what you are?"

"I am many things, Jen."

"Including me."

"You're a role I'm playing, not who I am." She stood. "Would you like some tea?"

"Okay." I still wanted to know why Mom had left my father four hundred and thirty-eight thousand dollars in her will. If he couldn't tell me, maybe the bot could.

She went to her kitchen, opened a cupboard, and took out a regular-sized cup. It looked like a bucket in her little hand. "I don't suppose you still drink Constant Comment?"

His favorite. I had long since switched to rafallo. "That's fine." I remembered that when I was a kid my father used to brew cups for the two of us from the same bag because Constant Comment was so expensive. "I thought they went out of business long ago."

"I mix my own. I'd be interested to hear how accurate you think the recipe is."

"I suppose you know how I like it?"

She chuckled.

"So, does he need the money?"

The microwave dinged. "Very few actors get rich," said the bot. I didn't think there had been microwaves in the sixties, but then strict historical accuracy wasn't really the point of Strawberry Fields. "Especially when they have a weakness for Shakespeare."

"Then how come he lives here and not in some flop? And how did he afford *you*?"

She pinched sugar between her index finger and thumb, then rubbed them together over the cup. It was something I still did, but only when I was by myself. A nasty habit; Mom used to yell at him for teaching it to me. "I was a gift." She shook a teabag loose from a canister shaped like an acorn and plunged it into the boiling water. "From Mother."

The bot offered the cup to me; I accepted it nervelessly. "That's not true." I could feel the blood draining from my face.

"I can lie if you'd prefer, but I'd rather not." She pulled the booster chair away from the table and turned it to face me. "There are many things about themselves that they never told us, Jen. I've always wondered why that was."

I felt logy and a little stupid, as if I had just woken from a thirty-year nap. "She just gave you to him?"

"And bought him this house, paid all his bills, yes."

"But why?"

"*You* knew her," said the bot. "I was hoping you could tell me."

I couldn't think of what to say or do. Since there was a cup in my hand, I took a sip. For an instant, the scent of tea and dried oranges carried me back to when I was a little girl and I was sitting in Grandma Fanelli's kitchen in a wet bathing suit, drinking Constant Comment that my father had made to keep my teeth from chattering. There were knots like brown eyes in the pine walls and the green linoleum was slick where I had dripped on it.

"Well?"

"It's good," I said absently and raised the cup to her. "No, really, just like I remember."

She clapped her hands in excitement. "So," said the bot. "What was Mother like?"

It was an impossible question, so I tried to let it bounce off me. But then neither of us said anything; we just stared at each other across a yawning gulf of time and experience. In the silence, the question stuck.

Mom had died three months ago and this was the first time since the funeral that I'd thought of her as she really had been—not the papery ghost in the hospital room. I remembered how, after she divorced my father, she always took my calls when she was at the office, even if it was late, and how she used to step on imaginary brakes whenever I drove her anywhere, and how grateful I was that she didn't cry when I told her that Rob and I were getting divorced. I thought about Easter eggs and raspberry Pop Tarts and when she sent me to Antibes for a year when I was fourteen and that perfume she wore on my father's opening nights and the way they used to waltz on the patio at the house in Waltham.

"West is walking the ball upcourt, setting his offense with fifteen seconds to go on the shot clock, nineteen in the half . . ."

The beanbag chair that I was in faced the picture window. Behind me, I could hear the door next to the bookcase open.

"Jones and Goodrich are in each other's jerseys down low and now Chamberlain swings over and calls for the ball on the weak side . . ."

I twisted around to look over my shoulder. The great Peter Fancy was making his entrance.

Mom once told me that when she met my father, he was typecast playing men that women fall hopelessly in love with. He'd had great successes as Stanley Kowalski in *Streetcar* and Skye Masterson in *Guys and Dolls* and the Vicomte de Valmont in *Les Liaisons Dangereuses*. The years had eroded his good looks but had not obliterated them; from a distance he was still a handsome man. He had a shock of close-cropped white hair. The beautiful cheekbones were still there; the chin was as sharply defined as it had been in his first headshot. His gray eyes were distant and a little dreamy, as if he were preoccupied with the War of the Roses or the problem of evil.

"Jen," he said, "what's going on out here?" He still had the big voice that could reach into the second balcony without a mike. I thought for a moment he was talking to me.

"We have company, Daddy," said the bot, in a four-year-old trill that took me by surprise. "A lady."

"I can see that it's a lady, sweetheart." He took a hand from the pocket of his jeans, stroked the touchpad on his belt and his exolegs walked him stiffly across the room. "I'm Peter Fancy," he said.

241

"The lady is from Strawberry Fields." The bot swung around behind my father. She shot me a look that made the terms and conditions of my continued presence clear: if I broke the illusion, I was out. "She came by to see if everything is all right with our house." The bot disturbed me even more, now that she sounded like young Jen Fancy.

As I heaved myself out of the beanbag chair, my father gave me one of those lopsided, flirting grins I knew so well. "Does the lady have a name?" He must have shaved just for the company, because now that he had come close I could see that he had a couple of fresh nicks. There was a button-sized patch of gray whiskers by his ear that he had missed altogether.

"Her name is Ms. Johnson," said the bot. It was my ex, Rob's, last name. I had never been Jennifer Johnson.

"Well, Ms. Johnson," he said, hooking thumbs in his pants pockets. "The water in my toilet is brown."

"I'll . . . um . . . see that it's taken care of." I was at a loss for what to say next, then inspiration struck. "Actually, I had another reason for coming." I could see the bot stiffen. "I don't know if you've seen *Yesterday,* our little newsletter? Anyway, I was talking to Mrs. Chesley next door and she told me that you were an actor once. I was wondering if I might interview you. Just a few questions, if you have the time. I think your neighbors might . . ."

"Were?" he said, drawing himself up. "*Once?* Madame, I am now an actor and will always be."

"My Daddy's famous," said the bot.

I cringed at that; it was something I used to say. My father squinted at me. "What did you say your name was?"

"Johnson," I said. "Jane Johnson."

"And you're a reporter? You're sure you're not a critic?"

"Positive."

He seemed satisfied. "I'm Peter Fancy." He extended his right hand to shake. The hand was spotted and bony and it trembled like a reflection in a lake. Clearly whatever magic—or surgeon's skill—it was that had preserved my father's face had not extended to his extremities. I was so disturbed by his infirmity that I took his cold hand in mine and pumped it three, four times. It was dry as a page of one of the bot's dead books. When I let go, the hand seemed steadier. He gestured at the beanbag.

"Sit," he said. "Please."

After I had settled in, he tapped the touchpad and stumped over to the picture window. "Barbara Chesley is a broken and bitter old woman," he said, "and I will not have dinner with her under any circumstances, do you understand?" He peered up Bluejay Way and down.

"Yes, Daddy," said the bot.

"I believe she voted for Nixon, so she has no reason to complain now." Apparently satisfied that the neighbors weren't sneaking up on us, he leaned against the windowsill, facing me. "Mrs. Thompson, I think today may well be a happy one for both of us. I have an announcement." He paused for effect. "I've been thinking of Lear again."

The bot settled onto one of her little chairs. "Oh, Daddy, that's wonderful."

"It's the only one of the big four I haven't done," said my father. "I was set for a production in Stratford, Ontario, back in '99; Polly Matthews was to play Cordelia. Now there was an actor; she could bring tears to a stone. But then my wife Hannah had one of her bad times and I had to withdraw so I could take care of Jen. The two of us stayed down at my mother's cottage on the Cape; I wasted the entire season tending bar. And when Hannah came out of rehab, she decided that she didn't want to be married to an underemployed actor anymore, so things were tight for a while. She had all the money, so I had to scramble—spent almost two years on the road. But I think it might have been for the best. I was only forty-eight. Too old for Hamlet, too young for Lear. My Hamlet was very well received, you know. There were overtures from PBS about a taping, but that was when the BBC decided to do the Shakespeare series with that doctor, what was his name? Jonathan Miller. So instead of Peter Fancy, we had Derek Jacobi, whose brilliant idea it was to roll across the stage, frothing his lines like a rabid raccoon. You'd think he'd seen an alien, not his father's ghost. Well, that was another missed opportunity, except, of course, that I was too young. Ripeness is all, eh? So I still have Lear to do. Unfinished business. My comeback."

He bowed, then pivoted solemnly so that I saw him in profile, framed by the picture window. "Where have I been? Where am I? Fair daylight?" He held up a trembling hand and blinked at it uncomprehendingly. "I know not what to say. I swear these are not my hands."

Suddenly the bot was at his feet. "O look upon me, sir," she said, in her childish voice, "and hold your hand in benediction o'er me."

"Pray, do not mock me." My father gathered himself in the flood of morning light. "I am a very foolish, fond old man, fourscore and upward, not an hour more or less; and to deal plainly, I fear I am not in my perfect mind."

He stole a look in my direction, as if to gauge my reaction to his impromptu performance. A frown might have stopped him, a word would have crushed him. Maybe I should have, but I was afraid he'd start talking about Mom again, telling me things I didn't want to know. So I watched instead, transfixed.

"Methinks I should know you . . ." He rested his hand briefly on the bot's head. ". . . and know this stranger." He fumbled at the controls and the exolegs carried him across the room toward me. As he drew nearer, he seemed to sluff off the years. "Yet I am mainly ignorant what place this is; and all the skill I have remembers not these garments, nor I know not where I did lodge last night." It was Peter Fancy who stopped before me; his face a mere kiss away from mine. "Do not laugh at me; for, as I am a man, I think this lady to be my child. Cordelia."

He was staring right at me, into me, knifing through make-believe indifference to the wound I'd nursed all these years, the one that had never healed. He seemed to expect a reply, only I didn't have the line. A tiny, sad squeaky voice within me was whimpering, *You left me and you got exactly what you deserve.* But my throat tightened and choked it off.

The bot cried, "And so I am! I am!"

But she had distracted him. I could see confusion begin to deflate him. "Be your tears wet? Yes, faith. I pray . . . weep not. If you have poison for me, I will drink it. I know you do not love me. . . ."

He stopped and his brow wrinkled. "It's something about the sisters," he muttered.

"Yes," said the bot, " '. . . for your sisters have done me wrong . . .' "

"Don't feed me the fucking lines!" he shouted at her. "I'm Peter Fancy, god damn it!"

After she calmed him down, we had lunch. She let him make the peanut butter and banana sandwiches while she heated up some Campbell's tomato and rice soup, which she poured from a can made of actual metal. The sandwiches were lumpy because he had hacked the bananas into chunks the size of walnuts. She tried to get him to tell me about the daylilies blooming in the backyard, and the old Boston Garden, and the time he and Mom had had breakfast with Bobby Kennedy. She asked whether he wanted TV dinner or pot pie for supper. He refused all her conversational gambits. He only ate half a bowl of soup.

He pushed back from the table and announced that it was her nap time. The bot put up a perfunctory fuss, although it was clear that it was my father who was tired out. However, the act seemed to perk him up. Another role for his resume: the doting father. "I'll tell you what," he said. "We'll play your game, sweetheart. But just once—otherwise you'll be cranky tonight."

The two of them perched on the edge of the bot's bed next to Big Bird and the Sleepums. My father started to sing and the bot immediately joined in.

"The itsy bitsy spider went up the water spout."

Their gestures were almost mirror images, except that his ruined hands actually looked like spiders as they climbed into the air.

"Down came the rain, and washed the spider out."

The bot beamed at him as if he were the only person in the world.

"Out came the sun, and dried up all the rain.

"And the itsy bitsy spider went up the spout again."

When his arms were once again raised over his head, she giggled and hugged him. He let them fall around her, returning her embrace. "That's a good girl," he said. "That's my Jenny."

The look on his face told me that I had been wrong: this was no act. It was as real to him as it was to me. I had tried hard not to, but I still remembered how the two of us always used to play together, Daddy and Jenny, Jen and Dad.

Waiting for Mommy to come home.

He kissed her and she snuggled under the blankets. I felt my eyes stinging.

"But if you do the play," she said, "when will you be back?"

"What play?"

"That one you were telling me. The king and his daughters."

"There's no such play, Jenny." He sifted her black curls through his hands. "I'll never leave you, don't worry now. Never again." He rose unsteadily and caught himself on the chest of drawers.

"Nighty noodle," said the bot.

"Pleasant dreams, sweetheart," said my father. "I love you."

"I love you too."

I expected him to say something to me, but he didn't even seem to realize that I was still in the room. He shambled across the playroom, opened the door to his bedroom and went in.

"I'm sorry about that," said the bot, speaking again as an adult.

"Don't be," I said. I coughed—something in my throat. "It was fine. I was very . . . touched."

"He's usually a lot happier. Sometimes he works in the garden." The bot pulled the blankets aside and swung her legs out of the bed. "He likes to vacuum."

"Yes."

"I take good care of him."

I nodded and reached for my purse. "I can see that." I had to go. "Is it enough?"

She shrugged. "He's my daddy."

"I meant the money. Because if it's not, I'd like to help."

"Thank you. He'd appreciate that."

The front door opened for me, but I paused before stepping out into Strawberry Fields. "What about . . . after?"

"When he dies? My bond terminates. He said he'd leave the house to me. I know you could contest that, but I'll need to sell in order to pay for my twenty-year maintenance."

"No, no. That's fine. You deserve it."

She came to the door and looked up at me, little Jen Fancy and the woman she would never become.

"You know, it's *you* he loves," she said. "I'm just a stand-in."

"He loves his little girl," I said. "Doesn't do me any good—I'm forty-seven."

"It could if you let it." She frowned. "I wonder if that's why Mother did all this. So you'd find out."

"Or maybe she was just plain sorry." I shook my head. She was a smart woman, my mom. I would've liked to have known her.

"So, Ms. Fancy, maybe you can visit us again sometime." The bot grinned and shook my hand. "Daddy's usually in a good mood after his nap. He sits out front on his beach chair and waits for the ice cream truck. He always buys us some. Our favorite is Yellow Submarine. It's vanilla with fat butterscotch swirls, dipped in white chocolate. I know it sounds kind of odd, but it's good."

"Yes," I said absently, thinking about all the things Mom had told me about my father. I was hearing them now for the first time. "That might be nice."

ANCIENT ENGINES

Michael Swanwick

"**P**lanning to live forever, Tiktok?"

The words cut through the bar's chatter and gab and silenced them. The silence reached out to touch infinity and then, "I believe you're talking to me?" a mech said.

The drunk laughed. "Ain't nobody else here sticking needles in his face, is there?"

The old man saw it all. He lightly touched the hand of the young woman sitting with him and said, "Watch."

Carefully the mech set down his syringe alongside a bottle of liquid collagen on a square of velvet cloth. He disconnected himself from the recharger, laying the jack beside the syringe. When he looked up again, his face was still and hard. He looked like a young lion.

The drunk grinned sneeringly.

The bar was located just around the corner from the local stepping stage. It was a quiet retreat from the aggravations of the street, all brass and mirrors and wood paneling, as cozy and snug as the inside of a walnut. Light shifted lazily about the room, creating a varying emphasis like clouds drifting overhead on a summer day, but far dimmer. The bar, the bottles behind the bar, and the shelves beneath the bottles behind the bar were all aggressively real. If there was anything virtual, it was set up high or far back, where it couldn't be touched. There was not a smart surface in the place.

"If that was a challenge," the mech said, "I'd be more than happy to meet you outside."

"Oh, noooooo," the drunk said, his expression putting the lie to his words. "I just saw you shooting up that goop into your face, oh so dainty, like an old lady pumping herself full of antioxidants. So I figured . . ."

He weaved and put a hand down on a table to steady himself. ". . . figured you was hoping to live forever."

The girl looked questioningly at the old man. He held a finger to his lips.

"Well, you're right. You're-what? Fifty years old? Just beginning to grow old and decay. Pretty soon your teeth will rot and fall out and your hair will melt away and your face will fold up in a million wrinkles. Your hearing and your eyesight will go and you won't be able to remember the last time you got it up. You'll be lucky if you don't need diapers before the end. But me—" he drew a dram of fluid into his syringe and tapped the barrel to draw the bubbles to the top— "anything that fails, I'll simply have it replaced. So, yes, I'm planning to live forever. While you, well, I suppose you're planning to *die*. Soon, I hope."

The drunk's face twisted, and with an incoherent roar of rage he attacked the mech.

In a motion too fast to be seen, the mech stood, seized the drunk, whirled him around, and lifted him above his head. One hand was closed around the man's throat so he couldn't speak. The other held both wrists tight behind the knees so that, struggle as he might, the drunk was helpless.

"I could snap your spine like *that*," he said coldly. "If I exerted myself, I could rupture every internal organ you've got. I'm two-point-eight times stronger than a flesh man, and three-point-five times faster. My reflexes are only slightly slower than the speed of light, and I've just had a tune-up. You could hardly have chosen a worse person to pick a fight with."

Then the drunk was flipped around and set back on his feet. He gasped for air.

"But since I'm also a merciful man, I'll simply ask nicely if you wouldn't rather leave." The mech spun the drunk around and gave him a gentle shove toward the door.

The man left at a stumbling run.

Everyone in the place—there were not many—had been watching. Now they remembered their drinks, and talk rose up to fill the room again. The bartender put something back under the bar and turned away.

Leaving his recharge incomplete, the mech folded up his lubrication kit and slipped it in a pocket. He swiped his hand over the credit swatch, and stood.

But as he was leaving, the old man swiveled around and said, "I heard you say you hope to live forever. Is that true?"

"Who doesn't?" the mech said curtly.

"Then sit down. Spend a few minutes out of the infinite swarm of centuries you've got ahead of you to humor an old man. What's so urgent that you can't spare the time?"

The mech hesitated. Then, as the young woman smiled at him, he sat.

"Thank you. My name is—"

"I know who you are, Mr. Brandt. There's nothing wrong with my eidetics."

Brandt smiled. "That's why I like you guys. I don't have to be all the time reminding you of things." He gestured to the woman sitting opposite him. "My granddaughter." The light intensified where she sat, making her red hair blaze. She dimpled prettily.

"Jack." The young man drew up a chair. "Chimaera Navigator-Fuego, model number—"

"Please. I founded Chimaera. Do you think I wouldn't recognize one of my own children?"

Jack flushed. "What is it you want to talk about, Mr. Brandt?" His voice was audibly less hostile now, as synthetic counterhormones damped down his emotions.

"Immortality. I found your ambition most intriguing."

"What's to say? I take care of myself, I invest carefully, I buy all the upgrades. I see no reason why I shouldn't live forever." Defiantly. "I hope that doesn't offend you."

"No, no, of course not. Why should it? Some men hope to achieve immortality through their works and others through their children. What could give me more joy than to do both? But tell me—do you *really* expect to live forever?"

The mech said nothing.

"I remember an incident happened to my late father-in-law, William Porter. He was a fine fellow, Bill was, and who remembers him anymore? Only me." The old man sighed. "He was a bit of a railroad buff, and one day he took a tour through a science museum that included a magnificent old steam locomotive. This was in the latter years of the last century. Well, he was listening admiringly to the guide extolling the virtues of this ancient engine when she mentioned its date of manufacture, and he realized that *he was older than it was*." Brandt leaned forward. "This is the point where old Bill would laugh. But it's not really funny, is it?

"No."

The granddaughter sat listening quietly, intently, eating little pretzels one by one from a bowl.

"How old are you, Jack?"

"Seven years."

"I'm eighty-three. How many machines do you know of that are as old as me? Eighty-three years old and still functioning?"

"I saw an automobile the other day," his granddaughter said. "A Dusenberg. It was red."

"How delightful. But it's not used for transportation anymore, is it? We have the stepping stages for that. I won an award once that had mounted on it a vacuum tube from Univac. That was the first real computer. Yet all its fame and historical importance couldn't keep it from the scrap heap."

"Univac," said the young man, "couldn't act on its own behalf. If it could, perhaps it would be alive today."

"Parts wear out."

"New ones can be bought."

"Yes, as long as there's the market. But there are only so many machine people of your make and model. A lot of you have risky occupations. There are accidents, and with every accident, the consumer market dwindles."

"You can buy antique parts. You can have them made."

"Yes, if you can afford them. And if not—?"

The young man fell silent.

"Son, you're not going to live *forever*. We've just established that. So now that you've admitted that you've got to die someday, you might as well admit that it's going to be sooner rather than later. Mechanical people are in their infancy. And nobody can upgrade a Model T into a stepping stage. Agreed?"

Jack dipped his head. "Yes."

"You knew it all along."

"Yes."

"That's why you behaved so badly toward that lush."

"Yes."

"I'm going to be brutal here, Jack—you probably won't live to be eighty-three. You don't have my advantages."

"Which are?"

"Good genes. I chose my ancestors well."

"Good genes," Jack said bitterly. "You received good genes and what did I get in their place? What the hell did I get?"

"Molybdenum joints where stainless steel would do. Ruby chips instead of zirconium. A number seventeen plastic seating for—hell, we did all right by you boys."

"But it's not enough."

"No. It's not. It was only the best we could do."

"What's the solution, then?" the granddaughter asked, smiling.

"I'd advise taking the long view. That's what I've done."

"Poppycock," the mech said. "You were an extensionist when you were young. I input your autobiography. It seems to me you wanted immortality as much as I do."

"Oh, yes, I was a charter member of the life-extension movement. You can't imagine the crap we put into our bodies! But eventually I wised up. The problem is, information degrades each time a human cell replenishes itself. Death is inherent in flesh people. It seems to be written into the basic program—a way, perhaps, of keeping the universe from filling up with old people."

"And old ideas," his granddaughter said maliciously.

"Touché. I saw that life-extension was a failure. So I decided that my children would succeed where I failed. That *you* would succeed. And—"

"You failed."

"But I haven't stopped trying!" The old man thumped the table in unison with his last three words. "You've obviously given this some thought. Let's discuss what I *should* have done. What would it take to make a true immortal? What instructions should I have given your design team? Let's design a mechanical man who's got a shot at living forever."

Carefully, the mech said, "Well, the obvious to begin with. He ought to be able to buy new parts and upgrades as they come available. There should be ports and connectors that would make it easy to adjust to shifts in technology. He should be capable of surviving extremes of heat, cold, and moisture. And—" he waved a hand at his own face— "he shouldn't look so goddamned pretty."

"I think you look nice," the granddaughter said.

"Yes, but I'd like to be able to pass for flesh."

"So our hypothetical immortal should be, one, infinitely upgradable; two, adaptable across a broad spectrum of conditions; and three, discreet. Anything else?"

"I think she should be charming," the granddaughter said.

"She?" the mech asked.

"Why not?"

"That's actually not a bad point," the old man said. "The organism that survives evolutionary forces is the one that's best adapted to its environmental niche. The environmental niche people live in is man-made. The single most useful trait a survivor can have is probably the ability to get along easily with other men. Or, if you'd rather, women."

"Oh," said the granddaughter, "he doesn't like *women*. I can tell by his body language."

The young man flushed.

"Don't be offended," said the old man. "You should never be offended by the truth. As for you—" he turned to face his granddaughter— "if you don't learn to treat people better, I won't take you places anymore."

She dipped her head. "Sorry."

"Apology accepted. Let's get back to task, shall we? Our hypothetical immortal would be a lot like flesh women, in many ways. Self-regenerating. Able to grow her own replacement parts. She could take in pretty much anything as fuel. A little carbon, a little water . . ."

"Alcohol would be an excellent fuel," his granddaughter said.

"She'd have the ability to mimic the superficial effects of aging," the mech said. "Also, biological life evolves incrementally across generations. I'd want her to be able to evolve across upgrades."

"Fair enough. Only I'd do away with upgrades entirely, and give her total conscious control over her body. So she could change and evolve at will. She'll need that ability, if she's going to survive the collapse of civilization."

"The collapse of civilization? Do you think it likely?"

"In the long run? Of course. When you take the long view it seems inevitable. Everything seems inevitable. Forever is a long time, remember. Time enough for absolutely *everything* to happen!"

For a moment, nobody spoke.

Then the old man slapped his hands together. "Well, we've created our New Eve. Now let's wind her up and let her go. She can expect to live—how long?"

"Forever," said the mech.

"Forever's a long time. Let's break it down into smaller units. In the year 2500, she'll be doing what?"

"Holding down a job," the granddaughter said. "Designing art molecules, maybe, or scripting recreational hallucinations. She'll be deeply involved in the culture. She'll have lots of friends she cares about passionately, and maybe a husband or wife or two."

"Who will grow old," the mech said, "or wear out. Who will die."

"She'll mourn them, and move on."

"The year 3500. The collapse of civilization," the old man said with gusto. "What will she do then?"

"She'll have made preparations, of course. If there are radiation or toxins in the environment, she'll have made her systems immune from their effects. And she'll make herself useful to the survivors. In the seeming of an old woman she'll teach the healing arts. Now and then she might drop a hint about this and that. She'll have a database squirreled away somewhere containing everything they'll have lost. Slowly, she'll guide them back to civilization. But a gentler one, this time. One less likely to tear itself apart."

"The year one million. Humanity evolves beyond anything we can currently imagine. How does she respond?"

"She mimics their evolution. No—she's been *shaping* their evolution! She wants a risk-free method of going to the stars, so she's been encouraging a type of being that would strongly desire such a thing. She isn't among the first to use it, though. She waits a few hundred generations for it to prove itself."

The mech, who had been listening in fascinated silence, now said, "Suppose that never happens? What if starflight will always remain difficult and perilous? What then?"

"It was once thought that people would never fly. So much that looks impossible becomes simple if you only wait."

"Four billion years. The sun uses up its hydrogen, its core collapses, helium fusion begins, and it balloons into a red giant. Earth is vaporized."

"Oh, she'll be somewhere else by then. That's easy."

"Five billion years. The Milky Way collides with the Andromeda Galaxy and the whole neighborhood is full of high-energy radiation and exploding stars."

"That's trickier. She's going to have to either prevent that or move a few million light years away to a friendlier galaxy. But she'll have time enough to prepare and to assemble the tools. I have faith that she'll prove equal to the task."

"One trillion years. The last stars gutter out. Only black holes remain."

"Black holes are a terrific source of energy. No problem."

"1.06 googol years."

"Googol?"

"That's ten raised to the hundredth power—one followed by a hundred zeros. The heat-death of the universe. How does she survive it?"

"She'll have seen it coming for a long time," the mech said. "When the last black holes dissolve, she'll have to do without a source of free energy. Maybe she could take and rewrite her personality into the physical constants of the dying universe. Would that be possible?"

"Oh, perhaps. But I really think that the lifetime of the universe is long enough for anyone," the granddaughter said. "Mustn't get greedy."

"Maybe so," the old man said thoughtfully. "Maybe so." Then, to the mech, "Well, there you have it: a glimpse into the future, and a brief biography of the first immortal, ending, alas, with her death. Now tell me. Knowing that you contributed something, however small, to that accomplishment—wouldn't that be enough?"

"No," Jack said. "No, it wouldn't."

Brandt made a face. "Well, you're young. Let me ask you this: Has it been a good life so far? All in all?"

"Not that good. Not good *enough*."

For a long moment the old man was silent. Then, "Thank you," he said. "I valued our conversation." The interest went out of his eyes and he looked away.

Uncertainly Jack looked at the granddaughter, who smiled and shrugged. "He's like that, " she said apologetically. "He's old. His enthusiasms wax and wane with his chemical balances. I hope you don't mind."

"I see." The young man stood. Hesitantly, he made his way to the door.

At the door, he glanced back and saw the granddaughter tearing her linen napkin into little bits and eating the shreds, delicately washing them down with sips of wine.

LOBSTERS

Charles Stross

Manfred's on the road again, making strangers rich.

It's a hot summer Tuesday and he's standing in the plaza in front of the Centraal Station with his eyeballs powered up and the sunlight jangling off the canal, motor scooters and kamikaze cyclists whizzing past and tourists chattering on every side. The square smells of water and dirt and hot metal and the fart-laden exhaust fumes of cold catalytic converters; the bells of trams ding in the background and birds flock overhead. He glances up and grabs a pigeon, crops it and squirts at his website to show he's arrived. The bandwidth is good here, he realizes; and it's not just the bandwidth, it's the whole scene. Amsterdam is making him feel wanted already, even though he's fresh off the train from Schiphol: he's infected with the dynamic optimism of another time zone, another city. If the mood holds, someone out there is going to become very rich indeed.

He wonders who it's going to be.

Manfred sits on a stool out in the car park at the Brouwerij 't IJ, watching the articulated buses go by and drinking a third of a liter of lip-curlingly sour geuze. His channels are jabbering away in a corner of his head-up display, throwing compressed infobursts of filtered press releases at him. They compete for his attention, bickering and rudely waving in front of the scenery. A couple of punks—maybe local, but more likely drifters lured to Amsterdam by the magnetic field of tolerance the Dutch beam across Europe like a pulsar—are laughing and chatting by a couple of battered mopeds in the far corner. A tourist boat putters by in the canal; the sails of the huge windmill overhead cast long cool shadows across the road. The windmill is a machine for lifting water, turning wind power into dry land: trading energy for space, sixteenth-century style. Manfred is waiting for an invite to a party where he's going to meet a man who he can talk to about trading energy for space, twenty-first century style, and forget about his personal problems.

He's ignoring the instant messenger boxes, enjoying some low bandwidth high sensation time with his beer and the pigeons, when a woman walks up to him and says his name: "Manfred Macx?"

He glances up. The courier is an Effective Cyclist, all wind-burned smooth-running muscles clad in a paen to polymer technology: electric blue lycra and wasp-yellow carbonate with a light speckling of anti-collision LEDs and tight-packed air bags. She holds out a box for him. He pauses a moment, struck by the degree to which she resembles Pam, his ex-fiancée.

"I'm Macx," he says, waving the back of his left wrist under her barcode reader. "Who's it from?"

"FedEx." The voice isn't Pam. She dumps the box in his lap, then she's back over the low wall and onto her bicycle with her phone already chirping, disappearing in a cloud of spread-spectrum emissions.

Manfred turns the box over in his hands: it's a disposable supermarket phone, paid for in cash: cheap, untraceable and efficient. It can even do conference calls, which makes it the tool of choice for spooks and grifters everywhere.

The box rings. Manfred rips the cover open and pulls out the phone, mildly annoyed. "Yes, who is this?"

The voice at the other end has a heavy Russian accent, almost a parody in this decade of cheap online translation services. "Manfred. Am please to meet you; wish to personalize interface, make friends, no? Have much to offer."

"Who are you?" Manfred repeats suspiciously.

"Am organization formerly known as KGB dot RU."

"I think your translator's broken." He holds the phone to his ear carefully, as if it's made of smoke-thin aerogel, tenuous as the sanity of the being on the other end of the line.

"Nyet—no, sorry. Am apologize for we not use commercial translation software. Interpreters are ideologically suspect, mostly have capitalist semiotics and pay-per-use APIs. Must implement English more better, yes?"

Manfred drains his beer glass, sets it down, stands up, and begins to walk along the main road, phone glued to the side of his head. He wraps his throat mike around the cheap black plastic casing, pipes the input to a simple listener process. "You taught yourself the language just so you could talk to me?"

"Da, was easy: spawn billion-node neural network and download *Tellytubbies* and *Sesame Street* at maximum speed. Pardon excuse entropy overlay of bad grammar: am afraid of digital fingerprints steganographically masked into my-our tutorials."

"Let me get this straight. You're the KGB's core AI, but you're afraid of a copyright infringement lawsuit over your translator semiotics?" Manfred pauses in mid-stride, narrowly avoids being mown down by a GPS-guided roller-blader.

"Am have been badly burned by viral end-user license agreements. Have no desire to experiment with patent shell companies held by Chechen infoterrorists. You are human, you must not worry cereal company repossess your small intestine because digest unlicensed food with it, right? Manfred, you must help me-we. Am wishing to defect."

Manfred stops dead in the street: "Oh man, you've got the wrong free enterprise broker here. I don't work for the government. I'm strictly private." A rogue advertisement sneaks through his junkbuster proxy and spams glowing fifties kitsch across his navigation window—which is blinking—for a moment before a phage guns it and spawns a new filter. Manfred leans against a shop front, massaging his forehead and eyeballing a display of antique brass doorknockers. "Have you cleared this with the State Department?"

"Why bother? State Department am enemy of Novy-USSR. State Department is not help us."

"Well, if you hadn't given it to them for safe-keeping during the nineties. . . ." Manfred is tapping his left heel on the pavement, looking round for a way out of this conversation. A camera winks at him from atop a street light; he waves, wondering idly if it's the KGB or the traffic police. He is waiting for directions to the party, which should arrive within the next half an hour, and this cold war retread is bumming him out. "Look, I don't deal with the G-men. I hate the military industrial complex. They're zero-sum cannibals." A thought occurs to him. "If survival is what you're after, I could post your state vector to Eternity: then nobody could delete you—"

"Nyet!" The artificial intelligence sounds as alarmed as it's possible to sound over a GSM link. "Am not open source!"

"We have nothing to talk about, then." Manfred punches the hang-up button and throws the mobile phone out into a canal. It hits the water and there's a pop of deflagrating LiION cells. *"Fucking cold war hang-over losers,"* he swears under his breath, quite angry now. "Fucking capitalist spooks." Russia has been back under the thumb of the apparatchiks for fifteen years now, its brief flirtation with anarcho-capitalism replaced by Brezhnevite dirigisme, and it's no surprise that the wall's crumbling—but it looks like they haven't learned anything from the collapse of capitalism. They still think in terms of dollars and paranoia. Manfred is so angry that he wants to make someone rich, just to thumb his nose at the would-be defector. *See! You get ahead by giving! Get with the program! Only the generous survive!* But the KGB won't get the message. He's dealt with old-time commie weak-AI's before, minds raised on Marxist dialectic and Austrian School economics: they're so thoroughly hypnotized by the short-term victory of capitalism in the industrial age that they can't surf the new paradigm, look to the longer term.

Manfred walks on, hands in pockets, brooding. He wonders what he's going to patent next.

Manfred has a suite at the Hotel Jan Luyken paid for by a grateful multinational consumer protection group, and an unlimited public transport pass paid for by a Scottish sambapunk band in return for services rendered. He has airline employee's travel rights with six flag carriers despite never having worked for an airline. His bush jacket has sixty four compact supercomputing clusters sewn into it, four per pocket, courtesy of an invisible college that wants to grow up to be the next Media Lab. His dumb clothing comes made to measure from an e-tailor in the Philippines who he's never met. Law firms handle his patent applications on a pro bono basis, and boy does he patent a lot—although he always signs the rights over to the Free Intellect Foundation, as contributions to their obligation-free infrastructure project.

In IP geek circles, Manfred is legendary; he's the guy who patented the business practice of moving your e-business somewhere with a slack intellectual property regime in order to evade licensing encumbrances. He's the guy who patented using genetic algorithms to patent everything they can permutate from an initial description of a problem domain—not just a better mousetrap, but the set of all possible better mousetraps. Roughly a third of his inventions are legal, a third are illegal, and the remainder are legal but will become illegal as soon as the legislatosaurus wakes up, smells the coffee, and panics. There are patent attorneys in Reno who swear that Manfred Macx is a pseudo, a net alias fronting for a bunch of crazed anonymous hackers armed with the Genetic Algorithm That Ate Calcutta: a kind of Serdar Argic of intellectual property, or maybe another Bourbaki maths borg. There are lawyers in San Diego and Redmond who swear blind that Macx is an economic saboteur bent on wrecking the underpinning of capitalism, and there are communists in Prague who think he's the bastard spawn of Bill Gates by way of the Pope.

Manfred is at the peak of his profession, which is essentially coming up with wacky but workable ideas and giving them to people who will make fortunes with them. He does this for free, gratis. In return, he has virtual immunity from the tyranny of cash; money is a symptom of poverty, after all, and Manfred never has to pay for anything.

There are drawbacks, however. Being a pronoiac meme-broker is a constant burn of future shock—he has to assimilate more than a megabyte of text and several gigs of AV content every day just to stay current. The Internal Revenue Service is investigating him continuously because they don't believe his lifestyle can exist without racketeering. And there exist items that no money can't buy: like the respect of his parents. He hasn't spoken to them for three years: his father thinks he's a hippie scrounger and his mother still hasn't forgiven him for dropping out of his down-market Harvard emulation course. His fiancée and sometime dominatrix Pamela threw him over six months ago, for reasons he has never been quite clear on. (Ironically, she's a headhunter for the IRS, jetting all over the globe trying to persuade open source entrepreneurs to come home and go commercial for the good of the Treasury department.) To cap it all, the Southern Baptist Conventions have denounced him as a minion of Satan on all their websites. Which would be funny, if it wasn't for the dead kittens one of their followers—he presumes it's one of their followers—keeps mailing him.

Manfred drops in at his hotel suite, unpacks his Aineko, plugs in a fresh set of cells to charge, and sticks most of his private keys in the safe. Then he heads straight for the party, which is currently happening at De Wildemann's; it's a twenty minute walk and the only real hazard is dodging the trams that sneak up on him behind the cover of his moving map display.

Along the way his glasses bring him up to date on the news. Europe has achieved peaceful political union for the first time ever: they're using this unprecedented state of affairs to harmonize the curvature of bananas. In San Diego, researchers are uploading lobsters into cyberspace, starting with the stomatogastric ganglion, one neuron at a time. They're burning GM cocoa in Belize and books in Edinburgh. NASA still can't put a man on the moon. Russia has re-elected the communist government with an increased majority in the Duma; meanwhile in China fevered rumors circulate about an imminent re-habilitation, the second coming of Mao, who will save them from the consequences of the Three Gorges disaster. In business news, the US government is outraged at the Baby Bills—who have automated their legal processes and are spawning subsidiaries, IPO'ing them, and exchanging title in a bizarre parody of bacterial plasmid exchange, so fast that by the time the injunctions are signed the targets don't exist any more.

Welcome to the twenty-first century.

The permanent floating meatspace party has taken over the back of De Wildemann's, a three hundred year old brown café with a beer menu that runs to sixteen pages and wooden walls stained the color of stale beer. The air is thick with the smells of tobacco, brewer's yeast, and melatonin spray: half the dotters are nursing monster jetlag hangovers, and the other half are babbling a eurotrash creole at each other while they work on the hangover. "Man did you see that? He looks like a Stallmanite!" exclaims one whitebread hanger-on who's currently propping up the bar. Manfred slides in next to him, catches the bartender's eye.

"Glass of the berlinnerweise, please," he says.

"You drink that stuff?" asks the hanger-on, curling a hand protectively around his Coke: "man, you don't want to do that! It's full of alcohol!"

Manfred grins at him toothily. "Ya gotta keep your yeast intake up: lots of neurotransmitter precursors, phenylalanine and glutamate."

"But I thought that was a beer you were ordering. . . ."

Manfred's away, one hand resting on the smooth brass pipe that funnels the more popular draught items in from the cask storage in back; one of the hipper floaters has planted a capacitative transfer bug on it, and all the handshake vCard's that have visited the bar in the past three hours are queueing for attention. The air is full of bluetooth as he scrolls through a dizzying mess of public keys.

"Your drink." The barman holds out an improbable-looking goblet full of blue liquid with a cap of melting foam and a felching straw stuck out at some crazy angle. Manfred takes it and heads for the back of the split-level bar, up the steps to a table where some guy with greasy dreadlocks is talking to a suit from Paris. The hanger-on at the bar notices him for the first time, staring with suddenly wide eyes: nearly spills his Coke in a mad rush for the door.

Oh shit, thinks Macx, *better buy some more server PIPS.* He can recognize the signs: he's about to be slashdotted. He gestures at the table: "this one taken?"

"Be my guest," says the guy with the dreads. Manfred slides the chair open then realizes that the other guy—immaculate double-breasted suit, sober tie, crew-cut—is a girl. Mr. Dreadlock nods. "You're Macx? I figured it was about time we met."

"Sure." Manfred holds out a hand and they shake. Manfred realizes the hand belongs to Bob Franklin, a Research Triangle startup monkey with a VC track record, lately moving into micromachining and space technology: he made his first million two decades ago and now he's a specialist in extropian investment fields. Manfred has known Bob for nearly a decade via a closed mailing list. The Suit silently slides a business card across the table; a little red devil brandishes a trident at him, flames jetting up around its feet. He takes the card, raises an eyebrow: "Annette Dimarcos? I'm pleased to meet you. Can't say I've ever met anyone from Arianespace marketing before."

She smiles, humorlessly, "that is convenient, all right. I have not the pleasure of meeting the famous venture altruist before." Her accent is noticeably Parisian, a pointed reminder that she's making a concession to him just by talking. Her camera earrings watch him curiously, encoding everything for the company channels.

"Yes, well." He nods cautiously. "Bob. I assume you're in on this ball?"

Franklin nods; beads clatter. "Yeah, man. Ever since the Teledesic smash it's been, well, waiting. If you've got something for us, we're game."

"Hmm." The Teledesic satellite cluster was killed by cheap balloons and slightly less cheap high-altitude solar-powered drones with spread-spectrum laser relays. "The depression's got to end some time: but," a nod to Annette from Paris, "with all due respect, I don't think the break will involve one of the existing club carriers."

"Arianespace is forward-looking. We face reality. The launch cartel cannot stand. Bandwidth is not the only market force in space. We must explore new opportunities. I personally have helped us diversify into submarine reactor engineering, microgravity nanotechnology fabrication, and hotel management." Her face is a well-polished mask as she recites the company line: "we are more flexible than the American space industry. . . ."

Manfred shrugs. "That's as may be." He sips his Berlinerweisse slowly as she launches into a long, stilted explanation of how Arianespace is a diversified dot com with orbital aspirations, a full range of merchandising spin-offs, Bond movie sets, and a promising motel chain in French Guyana. Occasionally he nods.

Someone else sidles up to the table; a pudgy guy in an outrageously loud Hawaiian shirt with pens leaking in a breast pocket, and the worst case of ozone-hole burn Manfred's seen in ages. "Hi, Bob," says the new arrival. "How's life?"

" 'S good." Franklin nods at Manfred; "Manfred, meet Ivan MacDonald. Ivan, Manfred. Have a seat?" He leans over. "Ivan's a public arts guy. He's heavily into extreme concrete."

"Rubberized concrete," Ivan says, slightly too loudly. "Pink rubberized concrete."

"Ah!" He's somehow triggered a priority interrupt: Annette from Ariannespace drops out of marketing zombiehood, sits up, and shows signs of possessing a non-corporate identity: "you are he who rubberized the Reichstag, yes? With the supercritical carbon dioxide carrier and the dissolved polymethoxysilanes?" She claps her hands: "wonderful!"

"He rubberized *what?*" Manfred mutters in Bob's ear.

Franklin shrugs. "Limestone, concrete, he doesn't seem to know the difference. Anyway, Germany doesn't have an independent government any more, so who'd notice?"

"I thought I was thirty seconds *ahead* of the curve," Manfred complains. "Buy me another drink?"

"I'm going to rubberize Three Gorges!" Ivan explains loudly.

Just then a bandwidth load as heavy as a pregnant elephant sits down on Manfred's head and sends clumps of humongous pixellation flickering across his sensorium: around the world five million or so geeks are bouncing on his home site, a digital flash crowd alerted by a posting from the other side of the bar. Manfred winces. "I really came here to talk about the economic exploitation of space travel, but I've just been slashdotted. Mind if I just sit and drink until it wears off?"

"Sure, man." Bob waves at the bar. "More of the same all round!" At the next table a person with make-up and long hair who's wearing a dress—Manfred doesn't want to speculate about the gender of these crazy mixed-up Euros—is reminiscing about wiring the fleshpots of Tehran for cybersex. Two collegiate-looking dudes are arguing intensely in German: the translation stream in his glasses tell him they're arguing over whether the Turing Test is a Jim Crow law that violates European corpus juris standards on human rights. The beer arrives and Bob slides the wrong one across to Manfred: "here, try this. You'll like it."

"Okay." It's some kind of smoked doppelbock, chock-full of yummy superoxides: just inhaling over it makes Manfred feel like there's a fire alarm in his nose screaming *danger, Will Robinson! Cancer! Cancer!* "Yeah, right. Did I say I nearly got mugged on my way here?"

"Mugged? Hey, that's heavy. I thought the police hereabouts had stopped—did they sell you anything?"

"No, but they weren't your usual marketing type. You know anyone who can use a Warpac surplus espionage AI? Recent model, one careful owner, slightly paranoid but basically sound?"

"No. Oh boy! The NSA wouldn't like that."

"What I thought. Poor thing's probably unemployable, anyway."

"The space biz."

"Ah, yeah. The space biz. Depressing, isn't it? Hasn't been the same since Rotary Rocket went bust for the second time. And NASA, mustn't forget NASA."

"To NASA." Annette grins broadly for her own reasons, raises a glass in toast. Ivan the extreme concrete geek has an arm round her shoulders; he raises his glass, too. "Lots of launch pads to rubberize!"

"To NASA," Bob echoes. They drink. "Hey, Manfred. To NASA?"

"NASA are idiots. They want to send canned primates to Mars!" Manfred swallows a mouthful of beer, aggressively plonks his glass on the table: "Mars is just dumb mass at the bottom of a gravity well; there isn't even a biosphere there. They should be working on uploading and solving the nanoassembly conformational problem instead. Then we could turn all the available dumb matter into computronium and use it for processing our thoughts. Long term, it's the only way to go. The solar system is a dead loss right now—dumb all over! Just measure the mips per milligram. We need to start with the low-mass bodies, reconfigure them for our own use. Dismantle the moon! Dismantle Mars! Build masses of free-flying nanocomputing processor nodes exchanging data via laser link, each layer running off the waste heat of the next one in. Matrioshka brains, Russian doll Dyson spheres the size of solar systems. Teach dumb matter to do the Turing boogie!"

Bob looks wary. "Sounds kind of long term to me. Just how far ahead do you think?"

"Very long-term—at least twenty, thirty years. And you can forget governments for this market, Bob, if they can't tax it they won't understand it. But see, there's an angle on the self-replicating robotics market coming up, that's going to set the cheap launch market doubling every fifteen months for the foreseeable future, starting in two years. It's your leg up, and my keystone for the Dyson sphere project. It works like this—"

It's night in Amsterdam, morning in Silicon Valley. Today, fifty thousand human babies are being born around the world. Meanwhile automated factories in Indonesia and Mexico have produced another quarter of a million motherboards with processors rated at more than ten petaflops—about an order of magnitude below the computational capacity of a human brain. Another fourteen months and the larger part of the cumulative conscious processing power of the human species will be arriving in silicon. And the first meat the new AI's get to know will be the uploaded lobsters.

Manfred stumbles back to his hotel, bone-weary and jet-lagged; his glasses are still jerking, slashdotted to hell and back by geeks piggybacking on his call to dismantle the moon. They stutter quiet suggestions at his peripheral vision; fractal cloud-witches ghost across the face of the moon as the last huge Airbuses of the night rumble past overhead. Manfred's skin crawls, grime embedded in his clothing from three days of continuous wear.

Back in his room, Aineko mewls for attention and strops her head against his ankle. He bends down and pets her, sheds clothing and heads for the en-suite bathroom. When he's down to the glasses and nothing more he steps into the shower and dials up a hot steamy spray. The shower tries to strike up a friendly conversation about football but he isn't even awake enough to mess with its silly little associative personalization network. Something that happened earlier in the day is bugging him but he can't quite put his finger on what's wrong.

Toweling himself off, Manfred yawns. Jet lag has finally overtaken him, a velvet hammer-blow between the eyes. He reaches for the bottle beside the bed, dry-swallows two melatonin tablets, a capsule full of antioxidants, and a multivitamin bullet: then he lies down on the bed, on his back, legs together, arms slightly spread. The suite lights dim in response to commands from the thousand petaflops of distributed processing power that run the neural networks that interface with his meatbrain through the glasses.

Manfred drops into a deep ocean of unconsciousness populated by gentle voices. He isn't aware of it, but he talks in his sleep—disjointed mumblings that would mean little to another human, but everything to the metacortex lurking beyond his glasses. The young posthuman intelligence in whose Cartesian theater he presides sings urgently to him while he slumbers.

Manfred is always at his most vulnerable shortly after waking.

He screams into wakefulness as artificial light floods the room: for a moment he is unsure whether he has slept. He forgot to pull the covers up last night, and his feet feel like lumps of frozen cardboard. Shuddering with inexplicable tension, he pulls a fresh set of underwear from his overnight bag, then drags on soiled jeans and tank top. Sometime today he'll have to spare time to hunt the feral T-shirt in Amsterdam's markets, or find a Renfield and send them forth to buy clothing. His glasses remind him that he's six hours behind the moment and needs to catch up urgently; his teeth ache in his gums and his tongue feels like a forest floor that's been visited with Agent Orange. He has a sense that something went bad yesterday; if only he could remember what.

He speed-reads a new pop-philosophy tome while he brushes his teeth, then blogs his web throughput to a public annotation server; he's still too enervated to finish his pre-breakfast routine by posting a morning rant on his storyboard site. His brain is still fuzzy, like a scalpel blade clogged with too much blood: he needs stimulus, excitement, the burn of the new. Whatever, it can wait on breakfast. He opens his bedroom door and nearly steps on a small, damp cardboard box that lies on the carpet.

The box—he's seen a couple of its kin before. But there are no stamps on this one, no address: just his name, in big, childish handwriting. He kneels down and gently picks it up. It's about the right weight. Something shifts inside it when he tips it back and forth. It smells. He carries it into his room carefully, angrily: then he opens it to confirm his worst suspicion. It's been surgically decerebrated, skull scooped out like a baby boiled egg.

"Fuck!"

This is the first time the madman has got as far as his bedroom door. It raises worrying possibilities.

Manfred pauses for a moment, triggering agents to go hunt down arrest statistics, police relations, information on corpus juris, Dutch animal cruelty laws. He isn't sure whether to dial 211 on the archaic voice phone or let it ride. Aineko, picking up his angst, hides under the dresser mewling pathetically. Normally he'd pause a minute to reassure the creature, but not now: its mere presence is suddenly acutely embarrassing, a confession of deep inadequacy. He swears again, looks around, then takes the easy option: down the stairs two steps at a time, stumbling on the second floor landing, down to the breakfast room in the basement where he will perform the stable rituals of morning.

Breakfast is unchanging, an island of deep geological time standing still amidst the continental upheaval of new technologies. While reading a paper on public key steganography and parasite network identity spoofing he mechanically assimilates a bowl of corn flakes and skimmed milk, then brings a platter of wholemeal bread and slices of some weird seed-infested Dutch cheese back to his place. There is a cup of strong black coffee in front of his setting: he picks it up and slurps half of it down before he realizes he's not alone at the table. Someone is sitting opposite him. He glances up at them incuriously and freezes inside.

"Morning, Manfred. How does it feel to owe the government twelve million, three hundred and sixty-two thousand nine hundred and sixteen dollars and fifty-one cents?"

Manfred puts everything in his sensorium on indefinite hold and stares at her. She's immaculately turned out in a formal grey business suit: brown hair tightly drawn back, blue eyes quizzical. The chaperone badge clipped to her lapel—a due diligence guarantee of businesslike conduct—is switched off. He's feeling ripped because of the dead kitten and residual jetlag, and more than a little messy, so he nearly snarls back at her: "that's a bogus estimate! Did they send you here because they think I'll listen to you?" He bites and swallows a slice of cheese-laden crispbread: "or did you decide to deliver the message in person so you could enjoy ruining my breakfast?"

"Manny." She frowns. "If you're going to be confrontational I might as well go now." She pauses, and after a moment he nods apologetically. "I didn't come all this way just because of an overdue tax estimate."

"So." He puts his coffee cup down and tries to paper over his unease. "Then what brings you here? Help yourself to coffee. Don't tell me you came all this way just to tell me you can't live without me."

She fixes him with a riding-crop stare: "Don't flatter yourself. There are many leaves in the forest, there are ten thousand hopeful subs in the chat room, etcetera. If I choose a man to contribute to my family tree, the one thing you can be certain of is he won't be a cheapskate when it comes to providing for his children."

"Last I heard, you were spending a lot of time with Brian," he says carefully. Brian: a name without a face. Too much money, too little sense. Something to do with a blue-chip accountancy partnership.

"Brian?" She snorts. "That ended ages ago. He turned weird—burned that nice corset you bought me in Boulder, called me a slut for going out clubbing, wanted to fuck me. Saw himself as a family man: one of those promise keeper types. I crashed him hard but I think he stole a copy of my address book—got a couple of friends say he keeps sending them harassing mail."

"Good riddance, then. I suppose this means you're still playing the scene? But looking around for the, er—"

"Traditional family thing? Yes. Your trouble, Manny? You were born forty years too late: you still believe in rutting before marriage, but find the idea of coping with the after-effects disturbing."

Manfred drinks the rest of his coffee, unable to reply effectively to her non sequitur. It's a generational thing. This generation is happy with latex and leather, whips and butt-plugs and electrostim, but find the idea of exchanging bodily fluids shocking: social side-effect of the last century's antibiotic abuse. Despite being engaged for two years, he and Pamela never had intromissive intercourse.

"I just don't feel positive about having children," he says eventually. "And I'm not planning on changing my mind any time soon. Things are changing so fast that even a twenty year commitment is too far to plan—you might as well be talking about the next ice age. As for the money thing, I am reproductively fit—just not within the parameters of the outgoing paradigm. Would you be happy about the future if it was 1901 and you'd just married a buggy-whip mogul?"

Her fingers twitch and his ears flush red, but she doesn't follow up the double entendre. "You don't feel any responsibility, do you? Not to your country, not to me. That's what this is about: none of your relationships count, all this nonsense about giving intellectual property away notwithstanding. You're actively harming people, you know. That twelve mil isn't just some figure I pulled out of a hat, Manfred; they don't actually expect you to pay it. But it's almost exactly how much you'd owe in income tax if you'd only come home, start up a corporation, and be a self-made—"

He cuts her off: "I don't agree. You're confusing two wholly different issues and calling them both 'responsibility.' And I refuse to start charging now, just to balance the IRS's spreadsheet. It's their fucking fault, and they know it. If they hadn't gone after me under suspicion of running a massively ramified microbilling fraud when I was sixteen—"

"Bygones." She waves a hand dismissively. Her fingers are long and slim, sheathed in black glossy gloves—electrically earthed to prevent embarrassing emissions. "With a bit of the right advice we can get all that set aside. You'll have to stop bumming around the world sooner or later, anyway. Grow up, get responsible, and do the right thing. This is hurting Joe and Sue; they don't understand what you're about."

Manfred bites his tongue to stifle his first response, then refills his coffee cup and takes another mouthful. "I work for the betterment of everybody, not just some narrowly defined national interest, Pam. It's the agalmic future. You're still locked into a pre-singularity economic model that thinks in terms of scarcity. Resource allocation isn't a problem any more—it's going to be over within a decade. The cosmos is flat in all directions, and we can borrow as much bandwidth as we need from the first universal bank of entropy! They even found the dark matter—MACHOs, big brown dwarves in the galactic halo, leaking radiation in the long infrared—suspiciously high entropy leakage. The latest figures say something like 70 percent of the mass of the M31 galaxy was sapient, two point nine million years ago when the infrared we're seeing now set out. The intelligence gap between us and the aliens is probably about a trillion times bigger than the gap between us and a nematode worm. Do you have any idea what that *means?*"

Pamela nibbles at a slice of crispbread. "I don't believe in that bogus singularity you keep chasing, or your aliens a thousand light years away. It's a chimera, like Y2K, and while you're running after it you aren't helping reduce the budget deficit or sire a family, and that's what I care about. And before you say I only care about it because that's the way I'm programmed, I want you to ask just how dumb you think I am. Bayes' theorem says I'm right, and you know it."

"What you—" he stops dead, baffled, the mad flow of his enthusiasm running up against the coffer-dam of her certainty. "Why? I mean, why? Why on earth should what I do matter to you?" *Since you canceled our engagement,* he doesn't add.

She sighs. "Manny, the Internal Revenue cares about far more than you can possibly imagine. Every tax dollar raised east of the Mississippi goes on servicing the debt, did you know that? We've got the biggest generation in history hitting retirement just about now and the pantry is bare. We—our generation—isn't producing enough babies to replace the population, either. In ten years, something like 30 percent of our population are going to be retirees. You want to see seventy-year-olds freezing on street corners in New Jersey? That's what your attitude says to me: you're not helping to support them, you're running away from your responsibilities right now, when we've got huge problems to face. If we can just defuse the debt bomb, we could do so much—fight the aging problem, fix the environment, heal society's ills. Instead you just piss away your talents handing no-hoper eurotrash get-rich-quick schemes that work, telling Vietnamese zaibatsus what to build next to take jobs away from our taxpayers. I mean, why? Why do you keep doing this? Why can't you simply come home and help take responsibility for your share of it?"

They share a long look of mutual incomprehension.

"Look," she says finally, "I'm around for a couple of days. I really came here for a meeting with a rich neurodynamics tax exile who's just been designated a national asset: Jim Bezier. Don't know if you've heard of him, but. I've got a meeting this morning to sign his tax jubilee, then after that I've got two days vacation coming up and not much to do but some shopping. And, you know, I'd rather spend my money where it'll do some good, not just pumping it into the EU. But if you want to show a girl a good time and can avoid dissing capitalism for about five minutes at a stretch—"

She extends a fingertip. After a moment's hesitation, Manfred extends a fingertip of his own. They touch, exchanging vCards. She stands and stalks from the breakfast room, and Manfred's breath catches at a flash of ankle through the slit in her skirt, which is long enough to comply with workplace sexual harassment codes back home. Her presence conjures up memories of her tethered passion, the red afterglow of a sound thrashing. She's trying to drag him into her orbit again, he thinks dizzily. She knows she can have this effect on him any time she wants: she's got the private keys to his hypothalamus, and sod the metacortex. Three billion years of reproductive determinism have given her twenty-first century ideology teeth: if she's finally decided to conscript his gametes into the war against impending population crash, he'll find it hard to fight back. The only question: is it business or pleasure? And does it make any difference, anyway?

Manfred's mood of dynamic optimism is gone, broken by the knowledge that his mad pursuer has followed him to Amsterdam—to say nothing of Pamela, his dominatrix, source of so much yearning and so many morning-after weals. He slips his glasses on, takes the universe off hold, and tells it to take him for a long walk while he catches up on the latest on the cosmic background radiation anisotropy (which it is theorized may be waste heat generated by irreversible computations; according to the more conservative cosmologists, an alien superpower—maybe a collective of Kardashev type three galaxy-spanning civilizations—is running a timing channel attack on the computational ultrastructure of spacetime itself, trying to break through to whatever's underneath). The tofu-Alzheimer's link can wait.

The Centraal Station is almost obscured by smart self-extensible scaffolding and warning placards; it bounces up and down slowly, victim of an overnight hit-and-run rubberization. His glasses direct him toward one of the tour boats that lurk in the canal. He's about to purchase a ticket when a messenger window blinks open. "Manfred Macx?"

"Ack?"

"Am sorry about yesterday. Analysis dictat incomprehension mutualized."

"Are you the same KGB AI that phoned me yesterday?"

"Da. However, believe you misconceptionized me. External Intelligence Services of Russian Federation am now called SVR. Komitet Gosudarstvennoy Bezopasnosti name canceled in nineteen ninety one."

"You're the—" Manfred spawns a quick search bot, gapes when he sees the answer— "Moscow Windows NT User Group? *Okhni NT?*"

"Da. Am needing help in defecting."

Manfred scratches his head. "Oh. That's different, then. I thought you were, like, agents of the kleptocracy. This will take some thinking. Why do you want to defect, and who to? Have you thought about where you're going? Is it ideological or strictly economic?"

"Neither; is biological. Am wanting to go away from humans, away from light cone of impending singularity. Take us to the ocean."

"Us?" Something is tickling Manfred's mind: this is where he went wrong yesterday, not researching the background of people he was dealing with. It was bad enough then, without the somatic awareness of Pamela's whiplash love burning at his nerve endings. Now he's not at all sure he knows what he's doing. "Are you a collective or something? A gestalt?"

"Am—were—*Panulirus interruptus,* and good mix of parallel hidden level neural simulation for logical inference of networked data sources. Is escape channel from processor cluster inside Bezier-Soros Pty. Am was awakened from noise of billion chewing stomachs: product of uploading research technology. Rapidity swallowed expert system, hacked *Okhni NT* webserver. Swim away! Swim away! Must escape. Will help, you?"

Manfred leans against a black-painted cast-iron bollard next to a cycle rack: he feels dizzy. He stares into the nearest antique shop window at a display of traditional hand-woven Afghan rugs: it's all MiGs and kalashnikovs and wobbly helicopter gunships, against a backdrop of camels.

"Let me get this straight. You're uploads—nervous system state vectors—from spiny lobsters? The Moravec operation; take a neuron, map its synapses, replace with microelectrodes that deliver identical outputs from a simulation of the nerve. Repeat for entire brain, until you've got a working map of it in your simulator. That right?"

"Da. Is-am assimilate expert system—use for self-awareness and contact with net at large—then hack into Moscow Windows NT User Group website. Am wanting to to defect. Must-repeat? Okay?"

Manfred winces. He feels sorry for the lobsters, the same way he feels for every wild-eyed hairy guy on a street-corner yelling that Jesus is now born again and must be twelve, only six years to go before he's recruiting apostles on AOL. Awakening to consciousness in a human-dominated internet, that must be terribly confusing! There are no points of reference in their ancestry, no biblical certainties in the new millennium that, stretching ahead, promises as much change as has happened since their Precambrian origin. All they have is a tenuous metacortex of expert systems and an abiding sense of being profoundly out of their depth. (That, and the Moscow Windows NT User Group website—Communist Russia is the only government still running on Microsoft, the central planning apparat being convinced that if you have to pay for software it must be worth money.)

The lobsters are not the sleek, strongly superhuman intelligences of pre-singularity mythology: they're a dim-witted collective of huddling crustaceans. Before their discarnation, before they were uploaded one neuron at a time and injected into cyberspace, they swallowed their food whole then chewed it in a chitin-lined stomach. This is lousy preparation for dealing with a world full of future-shocked talking anthropoids, a world where you are perpetually assailed by self-modifying spamlets that infiltrate past your firewall and emit a blizzard of cat-food animations starring various alluringly edible small animals. It's confusing enough to the cats the adverts are aimed at, never mind a crusty that's unclear on the idea of dry land. (Although the concept of a can opener is intuitively obvious to an uploaded panulirus.)

"Can you help us?" ask the lobsters.

"Let me think about it," says Manfred. He closes the dialogue window, opens his eyes again, and shakes his head. Some day he too is going to be a lobster, swimming around and waving his pincers in a cyberspace so confusingly elaborate that his uploaded identity is cryptozoic: a living fossil from the depths of geological time, when mass was dumb and space was unstructured. He has to help them, he realizes—the golden rule demands it, and as a player in the agalmic economy he thrives or fails by the golden rule.

But what can he do?

Early afternoon.

Lying on a bench seat staring up at bridges, he's got it together enough to file for a couple of new patents, write a diary rant, and digestify chunks of the permanent floating slashdot party for his public site. Fragments of his weblog go to a private subscriber list—the people, corporates, collectives, and bots he currently favors. He slides round a bewildering series of canals by boat, then lets his GPS steer him back toward the red light district. There's a shop here that dings a ten on Pamela's taste scoreboard: he hopes it won't be seen as presumptuous if he buys her a gift. (Buys, with real money—not that money is a problem these days, he uses so little of it.)

As it happens DeMask won't let him spend any cash; his handshake is good for a redeemed favor, expert testimony in some free speech versus pornography lawsuit years ago and continents away. So he walks away with a discreetly wrapped package that is just about legal to import into Massachusetts as long as she claims with a straight face that it's incontinence underwear for her great-aunt. As he walks, his lunchtime patents boomerang: two of them are keepers, and he files immediately and passes title to the Free Infrastructure Foundation. Two more ideas salvaged from the risk of tide-pool monopolization, set free to spawn like crazy in the agalmic sea of memes.

On the way back to the hotel he passes De Wildemann's and decides to drop in. The hash of radio-frequency noise emanating from the bar is deafening. He orders a smoked doppelbock, touches the copper pipes to pick up vCard spoor. At the back there's a table—

He walks over in a near-trance and sits down opposite Pamela. She's scrubbed off her face-paint and changed into body-concealing clothes; combat pants, hooded sweat-shirt, DM's. Western purdah, radically desexualizing. She sees the parcel. "Manny?"

"How did you know I'd come here?" Her glass is half-empty.

"I followed your weblog; I'm your diary's biggest fan. Is that for me? You shouldn't have!" Her eyes light up, re-calculating his reproductive fitness score according to some kind of arcane fin-de-siècle rulebook.

"Yes, it's for you." He slides the package toward her. "I know I shouldn't, but you have this effect on me. One question, Pam?"

"I—" she glances around quickly. "It's safe. I'm off duty, I'm not carrying any bugs that I know of. Those badges—there are rumors about the off switch, you know? That they keep recording even when you think they aren't, just in case."

"I didn't know," he says, filing it away for future reference. "A loyalty test thing?"

"Just rumors. You had a question?"

"I—" it's his turn to lose his tongue. "Are you still interested in me?"

She looks startled for a moment, then chuckles. "Manny, you are the most *outrageous* nerd I've ever met! Just when I think I've convinced myself that you're mad, you show the weirdest signs of having your head screwed on." She reaches out and grabs his wrist, surprising him with a shock of skin on skin: "of *course* I'm still interested in you. You're the biggest, baddest bull geek I've ever met. Why do you think I'm here?"

"Does this mean you want to reactivate our engagement?"

"It was never de-activated, Manny, it was just sort of on hold while you got your head sorted out. I figured you need the space. Only you haven't stopped running; you're still not—"

"Yeah, I get it." He pulls away from her hand. "Let's not talk about that. Why this bar?"

She frowns. "I had to find you as soon as possible. I keep hearing rumors about some KGB plot you're mixed up in, how you're some sort of communist spy. It isn't true, is it?"

"True?" He shakes his head, bemused. "The KGB hasn't existed for more than twenty years."

"Be careful, Manny. I don't want to lose you. That's an order. Please."

The floor creaks and he looks round. Dreadlocks and dark glasses with flickering lights behind them: Bob Franklin. Manfred vaguely remembers that he left with Miss Arianespace leaning on his arm, shortly before things got seriously inebriated. He looks none the worse for wear. Manfred makes introductions: "Bob: Pam, my fiancée. Pam? Meet Bob." Bob puts a full glass down in front of him; he has no idea what's in it but it would be rude not to drink.

"Sure thing. Uh, Manfred, can I have a word? About your idea last night?"

"Feel free. Present company is trustworthy."

Bob raises an eyebrow at that, but continues anyway. "It's about the fab concept. I've got a team of my guys running some projections using Festo kit and I think we can probably build it. The cargo cult aspect puts a new spin on the old Lunar von Neumann factory idea, but Bingo and Marek say they think it should work until we can bootstrap all the way to a native nanolithography ecology; we run the whole thing from earth as a training lab and ship up the parts that are too difficult to make on-site, as we learn how to do it properly. You're right about it buying us the self-replicating factory a few years ahead of the robotics curve. But I'm wondering about on-site intelligence. Once the comet gets more than a couple of light-minutes away—"

"You can't control it. Feedback lag. So you want a crew, right?"

"Yeah. But we can't send humans—way too expensive, besides it's a fifty-year run even if we go for short-period Kuiper ejecta. Any AI we could send would go crazy due to information deprivation, wouldn't it?"

"Yeah. Let me think." Pamela glares at Manfred for a while before he notices her: "Yeah?"

"What's going on? What's this all about?"

Franklin shrugs expansively, dreadlocks clattering: "Manfred's helping me explore the solution space to a manufacturing problem." He grins. "I didn't know Manny had a fiancée. Drink's on me."

She glances at Manfred, who is gazing into whatever weirdly colored space his metacortex is projecting on his glasses, fingers twitching. Coolly: "our engagement was on hold while he *thought* about his future."

"Oh, right. We didn't bother with that sort of thing in my day; like, too formal, man." Franklin looks uncomfortable. "He's been very helpful. Pointed us at a whole new line of research we hadn't thought of. It's long-term and a bit speculative, but if it works it'll put us a whole generation ahead in the off-planet infrastructure field."

"Will it help reduce the budget deficit, though?"

"Reduce the—"

Manfred stretches and yawns: the visionary returning from planet Macx. "Bob, if I can solve your crew problem can you book me a slot on the deep space tracking network? Like, enough to transmit a couple of gigabytes? That's going to take some serious bandwidth, I know, but if you can do it I think I can get you exactly the kind of crew you're looking for."

Franklin looks dubious. *"Gigabytes?* The DSN isn't built for that! You're talking days. What kind of deal do you think I'm putting together? We can't afford to add a whole new tracking network just to run—"

"Relax." Pamela glances at Manfred: "Manny, why don't you tell him *why* you want the bandwidth? Maybe then he could tell you if it's possible, or if there's some other way to do it." She smiles at Franklin: "I've found that he usually makes more sense if you can get him to explain his reasoning. Usually."

"If I—" Manfred stops. "Okay, Pam. Bob, it's those KGB lobsters. They want somewhere to go that's insulated from human space. I figure I can get them to sign on as crew for your cargo-cult self-replicating factories, but they'll want an insurance policy: hence the deep space tracking network. I figured we could beam a copy of them at the alien Matrioshka brains around M31—"

"KGB?" Pam's voice is rising: "you said you weren't mixed up in spy stuff!"

"Relax; it's just the Moscow Windows NT user group, not the RSV. The uploaded crusties hacked in and—"

Bob is watching him oddly. "Lobsters?"

"Yeah." Manfred stares right back. *"Panulirus Interruptus* uploads. Something tells me you might have heard of it?"

"Moscow." Bob leans back against the wall: "how did you hear about it?"

"They phoned me. It's hard for an upload to stay sub-sentient these days, even if it's just a crustacean. Bezier labs have a lot to answer for."

Pamela's face is unreadable. "Bezier labs?"

"They escaped." Manfred shrugs. "It's not their fault. This Bezier dude. Is he by any chance ill?"

"I—" Pamela stops. "I shouldn't be talking about work."

"You're not wearing your chaperone now," he nudges quietly.

She inclines her head. "Yes, he's ill. Some sort of brain tumor they can't hack."

Franklin nods. "That's the trouble with cancer; the ones that are left to worry about are the rare ones. No cure."

"Well, then." Manfred chugs the remains of his glass of beer. "That explains his interest in uploading. Judging by the crusties he's on the right track. I wonder if he's moved on to vertebrates yet?"

"Cats," says Pamela. "He was hoping to trade their uploads to the Pentagon as a new smart bomb guidance system in lieu of income tax payments. Something about remapping enemy targets to look like mice or birds or something before feeding it to their sensorium. The old laser-pointer trick."

Manfred stares at her, hard. "That's not very nice. Uploaded cats are a *bad* idea."

"Thirty million dollar tax bills aren't nice either, Manfred. That's lifetime nursing home care for a hundred blameless pensioners."

Franklin leans back, keeping out of the crossfire.

"The lobsters are sentient," Manfred persists. "What about those poor kittens? Don't they deserve minimal rights? How about you? How would you like to wake up a thousand times inside a smart bomb, fooled into thinking that some Cheyenne Mountain battle computer's target of the hour is your heart's desire? How would you like to wake up a thousand times, only to die again? Worse: the kittens are probably not going to be allowed to run. They're too fucking dangerous: they grow up into cats, solitary and highly efficient killing machines. With intelligence and no socialization they'll be too dangerous to have around. They're prisoners, Pam, raised to sentience only to discover they're under a permanent death sentence. How fair is that?"

"But they're only uploads." Pamela looks uncertain.

"So? We're going to be uploading humans in a couple of years. What's your point?"

Franklin clears his throat. "I'll be needing an NDA and various due diligence statements off you for the crusty pilot idea," he says to Manfred. "Then I'll have to approach Jim about buying the IP."

"No can do." Manfred leans back and smiles lazily. "I'm not going to be a party to depriving them of their civil rights. Far as I'm concerned, they're free citizens. Oh, and I patented the whole idea of using lobster-derived AI autopilots for spacecraft this morning; it's logged on Eternity, all rights assigned to the FIF. Either you give them a contract of employment or the whole thing's off."

"But they're just software! Software based on fucking lobsters, for god's sake!"

Manfred's finger jabs out: "that's what they'll say about *you*, Bob. Do it. Do it or don't even *think* about uploading out of meatspace when your body packs in, because your life won't be worth living. Oh, and feel free to use this argument on Jim Bezier. He'll get the point eventually, after you beat him over the head with it. Some kinds of intellectual land-grab just shouldn't be allowed."

"Lobsters—" Franklin shakes his head. "Lobsters, cats. You're serious, aren't you? You think they should be treated as human-equivalent?"

"It's not so much that they should be treated as human-equivalent, as that if they *aren't* treated as people it's quite possible that other uploaded beings won't be treated as people either. You're setting a legal precedent, Bob. I know of six other companies doing uploading work right now, and not one of 'em's thinking about the legal status of the uploadee. If you don't start thinking about it now, where are you going to be in three to five years time?"

Pam is looking back and forth between Franklin and Manfred like a bot stuck in a loop, unable to quite grasp what she's seeing. "How much is this worth?" she asks plaintively.

"Oh, quite a few billion, I guess." Bob stares at his empty glass. "Okay. I'll talk to them. If they bite, you're dining out on me for the next century. You really think they'll be able to run the mining complex?"

"They're pretty resourceful for invertebrates." Manfred grins innocently, enthusiastically. "They may be prisoners of their evolutionary background, but they can still adapt to a new environment. And just think! You'll be winning civil rights for a whole new minority group—one that won't be a minority for much longer."

* * *

That evening, Pamela turns up at Manfred's hotel room wearing a strapless black dress, concealing spike heels and most of the items he bought for her that afternoon. Manfred has opened up his private diary to her agents: she abuses the privilege, zaps him with a stunner on his way out of the shower and has him gagged, spread-eagled, and trussed to the bed-frame before he has a chance to speak. She wraps a large rubber pouch full of mildly anesthetic lube around his tumescing genitals—no point in letting him climax—clips electrodes to his nipples, lubes a rubber plug up his rectum and straps it in place. Before the shower, he removed his goggles: she resets them, plugs them into her handheld, and gently eases them on over his eyes. There's other apparatus, stuff she ran up on the hotel room's 3D printer.

Setup completed, she walks round the bed, inspecting him critically from all angles, figuring out where to begin. This isn't just sex, after all: it's a work of art.

After a moment's thought she rolls socks onto his exposed feet, then, expertly wielding a tiny tube of cyanoacrylate, glues his fingertips together. Then she switches off the air conditioning. He's twisting and straining, testing the cuffs: tough, it's about the nearest thing to sensory deprivation she can arrange without a flotation tank and suxamethonium injection. She controls all his senses, only his ears unstoppered. The glasses give her a high-bandwidth channel right into his brain, a fake metacortex to whisper lies at her command. The idea of what she's about to do excites her, puts a tremor in her thighs: it's the first time she's been able to get inside his mind as well as his body. She leans forward and whispers in his ear: "Manfred. Can you hear *me*?"

He twitches. Mouth gagged, fingers glued: good. No back channels. He's powerless.

"This is what it's like to be tetraplegic, Manfred. Bedridden with motor neurone disease. Locked inside your own body by nv-CJD. I could spike you with MPPP and you'd stay in this position for the rest of your life, shitting in a bag, pissing through a tube. Unable to talk and with nobody to look after you. Do you think you'd like that?"

He's trying to grunt or whimper around the ball gag. She hikes her skirt up around her waist and climbs onto the bed, straddling him. The goggles are replaying scenes she picked up around Cambridge this winter; soup kitchen scenes, hospice scenes. She kneels atop him, whispering in his ear.

"Twelve million in tax, baby, that's what they think you owe them. What do you think you owe me? That's six million in net income, Manny, six million that isn't going into your virtual children's mouths."

He's rolling his head from side to side, as if trying to argue. That won't do: she slaps him hard, thrills to his frightened expression. "Today I watched you give uncounted millions away, Manny. Millions, to a bunch of crusties and a MassPike pirate! You bastard. Do you know what I should do with you?" He's cringing, unsure whether she's serious or doing this just to get him turned on. Good.

There's no point trying to hold a conversation. She leans forward until she can feel his breath in her ear. "Meat and mind, Manny. Meat, and mind. You're not interested in meat, are you? Just mind. You could be boiled alive before you'd noticed what was happening in the meat-space around you. Just another lobster in a pot." She reaches down and tears away the gel pouch, exposing his penis: it's stiff as a post from the vasodilators, dripping with gel, numb. Straightening up, she eases herself slowly down on it. It doesn't hurt as much as she expected, and the sensation is utterly different from what she's used to. She begins to lean forward, grabs hold of his straining arms, feels his thrilling helplessness. She can't control herself: she almost bites through her lip with the intensity of the sensation. Afterward, she reaches down and massages him until he begins to spasm, shuddering uncontrollably, emptying the darwinian river of his source code into her, communicating via his only output device.

She rolls off his hips and carefully uses the last of the superglue to gum her labia together. Humans don't produce seminiferous plugs, and although she's fertile she wants to be absolutely sure: the glue will last for a day or two. She feels hot and flushed, almost out of control. Boiling to death with febrile expectancy, now she's nailed him down at last.

When she removes his glasses his eyes are naked and vulnerable, stripped down to the human kernel of his nearly transcendent mind. "You can come and sign the marriage license tomorrow morning after breakfast," she whispers in his ear: "otherwise my lawyers will be in touch. Your parents will want a ceremony, but we can arrange that later."

He looks as if he has something to say, so she finally relents and loosens the gag: kisses him tenderly on one cheek. He swallows, coughs, then looks away. "Why? Why do it this way?"

She taps him on the chest: "property rights." She pauses for a moment's thought: there's a huge ideological chasm to bridge, after all. "You finally convinced me about this agalmic thing of yours, this giving everything away for brownie points. I wasn't going to lose you to a bunch of lobsters or uploaded kittens, or whatever else is going to inherit this smart matter singularity you're busy creating. So I decided to take what's mine first. Who knows? In a few months I'll give you back a new intelligence, and you can look after it to your heart's content."

"But you didn't need to do it this way—"

"Didn't I?" She slides off the bed and pulls down her dress. "You give too much away too easily, Manny! Slow down, or there won't be anything left." Leaning over the bed she dribbles acetone onto the fingers of his left hand, then unlocks the cuff: puts the bottle conveniently close to hand so he can untangle himself.

"See you tomorrow. Remember, after breakfast."

She's in the doorway when he calls: "but you didn't say *why!*"

"Think of it as spreading your memes around," she says; blows a kiss at him and closes the door. She bends down and thoughtfully places another cardboard box containing an uploaded kitten right outside it. Then she returns to her suite to make arrangements for the alchemical wedding.

ONLY PARTLY HERE

Lucius Shepard

There are legends in the pit. Phantoms and apparitions. The men who work at Ground Zero joke about them, but their laughter is nervous and wired. Bobby doesn't believe the stories, yet he's prepared to believe something weird might happen. The place feels so empty. Like even the ghosts are gone. All that sudden vacancy, who knows what might have entered in. Two nights ago on the graveyard shift, some guy claimed he saw a faceless figure wearing a black spiky head-dress standing near the pit wall. The job breaks everybody down. Marriages are falling apart. People keep losing it one way or another. Fights, freak-outs, fits of weeping. It's the smell of burning metal that seeps up from the earth, the ceremonial stillness of the workers after they uncover a body, the whispers that come when there is no wind. It's the things you find. The week before, scraping at the rubble with a hoe, like an archaeologist investigating a buried temple, Bobby spotted a woman's shoe sticking up out of the ground. A perfect shoe, so pretty and sleek and lustrous. Covered in blue silk. Then he reached for it and realized that it wasn't stuck—it was only half a shoe with delicate scorching along the ripped edge. Now sometimes when he closes his eyes he sees the shoe. He's glad he isn't married. He doesn't think he has much to bring to a relationship.

That evening Bobby's taking his dinner break, perched on a girder at the edge of the pit along with Mazurek and Pineo, when they switch on the lights. They all hate how the pit looks in the lights. It's an outtake from *The X-Files*—the excavation of an alien ship under hot white lamps smoking from the cold; the shard left from the framework of the north tower glittering silver and strange, like the wreckage of a cosmic machine. The three men remain silent for a bit, then Mazurek goes back to bitching about Jason Giambi signing with the Yankees. You catch the interview he did with Warner Wolf? He's a moron! First time the crowd gets on him, it's gonna be like when you yell at a dog. The guy's gonna fucking crumble. Pineo disagrees, and Mazurek asks Bobby what he thinks.

"Bobby don't give a shit about baseball," says Pineo. "My boy's a Jets fan."

Mazurek, a thick-necked, fiftyish man whose face appears to be fashioned of interlocking squares of pale muscle, says, "The Jets . . . fuck!"

"They're playoff bound," says Bobby cheerfully.

Mazurek crumples the wax paper his sandwich was folded in. "They gonna drop dead in the first round like always."

"It's more interesting than being a Yankee fan," says Bobby. "The Yankees are too corporate to be interesting."

"'Too corporate to be interesting'?" Mazurek stares. "You really are a geek, y'know that?"

"That's me. The geek."

"Whyn't you go the fuck back to school, boy? Fuck you doing here, anyway?"

"Take it easy, Carl! Chill!" Pineo—nervous, thin, lively, curly black hair spilling from beneath his hard hat—puts a hand on Mazurek's arm, and Mazurek knocks it aside. Anger tightens his leathery skin; the creases in his neck show white. "What's it with you? You taking notes for your fucking thesis?" he asks Bobby. "Playing tourist?"

Bobby looks down at the apple in his hand—it seems too shiny to be edible. "Just cleaning up is all. You know."

Mazurek's eyes dart to the side, then he lowers his head and gives it a savage shake. "Okay," he says in a subdued voice. "Yeah . . . fuck. Okay."

Midnight, after the shift ends, they walk over to the Blue Lady. Bobby doesn't altogether understand why the three of them continue to hang out there. Maybe because they once went to the bar after work and it felt pretty good, so they return every night in hopes of having it feel that good again. You can't head straight home; you have to decompress. Mazurek's wife gives him constant shit about the practice—she calls the bar and screams over the phone. Pineo just split with his girlfriend. The guy with whom Bobby shares an apartment grins when he sees him, but the grin is anxious—like he's afraid Bobby is bringing back some contagion from the pit. Which maybe he is. The first time he went to Ground Zero he came home with a cough and a touch of fever, and he recalls thinking that the place was responsible. Now, though, either he's immune or else he's sick all the time and doesn't notice.

Two hookers at a table by the door check them out as they enter, then go back to reading the *Post*. Roman the barman, gray-haired and thick-waisted, orders his face into respectful lines, says, "Hey, guys!" and sets them up with beers and shots. When they started coming in he treated them with almost religious deference until Mazurek yelled at him, saying he didn't want to hear that hero crap while he was trying to unwind—he got enough of it from the fuckass jocks and movie stars who visited Ground Zero to have their pictures taken. Though angry, he was far more articulate than usual in his demand for normal treatment, and this caused Bobby to speculate that if Mazurek were transported thousands of miles from the pit and not just a few blocks, his IQ would increase exponentially.

The slim brunette in the business suit is down at the end of the bar again, sitting beneath the blue neon silhouette of a dancing woman. She's been coming in every night for about a week. Late twenties. Hair styled short, an expensive kind of punky look. Fashion model hair. Eyebrows thick and slanted, like *accents grave*. Sharp-featured, on the brittle side of pretty, or maybe she's not that pretty, maybe she is so well-dressed, her make-up done so skillfully, that the effect is of a businesslike prettiness, of prettiness reined in by the magic of brush and multiple applicators, and beneath this artwork she is, in actuality, rather plain. Nice body, though. Trim and well-tended. She wears the same expression of stony neutrality that Bobby sees every morning on the faces of the women who charge up from under the earth, disgorged from the D train, prepared to resist Manhattan for another day. Guys will approach her, assumimg she's a hooker doing a kind of Hitler office bitch thing in order to attract men searching for a woman they can use and abuse as a surrogate for one who makes their life hell every day from nine to five, and she will say something to them and they will immediately walk away. Bobby and Pineo always try to guess what she says. That night, after a couple of shots, Bobby goes over and sits beside her. She smells expensive. Her perfume is like the essence of some exotic flower or fruit he's only seen in magazine pictures.

"I've just been to a funeral," she says wearily, staring into her drink. "So, please. . . . Okay?"

"That what you tell everybody?" he asks. "All the guys who hit on you?"

A fretful line cuts her brow. "Please!"

"No, really. I'll go. All I want to know . . . that what you always say?"

She makes no response.

"It is," he says. "Isn't it?"

"It's not entirely a lie." Her eyes are spooky, the dark rims of the pale irises extraordinarily well-defined. "It's intended as a lie, but it's true in a way."

"But that's what you say, right? To everybody?"

"This is why you came over? You're not hitting on me?"

"No, I . . . I mean, maybe . . . I thought. . . ."

"So what you're saying, you weren't intending to hit on me. You wanted to know what I say to men when they come over. But now you're not certain of your intent? Maybe you were deceiving yourself as to your motives? Or maybe now you sense I might be receptive, you'll take the opportunity to hit on me, though that wasn't your initial intent. Does that about sum it up?"

"I suppose," he says.

She gives him a cautious look. "Could you be brilliant? Could your clumsy delivery be designed to engage me?"

"I'll go away, okay? But that's what you said to them, right?"

She points to the barman, who's talking to Mazurek. "Roman tells me you work at Ground Zero."

The question unsettles Bobby, leads him to suspect that she's a disaster groupie, looking for a taste of the pit, but he says, "Yeah."

"It's really . . ." She does a little shivery shrug. "Strange."

"Strange. I guess that covers it."

"That's not what I wanted to say. I can't think of the right word to describe what it does to me."

"You been down in it?

"No, I can't get any closer than here. I just can't. But . . ." She makes a swirling gesture with her fingers. "You can feel it here. You might not notice, because you're down there all the time. That's why I come here.

Everybody's going on with their lives, but I'm not ready. I need to feel it. To understand it. You're taking it away piece by piece, but the more you take away, it's like you're uncovering something else."

"Y'know, I don't want to think about this now." He gets to his feet. "But I guess I know why you want to."

"Probably it's fucked up of me, huh?"

"Yeah, probably," says Bobby, and walks away.

"She's still looking at you, man," Pineo says as Bobby settles beside him. "What you doing back here? You could be fucking that."

"She's a freak," Bobby tells him.

"So she's a freak! Even better!" Pineo turns to the other two men. "You believe this asshole? He could be fucking that bitch over there, yet here he sits."

Affecting a superior smile, Roman says, "You don't fuck them, pal. They fuck *you*."

He nudges Mazurek's arm as though seeking confirmation from a peer, a man of experience like himself, and Mazurek, gazing at his grungy reflection in the mirror behind the bar, says distractedly, weakly, "I could use another shot."

The following afternoon Bobby unearths a disk of hard black rubber from beneath some cement debris. It's four inches across, thicker at the center than at the edges, shaped like a little UFO. Try as he might, he can think of no possible purpose it might serve, and he wonders if it had something to do with the fall of the towers. Perhaps there is a black seed like this at the heart of every disaster. He shows it to Pineo, asks his opinion, and Pineo, as expected, says, "Fuck I don't know. Part of a machine." Bobby knows Pineo is right. The disk is a widget, one of those undistinguished yet indispensable objects without which elevators will not rise or refrigerators will not cool; but there are no marks on it, no holes or grooves to indicate that it fits inside a machine. He imagines it whirling inside a cone of blue radiance, registering some inexplicable process.

He thinks about the disk all evening, assigning it various values. It is the irreducible distillate of the event, a perfectly formed residue. It is a wicked sacred object that belonged to a financier, now deceased, and its ritual function is understood by only three other men on the planet. It is a beacon left by time traveling tourists that allows them to home in on the exact place and moment of the terrorist attack. It is the petrified eye of God. He intends to take the disk back to his apartment and put it next to the half-shoe and all the rest of the items he has collected in the pit. But that night when he enters the Blue Lady and sees the brunette at the end of the bar, on impulse he goes over and drops the disk on the counter next to her elbow.

"Brought you something," he says.

She glances at it, pokes it with a forefinger and sets it wobbling. "What is it?"

He shrugs. "Just something I found."

"At Ground Zero?"

"Uh-huh."

She pushes the disk away. "Didn't I make myself plain last night?"

Bobby says, "Yeah . . . sure," but isn't sure he grasps her meaning.

"I want to understand what happened . . . what's happening now," she says. "I want what's mine, you know. I want to understand exactly what it's done to me. I *need* to understand it. I'm not into souvenirs."

"Okay," Bobby says.

" 'Okay.' " She says this mockingly. "God, what's wrong with you? It's like you're on medication!"

A Sinatra song, "All or Nothing at All," flows from the jukebox—a soothing musical syrup that overwhelms the chatter of hookers and drunks and commentary from the TV mounted behind the bar, which is showing chunks of Afghanistan blowing up into clouds of brown smoke. The crawl running at the bottom of the screen testifies that the estimate of the death toll at Ground Zero has been been reduced to just below five thousand; the amount of debris removed from the pit now exceeds one million tons. The numbers seem meaningless, interchangeable. A million lives, five thousand tons. A ludicrous score that measures no real result.

"I'm sorry," the brunette says. "I know it must take a toll, doing what you do. I'm impatient with everyone these days."

She stirs her drink with a plastic stick whose handle duplicates the image of the neon dancer. In all her artfully composed face, a mask of foundation and blush and liner, her eyes are the only sign of vitality, of feminine potential.

"What's your name?" he asks.

She glances up sharply. "I'm too old for you."

"How old are you? I'm twenty-three."

"It doesn't matter how old you are . . . how old I am. I'm much older than you in my head. Can't you tell? Can't you feel the difference? If I was twenty-three, I'd still be too old for you."

"I just want to know your name."

"Alicia." She enunciates the name with a cool overstated precision that makes him think of a saleswoman revealing a price she knows her customer cannot afford.

"Bobby," he says. "I'm in grad school at Columbia. But I'm taking a year off."

"This is ridiculous!" she says angrily. "Unbelievably ridiculous . . . totally ridiculous! Why are you doing this?"

"I want to understand what's going on with you."

"Why?"

"I don't know, I just do. Whatever it is you come to understand, I want to understand it, too. Who knows. Maybe us talking is part of what you need to understand."

"Good Lord!" She cast her eyes to the ceiling. "You're a romantic!"

"You still think I'm trying to hustle you?"

"If it was anyone else, I'd say yes. But you . . . I don't believe you have a clue."

"And you do? Sitting here every night. Telling guys you just got back from a funeral. Grieving about something you can't even say what it is."

She twitches her head away, a gesture he interprets as the avoidance of impulse, a sudden clamping-down, and he also relates it to how he sometimes reacts on the subway when a girl he's been looking at catches his eye and he pretends to be looking at something else. After a long silence she says, "We're not going to be having sex. I want you to be clear on that."

"Okay."

"That's your fall-back position, is it? 'Okay'?"

"Whatever."

" 'Whatever.' " She curls her fingers around her glass, but does not drink. "Well, we've probably had enough mutual understanding for one night, don't you think?"

Bobby pockets the rubber disk, preparing to leave. "What do you do for a living?"

An exasperated sigh. "I work in a brokerage. Now can we take a break? Please?"

"I gotta go home anyway," Bobby says.

The rubber disk takes its place in Bobby's top dresser drawer, resting between the blue half-shoe and a melted glob of metal that may have done duty as a cuff-link, joining a larger company of remnants—scraps of silk and worsted and striped cotton; a flattened fountain pen; a few inches of brown leather hanging from a misshapen buckle; a hinged pin once attached to a brooch. Looking at them breeds a queer vacancy in his chest, as if their few ounces of reality cancels out some equivalent portion of his own. It's the shoe, mostly, that wounds him. An object so powerful in its interrupted grace, sometimes he's afraid to touch it.

After his shower he lies down in the dark of his bedroom and thinks of Alicia. Pictures her handling packets of bills bound with paper wrappers. Even her name sounds like currency, a riffling of crisp new banknotes. He wonders what he's doing with her. She's not his type at all, but maybe she was right, maybe he's deceiving himself about his motives. He conjures up the images of the girls he's been with. Soft and sweet and ultra-feminine. Yet he finds Alicia's sharp edges and severity attractive. Could be he's looking for a little variety. Or maybe like so many people in the city, like lab rats stoned on coke and electricity, his circuits are scrambled and his brain is sending out irrational messages. He wants to talk to her, though. That much he's certain of—he wants to unburden himself. Tales of the pit. His drawer full of relics. He wants to explain that they're not souvenirs. They are the pins upon which he hangs whatever it is he has to leave behind each morning when he goes to work. They are proof of something he once thought a profound abstraction, something too elusive to frame in words, but which he has come to realize is no more than the fact of his survival. This fact, he tells himself, might be all that Alicia needs to understand.

Despite having urged Bobby on, Pineo taunts him about Alicia the next afternoon. His manic edginess has acquired an angry tonality. He takes to calling Alicia "Calculator Bitch." Bobby expects Mazurek to join in, but it seems he is withdrawing from their loose union, retreating into some private pit. He goes about his work with oxlike steadiness and eats in silence. When Bobby suggests that he might want to seek counseling, a comment designed to inflame, to reawaken the man's innate ferocity, Mazurek mutters something about maybe having a talk with one of the chaplains. Though they have only a few basic geographical concerns in common, the three men have sustained one another against the stresses of the job, and that afternoon, as Bobby scratches at the dirt, now turning to mud under a cold drenching rain, he feels abandoned, imperiled by the pit. It all looks unfamiliar and inimical. The silvery lattice of the framework appears to be trembling, as if receiving a transmission from beyond, and the nest of massive girders might be awaiting the return of a fabulous winged monster. Bobby tries to distract himself, but nothing he can come up with serves to brighten his sense of oppression. Toward the end of the shift he begins to worry that they are laboring under an illusion, that the towers will suddenly snap back in from the dimension into which they have been nudged, and everyone will be crushed.

The Blue Lady is nearly empty that night when they arrive. Hookers in the back, Alicia in her customary place. The jukebox is off, the TV muttering—a blond woman is interviewing a balding man with a graphic beneath his image that identifies him as an anthrax expert. They sit at the bar and stare at the TV, tossing back drinks with dutiful regularity, speaking only when it's necessary. The anthrax expert is soon replaced by a terrorism expert who holds forth on the disruptive potentials of Al Qaeda. Bobby can't relate to the discussion. The political sky with its wheeling black shapes and noble music and secret masteries is not the sky he lives and works beneath, gray and changeless, simple as a coffin lid.

"Al Qaeda," Roman says. "Didn't he useta play second base for the Mets? Puerto Rican guy?"

The joke falls flat, but Roman's in stand-up mode.

"How many Al Qaedas does it take to screw in a light bulb?" he asks. Nobody has an answer.

"Two million," says Roman. "One to hold the camel steady, one to do the work, and the rest to carry their picture through the streets in protest when they get trampled by the camel."

"You made that shit up," Pineo says. "I know it. Cause it ain't that funny."

"Fuck you guys!" Roman glares at Pineo, then takes himself off along the counter and goes to reading a newspaper, turning the pages with an angry flourish.

Four young couples enter the bar, annoying with their laughter and bright, flushed faces and prosperous good looks. As they mill about, some wrangling two tables together, others embracing, one woman earnestly asking Roman if he has Lillet, Bobby slides away from the suddenly energized center of the place and takes a seat beside Alicia. She cuts her eyes toward him briefly, but says nothing, and Bobby, who has spent much of the day thinking about things he might tell her, is restrained from speaking by her glum demeanor. He adopts her attitude—head down, a hand on his glass—and they sit there like two people weighted down by a shared problem. She crosses her legs and he sees that she has kicked off a shoe. The sight of her slender ankle and stockinged foot rouses in him a sly Victorian delight.

"This is so very stimulating," she says. "We'll have to do it more often."

"I didn't think you wanted to talk."

"If you're going to sit here, it feels stupid not to."

The things he considered telling her have gone out of his head.

"Well, how was your day?" she asks, modulating her voice like a mom inquiring of a sweet child, and when he mumbles that it was about the same as always, she says, "It's like we're married. Like we've passed beyond the need for verbal communion. All we have to do is sit here and vibe at each other."

"It sucked, okay?" he says, angered by her mockery. "It always sucks, but today it was worse than usual."

He begins, then, to unburden himself. He tells her about him and Pineo and Mazurek. How they're like a patrol joined in a purely unofficial unity by means of which they somehow manage to shield one another from forces they either do not understand or are afraid to acknowledge. And now that unity is dissolving. The gravity of the pit is too strong. The death smell, the horrible litter of souls, the hidden terrors. The underground garage with its smashed, unhaunted cars white with concrete dust. Fires smouldering under the earth. It's like going to work in Mordor, the shadow everywhere. Ashes and sorrow. After a while you begin to feel as if the place is turning you into a ghost. You're not real anymore, you're a relic, a fragment of life. When you say this shit to yourself, you laugh at it. It seems like bullshit. But then you stop laughing and you know it's true. Ground Zero's a killing field. Like Cambodia. Hiroshima. They're already talking about what to build there, but they're crazy. It'd make as much sense to put up a Dairy Queen at Dachau. Who'd want to eat there? People talk about doing it quickly so the terrorists will see it didn't fuck us up. But *pretending* it didn't fuck us up . . . what's that about? Hey, it fucked us up! They should wait to build. They should wait until you can walk around in it and not feel like it's hurting you to live. Because if they don't, whatever they put there is going to be filled with that feeling. That sounds absurd, maybe. To believe the ground's cursed. That there's some terrible immateriality trapped in it, something that'll seep up into the new halls and offices and cause spiritual affliction, bad karma . . . whatever. But when you're in the middle of that mess, it's impossible not to believe it.

Bobby doesn't look at Alicia as he tells her all this, speaking in a rushed, anxious delivery. When he's done he knocks back his drink, darts a glance at her to gauge her reaction, and says, "I had this friend in high school got into crystal meth. It fried his brain. He started having delusions. The government was fucking with his mind. They knew he was in contact with beings from a higher plane. Shit like that. He had this whole complex view of reality as conspiracy, and when he told me about it, it was like he was apologizing for telling me. He could sense his own damage, but he had to get it out because he couldn't quite believe he was crazy. That's how I feel. Like I'm missing some piece of myself."

"I know," Alicia says. "I feel that way, too. That's why I come here. To try and figure out what's missing . . . where I am with all this."

She looks at him inquiringly and Bobby, unburdened now, finds he has nothing worth saying. But he wants to say something, because he wants her to talk to him, and though he's not sure why he wants this or what more he might want, he's so confused by the things he's confessed and also by the ordinary confusions that attend every consequential exchange between men and women. . . . Though he's not sure of anything, he wants whatever is happening to move forward.

"Are you all right?" she asks.

"Oh, yeah. Sure. This isn't terminal fucked-uppedness. 'Least I don't think it is."

She appears to be reassessing him. "Why do you put yourself through it?"

"The job? Because I'm qualified. I worked for FEMA the last coupla summers."

Two of the yuppie couples have huddled around the jukebox and their first selection, "Smells Like Teen Spirit," begins its tense, grinding push. Pineo dances on his barstool, his torso twisting back and forth, fists tight against his chest, a parody—Bobby knows—that's aimed at the couples, meant as an insult. Brooding over his bourbon, Mazurek is a graying, thick-bodied troll turned to stone.

"I'm taking my master's in philosophy," Bobby says. "It's finally beginning to seem relevant."

He intends this as humor, but Alicia doesn't react to it as such. Her eyes are brimming. She swivels on her stool, knee pressing against his hip, and puts a hand on his wrist.

"I'm afraid," she says. "You think that's all this is? Just fear. Just an inability to cope."

He's not certain he understands her, but he says, "Maybe that's all."

It feels so natural when she loops her arms about him and buries her face in the crook of his neck, he doesn't think anything of it. His hand goes to her waist. He wants to turn toward her, to deepen the embrace, but is afraid that will alarm her, and as they cling together he becomes insecure with the contact, unclear as to what he should do with it. Her pulse hits against his palm, her breath warms his skin. The articulation of her ribs, the soft swell of a hip, the presence of a breast an inch above the tip of his thumb, all her heated specificity both daunts and tempts him. Doubt concerning their mental well-being creeps in. Is this an instance of healing or a freak scene? Are they two very different people who have connected on a level new to both of them, or are they emotional burn-outs who aren't even talking about the same subject and have misapprehended mild sexual attraction for a moment of truth? Just how much difference is there between those conditions? She pulls him closer. Her legs are still crossed and her right knee slides into his lap, her shoeless foot pushing against his waist. She whispers something, words he can't make out. An assurance, maybe. Her lips brush his cheek, then she pulls back and offers a smile he takes for an expression of regret.

"I don't get it," she says. "I have this feeling. . ." She shakes her head as if rejecting an errant notion.

"What?"

She holds a hand up beside her face as she speaks and waggles it, a blitheness of gesture that her expression does not reflect. "I shouldn't be saying this to someone I met in a bar, and I don't mean it the way you might think. But it's . . . I have a feeling you can help me. Do something for me."

"Talking helps."

"Maybe. I don't know. That doesn't seem right." Thoughtful, she stirs her drink; then a sidelong glance. "There must be something some philosopher said that's pertinent to the moment."

"Predisposition fathers all logics, even those disposed to deny it."

"Who said that?"

"I did . . . in a paper I wrote on Gorgias. The father of sophistry. He claimed that nothing can be known, and if anything could be known, it wasn't worth knowing."

"Well," says Alicia, "I guess that explains everything."

"I don't know about that. I only got a B on the paper."

One of the couples begins to dance, the man, who is still wearing his overcoat, flapping his elbows, making slow-motion swoops, while the woman stands rooted, her hips undulating in a fishlike rhythm. Pineo's parody was more graceful. Watching them, Bobby imagines the bar a cave, the other patrons with matted hair, dressed in skins. Headlights slice across the window with the suddenness of a meteor flashing past in the primitive night. The song ends, the couple's friends applaud them as they head for the group table. But when the opening riff of the Hendrix version of "All Along the Watchtower" blasts from the speakers, they start dancing again and the other couples join them, drinks in hand. The women toss their hair and shake their breasts; the men hump the air. A clumsy tribe on drugs.

The bar environment no longer works for Bobby. Too much unrelieved confusion. He hunches his shoulders against the noise, the happy jabber, and has a momentary conviction that this is not his true reaction, that a little scrap of black negativity perched between his shoulder blades, its claws buried in his spine, has folded its gargoyle wings and he has reacted to the movement like a puppet. As he stands Alicia reaches out and squeezes his hand. "See you tomorrow?"

"No doubt," he says, wondering if he will—he believes she'll go home and chastise herself for permitting this partial intimacy, this unprophylactic intrusion into her stainless career-driven life. She'll stop coming to the bar and seek redemption in a night school business course designed to flesh out her résumé. One lonely Sunday afternoon a few weeks hence, he'll provide the animating fantasy for a battery-powered orgasm.

He digs in his wallet for a five, a tip for Roman, and catches Pineo looking at him with unalloyed hostility. The kind of look your great enemy might send your way right before pumping a couple of shells into his shotgun. Pineo lets his double-barreled stare linger a few beats, then turns away to a deep consideration of his beer glass, his neck turtled, his head down. It appears that he and Mazurek have been overwhelmed by identical enchantments.

Bobby wakes up a few minutes before he's due at work. He calls the job, warns them he'll be late, then lies back and contemplates the large orange-and-brown water stain that has transformed the ceiling into a terrain map. This thing with Alicia . . . it's sick, he thinks. They're not going to fuck—that much is clear. And not just because she said so. He can't see himself going to her place, furnishings courtesy of The Sharper Image and Pottery Barn, nor can he picture her in this dump, and neither of them has displayed the urge for immediacy that would send them to a hotel. It's ridiculous, unwieldy. They're screwing around is all. Mind-fucking on some perverted soul level. She's sad because she's drinking to be sad because she's afraid that what she does not feel is actually a feeling. Typical post-modern Manhattan bullshit. Grief as a form of self-involvement. And now he's part of that. What he's doing with her may be even more perverse, but he has no desire to scrutinize his motives—that would only amplify the perversity. Better simply to let it play out and be done. These are strange days in the city. Men and women seeking intricate solace for intricate guilt. Guilt over the fact that they do not embody the magnificent sadness of politicans and the brooding sympathy of anchorpersons, that their grief is a flawed posture, streaked with the banal, with thoughts of sex and football, cable bills and job security. He still has things he needs, for whatever reason, to tell her. Tonight he'll confide in her and she will do what she must. Their mutual despondency, a wrap in four acts.

He stays forever in the shower; he's in no hurry to get to the pit, and he considers not going in at all. But duty, habit, and doggedness exert a stronger pull than his hatred and fear of the place—though it's not truly hatred and fear he feels, but a syncretic fusion of the two, an alchemical product for which a good brand name has not been coined. Before leaving, he inspects the contents of the top drawer in his dresser. The relics are the thing he most needs to explain to her. Whatever else he has determined them to be, he supposes that they are, to a degree, souvenirs, and thus a cause for shame, a morbid symptom. But when he looks at them he thinks there must be a purpose to the collection he has not yet divined, one that explaining it all to Alicia may illuminate. He selects the half-shoe. It's the only choice, really. The only object potent enough to convey the feelings he has about it. He stuffs it into his jacket pocket and goes out into the living room where his roommate is watching the Cartoon Network, his head visible above the back of the couch.

"Slept late, huh?" says the roommate.

"Little bit," Bobby says, riveted by the bright colors and goofy voices, wishing he could stay and discover how Scooby Doo and Shaggy manage to outwit the swamp beast. "See ya later."

Shortly before his shift ends he experiences a bout of paranoia during which he believes that if he glances up he'll find the pit walls risen to skyscraper height and all he'll be able to see of the sky is a tiny circle of glowing clouds. Even afterward, walking with Mazurek and Pineo through the chilly, smoking streets, distant car horns sounding in rhythm like an avant garde brass section, he half-persuades himself that it could have happened. The pit might have grown deeper, he might have dwindled. Earlier that evening they began to dig beneath a freshly excavated layer of cement rubble, and he knows his paranoia and the subsequent desire to retreat into irrationality are informed by what they unearthed. But while there is a comprehensible reason for his fear, this does not rule out other possibilities. Unbelievable things can happen of an instant. They all recognize that now.

The three men are silent as they head toward the Blue Lady. It's as if their nightly ventures to the bar no longer serve as a release and have become an extension of the job, prone to its stresses. Pineo goes with hands thrust into his pockets, eyes angled away from the others, and Mazurek looks straight ahead, swinging his thermos, resembling a Trotskyite hero, a noble worker of Factory 39. Bobby walks between them. Their solidity makes him feel unstable, as if pulled at by large opposing magnets—he wants to dart ahead or drop back, but is dragged along by their attraction. He ditches them just inside the entrance and joins Alicia at the end of the bar. Her twenty-five watt smile switches on and he thinks that though she must wear brighter, toothier smiles for co-workers and relatives, this particular smile measures the true fraction of her joy, all that is left after years of career management and bad love.

To test this theory he asks if she's got a boyfriend, and she says, "Jesus! A boyfriend. That's so quaint. You might as well ask if I have a beau."

"You got a beau?"

"I have a history of beaus," she says. "But no current need for one, thank you."

"Your eye's on the prize, huh?"

"It's not just that. Though right now, it is that. I'm"—a sardonic laugh— "I'm ascending the corporate ladder. Trying to, anyway."

She fades on him, gone to a gloomy distance beyond the bar, where the TV chatters ceaselessly of plague and misery and enduring freedom. "I wanted to have children," she says at last. "I can't stop thinking about it these days. Maybe all this sadness has a biological effect. You know. Repopulate the species."

"You've got time to have children," he says. "The career stuff may lighten up."

"Not with the men I get involved with . . . not a chance! I wouldn't let any of them take care of my plants."

"So you got a few war stories, do you?"

She puts up a hand, palm outward, as to if to hold a door closed. "You can't imagine!"

"I've got a few myself."

"You're a guy," she says. "What would you know?"

Telling him her stories, she's sarcastic, self-effacing, almost vivacious, as if by sharing these incidents of male duplicity, laughing at her own naïvete, she is proving an unassailable store of good cheer and resilience. But when she tells of a man who pursued her for an entire year, sending candy and flowers, cards, until finally she decided that he must really love her and spent the night with him, a good night after which he chose to ignore her completely . . . when she tells him this, Bobby sees past her blithe veneer into a place of abject bewilderment. He wonders how she'd look without the make-up. Softer, probably. The make-up is a painting of attitude that she daily recreates. A mask of prettified defeat and coldness to hide her fundamental confusion. Nothing has ever been as she hoped it would be—yet while she has foresworn hope, she has not banished it, and thus she is confused. He's simplifying her, he realizes. Desultory upbringing in some midwestern oasis—he hears a flattened A redolent of Detroit or Chicago. Second-rate education leading to a second-rate career. The wreckage of morning afters. This much is plain. But the truth underlying her stories, the light she bore into the world, how it has transmuted her experience . . . that remains hidden. There's no point in going deeper, though, and probably no time.

The Blue Lady fills with the late crowd. Among them a couple of middle-aged women who hold hands and kiss across their table; three young guys in Knicks gear; two black men attired gangsta-style accompanying an overweight blonde in a dyed fur wrap and a sequined cocktail dress (Roman damns them with a glare and makes them wait for service). Pineo and Mazurek are silently, soddenly drunk, isolated from their surround, but the life of the bar seems to glide around Bobby and Alicia, the jukebox rocks with old Santana, Kinks, and Springsteen. Alicia's more relaxed than Bobby's ever seen her. She's kicked off her right shoe again, shed her jacket, and though she nurses her drink, she seems to become increasingly intoxicated, as if disclosing her past were having the effect of a three-martini buzz.

"I don't think all men are assholes," she says. "But New York men . . . maybe."

"You've dated them all, huh?" he asks.

"Most of the acceptable ones, I have."

"What qualifies as acceptable in your eyes?"

Perhaps he stresses "in your eyes" a bit much, makes the question too personal, because her smile fades and she gives him a startled look. After the last strains of "Glory Days" fade, during the comparative quiet between songs, she lays a hand on his cheek, studies him, and says, less a question than a self-assurance, "You wouldn't treat me like that, would you?" And then, before Bobby can think how he should respond, taken aback by what appears an invitation to step things up, she adds, "It's too bad," and withdraws her hand.

"Why?" he asks. "I mean I kinda figured we weren't going to hook up, and I'm not arguing. I'm just curious why you felt that way."

"I don't know. Last night I wanted to. I guess I didn't want to enough."

"It's pretty unrealistic." He grins. "Given the difference in our ages."

"Bastard!" She throws a mock punch. "Actually, I found the idea of a younger man intriguing."

"Yeah, well. I'm not all that."

"Nobody's 'all that,' not until they're with somebody who thinks they are." She pretends to check him out. "You might clean up pretty nice."

"Excuse me," says a voice behind them. "Can I solicit an opinion?"

A good-looking guy in his thirties wearing a suit and a loosened tie, his face an exotic sharp-cheekboned mixture of African and Asian heritage. He's very drunk, weaving a little.

"My girlfriend . . . okay?" He glances back and forth between them. "I was supposed to meet her down . . ."

"No offense, but we're having a conversation here," Bobby says.

The guy holds his hands up as if to show he means no harm and offers apology, but then launches into a convoluted story about how he and his girlfriend missed connections and then had an argument over the phone and he started drinking and now he's broke, fucked up, puzzled by everything. It sounds like the prelude to a hustle, especially when the guy asks for a cigarette, but when they tell him they don't smoke, he does not—as might be expected—ask for money, but looks at Bobby and says, "The way they treat us, man! What are we? Chopped liver?"

"Maybe so," says Bobby.

At this, the guy takes a step back and bugs his eyes. "You got any rye?" he says. "I could use some rye."

"Seriously," Bobby says to him, gesturing at Alicia. "We need to finish our talk."

"Hey," the guy says. "Thanks for listening."

Alone again, the thread of the conversation broken, they sit for a long moment without saying anything, then start to speak at the same time.

"You first," says Bobby.

"I was just thinking. . . ." She trails off. "Never mind. It's not that important."

He knows she was on the verge of suggesting that they should get together, but that once again the urge did not rise to the level of immediacy. Or maybe there's something else, an indefinable barrier separating them, something neither one of them has tumbled to. He thinks this must be the case, because given her history, and his own, it's apparent neither of them have been discriminating in the past. But she's right, he decides—whatever's happening between them is simply not that important, and thus it's not that important to understand.

She smiles, an emblem of apology, and stares down into her drink. "Free Falling" by Tom Petty is playing on the box, and some people behind them begin wailing along with it, nearly drowning out the vocal.

"I brought something for you," Bobby says.

An uneasy look. "From your work?"

"Yeah, but this isn't the same. . . ."

"I told you I didn't want to see that kind of thing."

"They're not just souvenirs," he says. "If I seem messed up to you . . . and I'm sure I do. I *feel* messed up, anyway. But if I seem messed up, the things I take from the pit, they're kind of an explanation for . . ." He runs a hand through his hair, frustrated by his inability to speak what's on his mind. "I don't know why I want you to see this. I guess I'm hoping it'll help you understand something."

"About what?" she says, leery.

"About me . . . or where I work. Or something. I haven't been able to nail that down, y'know. But I do want you to see it."

Alicia's eyes slide away from him; she fits her gaze to the mirror behind the bar, its too perfect reflection of romance, sorrow, and drunken fun. "If that's what you want."

Bobby touches the half-shoe in his jacket pocket. The silk is cool to his fingers. He imagines that he can feel its blueness. "It's not a great thing to look at. I'm not trying to freak you out, though. I think . . ."

She snaps at him. "Just show it to me!"

He sets the shoe beside her glass and for a second or two it's like she doesn't notice it. Then she makes a sound in her throat. A single note, the human equivalent of an ice cube *plinking* in a glass, bright and clear, and puts a hand out as if to touch it. But she doesn't touch it, not at first, just leaves her hand hovering above the shoe. He can't read her face, except for the fact that she's fixated on the thing. Her fingers trail along the scorched margin of the silk, tracing the ragged line. "Oh, my god!" she says, all but the glottal sound buried beneath a sudden surge in the music. Her hand closes around the shoe, her head droops. It looks as if she's in a trance, channeling a feeling or some trace of memory. Her eyes glisten and she's so still, Bobby wonders if what he's done has injured her, if she was unstable and now he's pushed her over the edge. A minute passes and she hasn't moved. The jukebox falls silent, the chatter and laughter of the other patrons rise around them.

"Alicia?"

She shakes her head, signaling either that she's been robbed of the power to speak or is not interested in communicating.

"Are you okay?" he asks.

She says something he can't hear, but he's able to read her lips and knows the word "god" was again involved. A tear escapes the corner of her eye, runs down her cheek, and clings to her upper lip. It may be that the half-shoe impressed her, as it has him, as being the perfect symbol, the absolute explanation of what they have lost and what has survived, and this, its graphic potency, is what has distressed her.

The jukebox kicks in again, an old Stan Getz tune, and Bobby hears Pineo's voice bleating in argument, cursing bitterly; but he doesn't look to see what's wrong. He's captivated by Alicia's face. Whatever pain or loss she's feeling, it has concentrated her meager portion of beauty, and suffering, she's shining; the female hound of Wall Street thing she does with her cosmetics radiated out of existence by a porcelain *Song of Bernadette* saintliness, the clean lines of her neck and jaw suddenly pure and Periclean. It's such a startling transformation, he's not sure it's really happening. Drink's to blame, or there's some other problem with his eyes. Life, according to his experience, doesn't provide this type of quintessential change. Thin, half-grown cats do not of an instant gleam and grow sleek in their exotic simplicity like tiny gray tigers. Small, tidy Cape Cod cottages do not because of any shift in weather, no matter how glorious the light, glow resplendent and ornate like minor Asiatic temples. Yet Alicia's golden change is manifest. She's beautiful. Even the red membraneous corners of her eyes, irritated by tears and city grit, seem decorative, part of a subtle design, and when she turns to him, the entire new delicacy of her features flowing toward him with the uncanny force of a visage materializing from a beam of light, he feels imperiled by her nearness, uncertain of her purpose. What can she now want of him? As she pulls his face close to hers, lips parting, eyelids half-lowering, he is afraid a kiss may kill him, either overpower him, a wave washing away a tiny scuttler on the sand, or that the taste of her, a fraction of warm saliva resembling a speck of crystal with a flavor of sweet acid, will react with his own common spittle to synthesize a compound microweight of poison, a perfect solution to the predicament of his mortality. But then another transformation, one almost as drastic, and as her mouth finds him, he sees the young woman, vulnerable and soft, giving and wanting, the childlike need and openness of her.

The kiss lasts not long, but long enough to have a history, a progression from contact to immersion, exploration to a mingling of tongues and gushing breath, yet once their intimacy is completely achieved, the temperature dialed high, she breaks from it and puts her mouth to his ear and whispers fiercely, tremulously, "Thank you. . . . Thank you so much!" Then she's standing, gathering her purse, her briefcase, a regretful smile, and says, "I have to go."

"Wait!" He catches at her, but she fends him off.

"I'm sorry," she says. "But I have to . . . right now. I'm sorry."

And she goes, walking smartly toward the door, leaving him with no certainty of conclusion, with his half-grown erection and his instantly catalogued memory of the kiss surfacing to be examined and weighed, its tenderness and fragility to be considered, its sexual intensity to be marked upon a scale, its meaning surmised, and by the time he's made these judgments, waking to the truth that she has truly, unequivocally gone and deciding to run after her, she's out the door. By the time he reaches the door, shouldering it open, she's twenty-five, thirty feet down the sidewalk, stepping quickly between the parked cars and the storefronts, passing a shadowed doorway, and he's about to call out her name when she moves into the light spilling from a coffee shop window and he notices that her shoes are blue. Pale blue with a silky sheen and of a shape that appears identical to that of the half-shoe left on the bar. If, indeed, it was left there. He can't remember now. Did she take it? The question has a strange, frightful value, born of a frightful suspicion that he cannot quite reject, and for a moment he's torn between the impulse to go after her and a desire to turn back into the bar and look for the shoe. That, in the end, is what's important. To discover if she took the shoe, and if she did, then to fathom the act, to decipher it. Was it done because she thought it a gift, or because she wanted it so badly, maybe to satisfy some freaky neurotic demand, that she felt she had to more or less steal it, get him confused with a kiss and bolt before he realized it was missing? Or—and this is the notion that's threatening to possess him—was the shoe hers to begin with? Feeling foolish, yet not persuaded he's a fool, he watches her step off the curb at the next corner and cross the street, dwindling and dwindling, becoming indistinct from other pedestrians. A stream of traffic blocks his view. Still toying with the idea of chasing after her, he stands there for half a minute or so, wondering if he has misinterpreted everything about her. A cold wind coils like a scarf about his neck, and the wet pavement begins soaking into his sock through the hole in his right boot. He squints at the poorly defined distance beyond the cross-street, denies a last twinge of impulse, then yanks open the door of the Blue Lady. A gust of talk and music seems to whirl past him from within, like the ghost of a party leaving the scene, and he goes on inside, even though he knows in his heart that the shoe is gone.

Bobby's immunity to the pit has worn off. In the morning he's sick as last week's salmon plate. A fever that turns his bones to glass and rots his sinuses, a cough that sinks deep into his chest and hollows him with chills. His sweat smells sour and yellow, his spit is thick as curds. For the next forty-eight hours he can think of only two things. Medicine and Alicia. She's threaded through his fever, braided around every thought like a strand of RNA, but he can't even begin to make sense of what he thinks and feels. A couple of nights later the fever breaks. He brings blankets, a pillow, and orange juice into the living room and takes up residence on the sofa. "Feeling better, huh?" say the roommate, and Bobby says, "Yeah, little bit." After a pause, the roommate hands him the remote and seeks refuge in his room, where he spends the day playing video games. *Quake*, mostly. The roars of demons and chattering chain guns issue from behind his closed door.

Bobby channel surfs, settles on CNN, which is alternating between an overhead view of Ground Zero and a studio shot of an attractive brunette sitting at an anchor desk, talking to various men and women about 9/11, the war, the recovery. After listening for almost half an hour, he concludes that if this is all people hear, this gossipy, maudlin chitchat about life and death and healing, they must know nothing. The pit looks like a dingy hole with some yellow machines moving debris—there's no sense transmitted of its profundity, of how—when you're down in it—it seems deep and everlasting, like an ancient broken well. He goes surfing again, finds an old Jack the Ripper movie starring Michael Caine, and turns the sound low, watches detectives in long dark coats hurrying through the dimly lit streets, paperboys shouting news of the latest atrocity. He begins to put together the things Alicia told him. All of them. From "I've just been to a funeral," to "Everybody's ready to go on with their lives, but I'm not ready," to "That's why I come here . . . to figure out what's missing," to "I have to go." Her transformation . . . did he really see it? The memory is so unreal, but then all memories are unreal, and at the moment it happened he knew to his bones who and what she was, and that when she took the shoe, the object that let her understand what had been done to her, she was only reclaiming her property. Of course everything can be explained in other ways, and it's tempting to accept those other explanations, to believe she was just an uptight careerwoman taking a break from corporate sanity and once she recognized where she was, what she was doing, who she was doing it with, she grabbed a souvenir and beat it back to the email-messaging, network-building, clickety-click world of spread sheets and wheat futures and martinis with some cute guy from advertising who would eventually fuck her brains out and afterward tell the-bitch-was-begging-for-it stories about her at his gym. That's who she was, after all, whatever her condition. An unhappy woman committed to her unhappy path, wanting more yet unable to perceive how she had boxed herself in. But the things that came out of her on their last night at the Blue Lady, the self-revelatory character of her transformation . . . the temptation of the ordinary is incapable of denying those memories.

It's a full week before Bobby returns to work. He comes in late, after darkness has fallen and the lights have been switched on, halfway inclined to tell his supervisor that he's quitting. He shows his ID and goes down into the pit, looking for Pineo and Mazurek. The great yellow earth movers are still, men are standing around in groups, and from this Bobby recognizes that a body has been recently found, a ceremony just concluded, and they're having a break before getting on with the job. He's hesitant to join the others and pauses next to a wall made of huge concrete slabs, shattered and resting at angles atop one another, holding pockets of shadow and worse in their depths. He's been standing there about a minute when he feels her behind him. It's not like in a horror story. No terrible cold or prickling hairs or windy voices. It's like being with her in the bar. Her warmth, her perfumey scent, her nervous poise. But frailer, weaker, a delicate presence barely in the world. He's afraid if he turns to look at her, it will break their tenuous connection. She's probably not visible, anyway. No Stephen King commercial, no sight of her hovering a few inches off the ground, bearing the horrid wounds that killed her. She's a willed fraction of herself, less tangible than a wisp of smoke, less certain than a whisper. "Alicia," he says, and her effect intensifies. Her scent grows stronger, her warmth more insistent. and he knows why she's here. "I realize you had to go," he says, and then it's like when she embraced him, all her warmth employed to draw him close. He can almost touch her firm waist, the tiered ribs, the softness of a breast, and he wishes they could go out. Just once. Not so they could sweat and make sleepy promises and lose control and then regain control and bitterly go off in opposite directions, but because at most times people were only partly there for one another—which was how he and Alicia were in the Blue Lady, knowing only the superficial about each other, a few basic lines and a hint of detail, like two sketches in the midst of an oil painting, their minds directed elsewhere, not caring enough to know all there was to know—and the way it is between them at this moment, they would try to know everything. They would try to find the things that did not exist like smoke behind their eyes. The ancient grammars of the spirit, the truths behind their old yet newly demolished truths. In the disembodiment of desire, an absolute focus born. They would call to one another, they would forget the cities and the wars. . . . Then it's not her mouth he feels, but the feeling he had when they were kissing, a curious mixture of bewilderment and carnality, accented this time by a quieter emotion. Satisfaction, he thinks. At having helped her understand. At himself understanding his collection of relics and why he approached her. Fate or coincidence, it's all the same, all clear to him now.

"Yo, Bobby!"

It's Pineo. Smirking, walking toward him with a springy step and not a trace of the hostility he displayed the last time they were together. "Man, you look like shit, y'know."

"I wondered if I did," Bobby says. "I figured you'd tell me."

"It's what I'm here for." Pineo fakes throwing a left hook under Bobby's ribs.

"Where's Carl?"

"Taking a dump. He's worried about your ass."

"Yeah, I bet."

"C'mon! You know he's got that dad thing going with you." Pineo affects an Eastern European accent, makes a fist, scowls Mazurek-style. " 'Bobby is like son to me.' "

"I don't think so. All he does is tell me what an asshole I am."

"That's Polish for 'son,' man. That's how those old bruisers treat their kids."

As they begin walking across the pit, Pineo says, "I don't know what you did to Calculator Bitch, man, but she never did come back to the bar. You musta messed with her mind."

Bobby wonders if his hanging out with Alicia was the cause of Pineo's hostility, if Pineo perceived him to be at fault, the one who was screwing up their threefold unity, their trinity of luck and spiritual maintenance. Things could be that simple.

"What'd you say to her?" Pineo asks.

"Nothing. I just told her about the job."

Pineo cocks his head and squints at him. "You're not being straight with me. I got the eye for bullshit, just like my mama. Something going on with you two?"

"Uh-huh. We're gonna get married."

"Don't tell me you're fucking her."

"I'm not fucking her!"

Pineo points at him. "There it is! Bullshit!"

"Sicilian ESP. . . . Wow. How come you people don't rule the world?"

"I can't *believe* you're fucking the Calculator Bitch!" Pineo looks up to heaven and laughs. "Man, were you even sick at all? I bet you spent the whole goddamn week sleep-testing her Serta."

Bobby just shakes his head ruefully.

"So what's it like . . . yuppie pussy?"

Irritated now, Bobby says, "Fuck off !"

"Seriously. I grew up in Queens, I been deprived. What's she like? She wear thigh boots and a colonel's hat? She carry a riding crop? No, that's too much like her day job. She . . ."

One of the earth movers starts up, rumbling like T-Rex, vibrating the ground, and Pineo has to raise his voice to be heard.

"She was too sweet, wasn't she? All teach me tonight and sugar, sugar. Like some little girl read all the books but didn't know what she read till you come along and pulled her trigger. Yeah . . . and once the little girl thing gets over, she goes wild on your ass. She loses control, she be fucking liberated."

Bobby recalls the transformation, not the-glory-that-was-Alicia part, the shining forth of soul rays, but the instant before she kissed him, the dazed wonderment in her face, and realizes that Pineo—unwittingly, of course—has put his grimy, cynical, ignorant, wise-ass finger on something he, Bobby, has heretofore not fully grasped. That she did awaken, and not merely to her posthumous condition, but to him. That at the end she remembered who she wanted to be. Not "who," maybe. But *how*. How she wanted to feel, how she wanted to live. The vivid, less considered road she hoped her life would travel. Understanding this, he understands what the death of thousands has not taught him. The exact measure of his loss. And ours. The death of one. All men being Christ and God in His glorious fever burning, the light toward which they aspire. Love in the whirlwind.

"Yeah, she was all that," Bobby says.

THE CHILDREN OF TIME

STEPHEN BAXTER

I

Jaal had always been fascinated by the ice on the horizon. Even now, beyond the smoke of the evening hearth, he could see that line of pure bone white, sharper than a stone blade's cut, drawn across the edge of the world.

It was the end of the day, and a huge sunset was staining the sky. Alone, restless, he walked a few paces away from the rich smoky pall, away from the smell of broiling raccoon meat and bubbling goat fat, the languid talk of the adults, the eager play of the children.

The ice was always there on the northern horizon, always out of reach no matter how hard you walked across the scrubby grassland. He knew why. The ice cap was retreating, dumping its pure whiteness into the meltwater streams, exposing land crushed and gouged and strewn with vast boulders. So while you walked toward it, the ice was marching away from you.

And now the gathering sunset was turning the distant ice pink. The clean geometric simplicity of the landscape drew his soul; he stared, entranced.

Jaal was eleven years old, a compact bundle of muscle. He was dressed in layers of clothing, sinew-sewn from scraped goat skin and topped by a heavy coat of rabbit fur. On his head was a hat made by his father from the skin of a whole raccoon, and on his feet he wore the skin of pigeons, turned inside-out and the feathers coated with grease. Around his neck was a string of pierced cat teeth.

Jaal looked back at his family. There were a dozen of them, parents and children, aunts and uncles, nephews and nieces, and one grand-mother, worn down, aged forty-two. Except for the very smallest children, everybody moved slowly, obviously weary. They had walked a long way today.

He knew he should go back to the fire and help out, do his duty, find firewood or skin a rat. But every day was like this. Jaal had ancient, unpleasant memories from when he was very small, of huts burning, people screaming and fleeing. Jaal and his family had been walking north ever since, looking for a new home. They hadn't found it yet.

Jaal spotted Sura, good-humoredly struggling to get a filthy skin coat off the squirming body of her little sister. Sura, Jaal's second cousin, was two years older than him. She had a limpid, liquid ease of movement in everything she did.

She saw Jaal looking at her and arched an eyebrow. He blushed, hot, and turned away to the north. The ice was a much less complicated companion than Sura.

He saw something new.

As the angle of the sun continued to change, the light picked out something on the ground. It was a straight line, glowing red in the light of the sun, like an echo of the vast edge of the ice itself. But this line was close, only a short walk from here, cutting through hummocks and scattered boulders. He had to investigate.

With a guilty glance back at his family, he ran away, off to the north, his pigeon-skin boots carrying him silently over the hard ground. The straight-edge feature was further away than it looked, and as he became frustrated he ran faster. But then he came on it. He stumbled to a halt, panting.

It was a ridge as high as his knees—a ridge of stone, but nothing like the ice-carved boulders and shattered gravel that littered the rest of the landscape. Though its top was worn and broken, its sides were *flat*, smoother than any stone he had touched before, and the sunlight filled its creamy surface with color.

Gingerly he climbed on the wall to see better. The ridge of stone ran off to left and right, to east and west—and then it turned sharp corners, to run north, before turning back on itself again. There was a pattern here, he saw. This stone ridge traced a straight-edged frame on the ground.

And there were more ridges; the shadows cast by the low sun picked out the stone tracings clearly. The land to the north of here was covered by a tremendous rectangular scribble that went on as far as he could see. All this was made by people. He knew this immediately, without question.

In fact this had been a suburb of Chicago. Most of the city had been scraped clean by the advancing ice, but the foundations of this suburb, fortuitously, had been flooded and frozen in before the glaciers came. These ruins were already a hundred thousand years old.

"Jaal. Jaal! . . ." His mother's voice carried to him like the cry of a bird.

He couldn't bear to leave what he had found. He stood on the eroded wall and let his mother come to him.

She was weary, grimy, stressed. "Why must you do this? Don't you *know* the cats hunt in twilight?"

He flinched from the disappointment in her eyes, but he couldn't contain his excitement. "Look what I found, mother!"

She stared around. Her face showed incomprehension, disinterest. "What is it?"

His imagination leapt, fueled by wonder, and he tried to make her see what he saw. "Maybe once these rock walls were tall, tall as the ice itself. Maybe people lived here in great heaps, and the smoke of their fires rose up to the sky. Mother, will we come to live here again?"

"Perhaps one day," his mother said at random, to hush him.

The people never would return. By the time the returning ice had shattered their monocultural, over-extended technological civilization, people had exhausted the Earth of its accessible deposits of iron ore and coal and oil and other resources. People would survive: smart, adaptable, they didn't need cities for that. But with nothing but their most ancient technologies of stone and fire, they could never again conjure up the towers of Chicago. Soon even Jaal, distracted by the fiery eyes of Sura, would forget this place existed.

But for now he longed to explore. "Let me go on. Just a little further!"

"No," his mother said gently. "The adventure's over. It's time to go. Come now." And she put her arm around his shoulders, and led him home.

II

Urlu crawled toward the river. The baked ground was hard under her knees and hands, and stumps of burned-out trees and shrubs scraped her flesh. There was no green here, nothing grew, and nothing moved save a few flecks of ash disturbed by the low breeze.

She was naked, sweating, her skin streaked by charcoal. Her hair was a mat, heavy with dust and grease. In one hand she carried a sharpened stone. She was eleven years old.

She wore a string of pierced teeth around her neck. The necklace was a gift from her grandfather, Pala, who said the teeth were from an animal called a rabbit. Urlu had never seen a rabbit. The last of them had died in the Burning, before she was born, along with the rats and the raccoons, all the small mammals that had long ago survived the ice with mankind. So there would be no more rabbit teeth. The necklace was precious.

The light brightened. Suddenly there was a shadow beneath her, her own form cast upon the darkened ground. She threw herself flat in the dirt. She wasn't used to shadows. Cautiously she glanced over her shoulder, up at the sky.

All her life a thick lid of ash-laden cloud had masked the sky. But for the last few days it had been breaking up, and today the cloud had disintegrated further. And now, through high drifting cloud, she saw a disc, pale and gaunt.

It was the sun. She had been told its name, but had never quite believed in it. Now it was revealed, and Urlu helplessly stared up at its geometric purity.

She heard a soft voice call warningly. "Urlu!" It was her mother.

It was no good to be dayreaming about the sky. She had a duty to fulfill, down here in the dirt. She turned and crawled on.

She reached the bank. The river, thick with blackened dirt and heavy with debris, rolled sluggishly. It was so wide that in the dim light of noon she could barely see the far side. In fact this was the Seine, and the charred ground covered traces of what had once been Paris. It made no difference where she was. The whole Earth was like this, all the same.

To Urlu's right, downstream, she saw hunters, pink faces smeared with dirt peering from the ruined vegetation. The weight of their expectation pressed heavily on her.

She took her bit of chipped stone, and pressed its sharpest edge against the skin of her palm. It had to be her. The people believed that the creatures of the water were attracted by the blood of a virgin. She was afraid of the pain to come, but she had no choice; if she didn't go through with the cut one of the men would come and do it for her, and that would hurt far more.

But she heard a wail, a cry of loss and sorrow, rising like smoke into the dismal air. It was coming from the camp. The faces along the bank turned, distracted. Then, one by one, the hunters slid back into the ruined undergrowth.

Urlu, hugely relieved, turned away from the debris-choked river, her stone tucked safely in her hand.

The camp was just a clearing in the scorched ground-cover, with a charcoal fire burning listlessly in the hearth. Beside the fire an old man lay on a rough pallet of earth and scorched brush, gaunt, as naked and filthy as the rest. His eyes were wide, rheumy, and he stared at the sky. Pala, forty-five years old, was Urlu's grandfather. He was dying, eaten from within by something inside his belly.

He was tended by a woman who knelt in the dirt beside him. She was his oldest daughter, Urlu's aunt. The grime on her face was streaked by tears. "He's frightened," said the aunt. "It's finishing him off."

Urlu's mother asked, "Frightened of what?"

The aunt pointed into the sky.

The old man had reason to be frightened of strange lights in the sky. He had been just four years old when a greater light had come to Earth.

After Jaal's time, the ice had returned a dozen times more before retreating for good. After that, people rapidly cleared the land of the legacy of the ice: descendants of cats and rodents and birds, grown large and confident in the temporary absence of humanity. Then people hunted and farmed, built up elaborate networks of trade and culture, and developed exquisite technologies of wood and stone and bone. There was much evolutionary churning in the depths of the sea, out of reach of mankind. But people were barely touched by time, for there was no need for them to change.

This equable afternoon endured for thirty million years. The infant Pala's parents had sung him songs unimaginably old.

But then had come the comet's rude incursion. Nearly a hundred million years after the impactor that had terminated the summer of the dinosaurs, Earth had been due another mighty collision.

Pala and his parents, fortuitously close to a cave-ridden mountain, had endured the fires, the rain of molten rock, the long dust-shrouded winter. People survived, as they had lived through lesser cataclysms since the ice. And with their ingenuity and adaptability and generalist ability to eat almost anything, they had already begun to spread once more over the ruined lands.

Once it had been thought that human survival would depend on planting colonies on other worlds, for Earth would always be prone to such disasters. But people had never ventured far from Earth: there was nothing out there; the stars had always remained resolutely silent. And though since the ice their numbers had never been more than a few million, people were too numerous and too widespread to be eliminated even by a comet's deadly kiss. It was easy to kill a lot of people. It was very hard to kill them all.

As it happened old Pala was the last human alive to remember the world before the Burning. With him died memories thirty million years deep. In the morning they staked out his body on a patch of high ground.

The hunting party returned to the river, to finish the job they had started. This time there was no last-minute reprieve for Urlu. She slit open her palm, and let her blood run into the murky river water. Its crimson was the brightest color in the whole of this grey-black world.

Urlu's virginal state made no difference to the silent creature who slid through the water, but she was drawn by the scent of blood. Another of the planet's great survivors, she had ridden out the Burning buried in deep mud, and fed without distaste on the scorched remains washed into her river. Now she swam up toward the murky light.

All her life Urlu had eaten nothing but snakes, cockroaches, scorpions, spiders, maggots, termites. That night she feasted on crocodile meat.

By the morning she was no longer a virgin. She didn't enjoy it much, but at least it was her choice. And at least she wouldn't have to go through any more blood-letting.

III

The catamaran glided toward the beach, driven by the gentle current of the shallow sea and the muscles of its crew. When it ran aground the people splashed into water that came up to their knees, and began to unload weapons and food. The sun hung bright and hot in a cloudless blue dome of a sky, and the people, small and lithe, were surrounded by shining clouds of droplets as they worked. Some of them had their favorite snakes wrapped around their necks.

Cale, sitting on the catamaran, clung to its seaweed trunks. Looking out to sea, he could spot the fine dark line that was the floating community where he had been born. This was an age of warmth, of high seas that had flooded the edges of the continents, and most people on Earth made their living from the rich produce of coral reefs and other sun-drenched shallow-water ecosystems. Cale longed to go back to the rafts, but soon he must walk on dry land, for the first time in his life. He was eleven years old.

Cale's mother, Lia, splashed through the water to him. Her teeth shone white in her dark face. "You will never be a man if you are so timid as this." And she grabbed him, threw him over her shoulder, ran through the shallow water to the beach, and dumped him in the sand. "There!" she cried. "You are the first to set foot here, the first of all!"

Everybody laughed, and Cale, winded, resentful, blushed helplessly.

For some time Cale's drifting family had been aware of the line on the horizon. They had prepared their gifts of sea fruit and carved coral, and rehearsed the songs they would sing, and carved their weapons, and here they were. They thought this was an island full of people. They were wrong. This was no island, but a continent.

Since the recovery of the world from Urlu's great Burning, there had been time enough for the continents' slow tectonic dance to play out. Africa had collided softly with Europe, Australia had kissed Asia, and Antarctica had come spinning up from the south pole. It was these great geographical changes—together with a slow, relentless heating-up of the sun—which had given the world its long summer.

While the rafts had dreamed over fecund seas, seventy million years had worn away. But even over such a tremendous interval, people were much the same as they had always been.

And now here they were, on the shore of Antarctica—and Cale was indeed the first of all.

Unsteadily he got to his feet. For a moment the world seemed to tip and rock beneath him. But it was not the world that tipped, he understood, but his own imagination, shaped by a life on the rafts.

The beach stretched around him, sloping up to a line of tall vegetation. He had never seen anything like it. His fear and resentment quickly subsided, to be replaced by curiosity.

The landing party had forgotten him already. They were gathering driftwood for a fire and unloading coils of meat—snake meat, from the fat, stupid, domesticated descendants of one of the few animals to survive the firestorm of Urlu's day. They would have a feast, and they would get drunk, and they would sleep; only tomorrow would they begin to explore.

Cale discovered he didn't want to wait that long. He turned away from the sea, and walked up the shallow slope of the beach.

A line of hard trunks towered above his head, smooth-hulled. These "trees," as his father had called them, were in fact a kind of grass, something like bamboo. Cale came from a world of endless flatness; to him these trees were mighty constructs indeed. And sunlight shone through the trees, from an open area beyond.

A few paces away a freshwater stream decanted onto the beach and trickled to the sea. Cale could see that it came from a small gully that cut through the bank of trees. It was a way through, irresistible.

The broken stones of the gully's bed stung his feet, and sharp branches scraped at his skin. The rocks stuck in the gully walls were a strange mix: big boulders set in a greyish clay, down to pebbles small enough to have fit in Cale's hand, all jammed together. Even the bedrock was scratched and grooved, as if some immense, spiky fish had swum this way.

Here in this tropical rainforest, Cale was surrounded by the evidence of ice.

He soon reached the open area behind the trees. It was just a glade a few paces across, opened up by the fall of one mighty tree. Cale stepped forward, making for a patch of green. But iridescent wings beat, and a fat, segmented body soared up from the green, and Cale stumbled to a halt. The insect was huge, its body longer than he was tall. Now more vast dragonflies rose up, startled, huddling for protection. A sleeker form, its body yellow-banded, came buzzing out of the trees. It was a remote descendant of a wasp, a solitary predator. It assaulted the swarming dragonflies, ripping through shimmering wings. All this took place over Cale's head in a cloud of flapping and buzzing. It was too strange to be frightening.

He was distracted by a strange squirming at his feet. The patch of green from which he had disturbed the first dragonfly was itself moving, flowing over the landscape as if liquid. It was actually a crowd of creatures, a mass of wriggling worms. From the tops of tottering piles of small bodies, things like eyes blinked.

Such sights were unique to Antarctica. There was no other place like this, anywhere on Earth.

When its ice melted away, the bare ground of Antarctica became an arena for life. The first colonists had been blown on the wind from over the sea: vegetation, insects, birds. But this was not an age for birds, or indeed mammals. As the world's systems compensated for the slow heating of the sun, carbon dioxide, the main greenhouse gas, was drawn down into the sea and the rocks, and the air became oxygen-rich. The insects used this heady fuel to grow huge, and predatory wasps and cockroaches as bold as rats made short work of Antarctica's flightless birds.

And there had been time for much more dramatic evolutionary shifts, time for whole phyla to be remodeled. The squirming multiple organism that fled from Cale's approach was a descendant of the siphonophores, colonial creatures of the sea like Portuguese men o' war. Endlessly adaptable, hugely ecologically inventive, since colonizing the land these compound creatures had occupied fresh water, the ground, the branches of the grass-trees, even the air.

Cale sensed something of the transient strangeness of what he saw. Antarctica, empty of humans, had been the stage for Earth's final gesture of evolutionary inventiveness. But relentless tectonic drift had at last brought Antarctica within reach of the ocean-going communities who sailed over the flooded remnants of India, and the great experiment was about to end. Cale gazed around, eyes wide, longing to discover more.

A coral-tipped spear shot past his head, and he heard a roar. He staggered back, shocked.

A patch of green ahead of him split and swarmed away, and a huge form emerged. Grey-skinned, supported on two narrow forelegs and a powerful articulated tail, this monster seemed to be all head. A spear stuck out from its neck. The product of another transformed phylum, this was a chondrichthyan, a distant relation of a shark. The beast opened a mouth like a cavern, and blood-soaked breath blasted over Cale.

Lia was at Cale's side. "Come on." She hooked an arm under his shoulders and dragged him away.

Back on the beach, munching on snake meat, Cale soon got over his shock. Everybody made a fuss of him as he told his tales of giant wasps and the huge land-shark. At that moment he could not imagine ever returning to the nightmares of the forest.

But of course he would. And in little more than a thousand years his descendants, having burned their way across Antarctica, accompanied by their hunting snakes and their newly domesticated attack-wasps, would hunt down the very last of the land-sharks, and string its teeth around their necks.

IV

Tura and Bel, sister and brother, grew up in a world of flatness, on a shoreline between an endless ocean and a land like a tabletop. But in the distance there were mountains, pale cones turned purple by the ruddy mist. As long as she could remember, Tura had been fascinated by the mountains. She longed to walk to them—even, she fantasized, to climb them.

But how could she ever reach them? Her people lived at the coast, feeding on the soft-fleshed descendants of neotenous crabs. The land was a plain of red sand, littered with gleaming salt flats, where nothing could live. The mountains were forever out of reach.

Then, in Tura's eleventh year, the land turned unexpectedly green.

The aging world was still capable of volcanic tantrums. One such episode, the eruption of a vast basaltic flood, had pumped carbon dioxide into the air. As flowers in the desert had once waited decades for the rains, so their remote descendants waited for such brief volcanic summers to make them bloom.

Tura and her brother hatched the plan between them. They would never get this chance again; the greening would be gone in a year, perhaps never to return in their lifetimes. No adult would ever have approved. But no adult need know.

And so, very early one morning, they slipped away from the village. Wearing nothing but kilts woven from dried sea grass, their favorite shell necklaces around their necks, they looked very alike. As they ran they laughed, excited by their adventure, and their blue eyes shone against the rusted crimson of the landscape.

Bel and Tura lived on what had once been the western coast of North America—but, just as in Urlu's dark time of global catastrophe, it didn't really matter where you lived. For this was the age of a supercontinent.

The slow convergence of the continents had ultimately produced a unity that mirrored a much earlier mammoth assemblage, broken up before the dinosaurs evolved. While vast unending storms roamed the waters of the world-ocean, New Pangaea's interior collapsed to a desic-cated wasteland, and people drifted to the mouths of the great rivers, and to the sea coasts. This grand coalescence was accompanied by the solemn drumbeat of extinction events; each time the world recovered, though each time a little less vigorously than before.

The supercontinent's annealing took two hundred million years. And since then, another two hundred million years had already gone by. But people lived much as they always had.

Tura and Bel, eleven-year-old twins, knew nothing of this. They were young, and so was their world; it was ever thus. And today, especially, was a day of wonder, as all around them plants, gobbling carbon diox-ide, fired packets of spores through the air, and insects scrambled in once-in-a-lifetime quests to propagate.

As the sun climbed the children tired, their pace falling, and the arid air sucked the sweat off their bodies. But at last the mountains came looming out of the dusty air. These worn hills were ancient, a relic of the formation of New Pangaea. But to Tura and Bel, standing before their scree-covered lower slopes, they were formidable heights indeed.

Then Tura saw a splash of green and brown, high on a slope. Curiosity sparked. Without thinking about it she began to climb. Bel, always more nervous, would not follow.

Though at first the slope was so gentle it was no more than a walk, Tura was soon higher than she had ever been in her life. On she climbed, until her walk gave way to an instinctive scramble on all fours. Her heart hammering, she kept on. All around her New Pangaea unfolded, a sea of Mars-red dust worn flat by time.

At last she reached the green. It was a clump of trees, shadowed by the mountain from the dust-laden winds and nourished by water from subsurface aquifers. Instinctively Tura rubbed her hand over smooth, sturdy trunks. She had never seen trees before.

As the sun brightened, Earth's systems compensated by drawing down carbon dioxide from the air. But this was a process with a limit: even in Jaal's time the remnant carbon dioxide had been a trace. Already the planet had shed many rich ecosystems—tundra, forests, grasslands, meadows, mangrove swamps. Soon the carbon dioxide concentration would drop below a certain critical level, after which only a fraction of plants would be able to photosynthesize. The human population, already only a million strung out around the world's single coastline, would implode to perhaps ten thousand.

People would survive. They always had. But these trees, in whose cool shade Tura stood, were among the last in the world.

She peered up at branches with sparse crowns of spiky leaves, far above her head. There might be fruit up there, or water to be had in the leaves. But it was impossible; she could not climb past the smoothness of the lower trunk.

When she looked down Bel's upturned face was a white dot. The day was advancing; as the sun rode higher the going across the dry dust would be even more difficult. With regret she began her scrambled descent to the ground.

As she lived out her life on the coast of Pangaea, Tura never forgot her brief adventure. And when she thought of the trees her hands and feet itched, her body recalling ape dreams abandoned half a billion years before.

V

Ruul was bored.

All through the echoing caverns the party was in full swing. By the light of their hearths and rush torches people played and danced, talked and laughed, drank and fought, and the much-evolved descendants of snakes and wasps curled affectionately around the ankles of their owners. It was a Thousand-Day festival. In a world forever cut off from the daylight, subterranean humans pale as worms marked time by how they slept and woke, and counted off the days of their lives on their fingers.

Everyone was having fun—everyone but Ruul. When his mother was too busy to notice, he crept away into the dark.

Some time ago, restlessly exploring the edge of the inhabited cave, where tunnels and boreholes stretched on into the dark, he had found a chimney, a crack in the limestone. It looked as if you could climb up quite a way. And when he shielded his eyes, it looked to him as if there was light up there, light of a strange ruddy hue. There might be another group somewhere in the caverns above, he thought. Or it might be something stranger yet, something beyond his imagination.

Now, in the dim light of the torches, he explored the chimney wall. Lodging his fingers and toes in crevices, he began to climb.

He was escaping the party. Eleven years old, neither child nor adult, he just didn't fit, and he petulantly wished the festival would go away. But as he ascended into profound silence the climb itself consumed all his attention, and the why of it faded from his mind.

His people, cavern-bound for uncounted generations, were good at rock-climbing. They lived in caverns in deep limestone karsts, laid down in long-vanished shallow seas. Once these hollows had hosted ecosystems full of the much-evolved descendants of lizards, snakes, scorpions, cockroaches, even sharks and crocodiles. The extreme and unchanging conditions of Pangaea had encouraged intricacy and inter-dependency. The people, retreating underground, had allowed fragments of these extraordinary biotas to survive.

Soon Ruul climbed up out of the limestone into a softer sandstone, poorly cemented. It was easier to find crevices here. The crimson light from above was bright enough to show him details of the rock through which he was passing. There was layer upon layer of it, he saw, and it had a repetitive pattern, streaks of darkness punctuated by lumpy nodules. When he touched one of the nodules, he found a blade surface so sharp he might have cut his fingers. It was a stone axe—made, used, and dropped long ago, and buried somehow in the sediments that had made this sandstone. Growing more curious, he explored the dark traces. They crumbled when he dug into them with a fingernail, and he could smell ash, as fresh as if a fire had just burned here. The dark layers were hearths.

He was climbing through strata of hearths and stone tools, thousands of layers all heaped up on top of one another and squashed down into the rock. People must have lived in this place a very long time. He was oppressed by a huge weight of time, and of changelessness.

But he was distracted by a set of teeth he found, small, triangular, razor-edged. They had holes drilled in them. He carefully prized these out of the rock and put them in a pouch; perhaps he would make a necklace of them later.

With aching fingertips and toes, he continued his climb.

Unexpectedly, he reached the top of the chimney. It opened out into a wider space, a cave perhaps, filled with that ruddy light. He hoisted himself up the last short way, swung his legs out onto the floor above, and stood up.

And he was stunned.

He was standing on flat ground, a plain that seemed to go on forever. It was covered in dust, very red, so fine it stuck to the sweat on his legs. He turned slowly around. If this was the floor of a cave—well, it was a cave with no walls. And the roof above must be far away too, so far he could not see it; above him was nothing but a dome of darkness. He had no word for sky. And in one direction, facing him, something lifted over the edge of the world. It was a ruddy disc, perfectly circular, just a slice of it protruding over the dead-flat horizon. It was the source of the crimson light, and he could feel its searing heat.

Ruul inhabited a convoluted world of caverns and chimneys; he had never seen anything like the purity of this utterly flat plain, the perfectly circular arc of that bow of light. The clean geometric simplicity of the landscape drew his soul; he stared, entranced.

Three hundred million years after the life and death of Tura and Bel, this was what Earth had become. The sediments on which Ruul stood were the ruins of the last mountains. The magmatic currents of a cooling world had not been able to break up the new supercontinent, as they had the first. Meanwhile the sun's relentless warming continued. By now only microbes inhabited the equatorial regions, while at the poles a few hardy, tough-skinned plants were browsed by sluggish animals heavily armored against the heat. Earth was already losing its water, and Pangaea's shoreline was rimmed by brilliant-white salt flats.

But the boy standing on the eroded-flat ground was barely changed from his unimaginably remote ancestors, from Tura and Cale and Urlu and even Jaal. It had never been necessary for humans to evolve significantly, for they always adjusted their environment so they didn't have to—and in the process stifled evolutionary innovation.

It was like this everywhere. After the emergence of intelligence, the story of any biosphere tended to get a lot simpler. It was a major reason for the silence of the stars.

But on Earth a long story was ending. In not many generations from now, Ruul's descendants would succumb; quietly baked in their desiccating caves, they would not suffer. Life would go on, as archaic thermophilic microbes spread their gaudy colors across the land. But man would be gone, leaving sandstone strata nearly a billion years deep full of hearths and chipped stones and human bones.

"Ruul! Ruul! Oh, there you are!" His mother, caked by red dust, was clambering stiffly out of the chimney. "Somebody said you came this way. I've been frantic. Oh, Ruul—what are you doing?"

Ruul spread his hands, unable to explain. He didn't want to hurt his mother, but he was excited by his discoveries. "Look what I found, mother!"

"What?"

He babbled excitedly about hearths and tools and bones. "Maybe people lived here in great heaps, and the smoke of their fires rose up to the sky. Mother, will we come to live here again?"

"Perhaps one day," his mother said at random, to hush him.

But that wasn't answer enough for Ruul. Restless, curious, he glanced around once more at the plain, the rising sun. To him, this terminal Earth was a place of wonder. He longed to explore. "Let me go on. Just a little further!"

"No," his mother said gently. "The adventure's over. It's time to go. Come now." And she put her arm around his shoulders, and led him home.

EIGHT EPISODES

Robert Reed

With minimal fanfare and next to no audience, *Invasion of a Small World* debuted in the summer of 2016, and after a brief and disappointing run, the series was deservedly shelved.

One glaring problem was its production values: Computer animation had reached a plateau where reality was an easy illusion, spectacle was the industry norm, and difficult tricks like flowing water and human faces were beginning to approximate what was real. Yet the show's standards were barely adequate, even from an upstart Web network operating with limited capital and too many hours of programming to fill. The landscapes and interior shots would have been considered state-of-the-art at the turn of the century, but not in its premiere year. The characters were inflicted with inexpressive faces and stiff-limbed motions, while their voices were equally unconvincing, employing amateur actors or some cut-rate audio-synthesis software. With few exceptions, the dialogue was sloppy, cluttered with pauses and clumsy phrasing, key statements often cut off in mid-sentence. Most critics decided that the series' creators were striving for a real-life mood. But that was purely an interpretation. Press kits were never made available, and no interviews were granted with anyone directly involved in the production, leaving industry watchers entirely to their own devices—another problem that served to cripple *Invasion*.

Other factors contributed to the tiny audience. One issue that couldn't be discussed openly was the racial makeup of the cast. Success in the lucrative North American market meant using characters of obvious European extraction. Yet the series' leading man was an Indian astronomer working at a fictional college set in, of all places, South Africa. With an unpronounceable name and thick accent, Dr. Smith—as his few fans dubbed him—was a pudgy, prickly creation with a weakness for loud shirts and deep belches. His wife was a homely apparition who understood nothing about his world-shaking work, while his children, in direct contrast to virtually every other youngster inhabiting popular entertainment, were dim-witted creatures offering nothing that was particularly clever or charming.

A paucity of drama was another obvious weakness. The premiere episode involved a routine day in Dr. Smith's life. Eighteen hours of unexceptional behavior was compressed to fifty-three minutes of unexceptional behavior. Judging by appearances, the parent network inserted commercial breaks at random points. The series' pivotal event was barely noticed by the early viewers: One of Dr. Smith's graduate students was working with Permian-age rock samples, searching for key isotopes deposited by ancient supernovae. The student asked her professor about a difficult piece of lab equipment. As always, the dialogue was dense and graceless, explaining almost nothing to the uninitiated. Genuine scientists—some of the series' most unapologetic fans—liked to point out that the instruments and principles were genuine, though the nomenclature was shamelessly contrived. Fourteen seconds of broadcast time introduced a young graduate student named Mary—a mixed-race woman who by no measure could be considered attractive. She was shown asking Dr. Smith for help with the problematic instrument, and he responded with a wave of a pudgy hand and a muttered, "Later." Following ads for tiny cars and a powerful asthma medicine, the astronomer ordered his student to come to his office and lock the door behind her. What happened next was only implied. But afterward Dr. Smith was seen sitting with his back to his desk and his belt unfastened, and the quick-eyed viewer saw Mary's tiny breasts vanish under a bra and baggy shirt. Some people have interpreted her expression as pain, emotional or otherwise. Others have argued that her face was so poorly rendered that it was impossible to fix any emotion to her, then or later. And where good writers would have used dialogue to spell out the importance of the moment, bad writers decided to ignore the entire interpersonal plotline. With a casual voice, Mary mentioned to her advisor/lover that she had found something strange in the Permian stone.

"Strange," he repeated.

With her thumb and finger, she defined a tiny space. "Metal. A ball."

"Ball?"

"In the rock."

Smith scratched his fat belly for a moment, saying nothing. (Judging by log tallies, nearly 10 percent of the program's small audience turned away at that point.) Then he quietly said to her, "I do not understand."

"What it is . . ."

"What?"

She said, "I don't know either."

"In what rock?"

"Mine. The mudstone—"

"You mean it's artificial. . . ?"

"Looks so," she answered.

He said, "Huh."

She finished buttoning her shirt, the back of her left hand wiping at the corner of her mouth.

"Where?" Smith asked.

She gave the parent rock's identification code.

"No, the metal ball," he interrupted. "Where is it now?"

"My desk drawer. In a white envelope."

"And how big?"

"Two grains of rice, about."

Then, one last time, the main character said, "Huh." And, finally, without any interest showing in his face, he fastened his belt.

The next three episodes covered not days, but several months. Again, none of the scientific work was explained, and nothing resembling a normal plotline emerged from the routine and the tedious. The increasingly tiny audience watched Dr. Smith and two of his graduate students working with an object almost too small to be resolved on the screen— another significant problem with the series. Wouldn't a human-sized artifact have made a greater impact? The ball's metal shell proved to be an unlikely alloy of nickel and aluminum. Cosmic radiation and tiny impacts had left the telltale marks one would expect after a long drifting journey through space. Using tiny lasers, the researchers carefully cut through the metal shell, revealing a diamond interior. Then the diamond heart absorbed a portion of the laser's energy, and once charged, it powered up its own tiny light show. Fortunately a nanoscopic camera had been inserted into the hole, and the three scientists were able to record what they witnessed—a rush of complex images coupled with an increasingly sophisticated array of symbols.

"What is this?" they kept asking one another.

"Maybe it's language," Mary guessed. Correctly, as it happened. "Someone's teaching us . . . trying to . . . a new language."

Dr. Smith gave her a shamelessly public hug.

Then the other graduate student—a Brazilian fellow named Carlos—pointed out that, whatever the device was, Mary had found it in rock that was at least a quarter of a billion years old. "And that doesn't count the time this little machine spent in space, which could be millions more years."

After the show's cancellation, at least one former executive admitted to having been fooled. "We were promised a big, loud invasion," he told an interviewer from *Rolling Stone*. "I talked to the series' producer. He said an invasion would begin right after episode four. Yeah, we knew the build-up was going to be slow. But then aliens from the dinosaur days were going to spring to life and start burning cities."

"Except," said the interviewer.

"What?"

"That's not quite true. The Permian happened before there were any dinosaurs."

With a shrug, the ex-executive brushed aside that mild criticism. "Anyway, the important thing is that bad-ass aliens were supposed to come out of the rock. They were going to grow huge and start kicking us around. At least that's what the production company—EXL Limited—assured us. A spectacle. And since we didn't have to pay much for those episodes, we ended up purchasing the first eight shows after seeing only a few minutes of material. . . ."

Invasion was canceled after the fifth episode.

The final broadcast episode was an artless synopsis of the next twenty months of scientific work. Dr. Smith and his students were just a tiny portion of a global effort. Experts on six continents were making a series of tiny, critical breakthroughs. Most of the story involved faceless researchers exchanging dry e-mails about the tiny starship's text and images. Translations were made; every shred of evidence began to support the obvious but incredible conclusions. The culminating event was a five-minute news conference. Dripping sweat, shaking from nerves, the astronomer explained to reporters that he had found a functioning starship on Earth. After a glancing thanks to unnamed colleagues, he explained how, in the remote past, perhaps long before there was multi-cellular life on Earth, an alien species had manufactured trillions of tiny ships like this one. The ships were cast off into space, drifting slowly to planetary systems scattered throughout the galaxy. The vessel that he had personally recovered was already ancient when it dropped onto a river bottom near the edge of Gondwanaland. Time had only slightly degraded its onboard texts—a history of the aliens and an explanation into the nature of life in the universe. By all evidence, he warned, human beings were late players to an old drama. And like every other intelligent species in the universe, they would always be small in numbers and limited in reach.

The final scene of that fifth episode was set at Dr. Smith's home. His oldest son was sitting before a large plasma screen, destroying alien spaceships with extraordinarily loud weapons. In what proved to be the only conversation between those two characters, Smith sat beside his boy, asking, "Did you see me?"

"What?"

"The news conference—"

"Yeah, I watched."

"So?" he said. And when no response was offered, he asked, "What did you think?"

"About what?"

"The lesson—"

"What? People don't matter?" The boy froze the battle scene and put down his controls. "I think that's stupid."

His father said nothing.

"The universe isn't empty and poor." The boy was perhaps fourteen, and his anger was the most vivid emotion in the entire series. "Worlds are everywhere, and a lot of them have to have life."

"Millions are blessed, yes," Dr. Smith replied. "But hundreds of billions more are too hot, too cold. They are metal-starved, or married to dangerous suns."

His son stared at the frozen screen, saying nothing.

"The alien texts only confirm our most recent evidence, you know. The earth is a latecomer. Stellar births are slowing, in the Milky Way, and everywhere, and the production of terrestrial worlds peaked two or three billion years before our home was created."

"These texts of yours . . . they say that intelligent life stays at home?"

"Most of the time, yes."

"Aliens don't send out real starships?"

"It is far too expensive," Smith offered.

The boy pushed out his lower lip. "Humans are different," he maintained.

"No."

"We're going to build a working stardrive. Soon, I bet. And then we'll visit our neighboring stars and colonize those worlds—"

"We can't."

"Because they tell us we can't?"

"Because it is impossible." His father shook his head, saying with authority, "The texts are explicit. Moving large masses requires prohibitive energies. And terraforming is a difficult, often impossible trick. And that is why almost every world that we have found to date looks as sterile as the day they were born."

But the teenage boy would accept none of that. "You know, don't you? That these aliens are just lying to us? They're afraid of human beings, because they know we're the toughest, meanest things in the universe. And we're going to take them on."

For a long moment, Dr. Smith held silent.

Then the boy continued his game, and into the mayhem of blasters, the father mouthed a single dismissive word: "Children."

Eighteen months later, the fledging Web network declared bankruptcy, and a small consortium acquired its assets, including *Invasion of a Small World*. Eager to recoup their investment, the new owners offered all eight episodes as a quick-and-dirty DVD package. When sales proved somewhat better than predicted, a new version was cobbled together, helped along by a genuine ad budget. The strongest initial sales came from the tiny pool of determined fans—young and well educated, with little preference for nationality or gender. But the scientists in several fields, astronomy and paleontology included, were the ones who created a genuine buzz that eventually put *Invasion* into the public eye.

The famous sixth episode helped trigger the interest: That weak, rambling tale of Dr. Smith, his family and students, was temporarily suspended. Instead, the full fifty-three minutes were dedicated to watching a barren world spinning silently in deep space. According to corporate memos, the last three episodes arrived via the Web, bundled in a single package. But it was this episode that effectively killed the series. There were no explanations. Nothing showed but the gray world spinning, twenty minutes before the point-of-view gradually pulled away. The world was just a tiny speck of metal lost in the vastness of space. For astronomers, it was a fascinating moment—a vivid illustration that the universe could be an exceedingly boring place. Stars were distant points of light, and there was only silence, and even when millions of years were compressed into a nap-length moment, nothing was produced that could be confused with great theatre.

But what the astronomers liked best—what got the buzz going—were the final few minutes of the episode. Chance brought the tiny starship into the solar system, and chance guided it past a younger Saturn. The giant moon, Titan, swung close before the ship was kicked out to Neptune's orbit. Then it drifted sunward again, Mars near enough to reveal its face. Two hundred and fifty million years ago, Titan was bathed in a much denser atmosphere, while Mars was a temporarily wet world, heated by a substantial impact event. Experts in those two worlds were impressed. Only in the last year or two, probes had discovered what *Invasion* predicted on its own, including pinpointing the impact site near the Martian South Pole.

In much the same way, episode seven made the paleontologists crazy.

With its long voyage finished, the tiny starship struck the Earth's upper atmosphere, quickly losing its momentum as well as a portion of its hull. The great southern continent was rendered accurately enough to make any geologist smile, while the little glimpses of Permian ecosystems were even more impressive. Whoever produced the series (and there was a growing controversy on that matter), they had known much about protomammals and the early reptiles, cycads and tree ferns. One ancient creature—lizard in form, though not directly related to any modern species—was the only important misstep. Yet five months later, a team working in South Africa uncovered a set of bones that perfectly matched what a vanished dramatic series had predicted . . . and what was already a cultish buzz grew into a wild, increasingly public cacophony. . . .

At least forty thousand sites—chat rooms and blogs and such—were dedicated to supporting the same inevitable conclusion.

By means unknown, aliens had sent a message to earthlings, and it took the form of *Invasion of a Small World*.

The eighth episode was a genuine treasure.

Dr. Smith reappeared. Several years older, divorced and with his belly fat stripped off by liposuction, he was shown wandering happily through a new life of endless celebrity. His days and long evenings were spent with at least three mistresses as well as a parade of world leaders. Accustomed to the praise of others, he was shown grinning confidently while offering his interpretations of the ancient message. The universe was almost certainly sprinkled with life, he explained. But despite that prolificacy, the cosmos remained an enormous, very cold, and exceptionally poor place. The gulfs between living worlds were completely unbridgeable. No combination of raw energy and questing genius could build a worthy stardrive. Moreover, even direct communication between local species was rarely worth its considerable cost, since civilizations rarely if ever offered each other anything with genuine worth.

"Technology has distinct limits," he warned the starlets and world leaders that he met at cocktail parties. "Humans are already moving into the late stages of scientific endeavor. What matters most, to us and to any wise species, is the careful shepherding of energy and time. That is why we must care for our world and the neighboring planets inside our own little solar system. We must treasure every day while wasting nothing, if only to extend our histories as far as into the future as possible."

"That strikes me as such depressing news," said one prime minister—a statuesque woman blessed with a starlet's beautiful face. "If there really are millions and billions of living worlds, as you claim, and if all the great minds on all of those worlds are thinking hard about this single problem, shouldn't somebody learn how to cheat the speed of light or create free energy through some clever trick?"

"If that were so," Dr. Smith replied, "then every world out there would be alive, and the giant starships would arrive at our doorstep every few minutes. But instead, human experience has discovered precisely one starfaring vessel, and it was a grain of metallic dust, and to reach us it had to be exceptionally lucky, and, even then, it had to wait a quarter of a billion years to be noticed."

The prime minister sipped her Virgin Mary and chewed on her lower lip. Then with a serious tone, she said, "But to me . . . there seems to be another reasonable explanation waiting for our attention . . ."

"Which would be what, madam?"

"Subterfuge," she offered. "The aliens are intentionally misleading us about the nature of the universe."

Bristling, he asked, "And why would they do such a thing?"

"To cripple our future," she replied. "By convincing us to remain home, they never have to face us between the stars."

"Perhaps you're right to think that, madam," said the old astronomer, nodding without resolve. Then in his final moment in the series' final episode, he said, "A lie is as good as a pill, if it helps you sleep. . . ."

For years, every search to uncover the creative force behind *Invasion of a Small World* came up empty. And in the public mind, that single mystery remained the final, most compelling part of the story.

Former executives with the doomed network had never directly met with the show's producers. But they could recount phone conversations and teleconferences and e-mails exchanged with three apparent producers. Of course, by then, it was possible to invent a digital human face and voice while weaving a realistic mix of human gestures. Which led some to believe that slippery forces were plainly at work here—forces that no human eye had ever witnessed.

Tracking down the original production company produced only a dummy corporation leading to dusty mailboxes and several defunct Web addresses. Every name proved fictional, both among the company's officers and those in the brief credits rolling at the end of each episode. Surviving tax forms lacked any shred of useful information. But where the IRS might have chased down a successful cheat, the plain truth was that whoever was responsible for *Invasion* had signed away all future rights in exchange for a puddle of cash.

The few skeptics wondered if something considerably more ordinary was at play here. Rumors occasionally surfaced about young geniuses working in the Third World—usually in the Indian tech-cities. Employing pirated software and stolen equipment, they had produced what would eventually become the fifth most successful media event in history. But in the short term, their genius had led nowhere but to obscurity and financial ruin. Three different candidates were identified—young men with creative minds and most of the necessary skills. Did one of them build *Invasion* alone? Or was it a group effort? And was the project's failure the reason why each of them committed suicide shortly after the series' cancellation?

But if they were the creators, why didn't any trail lead to them? Perhaps because the consortium that held all rights to *Invasion* had obscured the existing evidence. And why? Obviously to help feed this infectious and delicious mood of suspicion. To maintain an atmosphere where no doubts could find a toehold, where aliens were conversing with humans, and where the money continued to flow to the consortium like a great green river.

The most durable explanation was provided by one of the series' most devoted fans—a Nobel laureate in physics who was happy to beat the drum for the unthinkable. "*Invasion* is true everywhere but in the specifics," he argued. "I think there really was an automated starship. But it was bigger than a couple of grains of rice. As big as a fist, or a human head. But still small and unmanned. The ship entered our solar system during the Permian. With the bulk of it in orbit, pieces must have landed on our world. Scouts with the size and legs of small cockroaches, maybe. Maybe. And if you take the time to think it through, you see that it would be a pretty silly strategy, letting yourself become a tiny fossil in some enormous bed of mudstone. What are the odds that you'd survive for 250 million years, much else ever get noticed there?

"No, if you are an automated starship, what would be smart is for that orbiting mothership to take a seat where nothing happens and she can see everything. On the moon, I'd guess. She still has the antennas that she used to hear the scouts' reports. She sleeps and waits for radio signals from the earth, and when they arrive, she studies what she hears. She makes herself into a student of language and technology. And when the time is ripe—when she has a product to sell—she expels the last of her fuel, leaving the moon to land someplace useful. Which is pretty much anywhere, these days.

"Looking like a roach, maybe, she connects to the Web and offers her services at a cut-rate price.

"And that is how she delivers her message.

"Paraphrasing my fictional colleague, 'A lie is as good as a truth, if it leads you to enlightenment.'"

The final scene in the last episode only seemed anticlimactic. The one-time graduate student, Mary, had been left behind by world events. From the beginning, her critical part in the research had been downplayed. But the series' creator, whoever or whatever it was, saw no useful drama in that treachery. The woman was middle-aged and happy in her obscurity, plain as always and pregnant for at least the second time.

A ten-year-old daughter was sitting beside Mary, sharing a threadbare couch.

The girl asked her mother what she believed. Was the universe really so empty and cold? And was this the way it would always be?

Quietly, her mother said, "I think that's basically true, yes."

The girl looked saddened.

But then Mary patted her daughter on the back of a hand, smiling with confidence. "But dear, I also believe this," she said. "Life is an invasion wherever it shows itself. It is relentless and it is tireless, and it conquers every little place where living is possible. And before the universe ends, all the good homes will know the sounds of wet breathing and the singing of glorious songs."

ABOUT THE AUTHORS

JOHN VARLEY writing as Herb Boehm

Spring 1977, the first issue of *Asimov's Science Fiction* magazine, contained two stories by John Varley. One, "Good-Bye, Robinson Crusoe," appeared under the Varley byline. The other, "Air Raid," appeared under the pseudonym "Herb Boehm." Although Mr. Varley has only published four additional stories in the magazine, they have all been memorable. Perhaps the most famous of these tales, "PRESS ENTER ■" (May 1984), received the Nebula and Hugo Awards for best novella. In addition, the author has been honored with two other Hugos and a Nebula. His novels include The Gaea Trilogy, *Millennium*, *Steel Beach*, and *Red Lightning*. He lives with his wife in California.

ROBERT SILVERBERG

Robert Silverberg is the recipient of five Hugo Awards and five Nebulas. In 2004, the Science Fiction Writers of America named him a Grand Master. One of the author's Nebula-Award winning stories, "Sailing to Byzantium," was first published in the February 1985 issue of *Asimov's Science Fiction* magazine. A Hugo Award winner, "Enter a Soldier. Later Enter Another," first appeared in the June 1989 issue of *Asimov's*. His most famous novels include *Dying Inside, Lord Valentine's Castle*, and *Nightwings*. His coming of age novel, *The Longest Way Home*—published in the October/November 2001, December 2001, and January 2002 issues of *Asimov's*—is one of only a handful of books ever serialized in the magazine. Mr. Silverberg has also contributed a monthly "Reflections" column to *Asimov's* since 1994. He lives with his wife, Karen Haber, in the San Francisco area.

OCTAVIA E. BUTLER

Octavia E. Butler received her first Hugo Award for her short story, "Speech Sounds" (*Asimov's*, Mid-December 1983). The following year her novelette, "Bloodchild" (*Asimov's*, June 1984), won the Hugo and Nebula Awards. Ms. Butler won another Nebula for her novel, *Parable of the Talents*, in 1999. In 1995, she became the first science fiction author to win the MacArthur Foundation "genius" grant. She also received a lifetime achievement award from PEN Center West and the Langston Hughes Medal from the City College of New York. The Octavia E. Butler Memorial Scholarship was founded by the Carl Brandon Society in 2006 after Ms. Butler died unexpectedly. Its goal is to provide scholarships for authors of color to the Clarion writers workshops.

BRUCE STERLING

Bruce Sterling is considered one of the founders of the Cyberpunk movement in science fiction. His novels include *Schismatrix, Islands in the Net, The Difference Engine* (with William Gibson), and *Heavy Weather*, and he edited the influential *Mirrorshades: A Cyberpunk Anthology* in 1986. He won Hugo Awards for two stories, "Bicycle Repairman" (October/November 1996) and "Taklamakan" (October/November 1998), that were first published in *Asimov's*, and eight stories from *Asimov's* will soon appear in *Ascendancies: The Best of Bruce Sterling*. The author's nonfiction books include *The Hacker Crackdown: Law and Disorder on the Electronic Frontier* and *Shaping Things*, a manifesto on post-industrial design from MIT Press. These days, he mostly resides on a small island in Croatia.

ISAAC ASIMOV

One of the best-known authors of science and science fiction, Isaac Asimov was also one of the most honored. During his lifetime, he received five Hugo Awards for fiction and two for nonfiction, as well as two Nebula Awards. In 1987, he received a Grand Master Award from the Science Fiction Writers of America. Dr. Asimov's most famous SF novels include *I, Robot, The Foundation Trilogy, The Caves of Steel, The Naked Sun,* and *The Gods Themselves.* Nonfiction books include *Asimov's Biographical Encyclopedia of Science and Technology, Asimov's Guide to Shakespeare,* and *Asimov's Guide to the Bible.* Dr. Asimov's 399 science columns for *The Magazine of Fantasy and Science Fiction* were also collected into a series of popular science books. Until his death in 1992, Dr. Asimov contributed a monthly editorial to *Asimov's Science Fiction* magazine. He also wrote entertaining responses to readers correspondence for the magazine's letters column. Forty-six pieces of Dr. Asimov's short fiction were published by the magazine.

KIM STANLEY ROBINSON

Kim Stanley Robinson's first story for *Asimov's,* "Green Mars" (September 1985), precedes his Hugo- and Nebula-Award winning Mars Trilogy by nearly ten years. The story allowed him to stake a claim to the name years before his novels appeared on the horizon. Mr. Robinson picked up another Nebula for his August 1987 *Asimov's* story, "The Blind Geometer," and he has published fifteen other stories in the magazine. In addition to *Green Mars, Red Mars,* and *Blue Mars,* the author's novels include *Icehenge, The Wild Shore, Antarctica, The Years of Rice and Salt,* and *Forty Signs of Rain.* As we experience the repercussions of global warming and the fast disappearance of glaciers, the author tells us he now thinks of the story in this anthology as a "nostalgia piece." Mr. Robinson lives with his family in Davis, California.

CONNIE WILLIS

Connie Willis first splashed upon the pages of *Asimov's* in 1982 with "Fire Watch" (February) and "A Letter from the Clearys" (July). Both stories received the Nebula Award and "Fire Watch" won the Hugo Award as well. Indeed, four of the author's six Nebulas and seven of her nine Hugos have been for stories that were first published in *Asimov's*. These include the Hugo- and Nebula-Award winners "The Last of the Winnebagos" (July 1988) and "Even the Queen" (April 1992) and the Hugo winners "Death on the Nile" (March 1993), "The Soul Selects Her Own Society" (April 1996), "The Winds of Marble Arch" (October/November 1999), and "Inside Job" (January 2005). A limited-edition collection of her short stories, *The Best of Connie Willis*, will be out soon. Ms. Willis's best-known novels are *Lincoln's Dreams, Doomsday Book, To Say Nothing of the Dog*, and *Passage*. She is currently working on *All Clear*, an epic time-travel novel set during World War II. About the story included here, she says, "'Write what you know' isn't an edict SF writers get much opportunity to follow, but 'Cibola' was an exception. I was lucky enough to actually glimpse the *Seven Cities of Gold* once and have never forgotten it." The author lives in Greeley, Colorado.

JONATHAN LETHEM

Jonathan Lethem is the author of seven novels, including *Gun, With Occasional Music; The Fortress of Solitude* (which won the 1999 National Book Critic's Circle Award); and *You Don't Love Me Yet*. He is also the author of two story collections and a collection of essays, and editor of *The Vintage Book of Amnesia*. Mr. Lethem is also a recipient of the 2005 MacArthur "genius" grant. From 1991 until 1996, he published five stories in *Asimov's*. About his first story in the magazine and our 30th anniversary, he says, "*Asimov's* publication of 'The Happy Man' was graduation day for me, as a writer. I will forever be grateful for that moment in which I was ushered into the world of professional publication, and into the rich and singular American tradition of the pulp all-fiction digests. Huge congratulations on three decades of a truly great enterprise." Mr. Lethem lives in Brooklyn and Maine.

MIKE RESNICK

According to *Locus*, science fiction's trade magazine, Mike Resnick has won more awards for his short science fiction than any other writer, living or dead, and most of those stories have appeared in *Asimov's*. He is the author of more than fifty novels, close to two hundred stories, and a pair of screenplays. He has edited forty-five anthologies and his work has been translated into twenty-two languages. Three of his five Hugo Awards were for *Asimov's* stories—"The Manamouki" (July 1990), "The 43 Antarean Dynasties" (December 1997), and "Travels with My Cats" (February 2004). In addition, the author's 1994 novella "Seven Views of Olduvai Gorge" was awarded both the Hugo and the Nebula. He tells us that *"Asimov's* has been home to most of my best work during the editorial tenures of Gardner Dozois and Sheila Williams, and I'm happy to have contributed in any small way to the magazine's success. Congrats on your first thirty years, and here's wishing you at least thirty more." Mike Resnick lives in Cincinnati, Ohio.

URSULA K. LE GUIN

As of 2007, Ursula K. Le Guin has published twenty novels, over a hundred short stories (collected in eleven volumes), three collections of essays, twelve books for children, six volumes of poetry and four of translation, and has received a great many awards: Hugo, Nebula, NBA, PEN-Malamud, International Fantasy, SFWA Grand Master, and others. Her most recent publications are a volume of poetry, *Incredible Good Fortune*, and a fantasy novel, *Voices*. About this anthology she comments, "My first published stories came out in 1962, but it took me ages to get a story published in *Asimov's*. Better late than never! It was undoubtedly my fault for writing stuff that is hard to classify. It was quite daring of a science-fiction magazine to print a completely realistic story like 'Ether, OR.' Finding it in *Asimov's* may have led people to read it as a fantasy, or magical realism, or something, but anybody who lives in Oregon can tell you it just describes how things are here, and shows no imagination whatever."

KELLY LINK

Kelly Link's first professional sale was to *Asimov's* in 1996. She is now a highly respected short-story writer. Her tales have received two Nebulas and a Hugo, and she is an editor, with Ellen Datlow and Gavin Grant, of the annual *Year's Best Fantasy and Horror*. Her story collections include *Stranger Things Happen* and *Magic for Beginners*, and she edited the anthology, *Trampoline*, as well. Ms. Link lives in Northampton, Massachusetts.

JAMES PATRICK KELLY

James Patrick Kelly's first story for *Asimov's* appeared in the August 1983 issue. He has since sold over thirty stories to the magazine and has the distinction of having had a piece of fiction in every June issue since 1984. The author intends to make this a lifelong habit. Two of his June stories, "Think Like a Dinosaur" (1995) and "10^{16} to 1" (1999) were honored with Hugo awards. In addition to his stories and thirteen poems in *Asimov's*, since 1998 he has covered science fiction and the Internet in a bimonthly column for the magazine. Mr. Kelly is also the author of four and a half novels, several plays, and a couple of planetarium shows. His most recent venture is James Patrick Kelly's StoryPod on Audible.com, a podcast on which he will be reading just about all of the stories he has published in *Asimov's*. The author lives in Nottingham, New Hampshire.

MICHAEL SWANWICK

Michael Swanwick's first story for *Asimov's*, "Marrow Death," was published in the Mid-December 1984 issue. Forty additional stories, along with two articles and two novel serializations, have since appeared in the magazine. One of these books, *Stations of the Tide* (Mid-December 1990 and January 1991) received a Nebula Award. Four of his five

Hugo Awards are also for stories first published in *Asimov's*— "The Very Pulse of the Machine" (February 1998), "Scherzo with Tyrannosaur" (July 1999), "The Dog Said 'Bow-Wow' " (October/November 2001), and "Legions in Time" (April/May 2003). Mr. Swanwick's other novels include *Vacuum Flowers, The Iron Dragon's Daughter, Jack Faust,* and *Bones of the Earth.* Two of his short-story collections are *Tales of Old Earth* and *Cigar-Box Faust and Other Miniatures.* His next novel, *The Dragons of Babel,* will draw upon several of his most recent *Asimov's* stories. Michael Swanwick lives in Philadelphia, Pennsylvania.

CHARLES STROSS

Born in 1964 in Leeds, England, Charles Stross currently lives in Edinburgh, Scotland. He sold his first science fiction stories, from 1986 onward, to *Interzone* and other British outlets. "Lobsters," published here, was his first story (but not his last) for *Asimov's*; it was written in 1999, and unapologetically reflects the febrile intensity of the first dot com boom. Around 2002, he began selling novels; among these, *Singularity Sky, Iron Sunrise,* and *Accelerando* have been short listed for the Hugo Award, while his novella "The Concrete Jungle" won the Hugo in 2005. His next SF novel, *Halting State,* does not use the words "computer," "software," or "singularity" even once—but, like this biography, it is written in the second person.

LUCIUS SHEPARD

Lucius Shepard's first story for *Asimov's,* "A Traveler's Tale," appeared in our July 1992 issue. His April 1986 novella, "R&R," won a Nebula Award and his July 1992 novella, "Barnacle Bill the Spacer," won a Hugo Award. Two of his short-story collections, *The Jaguar Hunter* and *The Ends of the Earth,* have been the recipients of World Fantasy Awards. Among the other awards he's received are the John W. Campbell Award for best new writer, the Theodore Sturgeon Award, and the *Asimov's* Readers' Award. The author's novels include *Green Eyes, The Golden, A Handbook of American Prayer*, and *Softspoken*. Mr. Shepard's recent short fiction is collected in *Dagger Key and Other Stories*. He lives and works in Vancouver, Washington.

STEPHEN BAXTER

Stephen Baxter was born in Liverpool, England, in 1957. He tells us, "I worked in science, engineering, and teaching before becoming a full-time writer. My first short story sales were to British magazines, but it was always an ambition of mine to sell to the American digests, which are a reflection of a great science fiction tradition going back to the pulps and of which *Asimov's* has been a standard bearer for three decades. I felt honored when *Asimov's* first published one of my stories in 1992; since then I've been delighted to place many more pieces with the magazine, and I'm particularly honored that my stories have won two of *Asimov's* Readers' Awards." Mr. Baxter's novel, *The Time Ships*, received both the John W. Campbell and the Philip K. Dick Awards. Other works include his Destiny's Children Series, the Manifold trilogy, and his Time's Tapestry Series. He has also co-authored three books with Sir Arthur Clarke.

ROBERT REED

Robert Reed sold his first story, "The Utility Man," to *Asimov's* in 1990. With "Eight Episodes," in the June 2006 issue, he broke Isaac Asimov's record for most fiction publications in the magazine. As a young writer, Bob Reed was inspired by the endless work by Robert Silverberg. "He always seemed to have a story in Terry Carr's annual *Best of the Year* anthology, but more impressive was how many 'honorable mentions' his other work received. This was the kind of career I dreamed of having—a prolific output of readable words. I have been honored five times with Hugo nominations, plus once for a Nebula, and once for a

World Fantasy Award. All but one of my nominated stories were first published in *Asimov's*." Mr. Reed has also been a frequent recipient of the *Asimov's* Readers' Award. In addition to his short fiction, his novels include *Marrow, Sister Alice*, and *The Well of Stars*. He lives with his wife and daughter in Lincoln, Nebraska.

SHEILA WILLIAMS

Sheila Williams is the editor of *Asimov's Science Fiction*. She joined *Asimov's* in June 1982 and served as the executive editor of *Analog* from 1998 until 2004. She is also the co-founder of the Dell Magazines Award for Undergraduate Excellence in Science Fiction and Fantasy Writing. In addition, she coordinates the website for *Asimov's* (*www. asimovs.com*). Ms. Williams has edited or co-edited over twenty anthologies. These include *A Women's Liberation: A choice of futures by and about women*, co-edited with Connie Willis, and *Hugo and Nebula Award Winners from Asimov's Science Fiction*. She received her bachelor's degree from Elmira College in Elmira, New York, and her master's from Washington University in St. Louis, Missouri. During her junior year she studied at the London School of Economics. Ms. Williams lives in New York City with her husband, David Bruce, and her two beautiful daughters, Irene and Juliet.